Devilry Hunters

Devilry Hunters

Ashley M. Carter

This is a work of fiction. Names, characters, places and incidents either are the product of the author's imagination or are used fictitiously, and any resemblance to any actual persons, living or dead, events, or locales is entirely coincidental.

This book was printed in the United States of America.

To order additional copies of this book, contact:
Xlibris Corporation
1-888-795-4274
www.Xlibris.com
Orders@Xlibris.com
76055

When an evil from the depths of space plots to overwhelm Earth, a mystical guardian angel must locate the descendants of the once-powerful guardians of the planet to protect the world . . .

Acknowledgements

I would like to thank some wonderful people that helped make my dream a reality:

To my awesome Aunt Susie who I am blessed to be related to, I thank you for all your support and encouragement. Thank you for standing beside me on this long journey and for being a shining light in my life.

To my best friends Jon McKim and Lonna Hamilton, I want to thank you both for all the crazy fun times we have shared thus far and for helping me continue to laugh and smile through the hard moments.

A special thank you for my representative Rod Agbulos, without all your hard work and patience I would have been lost. Thank you for standing with me from the beginning to end, you are amazing.

To my consultant Archie Kent, I wish to thank you for giving me this opportunity to bring my story to the world.

I would also like to thank all the people at Xlibris that helped with the production and designing of my book. You are all truthfully wonderful people and I'm grateful for all your hard work and support.

Dedication

For my mother and sisters to which each heroine is based upon and this book is dedicated to. I thank all of you for showering me with your love and sharing with me the most cherished moments of my life. This is for you.

Prologue

The many untold wonders of our universe swirl in a dark abyss hidden from the human populations' most advanced, scientific equipment. We reside within a hidden world where the true meaning of world chaos originates from wars held between fifty-four planets for millenniums. So, what the Earthlings cannot see may turn out to be the end of their world itself. For hidden behind a curtain of stars in their atmosphere is a world far more dangerous and mysterious than they could ever imagine . . .

The vastness of the galaxy has extended beyond our fingertips and has given us dozens of spectacular omens. The dark emptiness of space is lost in both time and existence, yet the stars and planets stay content within the darkness they live. The giant star sun casts its fiery fingers through the darkness, lighting the path of the planets' merry dance. They beautifully display their poise, as the silence deepens, to the millions of stars watching their swaying elegance.

Joining the silent movement, a giant bull-nosed spacecraft quietly passed through the deepness of the galaxy. Thousands of stars reflected off the spacecraft's silvery, oval surface as it concealed over half of Jupiter's massive body. Large streams of air blew out the back of the craft while it slowly approached the moon. Venturing beneath, the spacecraft powered down in the dark shadows of the moon.

Within the spacecraft, mechanisms of adequate intelligence sparked dazzling lights throughout the darkness. Shadows consumed the interior of the craft, dissipating any chance of navigation. Portholes lining the walls in thirty-foot intervals proved fatal for a source of light. Large pipes wrapped around the craft's high ceilings sparked enormous volts of energy toward the core of the craft. Soft rays from Earth's moon peered in through the craft's dark control room.

The control room expanded with great depth across the front of the craft's nose. Huge display grids were woven into the floorboards while a crystal mapping system hung in the back of the chamber. The hologram projections from the grids cast a translucent glow upon a hump of scales towering over it.

Moving through the shadows of the chamber, large reptilian creatures jostled about. They moved quickly from the mapping system to the grid displays. Within the shadows, a pair of glowing, sinister giant eyes stared coldly at Earth's appearance. A gigantic scaly hand suddenly slammed down, destroying its armrest. The clenched fist trembled furiously when a high-pitched hiss streamed out of the darkness. A nearby creature approached the shadows bowing slightly.

"The Earthlings-s-s have yet to dis-splay our s-ship on their radars-s-s. We are free and ready for the firs-st s-stage, S-sire," the creature informed.

Uncoiling its hand, the creature hidden within the shadows extended three giant dragon talons toward Earth. "S-send forth the Nz-zers-s-s into the planet . . ." A low hiss speared through the darkness as the eyes massively expanded, "Des-stroy the Latrinian!"

Shooting through the dark tunnels, guiding the otherwise blind monsters by sound alone, a high-frequency led a small group of the reptilian creatures through the spaceship. A massive door dissolved, allowing them to pass into a large chamber filled with pods. As the creatures locked themselves inside a silver diamond-shaped pod, a gateway opened. Revealing the bright star and planet filled galaxy, the atmosphere quickly sucked the pod out into space. Setting controls and rerouting the direction, the pod descended toward Earth.

Inside the control room, the giant hand slowly scratched up and down the chair's broken arm as the silver pod zipped toward Earth.

"It will not be long . . . my minions-s-s will s-soon des-stroy the Latrinian and, then I s-shall finally be able to return to Latira . . . for my revenge!" The creature laughed sinisterly as its large white razor-sharp teeth flared through the darkness.

Earlier

Soft sirens hummed through an enormous room lined with machinery of unthinkable technique. Dispensing from the high ceilings, thin glass extended down to bubble into grids covered with ruins of data scrambled and unchecked. The noise forebode all occupants within the vicinity to scramble frantically about. Men and women alike pushed into chairs to roll before machines of large scale. Globes and orbs came to life beneath their touch. Screens brightened spontaneously, displaying the same twisted ruins. Set in the corner ceiling of the northern wall, a small orb flashed across the whole of the room, reflecting its red core over the scientists jostling about.

Sprinting quickly across the porcelain floor, a tall man gripped a stair rail and quickly climbed to the higher level of the chamber. Sliding around a young lady who raced toward the stairs, the man quickly plopped onto a wheeled chair and rolled over to the giant master computer. Pressing a small button, he twitched his mustache, moving his whiskers from his lips as he leaned toward a microphone.

"Captain to the LDCR."

Pushing away from the desk, he turned to roll toward a slender crystal plate suspended in the midst of the deck. Staring at the dismal shapes of scientists beyond its surface, the man released a long sigh as he touched several orb shapes in the plate.

"Come on, wake up, you piece of crap," he growled as he readjusted his round spectacles.

The crimson lights continued to flash across the white stonewalls of the LDCR (Latira's Database Control Room) as scientists moved around the crystal panel commonly known as the Central Processing Unit.

Sitting in front of the crystal plate, the man rubbed his hands across his white lab coat marred with a large cocoa stain. Pushing his eyes up to peer over the edge of his spectacles at the plate, he frowned as he watched lights dance across the crystal, forming a makeshift grin.

"Password . . ."

"CPU, we don't have time for games . . . there's a distress signal beckoning from a neighboring planet. If you want to be the one to explain to Esal that we were late rescuing them because of a simple game, be my guest!"

"Doc, systems are up, we're getting readings."

"Set them aside and align systems for beacons or warnings . . ." the bushy-haired man ordered as he set his hand on a panel next to the crystal plate. "CPU . . . I need you to locate the distress call."

"You didn't say please . . ."

"Dang it . . . I'm gonna say something, and it's not gonna be nice!" Doc growled as he grabbed his tangled locks of burgundy. "Would you for once cut me some slack?"

"No . . ."

Just then, a young man with hair the color of sea foam bounded up the stairs to the CPU's mainframe. As light from the overhanging lamps shimmered over the man's hair, the shaded patches turned to the dark hue of the depths of an ocean, a cerulean blue tint. He abruptly stopped as he saw the man lifting a chair to strike the crystal plate. Sprinting quickly across the porcelain tiles, the young man slid in front of the CPU's mainframe, catching the chair as it was swung down. Struggling effortlessly against the weight thrust into the swing, the young man snarled his nose as he slid his leg forward to unlock Doc's balance.

Gasping as his knee was pushed, Doc fell backward onto the ground to freeze as he saw the young man.

"What on holy Latira were you doing, Doc?" the young man growled with crystal blue eyes burning as he stared at the man. Lowering the chair as if it were a book, the young man raised an eyebrow. "What were you doing?" he inquired with a calmer breath exhaling through his nostrils.

"Esal . . ." Doc shrieked. "I . . . well, I was . . . I mean the, no, I was . . . I see you got my message?" he quickly smiled.

Staring at Doc, Esal slowly exhaled as he dropped the chair at his side, "Yes, Doc, I got the message. Sirens are only going off, but don't worry, I got your message."

Grinning like an impish child, Doc quickly stood and straightened his coat. "Well, that's good . . ." Clearing his throat, he pulled against the collar. "So we've got transmissions going out to every planet in hopes to get confirmations . . . we're currently seeking the location of the distress."

Peering at Doc, Esal smiled as he turned to set his hand to the crystal plate. "Good job, Doc . . . you did good."

Watching Esal's hand slip through the glass-covered crystal, Doc gasped as he watched the chemical material of the crystal swarm around Esal's hand.

"Is that safe?" Doc inquired.

Turning to glance at Doc, Esal frowned. "Have you never been around when I do this?"

Shaking his head, Doc moved closer to widen his eyes as thousands of lights danced through the plate from Esal's palm to his fingers.

"What're you doing, Captain?"

Lowering his head as a sudden light flashed through the plate, Esal pulled his hand out to peer at an orb in his palm.

"This is all data on the beacon distress, CPU?" Esal inquired as he glanced at the crystal plate.

Watching the flash of lights form the smile again, Doc sighed as the crystal plate rippled.

"Everything that was made prior to and after the distress call . . . I'd say the elapse time is probably thirty minutes before and after." The CPU's voice echoed through the LDCR.

Nodding, Esal turned to walk past Doc. "Care to see what it is?"

Staring at the CPU's mainframe, Doc turned to peer at Esal as he walked to the large machine setting several feet away.

"Did you seriously just do that?"

Nodding, Esal set the orb on an embossed tray as Doc walked to his side. Leaning into the machine's edge as a soft light lifted through the bottom of the orb, Esal's crystal blue eyes glowed as the light sprayed up into a drive of the machine.

"Wow . . ." Doc jumped as the light sprayed from the machine to shoot across the room to strike the western crystal wall. "How long has that been able to do that?"

"Since it was constructed three hundred millenniums ago," Esal nonchalantly responded as he turned to peer at the visuals springing across the crystal wall. "CPU, jump the orb ahead by twelve degrees."

Watching the image shift angle, Doc leaned into the railing as Esal narrowed his eyes.

"CPU, still that frame." Staring at it for several seconds, Esal peered across the ivory plains to the dark skies. "Enhance the south sector of the sky."

Watching a faint gray bubble zoom into place of the fields, Doc lifted his eyes to Esal. "What do you see?"

"You mean you don't see it?"

Esal shook his head as he tightened his hold on the railing. "CPU, can you clear that visual?"

"Give me a few seconds to try."

Leaning into his arms, Esal exhaled heavily as he watched the pixels of the crystal start to realign as the image began to reformate.

"There, stop!" Esal shouted as he saw the curve of the craft's front. "My god . . ." Straightening off the railing, Esal stared at the visual as Doc's mouth dropped open. "This can't be happening . . ." Licking his suddenly dry lips, Esal glanced back at the crystal plate. "CPU, move the time ahead before the distress was sent out!"

"One second . . ."

Gasping as he saw fires jumping across the crystal wall, Esal's eyes widened as he stared at the blood splattering the ivory fields.

That's Talouxia. His mind screamed in horror.

"What's going on, Esal?" Doc inquired as Esal's eyes drifted to the scaly hides scattered between the bloodied field and herbivores of Talouxia.

Staring at the dead to dying faces of the cat-faced race, Esal stepped back as he approached the stairs.

"Doc, send transmissions out to every neighboring planet of Talouxia. Inform them to take invasion precautions, but do not tell them what's happened. Am I clear?"

Nodding, Doc trotted up to the computer setting across from the machine spraying the light to the crystal wall. "Where you headed, Esal?"

"To a party . . ."

1

It was a night of elegance and poise, a night being touched by the blooming birth of the planet's new moon. Gently brushing through the curtain of ancient and young trees lining the borders of the kingdoms, the night's light cast over the vales of Latira. Smooth as a kiss, the light weaved through the river of spraying emerald meadow blades. Reflecting the shimmer of a faint snow, the light reached from the grassy meadows to the steeples of the castle bellowing in the distance.

Lights of fiery grace lifted from the castle, washing away the shadows of the night from the towering steeples to the garden. Dancing between the touches of darkness to the rays of fiery light, thick flags interlaid with silver lifted to the raising kiss of the wind to leave only the hum of their dance across the massive shingles stretching over the spiral roofs. Knights stood at each designated sector as the night's festivities continued on.

Sitting in the soft whistle of stirring trees, a gracefully youthful figured man held his head bowed to the chiming within the night. Inhaling as the wind touched the dark hues of his aqua green hair, he lifted his musky lids to watch his long bangs rock against his cheek. Lifting his eyes to the canopies, he slowly glanced down the expanse of the garden, watching the distorted touch of the moon against the wildlife. Brightness and shadow seemed to be lost into the glow of the moon, which extended its almost angelic kiss. Turning his eyes to the prism stream stretching across the skies, he gasped as he watched the moon turn dark and the skies bleed.

"Darkness will bring blood . . ." He gasped as he pushed from the ivory bench. "A ruin shall creep across the land."

Widening his eyes as he suddenly stared into an abyss of shadow, the young man slowly turned with a gasp. His breath froze in the back of his throat as the ground shifted and concaved. Groaning as he stumbled against the crumbling ground, he gasped as he fell into darkness. Narrowing his eyes from the biting wind, he grunted as a sharp light burst through the darkness. Turning to peer carefully at the light, he let his lips fall apart breathlessly as he watched someone spear through the light to extend a hand to him. Slowly lifting his heavy hand, he exhaled as his larger hand was gripped by soft velvet. Watching long strands of ebony silk flutter around him, he stuttered when the light flooded around the slender goddesslike figure.

Will you be the savior? He pondered silently.

Sitting in the motionless garden, a gracefully youthful figured man held his head bowed to the dead silence of the night. Slowly lifting musky lids, dark maroon orbs glowed in the darkness as the man turned his head toward the castle. Tilting his head up as the bustling joy of the festivities reached his ears, he pushed leisurely from the ivory bench. Touching the cottony texture of his staff, he released a long sigh as he started toward the thick stones leading toward the castle.

He must know . . . The man sighed as he glanced at the massive orb set at the top of his staff. Our doom is being set upon us, and I pray that he is the only one I can turn to now.

The dim lights spreading the expanse of Latira's grand halls bloomed to enormous ferocity as the dozens of precious gems settled on the ladies' gowns reflected the lights. From rubies to emeralds to amethysts and sapphires, the gems buckled in the flow of the gowns to cast rainbow shadows along the porcelain walls and floors. High-honored nobility walked the floors to enter the shimmering archway into the ballroom filled with royal families of the Solari. Heartwarming melodies spiraled around the room as a steady flow of skirts and capes brushed along the glasslike floors. The soft scuffling of leathered boots was joined with the soft taps of their beautiful partners' heels. Silk and velvet swirled together across the dance floor when a young woman paused at the edge of the crowd.

Bright sapphire irises sparkled in the light of the room as she glanced at each swirling partner gliding across the dance floor as if it were a river. Parting her strawberry lit lips to let a sigh escape, she turned slowly to search the crowd, her satin gown fluffing through the movement. Bowing her head slightly as she glanced at each individual, she smiled at a young man passing her.

"Princess of the Realms."

Turning again to watch a fair-aged man approach, the princess curtsied as the man bowed. "Duke of Chesna, how are you enjoying the party?"

"It's glorious, dear princess, just like your presence," the duke stated as he took her hand and kissed it. "I was hoping to have a chat with your brother, but he seems to have disappeared."

"He," the princess gasped as she turned to stare at an empty throne, "oh, not again!" She sighed as she stared at the gold-trimmed ivory form. What am I going to do with him?

"Does he still refuse to seek a queen?" The duke smiled as he took a sip of the wine in his hand.

Turning to peer at the duke, the Princess of the Realms frowned at his snide expression. "My brother's personal matters are no matter of yours, duke."

"They are a concern to the entire Solari, princess," the duke stated as he stepped closer to her. "The wars are failing to dwindle. Surely, you must understand the concern of the people. A woman at his side would prove that he is ready to step over boundaries and take care of his role as the defender of the Solari. He wasn't appointed as the Prince of the Realms for nothing."

"A queen won't prove anything, duke," the Princess of the Realms frowned as she pushed her shoulders back, straightening her frame. "Marrying won't make any difference in his duties. My brother is doing a fine job—"

"But he could certainly do better," the duke interrupted as he lowered his wine glass. "Or perhaps we should push you to marry . . ."

"You're drunk." The princess frowned as she stepped backward, her long hair stirring against her bare back while she turned away.

The party continued to spark of joyous laughter oblivious to the confrontation between the Princess of the Realms and the Duke of Chesna when Esal came racing down the long corridor leading toward the grand ballroom. Slowing to a soft trot as he came into view of the dozens of royal family members, he cleared his throat as he lowered his deep breaths. The silver glow of his armor danced off his broad thighs and biceps as he bowed his head to several couples enjoying the air of the garden. Sliding his leather glove over his stomach, Esal took a deep breath as light danced over his silver breastplate revealing the usually hidden etching of a tree. Rolling his chin to the soft velvet of his light blue cape, Esal paused at the ballroom's large archway while he pushed his sword into the flowing material. Lifting his leather boots reaching the low of his thighs, he slid carefully around the clergy to freeze as the staff beat into the porcelain floors.

"The captain of Latira's Guard."

Frowning as he turned to glance at the tall man, Esal scowled as soft shouts rang through the hall signifying the approach of young princesses. Grunting as he was pushed back slightly, Esal cringed as several princesses grabbed his arms and started jerking him from side to side.

"Ladies, wait!" Esal grunted as a princess grabbed his cheeks. Widening his eyes as she stood on her tiptoes to kiss him, Esal grunted as another princess attempted the same feat. "No, wait . . ."

"Girls, is this how you attempt to win over the fair captain?"

Stirring a slight movement from his bondage, Esal turned his crystal blue eyes to gasp as he watched the chamber's lights radiate off the woman standing behind him. Widening his eyes as he glanced down the snow-white gown strung tenderly to the lady's thin torso, he blushed as he watched the skirt flare away from the swan wings set on her hips. Each spreading feather brushed through the strawberry tips of her long golden hair. Large glass orbs buckled in the movement of her skirt while the gem chain hanging from her wings stirred against her thighs. The large glass ball attached to the chain resembled the strawberry colored swan eggs of her home planet.

"It's the ruler of Ouderia . . ."

"Fairy Princess Tiri!"

Tilting her head draping the glass teardrop past her electrifying sky blue eyes, the lady smiled as she walked up to set her hand on Esal's shoulder.

"You can't throw yourself at a fair man and hope this kind of action will win him your love." She sighed. "You must be gentle." She nodded as she loosened the girls' arms. "Court him as you would like to be courted."

Bowing their heads, the young princesses sighed heavily as Esal rubbed his neck. "Forgive us, Captain Esal . . ."

Staring at them, Esal smiled softly. "You're all right, ladies . . . please don't let this ruin your mood for the party. I'm only here on business, but I'm sure there are many other men here that would be honored to spend the evening at your sides."

Sighing as the girls walked away swooning, the Princess of Ouderia glanced at Esal to stare puzzled at his suddenly mesmerized expression.

"Esal . . ."

Glancing toward the direction he was staring, she widened her eyes for a moment to smile as she watched the Princess of the Realms brush through the crowd.

"You know you could always go talk to her."

Snapping out of his trance, Esal glanced at the Princess of Ouderia to blush as he saw her teasing stare.

"It's not like that!" Esal protested as he glanced away. "I'm here to see the prince."

"You can't say hi?" She grinned as Esal sighed. "You're simply adorable, Esal."

"Stop teasing me, Cynthia!" Esal frowned as he glanced at her. "The princess . . . we—" Sighing as he glanced at the ground, Esal closed his eyes. "We're just friends."

"And yet somewhere through the years someone fell in love." Cynthia softly giggled as Esal glanced at her with a frown. "It's not like it's a sin, Esal. You are after all—"

"Cynthia Tiri, Ruler of Ouderia, I would be honored if you'd share this dance with me!" A tall man interrupted as he bowed.

Staring at the bowed ebony curls, Esal smiled as he glanced at Cynthia. "Enjoy yourself, Cynthia."

Frowning as Esal kissed her hand, Cynthia lifted her hand as he softly giggled. "You're like an annoying little brother, Captain Esal!" Watching him bow to brush away into the crowd, Cynthia turned to the man as he straightened. "I'd be honored, King Pierre."

Smiling as Cynthia was lead onto the dance floor, Esal bowed his eyes as he turned to move through the crowd. Glancing at the hundreds of familiar faces, Esal paused as he stared at the empty throne.

Great . . . He sighed as he lifted his hand to rub between his eyes. *Now how am I supposed to do this without drawing attention?*

"I thought these gatherings held no interest to the young captain of my guard," a soft voice called near Esal's ear.

Widening his eyes as he released a surprised gasp, Esal turned quickly to stare into eyes darker than day and night. Peering into the pools of mesmerizing color, Esal's crystal blue eyes reflected the raven shade of the indigo blue eyes that belonged to the Prince of the Realms. Staring into the hope filled gaze, Esal watched the wonder spiral in the prince's eyes when he bowed his head. Gasping as the prince caught his arm, Esal lifted his eyes to stare at him bewildered.

"You are no man that need bow to me," the Prince of the Realms stated as he loosened his firm grip on Esal's arm. "I am not your superior."

Staring at the prince, Esal hung his head as he sealed his eyes. "You are my superior, sire, I am but your captain."

"A rule you decided to take by stepping down from your true calling," the prince stated, furrowing his brows as he stared at Esal's calm expression. "Esal . . ."

"You are my friend," Esal sighed as he slowly lifted his eyes to reveal the sparkle omitting from them. "I am not ashamed to serve under you if it means I can protect you."

Staring at Esal, the Prince of the Realms slowly released a disgruntled sigh as he hung his head. "It's no use trying to persuade you otherwise."

Lifting a soft smile to his lips, Esal lifted his hand to grip the prince's. "You know this truth, and yet every time you will try."

"Perhaps one day I hope you will listen," the prince stated as he lifted his other hand to touch Esal's imprisoning his hand in his grip. "Your safety is more important."

"Not to the eyes of the galaxy," Esal stated as he turned his head to his shoulder. "You're the Prince of the Realms, I'm your Captain of the Guard . . . tell me, which one is more important?"

"That's only because they don't know who you are!" The prince frowned gripping both Esal's shoulders. "If . . . if they knew . . ."

"They don't need to know," Esal smiled as he glanced at the prince. "This isn't important though, sire, I need to talk to you in private."

"You always were quick to change the subject." The prince sighed as he released Esal. "Fine, I'll let it go for now."

Bowing his head as he smiled slightly, Esal slowly turned his head as a sudden hush fell over the crowd.

Standing in the midst of the crowd, the Princess of the Realms peered at the sneering Duke of Chesna. Scrunching her nose as she tugged at her hand, the Princess released a soft grunt as he tightened his hold on her wrist.

"Unhand me now!"

Grinning as he watched her slender body struggle, the duke snickered as he watched her graceful curves jerk to free herself. "The entire Solari sees it, princess, it'd be better for everyone if you'd be wed to a man that can handle his duties."

"My brother has protected us—"

"We've been at war for countless centuries. Tell me how that's protecting us." The duke snarled as he pulled her toward him.

"Stop it!" the princess screamed quickly smacking her hand across his cheek.

Gasping as fire coursed up his cheek from the hard contact, the duke slowly glanced at the princess as he touched his aching cheek. Narrowing his eyes as he watched her step backward, the duke tightened his grip on her wrist forcing a cry from her lips.

Ignoring the gasps and whispers of the crowd, the duke lifted his hand from his cheek to swing it at the princess.

"Duke!" the prince's voice thundered through the crowd.

Screaming as the soft pad of his thumb was split open, the duke stumbled back as his hand was torn from the princess's wrist. Gripping his bleeding palm with a gasp, the duke quickly lifted his eyes with gritted teeth to watch the princess disappear behind a sheet of crystal armor. Gasping as a thin tip was hoisted to his neck, the duke swallowed a hard lump as he stared into the misty glare in Esal's crystal blue eyes.

"How dare you?" the duke growled as he narrowed his eyes. "Raising your sword to a nobleman!"

"You're no man, least of all a noble to raise your hand to a lady, this lady!" The soft tone of Esal's voice sent shivers up the duke's back as he stared into the crystal orbs. "Your title is what gives you the authority to do such audacious acts. But to raise your hand to the princess . . . I will not forgive it!"

Standing behind Esal, the princess released a gasp as she tightened her grip on his velvet cape. Glancing at his arm outstretched in front of her, the princess lowered her eyes as she stepped closer to his back.

Glaring at Esal as he continued to hold his sword at his throat, the duke glanced at the Prince of the Realms. "Will you just stand there and do nothing . . . your captain has struck me, drawn blood!"

"You raised your hand to hit my sister, duke." The Prince of the Realms frowned. "You'll bear a scar . . . better than losing your entire hand."

Glancing at Esal, the Duke of Chesna narrowed his dark eyes dangerously as he pointed at him. "You'd better stay clear of me, boy . . . I won't forget this!"

Pulling his sword back to sheath it, Esal exhaled slowly as he felt the princess's chest press against him. "Neither will I." Lowering his arm to grip the princess's hand, Esal turned to brush through the crowd with her following. Watching Esal and the princess move past her, Cynthia glanced at the prince as he stopped in front of the duke. Smiling as the duke's eyes brightened with a soft glow of fear, Cynthia stepped up to the prince as he started after Esal and his sister.

"Sire . . ."

Nodding to her, the prince turned to the crowd and waved his hand. "Continue."

Staring at Esal's cape stirring behind him, the princess slowly lifted her eyes to his wavy hair. Peering at the dark cerulean tints painted in the foamy blue tresses by the shadows, she slowly glanced at his hand captivating hers. Sighing as they cleared the archway leading to the ballroom, she lowered her eyes as she tightened her grip on his hand.

God forgive me . . . Esal thundered in his mind as he moved quickly through the hall.

Stumbling as Esal pushed through a door, the princess glanced around the night lit garden as Esal released her hand. Gaining her balance as he walked across the grassy path, she widened her eyes as Esal hammered his fist into a tree. Covering her mouth as a sapphire light exploded away from him, the princess watched Esal drop his head to the tree with a grunted exhale.

Smacking his fist into the tree, Esal grit his teeth as he slowly closed his eyes. "I could barely contain myself."

Watching him tremble in the faint light of the garden as the light surrounding him began to disappear. The princess slowly lowered her hand to her chest.

"But you did," she softly replied as she stepped toward him.

Opening his eyes as he felt her presence closing in on him, Esal slouched into the tree. "When I heard him make you cry, I . . ." Narrowing his eyes as he pictured the Duke of Chesna, Esal ground his teeth into his lip. "God, forgive me I wanted to hurt him!"

Dashing forward, the princess gripped his cape as she pressed against his back. "But you didn't, Esal . . . you were protecting me!"

Widening his eyes as he felt her tremble, Esal turned quickly to pull her against him as her sobs started. Cradling her head against his chest, Esal lowered his eyes as he hung his head. Closing his eyes as her jasmine scented hair stirred against his cheek, Esal stroked his hand across her bare back.

"You little idiot." He smiled as he stroked his hand through her hair. "I'd always protect you, princess. And not because I have to . . ."

Staring across his silver breastplate, the Princess of the Realms pushed deeper into him as she tightened her hold on his side. Groaning a whimper as she closed her eyes, she shivered as his fingers stretched over her back.

"Because I want to . . ."

His voice echoed in her ears drawing fresh tears to sparkle down her cheeks as she felt his embrace tighten tenderly around her. The warmth he was enveloping her in vibrated a sense of security through her being as she nestled closer to his slender built body. Inhaling a deep breath, she moaned softly as she inhaled the sweet aroma of a rainfall's fresh renewal rising off Esal.

Pausing at the entrance of the garden, the prince smiled as he saw Esal embracing his sister when Cynthia stopped at his side. Glancing at her to see her grin bemused, the prince shook his head with an exhale as he stepped down from the porcelain floor onto the cotton textured grass.

"Are you two all right?"

Lifting his eyes to watch the prince and Cynthia approach, Esal frowned at the amused look in Cynthia's eyes. *Great . . .*

Someone seems like it! Cynthia giggled quietly.

Glancing at her brother and Cynthia, the princess pushed slowly from Esal's embrace to wipe tears from her eyes. "Yes . . . I'm sorry, brother. I'm afraid I created a ruckus."

"Princess, the duke was going to hit you!" Cynthia gasped.

"But I . . ." she stuttered when Esal walked past her.

"You shouldn't feel ashamed about hitting a man like that, princess." Esal sighed as he walked to pause at the prince's side. "Your brother is the Ruler of the Solari, raising a hand against you is like doing it to him. It should be punishable by death." Closing his eyes, Esal hung his head. "But I'm not the one that can deal out that punishment."

Peering at Esal, the prince lowered his eyes as the younger man walked toward the garden's exit. "Esal . . ."

"Where are you going?" Cynthia sighed.

Pausing on the steps, Esal stared at the hall as he exhaled. "I've got to get back to the LDCR."

"Do you need me to come with you?" the prince inquired as he turned to face Esal's back. "You said you needed to talk to me."

Slowly turning to peer at the princess, Esal turned his eyes to the prince. "I can handle it . . . you just take care of your sister."

Walking up to Cynthia and her brother, the princess narrowed her eyes, "I can take care of myself."

Setting her hand on the princess's shoulder, Cynthia nodded, "I'll watch over her . . . no one will do anything with me around her."

Staring at the three, Esal sighed heavily as he closed his eyes, "All right, fine, sire, I need to borrow several minutes of your time."

Nodding, the prince turned to his sister, "I'll be back soon."

"It's not like the party's gonna end anytime soon," she smiled, "Cynthia and I will be all right without you."

"All right," the prince smiled as he started toward Esal. "I'll be back soon."

Staring at the floor, Esal started into the hall again when the princess called to him making him pause.

Watching him slowly turn his head, the princess released a soft breath, "will you come back also?"

Glancing away, Esal shook his head, "I don't have time for parties."

"Oh," she sighed dropping her eyes, "I see."

Staring blankly at the wall, Esal closed his eyes as he pushed into the hall and turned away from the garden. Parting her lips to protest, the princess sighed as she watched Esal disappear from the doorway with her brother following him.

"He'll be back."

Glancing at Cynthia, the princess shook her head, "I don't think so. You don't know Esal like I do. He hates royal parties."

Nodding, Cynthia grinned as she glanced at the princess. "Yes, but the party won't go on all night for you."

Staring at Cynthia puzzled, the princess blushed as she glanced away. "Cynthia . . ."

Giggling, Cynthia gripped the princess's hand. "Come on, let's head back."

Staring at Cynthia's fluffy golden hair, the princess lowered her eyes as her mind began to wonder. *I hope you come back* . . . Smiling, the Princess of the Realms closed her eyes as the noise of the party reached her ears. *I'll wait for you Esal.*

* * * * * *

Pushing a white iron door aside, Esal turned to the prince as he led him through the halls toward the LDCR. Turning back to the prince, Esal released a long sigh as he traced his hand over his side to his sword's steel hilt.

"I didn't know if you had heard the distress beacon . . ."

"Afraid not, there was too much ruckus going on at the party." The prince sighed as he followed Esal closely, "Have we identified from which planet the call was sent from?"

Nodding, Esal turned his eyes back before him as he turned another corner, "Doc has had the team working double time on this. He found the call was sent from Talouxia, he's sending transmissions out right now."

"You've done good, Esal. We should try to figure out when this happened," the prince replied as Esal paused in front of the stairs leading to the LDCR.

"I don't think you'd want to know that sire," Esal stated as he pushed the door open.

Peering at Esal as he walked into the bustling motion of the LDCR, the prince furrowed his brows. "Why wouldn't I?"

Lowering his eyes as he moved across the room, Esal started up the stairs leading to the CPU's mainframe deck when the prince caught his wrist.

"Esal, why wouldn't I want to know?"

Staring at the steel stairs, Esal released a long sigh as he tightened his hand on the railing. Slowly turning his head to peer at the prince, Esal dropped several steps to stare into the prince's dark blue eyes.

"I set up the beacons on each of the planets, sire, so that in case of an emergency a response could be acquired within a matter of seconds."

"I'm aware. It's why I wanted you to do it," the prince stated. "What's the problem?"

"I'm trying to show you," Esal replied as he started back up the stairs.

Releasing Esal's wrist, the prince exhaled as he pushed his raven boots onto the steel staircase.

Brushing past Doc as he continued to send out the transmissions, Esal walked to the crystal plate and tapped the screen. "Bring up the visual."

Listening to the soft clicks of the crystal falling into place, the prince turned to watch the light flood from the machine and strike the sapphire gem at the top center of the crystal wall. Watching the bloody fields appear, the prince's dark indigo eyes widened as they wandered over the falling and slain Talouxians.

Peering at the prince, Esal lifted his eyes to the crystal wall, "do you understand my meaning now, sire? The massacre was already over when the Talouxians hit the distress beacon. We couldn't have gotten there in time to save anyone."

"You don't know that . . ." the prince shouted, "there could be survivors still . . . why are we doing nothing to help them?"

"I can't make such a call and you know that!" Esal frowned.

The prince growled as he grabbed Esal's shoulder to spin him around. "You don't need my authority to save a nation and you also know you could be there saving those that haven't fallen!"

"But that's my point, sire, you aren't understanding," Esal sighed as he shook his head while glancing at the ground.

"Understand what?" the prince shouted as he tightened his hold on Esal. "You keep saying I don't understand . . . what am I supposed to understand?"

"Talouxia is gone!" Esal shouted as he pushed backward trying to free his arms.

"What . . ." the prince gasped as he loosened his hold on Esal. "What do you mean gone? Talouxia . . . a planet just can't be . . . Esal . . ."

Pushing his shoulder back as he shoved his hand into the prince's chest, Esal stepped backward as the prince quickly released his arms. Exhaling a heavy breath, Esal stared at the prince while lifting his hand to rub his arm.

"I meant that Talouxia's lost . . ."

"But . . ."

Peering carefully at the prince, Esal released a long sigh when the dark indigos turned to him. Closing his crystal blue eyes, Esal inhaled sharply as he turned to slide his fingers into the CPU's panel.

"CPU jump ahead five minutes before the Solar Windows shut down."

GIVE ME A MINUTE . . .

Watching the crystal wall fall dark as the CPU pushed the time ahead, the prince widened his eyes as the southern sector of the sky suddenly lit up.

"That can't be . . ."

Staring at the light illuminating the blurred shape of an oval spacecraft, the prince gasped as the visual's animation showed a ray descending from the craft to strike Talouxia. Parting his quivering lips as his eyes trembled, the prince watched the ground blast apart before the visual shut off.

"This . . ." the prince stuttered, "it's impossible . . ."

Both stood transfixed before the CPU's crystal mainframe, oblivious to the young girl that came leaping through the LDCR's entrance. Her pale eyes shot quickly around the craziness to brighten as she ducked backward to avoid the man rushing past with stacks of papers blocking his vision, thus making her invisible to him. A long breath eased through her as she instinctively hoisted her pumpkin eyes toward the CPU's deck where Esal stood with the stunned prince. Springing up the steps, several at a time, to drop to her knee as she reached the level, the clearing of her throat drew both men's attention as the skirt of her musky violet tunic fanned around her small body.

"Your Highness, Esal," she bowed her head quickly, the wavy curls of pumpkin shaded orange dancing across her shoulders. "I've been looking everywhere for you!"

"Jeannee . . ." The prince sighed, hoping things weren't about to get worse.

"Sire, I regret to inform that not long ago an unidentified spacecraft was found approaching the dimensional gateway," she informed.

"What?" Esal gasped.

"Where is the spacecraft heading?" the prince questioned.

"It's hard to tell, all we know so far is that it was sighted near the gateway leading to the other dimension!" Jeannee replied.

"The other dimension," the prince repeated.

She nodded before hoisting her pale gaze to his dark one. "Yes, it's unusual, considering there isn't anything of interest in the other dimension—"

"Don't misjudge the solar system . . . some of our oldest stories tell of Warriors from their universe!" the prince explained as a short man in a military uniform saluted behind the three. "Yes?"

"Sire, the spacecraft just passed through the gateway!"

Turning toward the man, the prince gazed at him in disbelief. "When?"

"Not ten seconds ago."

"There's no way a spacecraft can move through the gateway that fast!" Jeannee declared.

Turning to the wide eyed girl, the prince's brows creased as he pointed toward a computer, "Jeannee, I need to know where the spacecraft's heading."

"Right," she nodded while leaping to her feet and spinning to trot down the steps.

"Lieutenant, I want the ranks doubled and the guests escorted to a secure location."

"On your command, sire." The man saluted before dashing out of the room.

"Esal . . ." the prince took the younger man and pulled him away from the others. "I'm afraid we've made a critical mistake . . ."

"Sire, what are you talking about . . . it's possible that the craft just wasn't docked properly and was jarred lose at the last atmosphere shock." Esal stated.

"Not this time my friend. That spacecraft model hasn't been made for three thousand years . . ." the prince informed, "The only craft of that model left was one used to banish an evil malice that plagued this planet's valleys a millennium ago!"

Esal gazed at the prince in complete disbelief, "you aren't—you're talking about *that* war . . ."

The prince stared into the startled crystal eyes when Jeannee's holler called out to him urgently. "Yes."

"It's stopped, sire, the craft. It's just sitting in their world." Jeannee frowned.

"Where?"

"That fourth planet from their sun, it's powered down beneath its moon."

The prince gazed away from Jeannee toward Esal, "I need your help . . ."

2

$\mathcal{B}$ack at the Royal Families Party, the Princess of the Realms walked out the porcelain doorframe leaving the roaring chamber. She stood in the soft whistling hum of the native Angelician Night Seabirds as it gently bounced around her to fill the Palace walls. Gracefully lifting her soft satin hands, the princess tenderly pushed the diamond mask she'd been offered when she and Cynthia had reentered the ball nearly an hour ago, the brightness of her sapphire eyes sparkled like the lights that were leaking to the hall to reflect off the silver armor of the passing and stationary guards. A disappointed sigh softly escaped her throat as her thoughts returned to the young captain. Part of her had hoped he would've returned. Becoming lost in the soft melody of the night as she slid carefully through the crowd wandering around the halls to slip unnoticed onto one of the many garden balconies, she exhaled a deep breath as her gaze ventured toward the many sweet scented flowers. A gentle hum escaping the princess's lips brought a baby bird to her waiting fingers.

What a fool I am . . . she groaned as she gently stroked the baby's snowy breast.

The princess moaned softly to startle when the large globes at the corner of every hall began to suddenly flash a brilliant red as the warning sirens wailed. Guards throughout the kingdom ran through the halls, securely doubling up their posts as others escorted the party guests to a fortified chamber. The princess raced down a hall pushing through the guards until she came to a tall man with dark russet hair.

"Zek, what's going on?" the princess yelled.

Golden eyes turned curiously away from his regiment to gaze in mixed shock and irritation at the approaching girl. "Princess . . ." He frowned to glance at several of his shrinking men, "why are you not with the guests in the lockdown."

"Because I am not a guest, what is going on?" the princess urged.

"His Highness has ordered a lockdown, the Palace is to be fortified and we're sending ranks out across the galaxy," Zek replied.

"Why on earth would he do that . . ." she pondered.

Zek gazed at his fellow guards then back at the princess, "Princess, please allow my men to escort you—"

"No, take me to my brother now!"

Meanwhile

His heart was racing, his thoughts a jumbled mess. The large cloak breezing behind his small build would've drowned him if not for the brisk of his step and the slight menacing determination in his dark eyes. They swept from one dark corner to the next blindingly bright one, searching in empty spaces that clearly he alone knew could possibly hold some secret treasure. Or danger. His gloved hand held tightly to the sturdy ivory oak staff he was thumping against the porcelain floors, keeping a soft melody in time as he traversed the Palace, gliding toward the portal that would allow access from their world to the other. His dark eyes narrowed in irritation as he came upon the guard before the entrance.

Stopping before the guard, the Holy Priest of Ilberta tilted his staff waiting for the guard to move from his path.

"Not this time Priest, no one goes in or out. The Captain's about to open the path to the other universe and this door must remain closed!" The guard stated folding his arms.

I tried. He scowled before shifting his staff straight, the guard's eyes whipped instantly toward the glowing sphere atop its peak. "I do not care what your orders are unless you wish to be turned into a toad and boiled for next week's dinner, I suggest you move!" the Holy Priest warned.

The guard gazed at the Holy Priest for a few seconds before he stepped to the side allowing the Priest to move through the doorway.

Walking down a series of steel steps to the portal's threshold with Jeannee following close by, their boots clanging against the metal as he hoisted his eyes, Esal held the prince's dark gaze before the taller man nodded with a soft grin. Sitting within a crystal framed booth overlooking the gateway, several scientists busied themselves with bringing the ancient device to life as Esal's pale eyes centered on the large iron door that contained the passageway.

"Esal, you must be going insane! No one has ever gone to the other dimension, least of all one of the planets!"

"Jeannee calm down, if it wasn't possible to pass to the other world, why would we have the gateway?" Esal smiled.

"We use it to transport to the other areas of our galaxy! Access has never been granted to enter the other dimension," she exasperated.

"Jeannee," Esal frowned grabbing her arms. "I'll be all right. I'm the Captain of the guard, I can handle anything that comes my way, OK?"

Jeannee stood breathing heavily with Esal grasping her arms, her pale eyes searching his uncertainly. "OK," she sighed miserably, "all right, you just better come back . . . in one piece!"

Esal smiled brightly at Jeannee when the Holy Priest came trotting down the steps. His dark maroon eyes gazed steadily upon Esal as he stopped in front of the young Captain.

"Captain I need to speak with you privately . . ." the Holy Priest stated gazing at Jeannee.

"I don't have time Priest."

Moving several bangs from his eyes, the Holy Priest took Esal's arm, "It's important you hear this . . . it will help you with the search!"

"Search . . ." Esal questioned as the Holy Priest pulled him into a corner.

Once safely away from earshot, the Holy Priest turned toward Esal, "I know why you go to that blue planet . . . our prince believes that the craft happens to be one that has served as a prison to one of the biggest monstrosities, he wishes for you to go to investigate whether it is the ship, whether the creature within is still alive, still contained. I'll tell you now that it is there, alive . . ." wiping his brow as he took in a deep breath, he glanced slowly around before leaning toward Esal, "it is not alone."

"What?" Esal frowned.

"The beast, it is not alone."

"How can that possibly be, the prince told me it was the single survivor—"

"Evil has its ways of coming back."

Esal studied the Holy Priest for a long moment before his crystal eyes narrowed. "There's something you're not telling me . . . what is it?" He questioned when the darkness beyond him suddenly brightened with the light that began to pour from the humming portal.

The Holy Priest gazed to the portal before turning back toward Esal, "there are . . . circumstances that you wouldn't understand—"

"Priest, I need to go through that portal in the next couple seconds, if there's something I need to know about that world, I'd *really* appreciate you filling me in!"

"Just kill them, don't let them act first, don't let them search the planet!" The Priest rambled to glance at the portal.

"Search for what?"

Inhaling deeply, the Holy Priest grasped his staff firmly as he leaned his weight against it. "They've invaded the other universe because I've hidden our prince there."

Slowly, a small grin rose around the corners of Esal's lips as he stared steadily at the Holy Priest. "Really."

"Don't mock me boy!" The Priest growled, "You think that because of who you are you know everything there is to . . . well, surprise, you don't. Our prince, our true prince, has been living in secret down on that blue planet."

The seriousness in the Holy Priest's voice had wiped the smile from Esal's face as he stared in confusion at the elder man. "What do you mean? I don't understand what you're trying to say."

"Skip the understanding," the Priest urgently demanded while grabbing Esal's arm to lead him to the portal. "Just be aware that something happened that required me to take drastic action. I took it upon myself so that our prince would be safe, but they figured it out . . . I don't know how, but they did. They know that the strength, the heritage, the legacy of the Prince of the Realms rests with the young boy down on that planet. He doesn't know who he is, thinks of himself as normal, simple, hasn't a clue of the nobility or the power he possesses. Captain, you have to save him. It's what they've gone there for. If they kill him they kill the hope of this world and then that one as well."

His breath was heavy on his chest as he licked his dry lips, his pale eyes glancing toward the dark portal and the bright rings pulsing toward him from its depths.

"Esal . . ." the Priest pressed to narrow his eyes as the said youth remained silent, unresponsive. He stepped closer and grasped his arm to pull reluctant crystallized blue eyes on him, "Captain, do you understand what I've just told you? Our prince is about to be sought out to be murdered by these demon spawns, will you do nothing?"

"No," Esal snapped, his thin brows narrowing irritably as he stared up at the hyperventilating Priest. "I don't understand it at all . . . you're trying to tell me that the man I'm looking at right now isn't in **fact** my sovereign but a relic . . . and that his true self just **happens** to be on one of the planets of the other universe?"

"It was the only safe place."

His jaw tightened as he clenched his teeth in confused fury. "Safe . . ."

"Esal plea—" the Holy Priest pleaded to cut off at the soft shriek that echoed away from the viewing platform, drawing everyone's attention to the collapsing prince. A long breath eased through his chest as he watched Jeannee race past him, his gloved hand snapping forward to catch Esal's arm as the captain breezed past him.

The furious young man turned on the Priest, his clear eyes smoldering. "What're you doing let go . . ."

"There is no time for this, things are further in motion then I could've imagined."

"What're you rambling about old man, release me now!" Esal bit out while tugging at his snared wrist, "the prince—"

"If you want to help him, go to the blue planet . . . it is there that you will find your prince, it is there that you will ultimately be of use." The Holy Priest interrupted as he tugged the protesting youth ahead of him to hold him just before the edge of the portal. "You are of no use to him as he is here, he is nothing but a spirit, a remnant of what he was . . . it explains what is currently happening, he is being recalled to himself . . . body and spirit are calling out to one another. The invasion has begun his awakening. You must be there when it happens! He could blanket the entire universe in darkness if he is not controlled!"

His pale eyes vibrated slightly as he ran them carefully across the Priest's childlike face, searching the furious, guilt ridden, maroon depths of his eyes. The fury and worry that had once been within his own eyes had dissipated to be replaced with the gut wrenching knots that were numbing him from the inside out. His breath was shaky as it slipped through his parting lips.

"What am I supposed to do?"

"Fight," the Priest grasped the slumped shoulders and squeezed encouragingly, "like her, you are a light in endless darkness. Listen to your heart Esal, it is strong, it'll never steer you wrong." His own heart fluttered excitedly as he watched the young captain step away from him, his pale eyes peering up at him with determination and intent.

Tightening his grip on the hilt of his sheathed weapon, the leather binding his hands moaning slightly in protest, Esal nodded once while shifting so he was facing the pulsing doorway.

"Esal . . ." Jeannee pondered before grasping the rail and pulling herself from her knees beside the passed out prince and dozens of scientists and guards, "Captain what're you doing?"

He turned slowly to lift his gaze to her, smiling slightly. "It's going to be all right . . . take care of everyone til I return."

"What?" She frowned to part her lips in a gasp as he turned to brush through the blinding rings. "Esal?"

Watching him meld into the darkness for a moment longer before turning toward the stairs that would lead him to the unconscious prince, the Holy Priest's nose creased irritably as Jeannee's screams ground against his already aching head. He growled several things to the hyperventilating girl as Doc's narrowed gaze continued to watch the dimensional gateway, watching the edge of his captain's long cape fluttering within the blinding nothingness. A long breath eased through him as he turned his attention once more to the prince, his shaggy chocolate hair breezing suddenly past his cheeks as a blurry blue light zipped through the room to slip down the stairs and into the portal as it closed in on itself.

3

Earth—Friday, April 11, 2026

The wind quietly blew through the many towering trees within the miles of forestry surrounding the large city. Cuddly woodland creatures scampered across the soft forest floor and through the sturdy tree limbs so they could enter the crowded city. The roaring streets were crowded with buses, cars, and pedestrians when the city clock chimed half past two signaling the school day was coming to an end. Hastily moving through the busy streets, parents drove down the Boulevard in preparation to pick up their children as the school day came to an end.

The soft ticking of the clock echoed along the quiet halls of the school as the campus police patrolled the area for the remaining ten minutes. Their shoes echoed along the walls to join the faint tick of the clock as Professor Freché lectured to his AP Government class. With only a few minutes before the weekend, the students were plagued as the torment persisted. Over three-fourths of the class wasn't paying attention as Freché went over the material for their next upcoming test.

Slender fingers spun a pencil around finely sculpted knuckles, the thin wood remaining perfectly balanced as long raven strands fell over the copper sleeve of a beautiful girl's arm. Blowing a soft sigh past her pale cherry lips, she frowned as she rubbed her hand against her tense neck, ruffling the collar of her shirt. Dropping her head against her propped hand, she listened to the slow beat of the clock when she felt pressure against her back, softly at first to then turn persistent as she hesitated to turn toward the culprit.

"Psst Hikaru . . ."

Glancing backward, a slight bit of annoyance sparkling in her dark eyes, the girl turned to peer into the enchanting emerald eyes of the mischievous blonde behind her. Leaning further over her desk, the blonde widened an eye as a jade light flashed through her blonde locks.

"What?" Hikaru whispered.

"What? You sound almost disappointed that I'm interrupting your boredom!"

"No," Hikaru sighed shaking her head as she glanced at Freché then back at the blonde, "it's just that you always get us in trouble, Kimiko Shiru!"

"What, I do not!" Kimiko rebutted, "You have a fair enough hand in that trouble blame, Hikaru Neijo!"

Frowning, Hikaru blew a sigh out as her raven hair draped over her face, "fine . . . I relent and thus admit . . ." lifting her head as her brown eyes brightened, Hikaru nodded with a smile, "I give a fair share of trouble."

Turning to see Hikaru and Kimiko giggling, Freché lowered his ruler to his knees as he lifted his hand to rub the bridge of his nose. Lifting his eyes to scan the class, he sighed as he saw half the class doing anything and everything, but listened to him. Pausing as he saw a young man laying his head against his arms across his desk, Freché narrowed his eyes as he lifted his ruler.

"You'd think that after a while of talking over half of his students to sleep, Freché would get the picture to stop lecturing!" Kimiko whispered giggling. "Not like it matters though since we don't pay attention either way, huh Hikaru?" Kimiko chuckled when Professor Freché slammed his fist down on the desk across from her startling the girls.

"En Skilou!"

Quickly shooting up with a startled yelp, En lurched further back then intended and tipped his chair over onto his brother Jeremy Aino's feet. Releasing a soft shout, Jeremy banged his hand into his desk as he sank his teeth into his lower lip.

"En . . ." Jeremy ground out as he sucked in a low growl.

Standing in front of En's desk with crossed arms, Freché tapped the ruler against his tricep as he watched En smile nervously. Tumbling quickly out of his seat, En held his gaze on Freché as Jeremy released his breath.

"I assume you must have had another long night to explain why you were sleeping in my class again EN SKILOU!" Freché screamed when the afternoon bell rang. "Not so fast En," Freché growled as En picked up his books, "you'll stay after."

Fifteen minutes later

Students walked by Hikaru as she stood outside the classroom waiting for En with Kimiko and Jeremy. Tilting her head back against the wall as she sighed, she brushed her hand over her forehead moving raven bangs from her eyes. Rubbing her neck, Hikaru ran her hand down the orange collar of her jacket as several girls and boys brushed past her. Glancing after them, Hikaru frowned as they giggled while staring at the three. Smacking her briefcase against her knees, she tightened her grip as her thumbs brushed along the edge of her thigh-high white socks. Sighing as she lifted her black slipper shoe to the wall, she slowly glanced at Kimiko as her laughter hummed through the hall.

"So how do your feet feel Jeremy? It's not every day they get En dropped on them!" Kimiko burst out laughing.

"Cut it out Kimiko, it wasn't funny!" Jeremy yelled.

"Guys calm down," Hikaru replied to glance at Freché's classroom as En walked out,. "Hey guy, how did that go?"

A bright smile filled the corners of En's lips as he shut the door quietly behind him, "fine I suppose, can't be entirely sure cause I wasn't paying attention. I just smiled and nodded."

Shaking his head with a disgruntled exhale, Jeremy pushed off the wall to start down the hall. "You know, one of these days he's going to beat the shit out of you En."

"Ah, you're not still mad about me smashing your feet are you . . . Jeremy . . . Jeremy don't ignore me!" En shouted chasing after his brother.

Giving Freché's class a last glance before turning the corner, Hikaru glanced over the side of the walkway to the level below. Watching the other students merrily departing the school grounds, Hikaru glanced at Kimiko as she laughed.

"Oh come on, it's not my fault you squealed like a girl!"

"Would you stop already," Jeremy sighed as he stopped at the corner of the walkway. "I gotta head to fencing practice. I'll see you guys later."

"Are we gonna do something later?" Hikaru inquired as she settled her case against her shoulder.

Shrugging, Jeremy glanced back at the walkway, "I don't see a reason why not. We'll see how things are looking after practice."

"Okay, sounds like a plan," Kimiko smiled as Jeremy started down a hall with En. Glancing at Hikaru, Kimiko smiled mischievously, "so are you coming over to my house?"

Smiling, Hikaru shook her head, "you know I'd love to, but I promised my brother I'd start running with him after school."

"What?" Kimiko gasped sinking into her sagging shoulders. "But but but . . . Masumi gets you every day . . . it's my turn to have you!"

Sighing, Hikaru smiled as she turned to the same hall, "I'm glad I can be passed off so easily as a possession."

"What am I supposed to do til later then?" Kimiko pouted.

Grinning, Hikaru shrugged toward the hall, "you can run with me."

Frowning, Kimiko straightened as she brushed her thumb against her nose, "you mean mingle with the track rejects and get all sweaty and smelly with the lanky kids!"

"You're pretty lanky to Miss Shiru!" Hikaru teased with a giggle as she pointed toward Kimiko's body.

Slowly glancing down her small chest to her similarly small waist, Kimiko frowned as she lifted her eyes from her well distinguished hips.

"And your point is . . . you aren't exactly finely sculpted either Hikaru Neijo!" Kimiko pointed back at her. "So you have more in your bust than I do . . . and wider hips . . ." staring at Hikaru's well curved figure, Kimiko dropped her head with a defeated sigh, "OK, you look more like a girl then I do!"

Crossing her arms, Hikaru exhaled heavily as she stared at Kimiko, "done?"

"Possibly," Kimiko pondered. "It's my brothers fault . . . they've used me as a punching bag for too long!" She nodded.

"Please," Hikaru coughed a chuckle, "you dish out just as much as they do, if not more."

Nodding, Kimiko smiled conceitedly, "teaches 'em to mess with a girl. We're so much eviler than a guy can be . . . all we have to do is shoot a shot to their privates!" She snickered evilly.

Shaking her head, Hikaru glanced at the ceiling, "shows how much you know, you're the only one that would deliberately try to wound a guy in such a way Kimiko."

Crossing her arms, Kimiko pouted as she glanced down the other end of the hall, "whatever . . ."

Smirking, Hikaru lifted her case to her shoulder, "so are you coming or not?"

Shaking her head, Kimiko sighed, "I don't think so. Antony's been kinda edgy lately . . . I think it might be a good idea to just let him have his time with his guys."

"Have your dad and him been at it again?" Hikaru sighed lowering her smile.

Nodding, Kimiko stared at the ground, "yeah . . . dad's been real rough on Antony lately . . . I just think it'd be better if Antony uses this time to free some of his built rage."

"You know Antony loves your company more than anything!" Hikaru stated as she gripped Kimiko's shoulder. "He might need you today."

Nodding, Kimiko sighed, "yeah, but I don't have my clothes."

"Oh how convenient!" Hikaru smiled, "I swear you plan these things Kimiko!"

"I do not," Kimiko frowned then smiled. "OK, maybe I do, but I thought you were gonna come home with me, but I forget you like spending time with your brother."

"You like your brothers Kimiko." Hikaru sighed with a grin.

"Yeah, all five of them." Kimiko nodded with perched lips. "OK, I'm heading home . . . I'll see you later."

"Bye, Kimiko." Hikaru smiled as she waved Kimiko off. "Be careful heading home!" Watching her best friend disappear down the stairs, Hikaru turned to trot down the hall toward the track and field.

Smiling at a janitor she trotted past, Hikaru quickly turned a corner to grunt as she hammered into someone. Falling onto her butt, she cringed as she watched dozens of papers flutter around her.

"Oh gosh, I'm sorry!" Hikaru gasped as she caught several papers while sitting up. "I'm sorry . . ."

"You're all right," a masculine voice chuckled softly.

Gasping as she stared at the raven haired man, Hikaru felt her breath catch as she stared into his dark blue eyes. Blinking dumbfounded as she watched the overhanging lights dance over the snowy suit altering the fashion of the boy's attire, Hikaru smiled a nervous breath. "M-Mr. Chairman!"

Kneeling beside Hikaru as she lit up like a flame, the man smiled as her face contorted to nervous expressions. "You know you don't have to address me like that, after all we've practically grown up together." He smiled. "Will you please just call me Kimon?"

"Oh no . . ." Hikaru practically shouted to gasp. Lowering her eyes as her cheeks turned scarlet, Hikaru glanced at her feet. "I couldn't do that. You're the Acting Chairman, Mr. Youitan."

Frowning, Kimon moved his gloved hands along his white coat loosening the snap as he bent closer to Hikaru.

"Hikaru I grew up with your brother, we've been friends since you were able to walk. If I can call you by your name, you can call me by mine." He pleaded. "Besides, it doesn't sound right when you speak to me like that. I want you to be comfortable around me."

Slowly lifting her eyes, Hikaru stared at the green tendrils hanging from the scarlet orbs on Kimon's shoulders signifying his station of being the youngest Acting Chairman appointed in the history of the Academy.

"Mr. Chairman, there are certain protocols that must be addressed when at school. I must address you with respect and formality." Hikaru stated as she started to gather the papers into a pile. "I'm sorry I ran into you like that."

Sighing, Kimon started sliding the papers together when Hikaru's fingers brushed over his. Gasping as she suddenly snapped her hand backward, Kimon watched her bite her lower lip as she rubbed her hand.

"Sorry . . ."

Smiling, Kimon lowered his eyes with a soft snicker, "little Neijo . . ." dropping the papers, Kimon reached forward to grip her hand, "you're still as adorable as ever."

Widening her eyes as he kissed her hand, Hikaru held her breath as he slowly lifted his head to stare at her. "Kimon . . ."

"There you see," he smiled as he combed her bangs from her eyes, "that wasn't so hard was it?"

Staring blankly as he stood, Hikaru gasped as he started past her, "Kimon . . ."

Pausing, Kimon turned to peer at her as his arm lowered the papers to his hip, "yes, Hikaru?"

Pushing onto her feet, Hikaru trotted toward him. "You forgot these."

Staring at the offered papers, Kimon nodded as he took them, "thank you."

Nodding, Hikaru smiled impishly as she turned to race down the hall. "Oh . . ." she gasped as she skidded to a stop.

Watching Hikaru race back up the hall, Kimon smiled as she bent to pick her case off the floor.

"Bye Kimon."

"Try not to run into anyone else Hikaru!" Kimon chuckled. Sighing as Hikaru disappeared, Kimon lowered his eyes as he glanced at his gold cuffed sleeve. "She seems almost terrified to speak to me."

"You who, ooh Mr. Youitan!"

Sighing as he turned to watch the tall beauty rushing up to him, Kimon settled his eyes to a calm glance as she paused in front of him.

Smiling impishly like some small schoolgirl with a crush, the lady bated her eyes flirtatiously as she gripped Kimon's hand. "I missed you at lunch today!"

"Miss Syatlaoi," Kimon frowned, closing his eyes as he pulled his hand free. "You know that I can't be at school every second. My duties as the acting chairman require that I attend matters off school grounds if the Director should be busy."

"Yes, I know. Daddy had a board meeting today," she frowned crushed from his reaction, "I was just disappointed. I've had a long day and you usually help brighten it. And it's Claire, remember?"

"I'm sorry you had a bad day, Miss Syatlaoi, but I'm afraid I can't do much for it right now. I have some things to complete before the day ends. Perhaps you can tell me tomorrow."

Nodding merrily, Claire smiled brightly as Kimon brushed past her. "Until tomorrow then." Smirking as he continued down the hall, Claire glanced at the flabbergasted girls approaching her. "So . . ."

"Claire, you're astounding!" A girl with curly brown hair squeaked.

"Do you have no shame, Miss Claire?" A semishort girl with blonde hair impishly questioned. "I can't believe that you can just run up like that and . . . hug him! I don't think I could ever find the nerve to do something like that."

"Yes, well, Oakley, that's why you will never catch anything. You have to be willing to take what you want." Claire smiled.

"That's nice logic."

Scowling, Claire whipped her head around casting her long hair across her shoulder as she turned to stare at a young girl approaching.

"Fuí," Claire snarled as the girl paused several feet away from her. "What are you doing here?"

"You don't own the school, Syatlaoi." She sighed as she worked her hand up to push her wavy strawberry kissed blonde hair from her cheek.

"You will watch how you speak to Miss Claire, Maya!" Oakley snapped.

Raising an eyebrow as she smirked, Maya shook her head as she pulled her case off her arm. "I don't owe Claire Syatlaoi anything but a kick in the skirt."

Frowning as Maya closed her eyes, Claire stepped forward as she threw her hand out. Gasping as a solid ring of contacting flesh rang through the hall, Oakley and her companion covered their mouths in astonishment as Claire lowered her arm from Maya's cheek.

"I could have you expelled for this Fuí . . . you don't talk to me like that understand?" Claire growled.

Slowly opening her eyes, Maya softly exhaled as she rolled her head from her shoulder to glare at Claire. "This isn't the first time you've personally attacked me, but it will be the last!"

Gasping as Maya knocked her backward, Claire stumbled back to fall on her butt to cringe as Maya lifted her case.

"Don't . . ." Claire screamed lifting her arms.

Tensing her arm as she was ready to swing her case, Maya narrowed her eyes as she stared at Claire's quivering figure. Scoffing, Maya dropped her arm to her side as she turned away. "You aren't worth the time." She sighed as she started down the hall. "But you'll wish you hadn't done that."

Lowering her arms with a soft whimper, Claire watched Maya continue down the hall when Oakley gripped her arm. "Get off!" She screamed as she wrenched her arm free. Slowly lifting her eyes to glare at Maya, Claire pushed to her feet as Oakley glanced at the other girl. "You're the one that's going to regret this Maya Fui!"

Releasing an agitated sigh, Maya dropped her head with a frustrated growl as she moved down the halls of the school. Tilting her head to the side casting the tips of her hair along her shoulder, Maya inhaled when she suddenly jerked forward with a loud groan.

"Maya-Tama . . ." a tall girl merrily screamed as she hugged Maya's neck.

Stumbling forward as the girl threw her off balance, Maya released a long sigh as the girl chuckled. "Geez-us, Touko Keig what in the world is wrong with you?"

Sliding off Maya's back, Touko stared at her best friend with a soft frown, "Maya what's wrong?"

Staring at Touko, Maya slowly glanced away, "it's nothing . . . Claire just made me mad."

"Doesn't she usually do that?" Touko smiled as she pushed her long golden bangs behind her ear. "The only people in this school that like her is her dad!"

"And even then, I'm not sure he does!" Maya chuckled.

Staring at Maya as she laughed, Touko released a long sigh. "What did she do?"

"The usual, except this time she decided to hit me," Maya exhaled as she turned her bright blue eyes to peer at Touko.

"You," Touko grunted to bite her lower lip. "You didn't do anything back to her right . . . Maya, you didn't, right?"

"God knows I wanted to . . . but I didn't . . . took all my self-control not to hit her!" Maya frowned. "I can't wait for the day when someone puts that little witch in her place." Shaking her head, Maya glanced at Touko with a grin. "Come on, we better get to practice before coach starts to freak out."

"What about Kaho?" Touko inquired as she started after Maya. "Don't you need to pick her up?"

Shaking her head, Maya smiled. "No, Mom's got her. Kaho's starting to stay the few minutes mom has to stay after school. Guess, Kaho found something to keep her entertained. She won't tell me, but I think it has something to do with the Director's son."

"Oh, does Kaho have a crush?" Touko smiled.

Shrugging, Maya trotted down a set of stairs, "could be."

* * * * * *

"Timothy don't drive your power into your heels . . . move with the resistance not against it."

Trotting onto the track in a pair of white sneakers, loose shirt, and shorts, Hikaru watched the track team's captain bark out his orders. Shaking her head with a soft exhale, she bounded across the matted ground.

Working his fingers through the loose strands of raven hair, a tall young man watched his teammate rub his eyes in a near fit of defeat. "Count to ten, Antony." He grinned mischievously.

Opening his dark orbs to glance toward him, Antony shook his head, "I've counted to a hundred and back again . . ."

Chuckling to grunt as a solid slap struck his back, forcing him to stubble several feet, the raven haired man turned to a grinning Hikaru.

"How it be, cap'ain?"

"Antony's about to lose it," he smiled.

"More so then usual?" she inquired as she glanced at the chocolate haired young man.

"He must be at it with his dad again."

"How did—" Hikaru stammered to glance up at her brother, "how'd you know?"

"Antony and I've been friends since we were kids . . . I can tell."

Staring up at Masumi for a moment before slowly glancing toward Antony, watching the wind beat against his solid form, Hikaru lowered her eyes with a soft smile. "Sounds like Kimiko and I . . . do you think it's ironic that we're both your younger sisters?"

"I don't know," Masumi shrugged as Antony dropped back onto the grass. "Excuse me, I have to make sure he's not ready to blow."

Smiling as Antony looked at his approaching best friend in near desperation, Hikaru glanced into the sky as the wind disturbed her hair. Watching the lazy crawl of the cotton-formed clouds while combing her hair behind her ears, she let out a sharp gasp at the clear line that snapped like lightning through the now pulsing skies.

"Hey, Hikaru . . ."

Glancing back to her brother, her bright eyes fluttered as she blinked dumbfounded "huh?"

"Antony's decided on a city circuit, do you still want to come with us?"

"Seriously." Hikaru frowned then smiled. "Yeah, I'm coming."

Pushing off the grass, Antony smacked dew from his gray sweats. "Okay ladies and gents, we're gonna be having a change of scenery today." Frowning as groans and whines shot out at once, Antony slid a band onto his wrist with agitation. "Yeah that's right, endure the torture . . . you're gonna be able to run on water when I'm done with you."

Smiling as she watched the team follow Antony reluctantly, Hikaru slowly glanced at the still sky, her bright grin fading leisurely.

"You coming squirt?"

Gasping as she glanced toward her waiting brother, she trotted quickly toward him. "Coming."

* * * * * *

Walking slowly through the suddenly quieting school, Kimiko released a long sigh as she passed a mini garden, gratefully inhaling the soft aroma of the damp flowers as she came toward the staircase leading into the city.

"You must be thinking of something important to be in such a daze."

Glancing at the mirror image of a boy possibly an inch taller than her, Kimiko softened her eyes as the boy smiled earnestly at her. He held his twins adoring gaze with a chuckle breezing off his smiling lips when the wind forced itself past him, blinding him for a moment with his whipping hair. Hoisting his hand to block the pale blond strands from stinging his eyes further, his paler green eyes brightened for a moment as his sister's hands cupped his cheeks.

Her gaze had hardened, scrutinizing, as she carefully inspected his face as if she were searching for some hidden wounds. After several minutes of his face being nearly smushed within her grasp, she nodded and released her brother with a loud exhale.

"So how were classes?" He chuckled.

Watching him bend to lift their cases, Kimiko took hers as it was extended. "All right, I suppose, why?"

"No reason, you just seem to be in such a good mood."

"Oh whatever, shut it Esu . . . so what about you little brother?"

"Little . . . I know you must be joking, I'm older and taller than you."

"You're only an inch taller than me," Kimiko sighed, "if that," she challenged while touching his head.

Staring through his blond bangs, Esu pushed Kimiko's hand off his head. "An inch is an inch." He nodded to smile as his pale green eyes brightened.

Widening her eyes as he leaned forward suddenly to peak a quick kiss to her forehead, a gasp exploded through her chest as she threw her arms dramatically. "Eww . . . brother cuddles!"

"Come on, we have to go get Louise."

Wiping her forehead frantically, she turned to chase her twin down the stairs. "Remind me why you volunteered us to get the brat?"

"It's on the way home, Kimiko, it's been a routine for years . . . and Louise isn't a brat."

"You're right . . . he's just a boy."

Watching Esu shake his head with a smile, Kimiko grinned amusedly when she heard a vacuum-like hum. Glancing around the street, her bright eyes blinking in confusion to widen as she peered on impulse to the skies, she watched a faint light pulse across the pale blue skies like a wave. She watched entranced when Esu's voice snapped her back to reality.

"Huh . . ."

"What're you doing?" He puzzled as he glanced at the sky.

"Nothing," she stated with a shake of her head, "I just thought I'd seen something."

"What?"

Stopping next to her elder brother, Kimiko smiled to whisper conspiratorially, "I saw the light!"

Sighing, he started down the street. "Again you remind me of what a retard you are."

"Oh come on Esu, you know that was funny." Kimiko giggled as she chased after him. "Esu . . ."

* * * * * *

The sheer vapor of the clouds passed through the sky never remaining the same in appearance as the world moved, a slow rhythmic dance like a droplet ringing a disturbance in the water. The wind has no form, no visible shadow to follow its journey, just a voice to signal its approach or departure. A noisy flutter of wings is the occasional sound in the expanse of the silence.

Bursting through the cotton of the clouds, a boom like the snap of a tree ran through the sky. Moments later, a clear wave of energy pulsed from the disturbed cloud to ring the sky in an illusion that the sky was shifting. A second wave with a ring of half the sun's brightness reached through the sky to disappear at three yards distance. Crackles of thunder sang in the next wave as electrical snaps brought the wave of bright rings.

Running down the street, enjoying the burn that was reaching through her thighs to the rest of her sweating body, Hikaru inhaled a deep breath as she chanced a glance back to Antony and Masumi leading the wildly panting and whining track team. A soft chuckle rose through her to slip around her rapidly beating heart, her amused eyes turning right to lift to the skies and freeze.

"Wow, Kar!" She heard her brother shout before he stumbled quickly around her, Antony's chuckle falling on deaf ears as he said something that had her brother snapping at him quickly. Her legs began to tingle from the exertion of the run as the remaining track team passed her, annoyed to confused glances turning on her as she continued to peer into the sunny skies.

Her chest tightened as she stared up at the sky, watching the pulses that resembled ripples in a river. Slowly she turned, the loose strips of her long hair rising on a barely present breeze. Chocolate orbs widened drastically as the blinding rings were captured within and reflected within their depths.

"Hikaru . . ."

Standing at the corner, leaning into his knees, Masumi stared at his sister when his gaze wandered to the bare skies she was staring so intensely.

The burn had been replaced by a soft ache, she felt it slightly as she lifted her now heavy feet to start back the way she'd come. Sliding in and out of people littering the streets, her breath and heart increasing in speed as she became oblivious to her brother's shouts, Hikaru beat her feet into the cement as she raced through the city as if she were flying.

Walking slowly across the pulsing rings that served as a temporary floor within the air, Esal peered at the clear skies when he came to the edge of the portal. Widening his eyes as he saw the tall buildings reaching thousands of feet to the air, his gaze moved slowly over the cement paths and industries.

"So . . . this is the world my prince was sent to. The world I'm intended to protect from the wrath of a creature that should be dead." Lowering his eyes in shameful disgust, Esal slowly glanced back to the city to brighten his pale eyes in alarm at the sudden blob that dropped before his vision.

"Esal-pu mesa wuv yu an mesa sad yousa go owt mesa!"

"Gobu?" He rasped to lift his hand and close it carefully around the rubbery form of the blob. "What're—how'd you get here?" He questioned as he held the enormous eyed creature out before him.

"Mesa fallo yousa," it chirped excitedly to start throwing around a pair of short little arms.

"Was that such a good idea, what if the portal had closed before you got out?" He frowned, worry etched in the lines as he rubbed his thumb softly across the spongy stomach.

"Itsa skaire owt yousa," he whimpered to reach toward a now smiling Esal.

Releasing his hold to sigh as the blob zipped quickly across the space to plaster itself to his cheek, his cool rubbery body vibrating as he jabbered intangibly, Esal chuckled as the two large blue eyes pulled back to peer at him.

"All right, listen if you're going to be here with me I need you to be only visible when I say it's OK. 'Kay? This isn't home, we're in dangerous territory, I'll keep you safe, but I need your help in that as well, OK?" He nodded as he watched the little monster nod excitedly. "Good, now secure yourself." He ordered while pulling the hood of his white cape over his wavy locks, successfully covering Gobu as well as he pushed back to disappear beneath the tips of his hair. "Holding on?"

"Ah huh."

Nodding, Esal pushed from the portal's edge.

Running quickly down the street, carefully maneuvering around the pedestrians blocking her path as she continued toward the blinding light, Hikaru's eyes brightened when she saw something begin to fall through the sky. "Oh . . ." she rasped to grunt as her arm was caught, turning her to stare up at her alarmed brother. "Masumi . . ."

"What do you think you're doing?"

"Something's falling!"

"What?" He frowned, "what're you talking about?"

"The light," she protested to point toward the skies, her eyes lifting to narrow as she stared into its emptiness. "There was . . . where did . . ."

Masumi stared at the sky for a moment before letting his gaze fall once more to his little sister, his hand lifting to press beneath her sweaty bangs to rest on her clammy forehead. "Are you feeling OK?"

"I feel fine. Masumi there was something up there." She huffed while pushing his hand away. "You have to believe me!"

"Ok," he nodded to grasp her shoulder. "I believe you."

She glanced slowly across his tense face before shaking her head slowly, "you don't."

"I—" groaning as she pushed his hands away to then slip past him, Masumi turned after her, "Kar . . ."

"They're waiting," she called while trotting toward Antony to breeze past him, tears on the border of her eyes.

Later

If the run back to the school had been unbearable then this was positively hell for young Masumi Neijo. She hadn't said a thing since, had maintained her unbelievable speed almost several yards ahead of them without the slightest impression to slow her pace. Even now, as he helped Antony check in all the track gear and equipment, she refused to speak, even glance at him.

"So what exactly happened?" Antony finally inquired as he threw the soggy towel from his neck to his distracted friend. "She suddenly pmsing?"

"No," Masumi sighed to duck beneath the towel. "She thought she saw something and I . . . well, I didn't."

"And now she's pissed?" He grinned to pop the lock on his locker and jerk the door wide. His amused eyes turning from a scowling Masumi to search the top shelf for the necklace he was now slipping over his head, the silver cross bouncing slightly as he let it loose. "Your sister is scary alike to Kimi."

"I'm gonna have to endure this ice age for the next month!" Masumi scowled to slam his locker shut, ripping his duffle up to sling it over his shoulder.

"Girls," Antony sneakered to grab his jacket and bag while kicking his locker shut. "Possibly the biggest drug and nuisance God ever created."

"Are we sure he really created them?" Masumi smiled. "Hikaru and Kimiko are a bit evil to be from Him. Aren't things He gives us usually supposed to be blessings, gifts?"

"Can we give these ones back?" Antony chuckled as he pushed the locker room door open to follow Masumi.

"I've tried negotiating that one."

"Oh yea?" Antony quirked one of his dark brows.

"Gramps got me good."

"You let him hit you with that cane?" He burst out laughing. "Man that's pathetic, Gramps is like 200 years old!"

"No he's not!" Masumi chuckled to swing his duffle.

"Yea yea," he sighed while pulling his jacket on. "So where's little Neijo?"

"She's mad at me, prolly already left."

* * * * * *

She wasn't mad, not crazy. Hadn't been hallucinating, she knew what she'd seen and it was real, not some fantasy. Masumi not believing her had stung a little, but then the more she thought back to it, not a single person had seemed aware of what was within the sky when she'd first laid her eyes upon it. Even she wasn't entirely positive what it had been, but it had made her skin hum, her blood pulse with a tingling feeling like electricity had been crackling angrily within her.

Releasing a long sigh as she turned her gaze to the clear skies, carefully searching each fluffy cloud rolling lazily on its way, she continued across the school patio when a soft chuckle drew her gaze whipping quickly down. She turned quickly to a porcelain bench and the young girl that was sitting on it, her long hair fluttering with the white ribbon that was tying it back.

"Hello Hikaru." She greeted with a small bow of her head.

"Yuri?" She questioned to let her case fall from her shoulder as she approached the small freshman. "What're you doing . . . Kimo—" She scowled to tip her head to the side in irritation, "drats."

"You don't have to be ashamed of calling him by name." She exhaled softly to scoot and then pat the bench.

Slumping her shoulders, Hikaru plopped to the bench with a weary groan. "He's the chairman's second, Yuri. I have to speak about him with respect."

"As though saying his name isn't respectful enough?" Yuri smiled, her eyes turning to peer up at the sky.

"Everyone will just think I'm trying to get friendly with him."

"You are friendly with him," she chuckled to turn her dark sapphire eyes toward a now pouting Hikaru. "We all grew up together, how can't we be?"

"Yea, but . . . I don't want people to think of me as that kind of person."

"You mean like Claire?" She nodded to set her hand on Hikaru's. "You could never be like that selfish woman. You are sweet, determined, haven't ever said a single bad thing about anyone that I've heard. Your heart is kind."

A smile finally lifted back to her cheeks as she glanced at Yuri. "Thank you." A quick inhale and she was pushing off the bench, stretching her arms above her head as she glanced back at the grinning freshman. "So what're you still up here for . . . your brother didn't forget you did he?"

"Course not," she smiled, "he's finishing up his work. He didn't want to have to do any at home."

"So you've been here waiting since school got out hours ago?"

"Oh no," she giggled. "No, I was at the elementary school, I just recently got back up to school."

"Oh," Hikaru chirped to tilt her head as her curiosity spiked. "What where you doing there?"

Grinning softly as her gaze fell to her lap, she shook her head slightly while lifting her hand to brush her fingers through the loose strands guarding her eyes. "Well, I help with their art and music lessons from time to time, but I really spend most my time with the Director's son. You see, he'd just recently been in a pretty bad accident and most the doctors hadn't expected him to last the night after . . ."

"Geez, I'm sorry Yuri that's terrible!"

"But he's doing all right, it was a five car pileup and he came away with a minor fracture to his fibula, little bruising and a few cuts. It was a complete miracle." Yuri smiled, "he's been up and around for about a month." Her eyes brightened suddenly, "Actually while I remember, tomorrow night we're holding a sort of celebration party for him. There won't be many people there my age so if you aren't busy, would you like to go with me?"

"Yuri Youitan!"

Glancing across the courtyard as Yuri turned in search of the person calling out to her, the tiny hairs on the back of her neck and across her arms rose as Hikaru stared at the tall girl brushing toward them with her henchmen in tow.

Fantastic . . .

"Claire." Yuri frowned softly.

"I know you aren't thinking of inviting her to the party. Right?"

"You aren't right?" Both the girls mimicked.

"Yes," Yuri stated flatly as her brows knotted, "I am and already did invite Hikaru to the party."

"This was a distinguished-guests-only invitation," she snottily remarked to peer scornfully toward Hikaru.

"I take it you're going?" Hikaru sighed.

"Of course, Miss Claire's been invited," Oakley scoffed to uncross her arms and set them to her hips as her friend nodded quickly. "Miss Claire's the most refined and distinguished person in town, you'd have to be crazy not to have her invited."

"Or incredibly intelligent," Hikaru mumbled to which Yuri giggled.

"Look, I imagine that even lowly commoners such as yourself must wish that every once in a while that they may be able to be treated like they are somebody, but that's just not something that'll ever happen for you Neijo . . . best give up hope now. You'll be pushing pennies for the rest of your life like that retarded guardian of yours." She chuckled to grunt as she was suddenly jerked forward, her eyes widening as she stared into Hikaru's furious depths. "Let go of me!"

"You can say what you like about me, I don't really care, but if you ever—ever disrespect my grandpa or any other member of my family again, I will make you regret every syllable you uttered!" Hikaru growled softly, her calm had shivers racing down Claire's spine.

"How dare you!" Claire hissed to grasp Hikaru's hands, "you can't talk to me like this! Unhand me, Hikaru Neijo!" Yelping as she was pushed backward to stumble then fall unceremoniously to her butt, Claire's pale eyes snapped up to glare into Hikaru's furious chocolates.

She held the vengeful gaze a moment longer before turning to Yuri, her expression softening as she regarded the sapphire eyed ravenette. "I'll talk to you later Yuri."

"All right," she nodded to watch Hikaru sling her case over her shoulder and start down the school's front steps. Exhaling softly to turn toward Claire as Oakley and the other girl helped her to her feet. A soft grin twinkled in the corner of her lips as she picked her own case up off the bench. "Claire . . ."

"What?" She shouted to turn to the freshman. "Do you have something to say to?"

Nodding once, Yuri turned to the stairs but not before stating with a smile. "I'm telling Kimon."

4

The wind blew softly through the surrounding trees on the eleventh day of April in the year 2026 while the sun shone brightly over the city. Thumping a stick along a fence, Hikaru briskly walked toward her grandfather's plantation at the top of Cendlock Hill. Dropping the stick at the fence line, she started trotting up a flight of stairs as sweet fragranced cherry blossoms floated down around her. Reaching the top of the hill, she reached over the wooden fence and lifting the latch pushed open the gate to walk across the lawn while the gate resettled in its station. Feeling grumpy and sour, Hikaru walked past many of her grandfather's pupils without a 'hello'.

A skilled mentor in the art of taekwondo, Grandpa Neijo taught his pupils that strength was not always the stronger weapon. His noble and honorable teachings inspired youths and adults of all ages to join his dojo. Five days of the week, Grandpa Neijo freely taught younger children while their parents were at work.

"You have all successfully fulfilled the first stage of Tai Chi Chuan," the old steady voice of Grandpa Neijo stated as he sat in front of his students.

"Why do we need the first stage, sensei? This was so boring, why couldn't we've just gotten to the point?" a young boy questioned.

"We must first focus on the gentle slow and nonjarring movements which produce a high degree of relaxation in order to balance the unification of your mind and body. If you fail to accomplish that stage you won't be able to stretch and tone your bodies' muscles, which would eventually enable you to circulate the internal healing energy, which is your chi. After completing the trials you are left feeling alert, revitalized, yet relaxed with increased focus, harmony, and strength for your daily lives. You cannot control your chi if you go head long into it Ethan Pritchard!" Grandpa explained.

"Other than yourself, has anyone ever mastered the final trial sensei?" A young rambunctious brown-headed girl questioned.

"Of course, Mamoru Aino, many have been able to call upon their Chi, however, the internal healing energy of our innersoles has become more difficult to call upon in this new age. With all the corruption and evils of our world, the magic is diminishing, which makes it harder to discover!" Grandpa sadly explained.

"If the magic is gone. Why are we attempting to find it?" Ethan questioned.

"The magic isn't gone Ethan, you weren't listening, I said it's getting harder to call upon!" Grandpa replied. "But if the world is to become balanced again I pray it will be done through all of you!"

"Through us, what makes you think we will be the ones to balance the world sensei?" Mamoru Aino questioned.

"The youths of the world are still innocent, it's easier for you to obtain the pure essences in life," Grandpa softly stated.

Hikaru gazed at the twenty students lined up in four rows of five attentively sitting in front of her grandfather when a thick hum trailed to her ears. Glancing to her right, Hikaru spied a young man wearing a white kimono in the center of the training mat.

Adopted by Grandpa Neijo when he was very young, Hagane Rouse was one of Grandpa's more skilled students. Short russet strands blew loosely before his brown eyes that steadily gazed ahead of him. She watched him in wonder as he elegantly moved across the tile floor as if it were a cloud, his swift graceful movements joined by the soft breeze and cherry blossom petals came together in a perfect unison.

Turning back toward the house, Hikaru strolled across the large pebble-stoned sidewalk and stepped onto the patio when Masumi opened the sliding door.

"Hey, squirt," he smiled as Hikaru approached him. "Are you still not talking to me?"

"I don't want to talk about it!" she quickly replied to shut the door just as quickly on Masumi's face.

"All right then," he sighed to glance slowly across the lawn.

Moments later

Once again, the wind blew softly through the streets, the sun shining its light less intensely down upon the busy city. The later afternoon hours came into realization when elementary schools, grade schools, and middle schools began to come to an end. Young boys and girls laughed and joked contently while they strolled past the Neijo's plantation.

Feeling bored and uncomfortably grumpy, Hikaru leaned against the fence surrounding the plantation watching the little kids walk by to turn her gaze back to watch her adopted brother strolling up, wiping sweat from his neck.

"I am so depressed!" she mumbled as he rested his arms on the rail beside her.

"That has become evident," Hagane softly replied. "All Grandpa Neijo's pupils have left, and you weren't there to say bye like you usually do."

"I didn't feel like it today."

"What's wrong, Hikaru? And don't say nothing, I can tell when you're lying to me." He grinned. "Is it still Masumi?"

"No, I'm used to him not believing me. I kinda got into it with Claire," Hikaru stated. "Again."

"You know you're just adding fuel to her fire when you rise to the occasion," Hagane softly explained.

"With her, for once I didn't care!" Hikaru replied.

"It takes a bigger person to just walk away," Hagane stated.

"Maybe for you . . ." Hikaru grumbled.

"Try it next time. If she starts something, just walk away."

"You're joking, right?"

"Nope," he replied with a wide grin.

"Yeah, whatever," Hikaru exclaimed, walking away.

Walking down the pebbled sidewalk, Hikaru strolled into the backyard and sat upon a millstone beside a small fountain centering the yard. Her large brown eyes steadily stared at the old ancestral shrine at the back fence of the plantation, her thoughts racing back to the many times her father would retreat to the millstone with her.

She would sit quietly on his warm lap to listen to his tales of old—of times when a hero had more than strength, his noble deeds and valor ran his heart and the will of his mind. Tears streamed from Hikaru's eyes like they did every time she thought of her father. A remembrance of the little joyous time they had spent together before the event of his death was engraved within Hikaru's heart.

Wiping the tears off her cheeks, Hikaru sat staring at the rickety shrine when a mystic voice whispered along the wind. Like a wind chime blowing off the wind, the voice echoed like the hum of when a crystal is lightly tapped. Gazing around the backyard, the soft voice continuing to echo in the emptiness, she pushed slowly to her feet to take several steps toward the shrine, looking for the perpetrator when she was suddenly engulfed by a black abyss.

Giant rays of light sparked past Hikaru in the darkness, a soft squeak escaping as she lifted her arms to guard her face when she suddenly fell through the earth. Sliding rapidly through some long shallow chasm, blinding rays of light breezed past her when she suddenly spied a tiny white light sparkling below. Staring down at the white light as it grew bigger, Hikaru suddenly found herself quickly clearing the chasm into light.

Pushing her skirt down over her legs as the wind whipped past her while holding her breath, Hikaru slowly opened her tightly pinched eyes to peer dazed at the clouds rolling lazily around and through her. Slowly glancing around to gasp as she realized she was floating at least fifty thousand feet from solid ground, the vibrant mood of the day quietly breezing past, Hikaru inhaled several raspy breaths as she glanced toward the air traffic tower hovering not far away. Her eyes expanded as she spied a tall figure standing at its peak.

A large hood draping over the being concealing even the hair color from Hikaru's wide eyes, had her curiosity bubbling over so that she tried desperately to find some way toward the tower. Then as she just began to envision herself flapping her arms like some bird, the person slowly gazed back to peer into the sky. A look of surprise flowing over his face convinced Hikaru that he was just as astonished to see her floating there as she was herself. Him, it was a man, a man with piercing pale blue eyes. A large smile broke out across his tanned complexion until a loud screech mysteriously split the sky.

Hikaru watched the young man stumble below her when as she attempted to ask for assistance, the bright rays sprayed out once again around her. Momentarily shielding her eyes from the blinding light, Hikaru slowly peaked to gaze at her grandfather's shrine. Gazing around the backyard, Hikaru saw Masumi and Gramps come running onto the back porch as Hagane screamed from the front of the house.

"Grandpa Neijo!" Hagane screamed. "Come quick!"

Hikaru stared at Masumi and Hagane as they pulled Gramps off the porch when a shadow slowly started to creep over her. Gazing toward the south, Hikaru peered into the sky to see a massive burning cloud approaching the city. Fire and brimstone radiated from the cloud as it descended along with a mind-splitting scream.

Breathless, Hikaru watched a fiery meteor escape the cloud to soar over the tower before she raced to the back fence following the descending rock. Stunned, Hikaru watched the meteor crash into the forest to explode into a massive, blinding cloud of fire.

"Hikaru, come on!" Masumi yelled grabbing his baby sister.

"No! Wait Masumi, I want to—I need to see this!" Hikaru stated squirming in her brother's arms knocking him backward against the grass.

"It's coming this way!" Masumi yelled scooting across the ground.

Hikaru and Masumi sat upon the quivering grass as they watched the explosion shoot a black cloud a hundred thousand feet above the forest canopy. Captivated within Hikaru's brown eyes as Masumi pulled her to the bomb shelter the black cloud blew massive flaming rocks into the sky as the cloud swept toward the city.

The meteor's impact sent a shockwave through the city destroying buildings, uprooting mighty towering trees, and splitting streets in half when the piercing roar hammered into the city shattering any glass material left standing.

In the center of the city, Esal stood in a slight daze at the tower's peak with Gobu holding a steel wall to balance himself, his pale eyes turning murky as they reflected the quickly approaching cloud. Pushing off the wall, he raced to the edge of the platform and throwing his cape back drew his crystalline sword. Severing it through the steel tower, he pulled a crystal cloth out and wrapped it hurriedly around Gobu's pudgy stomach.

"Go!" Esal yelled over the roar as he threw Gobu into the air.

Pushing off his leather clad hands, Gobu zipped into the air to race across the skies, defying the speed of light as he shot straight toward the roaring fires before Esal dropped to his knees behind his sword. His hair fell loosely before his closed eyes as silver engravings suddenly pulsed from the midst of the blade, casting a heavenly glow into the cloudy darkness.

As he sailed through the trembling buildings, the crystal cloth blowing behind Gobu began to glow—the same symbols that a moment ago had appeared on Esal's sword burned a steady crimson. Blowing through the streets, Gobu watched the cloud nearly cross over the city border to shoot quickly through several shattered windows.

Whizzing in front of the cloud, the crystal cloth upon Gobu's back shot a barrier out as the little Arinumian sped off.

Slamming into the crystal barrier, the cloud pushed along the wall after Gobu to his dismay. Screaming while his bugged out eyes shot back into his chubby body, Gobu's tiny sponge arms rapidly swiped through the air trying to quicken his pace. Pushing along the wall, the cloud blew past Gobu ripping the crystal cloth from his body. Moving away from the cloud, Gobu frantically gazed around for the crystal cloth while at the tower Esal stood to his feet gazing at the cloud as the barrier began to shatter. Staring at the cloud, Gobu gazed over at Esal with large eyes to whimper out across the roaring sky.

Pushing his hood back, Esal unclasped the silver feather brooch across his neck and let his white cloak fall to his feet. Closing his eyes, Esal bowed his head as a stern look of concentration flowed across his face. Splitting through the cloth and armor upon his back, two magnificent crystal wings sprouted out into the darkness. Standing to his feet, Esal approached the edge as crystal dust blew from the parting wings separating the darkness.

Floating before the cloud, Gobu gazed at the burning cloud, whimpering while it approached when Esal suddenly grabbed him. Safely within Esal's arms, Gobu watched as the crystal wings blew a strong gust against the cloud. Releasing Gobu, Esal unsheathed his crystalline sword and swept toward the cloud with the little Arinumian close behind.

The silver engravings on the crystal blade cast a heavenly glow around Esal as he speared through the cloud into darkness. Flying through the cloud, Esal came to the blazing core and swiping the glowing blade shot a ray into the fire. The ray disintegrated the core and spread throughout the darkness, crumbling the meteor's debris and extinguishing the spraying flames as it passed beyond the barrier's edge nearly escaping into the city.

In the city, people came out of buildings and other hiding areas as light began to descend upon them. They walked into the dismantled city and gazed confusingly at the bright glowing skies that had previously displayed the monstrous cloud.

At the Neijo plantation, Hikaru lifted the shelter hatch and climbed out onto the grass gazing into the clear sky. While Hikaru walked toward the back fence, Masumi stumbled up the steps and released a nervous sigh as Hagane assisted Grandpa Neijo out of the shelter.

"What just happened?" Masumi questioned.

"It looked like a meteor fell into the forest," Grandpa Neijo replied.

"You've got to be shitting me!" Masumi exclaimed.

"Masumi, watch your mouth!" Hagane ordered leading Gramps toward the house.

"Watch my mouth, you've got to be shitting me!" Masumi exasperated.

"Masumi, everything's all right, now come back inside," Hagane replied.

"Okay, am I the only idiot around here that thinks a meteor crashing outside the city to be a bit strange?" Masumi yelled at Hagane as he shut the sliding door.

"Masumi, that was spectacular!" Hikaru yelled grabbing his arm.

"WHAT . . ." Masumi gasped. "HIKARU, A METEOR JUST CRASHED INTO THE CITY!"

"Yes, I'm aware of that," Hikaru stated.

"How are you so calm?" Masumi exclaimed.

"Masumi shut up and listen. I am trying to tell you that someone just saved the entire city! There was a man upon the tower dressed like a white knight . . ."

"White knight," Masumi repeated. "Whatever, Hikaru, if you want to make a fool out of someone, go see Kimiko. I'm not going to listen to another one of your make-believe tales!"

"But, Masumi, I'm not making it up . . ." Hikaru yelled as Masumi walked in the house and shut the door. "I'm not making it up," Hikaru whispered gazing toward the area that had previously contained the cloud.

* * * * * *

A deep silence had suddenly consumed the vibrant forest after the meteor struck Earth, shattering her fertile layer as the afternoon turned to dusk. Within the dark forest, a large gray cloud looming over the fallen meteor slowly dissipated into the diminishing brightness of the sky bringing upon the night. A trail where the meteor had struck the ground stretched across two miles of the forest floor with many giant trees lying stretched over one another beside the large trench. The wind remained silent as it softly breezed through the forest, creatures on the floor and in the trees hid themselves deep in the shadows.

Large layers of the smoldering meteor lay scattered about the forest in heaps when Esal softly landed within the trench. The large crystal wings folded elegantly behind Esal as he gazed up at the smoking meteor. With Gobu close behind, he stepped over broken fragments of burning rock pressed into the trench to stop a few feet away from the meteor. Jumping out of the trench to walk around the meteor, his clear eyes gazed at every steam pocket carefully til he spied a small fissure.

Lifting his sword, Esal speared the blade through the rock and shifted it breaking the meteor open. Stepping back as the blazing piece fell, Esal shielded his eyes from the spraying steam and walked into the fog. Slowly peering around, Esal found himself standing within what looked like some sort of research facility. Lights flashed across keyboards and database screens as Esal turned to jump back into the forest, his gaze falling on the forest floor to narrow at the enormous prints in the dirt. Looking off in the indicated direction, a rosy glow cast over Esal's tanned face as his crystal blue eyes stared at the sun falling behind the city.

"It's already begun!" Esal softly breathed staring at the city as it fell dark.

5

Earth—Saturday, April 12, 2026, 1:45am

The moon's first, dim rays poured down from the empty skies to shimmer upon the quiet peaceful streets. The wind silently swept through the city without recognition, most of the smoldering debris covered the bare streets in the presence of Hikaru as she stood alone in the twilight. A tiny satin moonbeam fell gently over her small form, her gaze boring into the utter darkness that had consumed the city. Shadows spread over the nearby buildings to creep across the sidewalks as they moved into the street. Standing bare foot in the desolate street, the cold damp cement swept chills up Hikaru's body provoking her nerves.

Glancing around nervously, Hikaru slowly stepped back onto the borderline of the satin beam causing large rays of light to explode out into the empty abandon street. Quickly glancing backward, Hikaru watched the rays turn around to gently breeze past her frame, sweeping her hair into the air. Pushing her blowing hair out of her face, Hikaru gazed wide-eyed at the rays as they bounced around the street highlighting the area. Rising into the sky to leisurely fall back to the ground like a feather, the satin moonbeams fell over dark figures jumping about within the darkness. Watching the quick elegant pace of the figures before her, Hikaru gazed upon a figure firmly standing within the darkness.

As musical wind chimes ring on the wind, a masculine voice echoed throughout the darkness like crystallized porcelain bells. "The smoldering darkness quickly rides among the wind of deceit . . . desolate and unwavering, it devours the pure heart!"

"What? Wait, don't leave . . . I don't know what you're talking about!" Hikaru screamed out as the figures disappeared into the darkness.

Once again Hikaru nervously gazed around her surroundings, shivers coursing through her as she stood alone within the spreading darkness. Freezing in her pajamas from standing bare foot in the cold damp street, Hikaru whiningly moaned when a low hiss echoed through the street, piercing the shadows. Slowly glancing across her shoulder to gasp as she stared into two large eyes, she watched mortified as a scaly face began to emerge with the snarling fangs that stole her breath away. Stepping back as the creature lunged at her face, Hikaru screamed out into the empty street.

Falling over the side of her bed, Hikaru accidentally pulled her sheets and pillow with her to the floor. Slowly gazing around, enthusiastically identifying the familiar sight of her room, Hikaru sat back on her bed with a sigh of relief.

What a nightmare . . .

Heart pounding intensely beneath her thin shirt, she slowly reached out to lift her sheets and pillow off the floor. Dropping her pillow at the front of her bed, Hikaru lifted her sheets up to her chest while the cool breeze pushed through her window. She watched the wind gently blow her curtains in a slight trance when her bare feet hit a fluffy object. Gazing down at the dark floor, Hikaru spied an old stuffed bear lying at her feet.

"Oh, Cleo, what are you doing on the cold floor?" Hikaru smiled before she picked the small brown bear off the floor.

Sitting back down on her bed, Hikaru slid her fingers through the soft curls on the stuffed animal when a tiny light flickered through the window. Gazing at her window, Hikaru watched the tiny rays try to poke through the miniblinds as the curtains abruptly dropped. Setting the stuffed bear beside her pillow, Hikaru pushed her covers off her legs and approached the window when a soft melody from the falling rain reached her ears. Pushing away the curtains, Hikaru pulled up the miniblinds to peer out the window to be momentarily blinded by a ray of light.

Quickly shutting her eyes, Hikaru leisurely reopened her night worn eyes to gaze through the light to peer around the dark backyard. The night rain dropped across the backyard, thumping upon the roof, splashing into the fountain, splattering over the stepping stones, and spit upon the grass under Hikaru's watchful eyes. Hikaru gazed around the dark yard 'til her eyes befell a streetlamp's light flickering and determined it to be what was trying to invade her room.

Dropping the miniblinds, Hikaru walked toward her bed when a white glow stretched up her figure. Turning around, so the glow spread over her confused face, Hikaru walked up to the window and pulled the blinds up to gaze outside. Within the darkness, Hikaru's brown eyes gazed at the same bright ray from her dream glowing around the old rickety shrine in the center of her grandfather's plantation. Astonished, Hikaru watched the termite infested wood revert to the sturdy foundation it had once been. The weather-worn roof was patched up, the broken monuments were revitalized, the shattered windows were pieced together, the collapsed porch pushed back into place, the crumbled steps were freshly cut stones, and the boarded doors were visible.

Racing across her room, Hikaru opened her white-whicker door and raced down the hall to her brother's room. Pushing open the door, Hikaru raced up to Masumi's bed and violently shook him trying to rouse him from his slumber. Hikaru watched her brother turn away to stare at him for a few seconds before she crawled over him to the other side of the room. Dropping onto her knees, she shook him to where they were bouncing on the bed until Masumi pushed Hikaru off his bed and gazed down at her with sleepy eyes.

"The shrine's come to life," Hikaru whispered pointing at his window.

Masumi gazed at his little sister with disgust before rolling his eyes and dropping his head back onto his pillow. Pulling herself off the ground, Hikaru crawled back onto her brother's bed and shook him while she called his name to only get knocked off the bed again. Hikaru sat on the floor gazing at her brother when her frustration erupted. Pulling herself off the ground, Hikaru walked to the other side of the bed and, lifting the mattress, threw her brother onto the floor. Crawling over the mattress, Hikaru gazed down at her brother as he refused to get off the cold floor. Finally giving up, Hikaru walked out of her brother's room into the hall toward her room where as she passed the hall window, a golden glow radiated across Hikaru's skin. Leisurely stopping in the center of the hall, Hikaru glanced through the window to peer at the glowing shrine. Turning away from the window, Hikaru raced toward the kitchen to stroll out into the lightly drizzling rain.

The ground was bitterly cold beneath Hikaru's bare feet as she walked across the pebbled sidewalk past the millstone sitting beside the fountain. Peering into the fountain, Hikaru gazed at her reflection cast within the dark waves for a moment before trotting toward the shrine. Halting before the once-rickety steps, Hikaru gazed in astonished wonder at the spectacular building and the lion statues sited highly upon the marble. Reaching out toward the statue, her fingers leisurely extended to brush the open mussel of the watchful lion. She gazed at the noble dignity within these creatures' eyes with respect when they suddenly turned to gaze upon her. A fiery glow lit up the two statues before Hikaru and disappeared as mysteriously as it had appeared. A soft sweet-scented breeze blew up around Hikaru's figure into the purple and pink sky of blanketing darkness.

Straightening her stature, Hikaru lifted her cold wet foot and stepped down onto the firm steps leading to the shrine. Walking across the shimmering red pine patio, Hikaru stopped before a pair of large iron doors with golden symbolized engravings. Tenderly sliding her fingers gently along the engravings, the soft touch of Hikaru's fingertips caused the heavy doors to retract. Small sweat beads trickled down Hikaru's soft skin as her fingers rolled up her hot sticky hands, her heart immediately began to race. Her breath came in hot short rhythms when she slowly passed under the golden archway.

Dark eyes gazed on in unbelieving astonishment as she gazed around the mighty hall of the old shrine that for years had long since been abandoned. Hikaru's bare feet stepped across large oval granite stones surrounded by small streams of crystal clear waters scented of honeysuckle blossoms. Behind the large columns holding the long high roof on the left side was a massive foundation of stone holding triple falls that joined at the bottom to flow into the hall's center. Lying to the right was a tall budding tree growing in a small puddle.

Jumping off the last granite stone, Hikaru landed on a soft velvet rug stretched toward a large kindling fire where a tall figure stood hidden in the glow of the sprouting flames. She cautiously moved closer toward the jumping flames to see the fiery glow cast upon the white armor of the young man she had seen earlier standing on top of the tower. A white hood drooped over the young man's head concealing his face, yet she could see the reflection of the flames within pale eyes that turned to gaze at Hikaru.

"It's you," Hikaru whispered. "You were on the tower . . ."

A soft exhale eased through Esal's tight chest as he let his eyes shift toward the curious girl. He nodded slowly to watch a dazzling smile lift across her rosy cheeks.

"Wow . . . I—I umm, who are you?"

His gaze shifted back to the crackling fire to frown slightly. "I am not of your world."

Hikaru stared at him in a puzzled daze before her mouth once again moved, "wha—what do you, I don't understand what does that mean?"

"How can you see me?"

She stared at him speechlessly.

"On that skyscraper, now . . . how can you see me?" Esal sighed to turn toward her completely, "I should be invisible to this world's eyes. It ensures mine and your safety."

"I . . . I don't know, I'm not supposed to see you?"

Glancing back to the flames, Esal peered slowly back to Hikaru. "I come from another world. One that's hidden within your own. It's much older and far more dangerous then you could ever imagine, would ever want to imagine."

"Another world?" She glanced slowly toward the shrine before glancing back toward Esal. "Why are you here?"

"I'm here to save you," he stated while watching the flames.

"From the creatures?"

His eyes widened before he snapped his gaze toward Hikaru. "How did you—have you seen them? Where?" He demanded as she nodded.

"In a dream . . . a nightmare," she stated to peer at the fire, her hands rising to rub her arms. "It was bizarre, it felt so real . . ."

"Were you hurt?"

She shook her head to glance at herself suddenly. "I don't think so." Hikaru stated as Esal walked away from the flames toward the crystalline tree where he slowly began to trace his fingers through several of the crevasses.

"The things you saw . . . what did they look like? Did you see them?"

"Kind of," Hikaru nodded. "They were tall, umm . . . really fast, big yellow eyes, and they were hissers."

A smile lifted to Esal's lips as he turned to peer at Hikaru. "I'm here for them. To stop them from destroying my world and as a consequence yours."

"Mine?" Hikaru gasped. "What're they—how will they destroy Earth?"

"Tear it apart, inch by inch til they uncover what they've come for."

"And that is?"

He turned from her then, his eyes staring into the clear pool for a moment before she came to his side.

"Why are they here? Why are you here . . . why couldn't you have just done this in your world?"

"Because he's hiding here," Esal sighed to glance at her sorrowfully, "according to the Holy Priest, a man that can see almost everything, a good deal of the princes and princesses of our universe were killed in a massacre against these creatures, they were sent to this planet to be reborn and live peacefully."

"So what's the problem . . ." Hikaru inquired.

"The only creature to survive the massacre knows the prince and his subjects were sent here and that they have no memory of their past lives . . . it's coming here to kill the prince and anyone that gets in the way!"

Exhaling a heavy breath, Hikaru drew her arms up tightly across her chest, "why're you telling me all this . . . why can I see you if I shouldn't . . . and why am I dreaming about something that I shouldn't even know existed? What does any of this have to do with me?"

He studied her for a long moment before shifting, his cape breezing in the movement, "For every planet, young or old, this universe or mine, there will be those that are to fight for her. Protect her from all harm and destruction. I think that . . . I believe you may be one of these people."

Hikaru gazed at Esal for a few minutes in a daze before she caught wind of what he was saying. "You're joking right?"

"No," he frowned, "why would I joke about such a thing in such a time? My prince is being hunted. I don't have time for such—games."

"So I'm just supposed to take your word for it? I'm supposed to accept that I may be some kinda freak or whatever . . . I can't be a hero!"

"Why is that? Why can't you believe what's right before your eyes? How else do you explain that you can see me or that you've envisioned a monster that until now, never existed for you?"

"Because it's impossible I tell you, there's no way . . . I couldn't even keep the class hamster alive!" Hikaru declared.

"I haven't a clue what that means, but I assure you, the only explanation for all this is because you must be one of this planet's guardians." Esal stated.

Hikaru started pacing at a slow pace, "but I'm an ordinary goofy girl that gets in a lot of trouble with her best friend!"

"It shows you aren't afraid to make a stand for something you think is right."

"But I'm not very old!" Hikaru stated.

"We have twelve-year-olds come to assist in wars . . . age means nothing when you're willing to stand for a greater cause."

Got an answer for everything don't ya . . .

Hikaru stopped pacing to turn toward Esal, "I'm a coward . . . hero's are brave and strong, everything that I am not."

He walked up before Hikaru and gently took her hand in his, "you'll find the strength to master your fears. Everyone fears something, but that doesn't make them a coward or any less a warrior than another!"

She lifted her gaze to peer into Esal's crystal blue eyes, "do you really think that I'm a warrior . . . me a girl?"

"Some of our best soldiers are women . . ." Esal tenderly replied. "I think you're a born warrior, destine to govern over the evils that would threaten your beloved home."

"What am I supposed to do?" Hikaru asked.

"For now, stay alive. We won't rush into things yet, you'll know what to do when the time comes."

"The time comes . . . what time comes?" Hikaru questioned. "Why must you speak in riddles?"

"I don't intend to, it just happens. I can't explain everything yet. Some things are best left alone for right now. When the time comes, you'll know!" Esal stated.

"I suddenly feel very frightened," Hikaru replied grasping her arms.

Smoothing his strong hands down Hikaru's arms, Esal softly replied, "You've nothing to fear, I'll always be there to protect you and soon you'll discover your own power."

Hikaru walked away from Esal, stepping across the oval stones toward the rock formation, "I can't choose whether I want to do this or not can I?"

Esal gazed at Hikaru in surprise, "you always have a choice." Following across the stones, Esal stopped by Hikaru as she ran her fingers through the stream, "But know this: Things are in motion now that cannot be undone. Those things have identified you and will come back. Their mission will not end 'til you or they are dead. You must take the knowledge I've given you and use it in what way seems best to you. Your once peaceful life has now taken a long leap into a pit too deep to climb out of. You don't have to take the responsibility that I'm asking, but whether you like it or not, you are a threat. I can't alter that."

Hikaru stared at the clear water pushing past her throughout the shrine before gazing up at Esal, "I don't know if I can do this!"

Esal dropped down and pulled Hikaru toward him, "You won't be alone. I will be here to protect you."

Hikaru turned to watch the water pour over the rocks, her thoughts in a jumbled mess when his smooth voice broke the silence again. She turned her dark surprised eyes on him to nearly melt as she stared at his beautiful face twisted up in an entrancing smile.

"You asked before who I was," he sighed to glance at the waterfall, "I was our ruling planet's captain of the guard, but now, I am simply a visitor . . . a friend, your friend." He glanced toward her again to shake his head at her entranced stare. Reaching out to comb some of her bangs from her eyes, watching her eyes flutter, breaking the spell, Esal leaned closer. "I am your protector, you can call me Esal."

"E-Esal . . ." she repeated to grin, "Hikaru. My name is Hikaru."

6

$\mathcal{L}$ight from the morning moon began to pour over the towering trees around the border of the Neijo plantation as Masumi stirred from his sleep. Opening his tired hazel eyes, he frowned as he realized he was lying on the floor.

Did I fall off the bed?

Then he remembered. Hikaru had come in last night claiming something about the shrine coming to life. Pulling himself off the cold floor, Masumi staggered toward his door and walked toward the kitchen. Walking past the den, Masumi glanced in and saw Hagane meditating in the center of the room.

"Have you seen our annoying little sister?"

"No, I haven't seen Hikaru, but I think she may be outside."

"What would she be doing out there," Masumi wondered continuing to walk toward the kitchen.

Walking across the kitchen floor, Masumi opened the back door and gazed out into the drizzling rain for Hikaru to find her sitting on the shrine's broken steps. Grabbing a rain jacket from a hook, Masumi trotted out into the rain toward the shrine to fetch his little sister.

Sitting upon the rejuvenated steps, Hikaru quietly listened to the rain hit the shrine making a soft melody trail into the air when she caught wind of her brother. Turning to gaze at him as he approached, Hikaru complied when he took her arm and pulled her under the jacket with him. The two held the jacket above their heads as they ran toward the house, escaping the rain. Once inside, Hikaru wiped the rain droplets from her arm while Masumi hung the dripping jacket back on the wall.

"What were you doing in the rain?"

"I wasn't getting wet 'til you pulled me into it!" Hikaru stated.

"What if the building suddenly collapsed on you?" Masumi questioned.

"You exaggerate too much the shrine is too fortified to collapse."

"Oh, yeah I forgot, since it's alive it wouldn't collapse," Masumi laughed.

"Go ahead make jokes, but I'm serious."

"Yeah, I can see that, are you sure you're feeling OK, Hikaru?"

"I feel fine despite my brother not believing me, but that's all right. I don't need you to believe me, I don't need to prove anything. I know I'm right!" Hikaru stated walking away. Masumi stood in the center of the kitchen staring after his little sister before moving toward the refrigerator.

The hours after noon passed slowly. Hikaru found herself hanging upside down on her bed, staring up at the ceiling and the dancing images the rain was casting over its shadowed surface. It wasn't long after her meeting with Esal that she realized all her senses seemed heightened. She could hear her brother as he sang four rooms down in the shower, each loud obnoxious syllable seemed as if he were screaming in her ear. She could smell the cherry blossom tree at the front of the house as if she was standing directly beneath it. She could feel the wind, cold and wild through the pouring rain. Could taste the fresh chill of the rain as it fell against the grass. Could see the swaying tree tops through the ceiling though her eyes were tightly sealed.

She could see Kimiko racing up the steps toward the house. She could feel her chilled hand on the fence as she hopped over it. Saw her race across the sidewalk to hop onto the porch before entering the house. She could hear the rain dripping off her as she pulled off her raincoat and hung it on a hook. She could smell her five brothers on her through the sugar vanilla scent she always wore.

Sitting up in her bed, Hikaru gazed at the door knowing Kimiko was walking through it in the next few seconds. The whicker door flew open as Kimiko raced into Hikaru's room and sat beside her on the bed. Kimiko's emerald eyes and white pearl smile conveyed the want of something she knew she would get from Hikaru.

Smiling Hikaru turned her face away and asked, "What do you want now?"

"I'm hurt, what makes you think I want something? It is possible that I just came to see you!" Kimiko replied to get a look from Hikaru suggesting she wasn't going to be fooled. "All right, I want you to come with me to my house so I don't get bombarded by my brothers. They're all cooped up in the house so they immediately think it's time to kill Kimiko!"

Letting out a laugh, Hikaru dropped back onto her bed. "You see, I knew it. You don't come over like you did unless you need something."

"What do you mean?"

"Jumping over the gate, you don't do that unless you're really desperate!"

Kimiko stared at her in confusion, her bright eyes glancing toward the window for a moment before turning back on Hikaru. "How did know that?"

Lifting her head from the pillows to tip it to the side, Hikaru's brows tightened as she stared at Kimiko. "Know what?"

"That I jumped over the gate. You can't see the front of the house from your room."

She instantly realized her mistake. "I uh—I saw you, how else would you explain it?"

Kimiko gazed at Hikaru in wonder, "I don't know, but anyway, how 'bout it? Will you come over?"

"Actually, how 'bout you come with me." Hikaru asked.

"Where . . ."

An almost wicked grin crossed Hikaru's face as she proceeded to tell her best friend all about her encounter with Claire and the party Yuri had invited her to.

"You're joking right?" Kimiko asked gazing at Hikaru's serious face.

"It's Claire, Kimiko, when do I ever joke with her involved?"

She stared at Hikaru seriously before she chuckled, "Okay, I'll go . . . but we need to get the boys?"

"Why?"

"Because if a fight breaks out, I'd rather have the Four Musketeers together than two!" Kimiko giggled.

Smiling, Hikaru inhaled a deep breath, "May we always be connected through our suffering, now and forever . . . All for One . . ." clasping hands with Kimiko the two declared, "And One for All!"

Earth—Saturday, April 12, 2026, 10:15pm

At the Children Mercy Elementary, the school's auditorium was overly crowded with many people from across the town. A classical jazz band set up on a portable stage played music for the people to dance at the center of the room while others simply watched, listened, or talked. A large refreshments table set up at the west end of the room was crowded by young and elderly folks. The large windows' curtains were drawn shut hiding the rain and night lights from sight. Hanging above the stage, a gigantic colorful banner read: **Congratulations Takkun!**

Back against the wall in the midst of the rows of chairs, Yuri sat alone watching the many faces of the people she did not know surrounding her. Gazing through the crowd, Yuri found her brother talking to the elementary school principal, Susy Fuí. She was taller than Yuri, measuring about five foot nine and she was tan faced with aqua eyes. She had a large beautiful smile that was almost always on her face. Her long golden hair was pulled up into two buns today and she was wearing a tan business suit.

Normally, Yuri would join her brother, but Claire was standing not to far away from Kimon and since she was infuriated with her, she had no desire to be anywhere near her tonight. At points, Yuri sadly realized she was scanning the room in hopes of finding Hikaru coming toward her.

Glancing away for a second, Kimon saw his little sister sitting alone and could immediately tell she was lonely. He watched her as she quietly sat gazing around, returning smiles where met when she saw him watching her. Extending his hand, Kimon offered Yuri to come over with him to only get a quick shake of her head and mouthed, 'I'm not going anywhere near *Her*!' Releasing a sigh, Kimon dropped his hand as Yuri turned away.

10:25pm

The rain hammered down upon Hikaru, Kimiko, En, and Jeremy as they raced down the street toward the elementary school steps. Bounding up the steps, En reached the top first and opened the doors as he waited for the others.

"Come on, come on, come on. Hurry up!" En yelled, jumping in the pouring rain.

After the others passed him, En raced through the doors into the school. Hikaru gazed around the school while the others squeezed their clothes out.

"The auditorium's that way," Hikaru stated after her acute senses picked up the echoes down the hall.

"How do you know that?" Jeremy asked.

"I hear voices from that direction," answered Hikaru biting her lower lip realizing she did it again.

"I don't hear any voices!" Jeremy stated.

"Oh, be quiet, Jeremy, the auditorium is that way," Kimiko stated pointing the way Hikaru suggested. "Trust me. I normally have to come with Antony to get Louise out of the principal's office and the auditorium is a couple doors down." Kimiko replied gazing at Hikaru in wonder.

"Okay, let's go," Hikaru quickly replied running down the hall.

"We have to run?" Jeremy whimpered.

The four friends raced down the hall as voices finally began to echo past them as they approached the auditorium. Turning the corner, the four slowed down when they neared several people talking in the foyer. Straightening their statures when the people gazed in there direction, the three nudged Hikaru forward following closely with big smiles on their faces. Pushing through the doors, Hikaru walked into the auditorium astonished to see how many people were standing before them.

"Well, there're certainly a bunch of people here, huh, En!" Hikaru giggled shutting his mouth.

"A bunch, this is like a circus!" En stated putting his hand on his head.

"Don't be ridiculous," Kimiko replied.

Walking into the crowd, Hikaru glanced back at her friends, "come on guys, we have to find Yuri!" Proceeding on, Hikaru pushed her way through people with En, Jeremy, and Kimiko looking for Yuri.

10:30pm

Quietly lifting herself out of the chair, Yuri strolled across the black and white tile floors toward the large windows. Pushing back the curtain, Yuri watched the almost invisible rain pour over the dark streets. Releasing a mournful sigh, Yuri held the curtain as she sat down beside the window continuing to watch the rain. Letting the curtain fall back into place, Yuri straightened her skirt and dropped her chin into her hands.

"Excuse me miss, could you tell me where the life of the party is?" A deep scruffy voice questioned.

A large smile crept up Yuri's face as she glanced up at Hikaru. "Well, I'm not sure if there is much life to this party as of yet!"

Giggling the two girls hugged each other when Kimiko, En, and Jeremy strolled up behind them.

"Oh, look, group hug!" En chuckled throwing his arms around the girls.

Pulling out of the hug, Yuri turned toward all her friends, "you all came . . . oh thank you so much!"

"Well, you know us. We like to make an entrance!" Kimiko giggled.

Standing in the center of the crowd, Claire stood swaying beside Kimon when she glanced over and saw Hikaru and gang with Yuri. Letting out a scowl, Claire walked through the crowd in their direction.

Gazing after Claire, Kimon watched her head toward Yuri, "Oh no . . ."

Pushing through the last people, Claire stopped behind Jeremy, "Well, just when you think everything's all right, a group of losers enters the party. I thought I made it clear that you freaks weren't welcome here!"

"What is with you . . . can you ever be nice?" Jeremy asked.

"I'm nice to people that deserve it, you are nothing so you deserve nothing!" Claire declared.

"I swear. I'm goin' kick your ass!" Kimiko stated rolling up her sleeves.

"Don't bother, Kimiko, she's not worth it!" En stated grabbing Kimiko's arm.

"I'm worth more than you!" Claire spat coldly at En attracting attention.

"Evidently, enough to be able to ridicule others for no reason . . ."

Turning around Claire gazed at Kimon in surprise, "Kimon, don't worry. You don't need to defend them. It's a waste of time."

"Back off, Claire . . ." Kimon sternly ordered. "Go back to your friends and leave them alone."

"Wow, I never expected that from you," Kimiko stated after Claire stormed off.

"I stick up for those that deserve it," Kimon replied gazing at Hikaru, who glanced away. "I'm glad you guys came."

"Excuse me, we aren't guys. We're girls!" Kimiko stated.

"I beg your pardon!" Kimon smiled at Kimiko after she corrected him. "I don't mean to intrude, but I believe that there's a young seven-year-old that is looking for you, Yuri!"

"Oh, yeah, where is Takkun, Kimon, I want to introduce him to my friends," Yuri stated taking Hikaru's hand.

"That's the point, Yuri. He told me to go get you so you can find him," Kimon smiled brightly.

"All right, come on let's start looking!" Yuri demanded pulling Hikaru with her.

7

10:35pm

The rain was cast upon the city in blinding sheets as Esal jumped effortlessly across the roofs of the towering buildings. Heaving himself over a railing, Esal gracefully glided down into an alley not three blocks from the elementary school. Pulling his hood further over his face, he strolled out of the alley. The rain slid off the soaked cloak to the flooding streets as he kneeled to examine a large alien imprint in the mud. The deep rift in the heel estimated the height at eleven foot and a quarter, the three talons deeply compressed into the soil indicated the creatures were moving at least 45mph. The single file line across the lawn cried out to Esal's senses, adding to his knowledge of the creatures patterns to seclude their numbers, which Esal estimated to be no more than seven, no less than four.

While he studied the mud prints, Gobu dropped down from a tree to hover next to Esal before following the imprints toward the elementary school. Floating through a bush, Gobu emerged out the other side with water slipping down his back, his giant eyes searching his surroundings. After spying the school, Gobu quickly turned and speed off toward Esal in a hurry. Knelt beside the imprint, Esal slowly glanced toward the frantic gurgling when Gobu zipped past him blowing his hood back. Glancing back, Esal's face scowled as he watched the little blob slam into a building. A large smile crept over Esal's face as he lifted himself from the ground and walked toward the building to peel Gobu off it.

"Gobu I thought we agreed you weren't going to come charging back to retrieve me because of your inability to stop!" Esal chuckled.

Floating into the air, Gobu shook his head to stop the spinning then turned his attention back to Esal. "Esal-pu, zee uglies at zee zchool!"

"That's where the prints led?"

"Ah huh," Gobu gurgled, shaking his head while pointing at the school.

10:40pm

Hikaru followed Yuri through the crowd with Kimiko, En, and Jeremy close behind while Yuri searched for Takkun Tenko. While Yuri lead Hikaru politely through the crowd, Kimiko cleared the path for En and Jeremy as she shoved and pushed people out of her way.

"So what does the kid look like Yuri?" Jeremy asked following En.

"He's short—"

"I could've guessed that!" Jeremy called up to her.

Suddenly stopping where she stood, Yuri turned to face Jeremy, "if you hadn't of been rude, you would've heard the rest, but you cut me off before I could finish!"

"Yeah man, get a hold of yourself!" En mused smacking the back of Jeremy's head and cowering backward as Jeremy came at him.

Smiling brightly, Hikaru giggled as she watched En and Jeremy wrestle with one another as Yuri told Kimiko about Takkun when a white light suddenly shone across Hikaru's eyes. Shielding her eyes, Hikaru lifted her hand above her eyebrows and scanned the room for the familiar light from her dream and the shrine.

What's going on . . . is it another dream . . . is it Esal?

Turning around, Hikaru gazed into the blinding ray to discover she could make out a figure concealed within the light. The white light floated about the woman who was quickly approaching Hikaru like fog hovers above a stream. Her long white hair streamed past her bronzed face, her lavender eyes gazed steadily upon Hikaru as a crystal gem centering her forehead sparkled brightly. A long white rob draped over her arms trailed behind the crystal white gown she wore, her tall figure swayed as she strolled across the floor.

Hikaru stared dumbfounded when Yuri's voice called out bringing her back to reality. She stared at the tall woman she had just visualized in pure white garments standing before her in a gray business jacket and skirt with her blonde hair pulled up into a bun.

"Mrs. Tenko . . . it's so nice to see you again!" Yuri stated taking the woman's hand. "Where's Takkun?"

"You know my son. Here one minute, gone the next!" Mrs. Tenko smiled.

"Mrs. Tenko I would like you to meet my best friends in the whole world . . . this is Kimiko Shiru and Hikaru Neijo . . . and those two killing each other are En Skilou and Jeremy Aino. I'll introduce you to them when their done." Yuri giggled.

"I'm pleased to meet you both," Mrs. Tenko stated gazing at Hikaru.

While Mrs. Tenko spoke with the girls, a small boy snuck up and leapt out at Yuri. "Boo!"

Startled, Yuri turned and quickly caught Takkun in a hug as he tried to skedaddle, "there you are . . . where have you been . . . I've been looking everywhere for you!"

"I know. I'm just good at hiding . . . did I scare you?" Takkun excitedly asked.

"No, I'm just good at pretending!" Yuri smiled.

After En and Jeremy resolved their little conflict, the brothers stood talking with Kimiko and Hikaru when a firm hand grasped En's shoulder, turning him around to gaze into bright blue eyes.

"Maya! What are you doing here?" En asked quite bashfully.

"My mother's the principal and my little sister is friends with Takkun . . . did you forget?" She smiled.

"N-n-no . . . I didn't forget, I-I-I just . . . what I mean is . . ."

Maya gazed at En with a smirk before taking his hand, "Guys I'm stealing En for a few minutes . . . you can have him back when I'm finished."

Hikaru, Kimiko, and Jeremy watched as Maya nearly dragged En toward the dance floor before bursting out laughing.

"What just happened?" Hikaru asked. "What was wrong with him?"

"Hikaru, you know perfectly well that En has a major crush on Maya . . . has since kindergarten!" Jeremy declared.

"Sounds like someone else I know . . ." Kimiko chuckled to get an evil glare from Hikaru as she walked away. "Oh, come on Hikaru . . . I was playing!"

10:45pm

The rain seeped over the school's roof creating a torrent around the foundation when Esal and Gobu arrived at the site. The water sitting on the school lawn trailed to the street, flooding the gutters as Esal cautiously approached the school embankment. His crystal blue eyes stood out in the dark atmosphere scanning the perimeter, the few wet bangs in his face dripped onto his bronzed cheeks.

Inside the school, Hikaru squeezed her way through people to sit beside the window and its blowing curtain. Her dark brown eyes watched the multitude of people curiously when her name was softly called out through the racket.

Lifting herself to her feet, Hikaru started to skim the crowd when she was called again, only louder. Hikaru glanced around the auditorium trying to identify the voice beckoning when her eyes befell the monstrous windows behind her. Dazzled, Hikaru stared at the curtain blow amidst a wind that should've been shut out by the closed windows. Striding toward the window, Hikaru grabbed the curtain and yanked it aside to gaze through the open window at the showering screen outside.

The rain beat heavily across the ground where two large prints were smashed into the wet soil beside a tree alongside the building. Three long talons clung securely to a small limb bearing the creature's massive weight while its large muscular arms moved it closer to the window. Reaching out through the hammering storm, two talons extended toward the window coaxing the girl standing near it.

Peering entranced out into the darkness, Hikaru extended her hand out into the rain to press her fingertips against two ivory talons. As she slid her fingers down the talons, a bright flash of light highlighted a gigantic creature leaping toward the window. Quickly pulling her hand away, Hikaru lurch backward to fall against the ground right as the Nzer hammered into the floor scraping up tile as it skimmed across.

The crowd of people cleared the area the Nzer had landed as it leapt onto its feet and gazed quickly around its surroundings. Releasing a high shrilled screech, the windows throughout the auditorium shattering into millions of tiny shards, the Nzer hammered people into the ground.

Lifting herself onto her knees, Hikaru watched the Nzer checking the dead bodies as four others leapt through the window and raced up beside it. Brushing glass from her shoulder, Hikaru stood to her feet watching the Nzers searching the slain bodies when she heard Kimiko yell.

"Hikaru look out!"

Spying Kimiko behind four of the creatures, she watched Jeremy struggling to hold her while she frantically pointed behind Hikaru. Turning around, Hikaru gazed into one of the Nzer's scaly faces and its blaring white teeth. Falling backward, Hikaru watched as the creature looming over her was severed by a crystalline sword.

Heaving the body quickly out into the rain before it could alert the others. Esal took Hikaru's hand and lifted her to her feet. Releasing her breath, Kimiko gazed curiously at the white cloaked man standing beside Hikaru.

"Are you hurt?"

"No, I'm fine . . . what are they doing?" Hikaru asked pointing at the other Nzers.

"They're looking for you," Esal replied wiping his sword of the Nzer's blackened blood.

"But they killed those people . . ."

"Yeah, well they don't want to play happily with you . . ." Esal reminded.

"Well, what do we do?" Hikaru questioned when a loud wail pierced the air.

Esal and Hikaru gazed over at the Nzers who were staring directly at the two. One of the Nzers with a long scare across its lost eye rose to its eleven-and-three-quarter length and bellowed out.

"Evalëantían . . ."

"Oh, this is not good!" Esal yelled taking Hikaru's arm.

"What are you doing?" Hikaru yelled.

"We're leaving . . ."

"Where are we going?" Hikaru questioned when another Nzer leapt through the window. "Esal . . ."

Pushing Hikaru down, Esal caught the Nzers front talons and swung it around into its nearest companion. Lifting his sword, Esal turned to Hikaru and nodded toward the darkness behind her.

"Go, I'll try to hold them off for you to get a head start!"

"A head start to where?" Hikaru asked racing up to the window.

Dodging a muscular arm, Esal blew the Nzer back and turned toward Hikaru, **"GET OUT OF HERE—NOW!"**

Dismayed, Kimiko watched Hikaru leap from the window while the man fed off the creatures. The large white cloak whirled about his body as he held the creatures back 'til one pushed past the other overtaking the man. The creature and Esal fell out the window beyond Kimiko's eyes before the rest of the creatures leapt out into the darkness. Squirming in Jeremy's arm, Kimiko whacked En in the head knocking him backward onto the floor.

"Ouch! What was that for . . ." En questioned. "Hurt him, not me. I'm not the one that's holding you!"

"Tell your brother to put me down . . ." Kimiko ordered.

"Promise not to hurt me . . ." Jeremy asked.

"Only if you don't hurry!" Kimiko bellowed.

Pulling Yuri out from under him, Kimon stood to his feet and gazed around at the dead and dying people. "We need to call an ambulance . . . Yuri stay with Mrs. Tenko and your friends I'll be right back!" Kimon ordered.

Once freed from Jeremy's arms, Kimiko watched Kimon run into the hall. "What about Hikaru . . ."

"Whe—where is Hikaru . . ." Yuri questioned.

11:15pm

The rain poured down upon the slumbering city as Hikaru raced down the desolate streets searching for cover. Large puddles covering the streets vaulted water against her legs as she sprinted across the street to a warehouse under construction.

Bolting toward the warehouse, Hikaru frantically tugged at the boards covering the doorway. Hearing the fast approaching Nzers' shrilling bellow, Hikaru kicked the board 'til it fell out of place. Squeezing her body through the opening, Hikaru pushed past the boards into the warehouse as a large arm grabbed her ankle.

Falling against the floor, Hikaru turned to start kicking the hand holding her ankle when she saw Esal's crystalline sword sever through the arm. Quickly pulling out of the hand, Hikaru raced into the warehouse and dropped behind a tank as the Nzers crashed through the boards with Esal. Slowly peeking around the tank's side, Hikaru watched Esal roll over his back when the Nzer quickly slammed its talons through the floor.

"Go, Hikaru . . . keep going!" Esal yelled slicing past the Nzer's chest.

Scrambling to her feet, Hikaru raced deeper into the warehouse pushing past boxes and equipment as she turned the corner spying an elevator shaft. Bolting toward the shaft, Hikaru slammed her palm against the button pressing it continually while watching the area behind her.

When the elevator doors slowly slid open, Hikaru was dismayed to find there was no access elevator within the shaft. To make matters worse, Hikaru's troubles were added to when a smaller sized Nzer crept around the corner and spied her.

Losing her breath, Hikaru quickly scanned the shaft for something to climb as the Nzer started to race toward her. Turning toward the Nzer, Hikaru backed to the edge of the floor and waited for the approaching alien malice. As the Nzer leapt, Hikaru dropped down into the duct taking hold of the floor to slam into the side of the shaft as the Nzer fell past her to the bottom.

Pulling herself up, Hikaru gazed down at the Nzer as it smashed against the bottom of the shaft with a wail. She watched it curiously and quite proud of herself when the shaft doors gradually resealed. Quickly glancing around, Hikaru bolted to a stairwell and slammed through the door to start climbing up the stairs.

11:45pm

Quickly climbing the stairwell, Hikaru ran out onto the eighteenth floor and continued toward the roof access. Pushing through the door, Hikaru trotted out into the rain and scanned the roof for any of the Nzers. Racing to the edge of the roof, Hikaru peered over the railing in search of a fire escape when a very large Nzer swiped its talons at her. Falling backward as the Nzer climbed over the railing, Hikaru scooted across the roof as another broke through the roof. Large pieces of cement fell off the Nzer's body as four more climbed over the other side of the roof.

Quickly standing to her feet, Hikaru stepped away from the Nzers as they came toward her in an arch. Hikaru's heart pounded uncontrollably as she watched the Nzer missing the eye lick its forked tongue across its massive fangs. Backed against the railing, Hikaru stared appalled when the larger Nzer leapt at her to come down upon Esal's crystalline blade.

"Esal . . ."

"Stay behind me Hikaru!" Esal yelled slicing through the charging Nzers.

"You've ins-serfered for the las-s time, Evalëantían!" A charging Nzer hissed.

Gasping as the large Nzer dove toward him, Esal shifted his weight to grimace as its thick hand cut past his arm. Grunting as he was smacked with the jutted curve of the Nzer's hip, Esal stumbled backward into Hikaru toward the railing. Sucking in a deep breath, Hikaru's eyes widened as her legs scraped over the roof's railing. Hitting the side of the rail as Hikaru fell over the other side, Esal pushed up quickly to grab her foot before she plummeted down the twenty-story building.

Huffing a yelping pant, Hikaru stared at the dark shadows below her as Esal tightened his grip on her foot.

"Esal . . ."

Gritting his teeth as he held Hikaru's leg, Esal sliced his sword at charging Nzers throwing them backward. "Damn . . ." Esal cursed as he cast his sword to the ground to turn and grasp Hikaru's foot with both his hands. "Hikaru . . . you need to try to reach up to me!"

Arching up so she could see Esal, Hikaru gasped as she watched the rain slide down his face like a slow rhythm of a stream. Watching his face wrinkle in determination, Hikaru slowly extended her hand toward him.

"Don't drop me!"

Shaking his head slowly, Esal grinned softly as he groaned, "I'd never let you go . . . I'd die first!"

"Then do it!"

Turning to see a Nzer cutting its arm across his shoulder to his face, Esal let a soft cry out as the thick thorned talons pierced his armor cutting the soft flesh of his arm. Jerking his head to the side as the talons nicked his neck, Esal widened his eyes as the Nzer dropped its body against his. Shifting his weight, Esal grit his teeth as he used his hips like a sludge hammer against the Nzer.

"Esal . . ." Hikaru gasped as the Nzer snapped at him.

Narrowing his eyes, Esal's bangs blasted up as energy erupted from his body. ***"GET OFF!"***

Watching the Nzer blast backward, Hikaru smiled as Esal glanced at her. Exhaling slowly, Esal pulled against Hikaru's leg til his hand clasped tightly around her smaller palm.

"I've gotcha . . ." he sighed as he pulled her toward him.

"Esal-pu!"

Gasping as a talon pierced his side, Esal sucked in a breath as his grip was cut from Hikaru's ankle.

"*No . . . Hikaru—*" Esal bellowed as a Nzer slammed him against the roof's banister.

The rain fell gently into rhythm along Hikaru while she plummeted toward the ground. Tears streamed from her pinched eyelids lifting away from her cheeks to float momentarily in the dark sky. Her jet black hair whipped furiously through the air as bright white rays erupted from behind Hikaru to stream along her figure throughout the darkness.

12:00am

8

The previous path the tears had abandon to the air stained Hikaru's cheeks, chilling them as she neared the streets below. Her fingers nearly touched the water streaming along the gutters when a black feather leisurely fell past her eyes. Her senses erupted when firm hands gripped her waist line and pulled her away from the concrete laying beneath her brown eyes.

A strong musky smell of sweat sliding down a broad bare chest suddenly filled Hikaru's nostrils and blurred her senses for a moment. Gasping as a crystallized chime rang through her ears, Hikaru slowly glanced toward a golden cross dangling past her brown eyes. The muscular arms holding her within the air pulsed through the man's fingers crawling along Hikaru's skin. Staring at the pool of water beneath her, Hikaru could see the man's bright blue eyes radiating in the darkness within the water.

"It's not yet your time . . . your days shan't be numbered as of yet."

Yelping as she was dropped onto the puddle, Hikaru stared at the water ripple around her when a shadow leapt across the glassy black water. Slowly lifting her eyes to a building across the street, Hikaru narrowed her eyes as she saw something disappear over the edge. Pushing her hands against the cool street, Hikaru slowly turned to glance up the warehouse building as Nzers' shrieks drifted on the wind.

Slowly stepping back to the building's edge, a tall man completely veiled in shadows stared at Hikaru as she peered at the building she had fallen from. Tensing his shoulders as a smaller man walked up to settle his weight against the railing, the tall man sighed as his brown eyes watched Hikaru sprint back toward the building.

"Should you've intervened this time?"

Sealing his brown eyes, the man smirked slightly. "Isn't that what we're always doing?"

Turning clear blue eyes toward the taller man, the boy sighed as he glanced back at the building. "Is there something special about that girl or something?"

Nodding his head, the man slowly lifted his eyes to peer into the dark skies as thunder rolled. "You realize that the left half of the Trinity is here."

"Is he now . . ." the boy smirked as he turned to start walking back across the roof. "That's no concern of mine."

"Ya—"

"I've forgotten all about that life!" The boy growled as he paused. "You should to, if you know what's good for you."

Watching the boy walk away, the man sighed as he closed his eyes while lifting his face back to the skies, "shadows have ways of not being able to forget . . . they see everything, just as I can!"

12:01 am

Grunting as he was knocked down into the stone wall, Esal leaned heavily into the rail as he slowly struggled to his feet. Hoisting his suddenly lead weighted sword, Esal panted painfully as he watched the Nzers encircle him. Gritting his teeth as he tightened his hold on his hilt, he narrowed his eyes as he lunged forward to pierce a Nzer then turn quickly to slice the crystal blade through another's arm. Grunting as a heavy body hammered into him, Esal knocked into the roof as his sword clanked across the floor with a sickening ring. Peering at his sword when a thick hand grasped his neck, Esal grunted as his head was hammered into the roof.

Beating her feet quickly into the dust-sprinkled floors, Hikaru ran her hand across a wall as she slid around its corner. Stumbling as her knee hit a box, Hikaru grunted as she took several steps to regain her balance. Sprinting across plastic sheets and broken boards, Hikaru came to the stair door when a soft scream drifted through a resounding of thunder.

Esal . . .

Busting through the door, Hikaru sprang up the steps as the door settled back to its frame. Climbing two to three steps at a time, Hikaru inhaled sharply as she wound up to the roof. Widening her eyes as she saw light start to pour around a corner, Hikaru grunted as she stumbled against the stairs. Pushing forward suddenly, Hikaru knocked into the door to stumble out across the roof.

Chuckling soft hisses, the Nzers all gathered around the largest which pinned Esal to the roof. Inhaling sharply, the Nzer bent down to rub its nose against Esal's cheek as the muscles in its neck tightened. Cutting its talons across Esal's spilt wrists, the Nzer chuckled against Esal's cheek as its teeth cut his soft skin.

"Get off him!" Hikaru screamed as she started toward the Nzer.

Moving his eyes across the roof, Esal gasped as he saw Hikaru, "no way . . . Hikaru?" Grunting as the large Nzer gripped his neck, Esal grit his teeth as he tried to lift his bleeding hands.

Gasping as she watched a light blast out of Esal, Hikaru widened her eyes as a cross of light cut several Nzers in half. Jumping as the large Nzer hoisted Esal above it,

Hikaru dove forward suddenly to hammer into its stomach. Stumbling forward to land on her stomach, Hikaru glanced at Esal as he dropped next to her.

"Esal . . ."

Clutching his wrist, Esal slowly lifted his eyes to her. "Are you OK?"

"You're worse off than me!" Hikaru gasped as she took his other wrist. "Esal you're going to die if we don't stop the bleeding!"

"We'll have time for that later . . ." Esal groaned as he pushed onto his feet. Turning to his sword across the roof, Esal narrowed his eyes as a white light radiated around his body.

Gasping as she saw the sword lift, Hikaru smiled as it sprang forward to Esal's ready hand. Turning to watch the larger Nzer push up, Hikaru narrowed her eyes as Esal released soft gasping pants.

"Esal . . ."

"I'm OK . . ." Esal groaned as sweat slicked slowly down his cheek to crawl along the curve of his jaw.

Watching it fall to strike his armor, Hikaru slowly lifted her eyes from one blazing bloody cut to the next. "No you aren't . . . you're hurt really badly."

Sliding his legs further apart as the Nzer started toward them, Esal ground his teeth together as his left arm fell from his sword.

Widening her eyes as she watched the sword tip clatter to the ground, Hikaru jumped at the sickening ring of the crystal beating against the stones. *It sounds like its crying . . .*

Grinning as it watched Esal slouch his weight heavily into his knees, the Nzer lunged forward suddenly with a chuckling hiss. "Kill it while it's-s-s weak!"

Shaking her head as Esal lifted his sword to grimace before the sickening tang rang through the shadows again, Hikaru shook her head as she raced toward Esal.

"Die Evaleantian!"

Gritting his teeth as he gripped his torn arm, Esal stared at the Nzer as its talons flexed dangerously in anticipation of his warm blood.

"Esal . . ."

Widening his eyes as he felt Hikaru's slender body press against him, Esal turned his head to watch her hand close about his hand grasping the sword's handle. Gritting her teeth as she threw weight into her arm, Hikaru shouted as she hoisted Esal's arm supporting the sword's weight. Narrowing his eyes as he twisted his wrist, Esal skewered the blade through the Nzer's neck severing it clean as Hikaru held tight to his arm.

Glancing at the respectfully clean blade, Hikaru turned to the rolling Nzer head as the others began to hiss and growl menacingly.

"Let's-s-s s-see you do that trick twic-ce!" The red marked Nzer hissed as it dashed toward Esal and Hikaru.

Grunting as Esal wrenched his blade from her grip, Hikaru watched him sheath it to his scabbard. Grinning nervously as he turned to stare angrily at her, Hikaru yelped as he snatched up her hand and pulled her across the roof. Pushing her toward the door, Esal spun with a soft cry to slice his sword through a Nzer.

Smacking into the roof's door, Hikaru turned to watch Esal kick the Nzer away before trotting toward her.

"Go . . ."

Yanking the door open, Hikaru stumbled inside to grunt as she nearly fell down the stairs. Catching herself on the rail to blow out a relieved sigh, Hikaru turned to watch Esal slam the door as he proceeded toward her. Grunting as he hoisted her against his hip, Hikaru squealed as she watched him bound over the rail to sail down the center of the stairwell.

"Esal!"

Grunting as Esal hit the bottom of the stairwell, Hikaru sighed softly when she hiccupped. Covering her mouth as she was tugged through the door to the floor, Hikaru watched Esal slam the door to the stairs and burn the wood into the frame.

"How did you do *hwk* that?" Hikaru inquired.

Glancing at Hikaru as she hiccupped again, Esal frowned, "what's wrong with you?"

"You scared the crap outta me and now I have the hic*hwk*cups . . ." Hikaru sighed, "what're we gonna do?"

Glancing at the door as a Nzer arm thundered through the wood, Esal quickly pulled his sword up through the stretching fingers.

Grinning as the arm shot back in toward the wailing Nzer, Hikaru grunted as she was tugged backward.

"You have to get outta here, Hikaru."

"Why *hwk* do I have to leave?"

Glancing at her as if she were insane, Esal chuckled, "you're kidding right . . . Hikaru, they're trying to kill you!"

"Looks like they were *hwk* more content with—" Grunting as she was pulled around a corner, Hikaru wheezed as she was pushed into the wall, "you."

Peering at the dark hall before dropping his eyes to Hikaru, Esal leaned toward her as he grasped her arms.

"Listen carefully Hikaru . . . those creatures are a dead race—"

"Well they look very much *hwk* alive!"

"Quiet and listen," Esal ordered as he covered her mouth, "there was a war in my universe a very long time ago. These creatures were wiped out save for one. One which isn't among the near dozen that have been attacking us."

Staring at Esal, Hikaru shook her head, "if only one wasn't killed how are there so many . . . was it pregnant or something?"

"No . . ." Esal sighed as he took Hikaru's hand and pulled her after him.

"Then how is *hwk* this possible?"

Glancing around the corner, Esal shook his head, "there're other forces at work here . . . dark forces."

Staring at Esal, Hikaru shivered when the wall exploded behind her.

"Get down . . ." Esal shouted as he spun around.

Dropping beneath Esal's arms as his sword whipped forward, Hikaru watched the Nzer's torso spilt apart from the reflection of the blade. Gripping Esal's side as he pulled his sword and body back into balance, Hikaru slid up to his back as several Nzers dove toward them. Taking firm hold of Esal's cape, Hikaru watched one Nzer fall dead to Esal's feet while the other jumped backward.

They are after me.

Stepping closer to Esal, Hikaru buried her nose and fingers into the soft silk of his cape while she stared at the Nzers. Moving his sword across his waist, Esal watched the Nzers when he felt a presence loom over them. Turning to watch a Nzer rear behind Hikaru, Esal narrowed his eyes as he shifted his weight.

Hearing a soft hiss ring in her ear, Hikaru grunted as Esal pushed back against her. Watching his arm swing in front of her chest like a shield, Hikaru widened her eyes with a gasp as she saw the Nzer drop its jaw open releasing a glass shattering screech. Inhaling a startled breath as the dragon-like talons sprang forward, Hikaru's lips fell apart as blood sprayed in the motion of the Nzer's thick arm.

Wincing a hiss, Esal pushed Hikaru as he brought his sword up from the Nzer's abdomen to its thick shoulder.

Gripping Esal's shoulder as the black blood burst into the air, Hikaru grunted as she was pulled down the hall into the construction spread across the building.

"Esal you're hurt!"

"I'm fine," Esal breathed as he held securely to Hikaru's soft hand. "I've got to get you outta here now." Stumbling across several boards, Esal pushed Hikaru toward the dismantled entrance as he grasped a wooden carton. "Go to your family's shrine."

Watching Esal hurdle the carton, Hikaru shook her head as she gripped his waist steadying his swaying body. "Esal you're ready to pass out . . . you've lost too much blood!"

"I told you I'm fine," Esal growled as he pushed her hands off, "I'm telling you to get outta here!"

"Why Gramps shrine?"

"It's holy, the Nzers can't enter . . ." Esal grunted as he gripped his sword's hilt, "go Hikaru, I'll be right behind you."

"Yeah, I heard that at the school," Hikaru sighed as she ran into the street. Shrieking as a Nzer dropped in front of her, Hikaru dropped backward as it swung at her, "Esal . . ."

Turning to see Hikaru fall to the Nzer's feet, Esal grit his teeth as he ran toward her with Nzers on his heels.

Staring at the Nzer as it moved toward her, Hikaru closed her eyes with a whimper when a crystal chime rang through the air. Gasping as the Nzer screeched, Hikaru slowly opened her eyes to see a white light flooding from the contact of Esal's sword piercing its chest. Jumping as the sword trembled moments before the Nzer exploded, Hikaru watched the ash flutter to the ground in bewilderment. Watching a wave pulse from the sword, Hikaru exhaled as the sword dropped through the concrete.

"Go Hikaru!" Esal shouted as a thick body struck his lower back.

Turning to watch Esal hit the ground, she gasped as he saw the Nzer raise over him.

No!

Don't let him die

"What . . ." Hikaru gasped as she turned to see the sword pulsing through the concrete. Staring at the vibrating blade, Hikaru slowly pushed off her legs as the Nzers screams echoed through the hollow building.

Grunting as the talons cut through the armor on his back, Esal shifted to avoid his spine being severed.

"Get off!" Esal growled as a wave of energy burst from the frame of his body.

"Hang on Esal!"

Glancing at Hikaru, Esal gasped in horror as he watched her trot up to his pulsing sword.

"Hikaru don't—" Esal started as a Nzer leapt on him.

"I'm going to help you," Hikaru grunted as she pulled on the hilt.

Cracking his elbow into the Nzer's face, Esal pushed up as Hikaru pulled on the sword. Gasping as the blade turned rosy, Esal widened his eyes as the wave pulsed off the crystal.

"Hikaru don't touch her!"

Watching a Nzer catch Esal's hip, Hikaru grit her teeth as she tightened her grip on the hilt. The muscles in Hikaru's arm tensed as her fingers turned white around her knuckles.

"I-I won't let you . . ."

Sliding several inches from the street, the sword released a thick chime as Hikaru's face furrowed in determined desperation.

"You aren't dying for me!"

Ripping the sword from the street with a disgruntled scream, Hikaru stumbled backward as the force and weight of the blade threw her off balance.

Gasping as he watched a light blink through the blade, Esal pushed against the street as he saw Hikaru drop onto her hands and knees.

"Hikaru . . ." grunting as a Nzer cut his abdomen, Esal released a thick shout as he was slammed into a crate shattering it as he proceeded toward the floor.

Rubbing her hip with a soft pout on her lips, Hikaru slowly glanced into the building as she heard Esal's shout. Wrinkling her nose as she watched a Nzer pull on his hair, Hikaru reached toward the sword to curl her fingers around the hilt as she pushed onto her feet. Yelping as flames jumped up the blade to burn her hand, Hikaru stumbled backward as she released the sword.

Sighing as the sword struck the ground, Esal closed his eyes as the sickening ring of crystal striking concrete called through the darkness. Grunting as he was ripped backward, Esal choked out a gasp as he was lifted up a Nzer's scaly chest to scream as fangs tore at his shoulder.

"Esal!" Hikaru screamed as she cradled her hand, her eyes snapping toward the sizzling sword lying across the street. She bit into her lower lip as she stared at the rosy blade.

Furrowing her brows as thunder echoed overhead, Hikaru grit her teeth as she dropped her hand and jumped at the sword. Scratching her fingers up the hilt, Hikaru released a thick shout as the flames wrapped around her arm to cut at her face.

Gasping as he watched the flames leap from the blade to engulf Hikaru, Esal ground his teeth together as a wave blasted out of him to blow the Nzer backward. Hitting the pile of boxes with a hard grunt, Esal slowly lifted his hand to his torn shoulder as Hikaru screamed. Lifting his eyes to watch her hunch over in the midst of the flames, Esal pushed his legs beneath him to grunt as he collapsed back to his knees. Smacking his head to the floor, Esal blew out a soft breath as he heard a Nzer crawl up to him.

Gripping her burning wrist binding the blade's hilt, Hikaru stared narrow eyed at the blade as it released a small pulse. Pinching an eye closed as she grit her teeth, Hikaru snapped her head to the side with a scream as her cheek was torn open. Wincing as she felt her blood slide down her jaw to stick in the edges of her hair and shirt collar, Hikaru slowly peered at Esal as he struggled to stand.

"Whatever power is in me . . ." Hikaru groaned as she tightened her fingers around the hilt. Hitching her breath as she felt her blood start to boil, Hikaru stared at the blade as a figure pulsed over the reflection. "Help me save him!"

Gasping as the weight of the sword vanished, Hikaru stepped backward when the core of the flames turned snowy. Staring at the blade as it turned violet, Hikaru blinked in confusion when the flames started to ring around the sword. Wrinkling her nose as she hoisted the sword above her shoulder, Hikaru released a deep huffing breath as she watched Esal lift his eyes to her.

"How . . ." gasping as he watched white flames pulse over the sword like sparks of lightning, Esal widened his eyes as he saw cherry flames pulse through Hikaru's eyes. "Hikaru let go of the sword!"

"When I'm—" inhaling as she threw her weight into the sword, Hikaru screamed as she thrust the sword down. "DONE!"

Widening his eyes as he watched a white ray blast from the tip of the sword, Esal ducked as it flew forward to hammer through the Nzer crawling onto his back.

Dropping the sword noisily to the street, Hikaru swayed to the side as her legs buckled dragging her to the street.

"Hikaru!" Esal shouted as he pushed off his knees. Grunting as the building shook, Esal grasped a machine as boards and steel began to crumble to the ground. "It's caving in . . ." he gasped as he pushed off the machine to race around falling debris.

Staring at the building as she watched debris start to fall, Hikaru slowly closed her eyes when Esal dove through the shattered entrance. Grunting as he struck his shoulder into the street, Esal wheezed as he pushed to his knees. Turning to watch the building collapse, Esal exhaled shakily as he crawled quickly across the street to drop over Hikaru. Holding his breath as dust and debris flew over them, Esal curled his arms around Hikaru when he heard the distant call of sirens.

9

Thunder rumbled through the smothering texture of the rainclouds veiling the night's darkness from the city. Sheets of rain poured from the heavens like a river as sirens were drowned by the crackle of thunder and lightning. Huddles of people lined the streets outside the elementary school as several more squad cars pulled up to the curb. Whispers trailed through the wonder gazing crowd as the lights fell off the glazed surface of a black sedan.

Pushing his door open, a tall man with night painted hair stepped out into the light rain to stare at the crowd before turning his eyes toward the school. Lifting his hand to his soaked bangs, he moved his musky green eyes carefully over each movement before dropping his arm into his leather coat. Closing the door before proceeding toward the stairs leading to the school, he glanced at the line of ambulances caring for the injured while others zipped bags closed.

Rubbing her numb arms, Yuri stared at the dozens of sobbing people near the ambulances when a warm arm wrapped her shoulders. Closing her eyes as she inhaled the soft drench of fresh rain racing over Kimon, she slowly lifted her sapphire eyes to his piercing blue eyes.

"Are you OK?"

Shaking her head, Yuri glanced around, "Hikaru's not been accounted for."

"I'm sure she's around here somewhere," Kimon sighed as the cop walked up to him.

"Are you Kimon Youitan?" Turning to stare at the drenched man, Kimon nodded as he flashed his badge. "Thanks for the call, now I'd like to hear what went on here."

Stumbling around people as she stared at each face, Kimiko released a frustrated sigh as she bounded quickly toward the other side of the crowd.

"Hikaru Neijo!"

Sitting on the steps of the school, En held his head balanced in his chilled hands when Maya sat next to him. Pulling the sheer jacket around her bare shoulders, she released a soft sigh as she reached her hand around his waist. Exhaling softly, En pushed back slowly to drop his arms and lower his head against Maya's chest.

"She's OK, En . . . she probably . . . maybe she got out with some of the others." Maya softly stated.

Staring blankly as he moved his head against Maya's warm chest, En closed his eyes with a frown, "then where is she?"

Sliding carefully through the crowd, Jeremy paused as he saw Claire standing beside her father. Exhaling slowly, he scratched his head as he dropped back to stare into the rain.

"What a mess . . ."

Smoothing her fingers down Takkun's back, Sinobu stared across the street to the shadowed buildings as she heard a thick ring call through the thunder and lightning. Narrowing her eyes as she pulled Takkun's slumbering body tighter against her chest, Sinobu lifted her lavender eyes to the dancing lightning. *Can it be happening already . . .*

Pushing through the last edge of people to lean into her knees while drawing in thick breaths, Kimiko slowly hoisted her gaze to the dark city. Staring through the light drizzle to the mist sweeping almost eerily across the streets, she started down the steps when Jeremy suddenly caught her arm.

"Hey . . ."

"Where do you think you're going?"

Staring at him, Kimiko wrinkled her nose as she jerked her arm to the side, "where you think . . . I'm going to find my best friend!"

"Kimiko . . ." Jeremy struggled as he yanked her backward toward him. "Hikaru's missing . . . we don't need to add you to the list!"

"Let me go!"

Wincing as she hit him, Jeremy grunted as his cheek was smacked. Closing his eyes as he felt Kimiko's weight surge into him, he braced his arms around her waist as she clinched her fists in his shirt.

"We're gonna find her, Kimiko . . ." Smiling, Jeremy chuckled. "Who knows she may be already home for all we know."

Stroking his fingers through Yuri's long hair, Kimon shook his head as he stared at the cop. "I've already told you . . . I don't know what they were . . . all I can tell you is that while you're here asking questions those things, people, are out there still . . . possibly wrecking havoc on other innocent people!"

"Mr. Youitan, try to stay calm," the cop sighed as he pulled his hand out of his coat. "I'm just doing my job . . ."

"Well, then do it, Detective Shang . . ." Kimon sighed, "a friends still missing and those people are out there."

Nodding, Shang rubbed between his eyes. "We're going to do all we can . . ."

"Thank you." Kimon nodded as he led Yuri away.

Tilting his head to the air, Shang lifted a soft scowl to his lips as he glanced across the city. "You're in good hands, Mr. Youitan . . ."

Stopping in front of the steps, Kimon watched En lift his eyes to him when Jeremy emerged from the crowd leading Kimiko. Sighing as he closed his eyes, Kimon turned to the city as Yuri lifted her hand up his chest.

"I don't know what to do . . ."

"Searching would be a good idea," Kimiko frowned when Jeremy squeezed her hand.

Turning to see Sinobu approaching, Kimon smiled a nod as she stopped beside him. "Mrs. Tenko."

"Are you all all right?"

"No . . ." Kimiko frowned.

Lowering her eyes, Sinobu sighed, "I'm sure your friend is fine."

* * * * * *

Standing in front of the clearing dust, a cop stared at the crumbled building as the squad car lights flashed through the cloud.

"Just what the hell was going on tonight?"

Watching chilled steam rise through the rain from his exhale, Esal glanced down the street as he cradled Hikaru closer to his chest. Releasing a soft cough, he groaned as he pushed his aching legs into motion. Flexing his fingers across the edge of her back, he lowered his head against the beating rain to watch it slid off his cape concealing Hikaru from the chill. Lifting his eyes to Cendlock Hill, he dropped his lips apart to tremble as he closed his eyes. Gritting his teeth as he started to climb the stairs, he exhaled heavily as his eyes wandered over the glassy shimmer of the rain streaking the grass.

Kicking the gate open, Esal stumbled slightly as his boots dragged along the stoned pathway. Panting as he moved his eyes over the lawn to the homestead, Esal inhaled sharply before proceeding toward the porch. Grinding his teeth into his lower lip as he felt the sticky film of his drying blood stirring against his quickening movements, Esal dropped his head as lightning lit the skies.

"Someone help me!"

Stumbling onto the porch, Esal sighed as he heard the quick beat of feet against the wood. Closing his eyes as he watched the door slide open, Esal stared at Masumi.

"Wha . . ." Masumi stuttered as he stared at a drenched boy. Peering at the wrapped figure in his arms, Masumi's eyes widened as he recognized the petite form. "Hikaru . . . Hagane get out here!"

Standing across the street, a tall thick shouldered man watched the scene when lightning sprayed over the golden cross dancing against his bare chest. Clear brown eyes stared through the rain watching the exchange below when his eyes shot around to see a figure emerge on the roof behind him.

"Night-watching again?"

"It's our job," the man replied as he watched the smaller-framed man stop beside him.

Sliding his hand up through his drenched hair, the man smiled as his musky green eyes glanced at the other man. "What're you going to do?"

"Depends on what's going on." Glancing into the green eyes, the man sighed. "What happened at the school?"

"I got a lot of 'I don't know.' They really don't have any clue what's about to happen." Shang sighed as he flung his drenched bangs off his hand.

"Do you know what's about to happen?"

Shaking his head, Shang smirked, "I was hoping you would tell me."

"What's to tell?"

Turning to watch the blond boy emerge, Shang sighed. "You're cheery tonight."

Staring at Shang as he walked to the edge, the blond sighed. "It's not a prank, it's not a band of disgruntled thugs either . . . it's the start of the end."

Staring at the blond, Shang glanced at the older man. "What's he talking about?"

"You know what he's talking about." He sighed as he glanced at the blond. "The revolution is starting."

"Has started . . ." the blond corrected. "The girl wielded the sword . . . she won't be able to turn back now. She's tapped into power not many live to tell about."

"The Trinity . . ." Shang sighed.

Shaking his head, the blond snarled. "No . . . something worse . . ."

Earth—Sunday, April 13, 2026-10:25am

The lazy flow of air brushing over the city carried the distant call of sirens and bells chiming the morning hours when the first glimpses of the sun cascaded from the still hovering rainclouds. Floating over a dying streetlamp, Gobu gurgled a whimper when he dropped toward Cendlock Hill. Beads of water sprinkled the grass blades like gems. A soft mist curled against the ground to reach for the high settlement of the porch.

Dim candle lights flooded the interior of the Neijo plantation when Hagane emerged from the den to walk down the hall toward the kitchen. Pausing as he came to Hikaru's wicker door, he released a long sigh as he turned toward it. Slowly pushing the door open to see Masumi leaning into the bed from the chair setting along the bed's side, Hagane lowered his eyes with a smile as he closed the door again.

Flexing her fingers beneath the firm hand holding hers, Hikaru moaned as she slowly stirred. Lifting heavy lids from musky brown eyes, she stared at her ceiling before rolling her head to the side to stare at Masumi. Lifting her head from the pillow, Hikaru searched over his slender figure carefully when she saw the discomforting position. Smiling as she pushed up, she gently touched his cheek, combing his bangs from his unconscious face. Staring at his calm expression lined with worried brows, Hikaru tilted her head to the side as she lay on her stomach.

Moaning as he stretched his fingers out across the sheets, Masumi slowly rolled his lids back to let his glassy hazel eyes stare blankly. Pushing up after several minutes of staring into Hikaru's bright brown eyes, Masumi stuttered dumbfounded as she sat up giggling.

"Hikaru . . ."

"Do you realize you're only peaceful when you sleep," she smiled as she lifted her hand to touch Masumi's cheek. Pausing as she saw the gauze wrapping her burnt palm, Hikaru gasped as she remembered the past night. "Where's Esal!"

Gasping as she nearly sprang from the bed, Masumi pushed against Hikaru's shoulders. "Wow . . . what're you talking about?"

Glancing around frantically, Hikaru peered at her hand, "how did I get here? Did he bring me home?"

"He? Hikaru you're not making a bit of sense!"

"How did I get home Masumi? Did Esal bring me here?"

"No one brought you," he frowned to release her, "Kar you came home by yourself . . . a little disorientated . . ."

"Alone . . ." Hikaru rasped to peer at the sheets bunched in her lap, "but I was . . . the school, what happened at the school, has it been on the news? Was anyone hurt?" She grasped his arms firmly while leaning toward him.

"I haven't a clue what you're talking about!" He growled to jerk free, "were you drinking last night? Gramps is gonna kick your ass if he finds out you were—"

"What?" She scowled to shake her head with a disgusted scoff, "of course I wasn't drinking you idiot . . . I'm trying to figure out what happened last night!"

"Well let me remind you then," Masumi frowned, "you and Kimiko ran off to some kind of party with En and Jeremy, missed curfew to which I had to listen to Gramps howl about for hours til he passed out, and then when you did finally decide to show up . . . you were like a freaken zombie coming in here, stumbling and nearly falling on your face as you made it to your room where you passed out. There better?"

"I don't—" she started to stop, her brows drawing tight as she peered at her confused brother. *Did I . . . was it all a dream?*

Hikaru

Her eyes drifted slowly toward her window, expanding slightly as she stared at the glowing shrine. *Esal . . .*

It was soothingly quiet within these sanctified walls, drowning out all the chaos and emotion that always plagued him whenever he traveled to a foreign planet. He was able to hear Her true voice for the first time since his arrival, hear Her fears and feel the pains that were crippling Her. Within this monument that had been built in memory for the lost, he understood why the Priest had chosen Earth.

A heavy breath passed through his aching chest as his pale eyes slowly opened, staring blankly at the golden ceilings when he felt her rapidly approaching presence. Wincing to grind his teeth as he picked himself up off the chilled floors, Esal turned to the entrance as the heavy doors blasted open.

"Esal?"

He was caught off guard by the ravenette leaping into his arms, his wide eyes softening at the sobs reaching his ears. Water from the pool vaulted across the floors as they toppled backward. Esal choked out a deep breath to glance at Hikaru with a chuckle as she buried her face into his chest, her grip tightening around his waist as his hand fell one to her shoulder the other to the top of her head.

"You aren't a dream . . ." she sobbed to bury her face further into his chest, "oh thank God you aren't a dream! Tell me you're real! Tell me I'm not crazy! Tell me that you are really here and that everything that happened last night was real!"

His brows furrowed as he grasped her arms firmly, pushing her back to peer into her watery chocolates. "What're you talking about Hikaru? Of course I'm real, I'm floating right here in front of you."

"Ooh," she gasped to quickly jerk back, water vaulting across the tiled floor again, "God I'm so sorry, you're hurt and here I am tackling you!"

"I'm OK," he chuckled to stand as she blushed a deep crimson, "my injuries aren't as bad as you think they are . . . this little shrine of yours actually helped out a great deal."

"The memorial?" Hikaru frowned, "how?"

"It seems the same healing minerals that flow through the currents of my home world have found their way to your world." He smiled to shake his head, "in a memorial for your lost parents."

Glancing slowly toward the crystal clear streams and small pools stretching throughout the shrine, Hikaru turned back to Esal with a smile. "Maybe this wasn't a coincidence . . . you and I meeting. Maybe its fate."

He nodded to smile brightly, "I don't think there's any other way to describe it."

"Esal . . ." she pursed her lips to glance into her lap, his soft chuckle echoing through the shrine as she remained silent for a moment. "If—everything that happened last night was real . . . how come I don't remember coming home?"

"You had passed out after wielding my sword, a weapon I might add you shouldn't have touched. She could've killed you."

"I passed out?" She frowned, "then why does my brother think I came home on my own? You had to have brought me right, a passed out person can't walk home . . . and why isn't there anything about the attack on the school last night? Shouldn't there be something on the news? And why would your sword kill, its not like I was gonna stab myself?"

Esal stood staring at her, a small grin slowly rising in volume the longer she went on with her rant. "Well . . . that is a curious situation. I'm afraid I'm responsible for everything. You see, I can't have your world aware of all that's happening. I can't have a panic breaking out. It'll only drive these monsters further. They feed off the negative emotions of a species. So I—I took all the memories of this past night . . . all the pain, the fear, the destruction . . . and I destroyed them. Made it seem as though nothing had really happened."

"What?" Hikaru gasped, "you can't do that Esal, those are peoples rightful memories you had no right?"

"I had every," he scowled, "I brought on this pain, I gave that horror to those people because I wasn't quick enough to stop them from finding you! And to keep your secret, our secret, I made your brothers believe that you came home alone. Exhausted to the point that you weren't coherent."

"Exhausted?" Hikaru scoffed, "Masumi thinks I was drunk!"

"I am sorry for that but Hikaru you have to understand . . . what I am doing, this mission . . ." his brows creased in dread as he grasped her arms firmly, "everyone could die unless I keep them unaware!"

"But why? I don't understand why that is?"

"I can't explain it in any way that will help you to understand it." He sighed to cradle her cheeks. "You aren't of my world, Hikaru, you could never come to understand everything involved. Just please, trust me. This isn't my first mission. I know what I am doing. You are safe with me, I promise. I will protect you and your home."

Exhaling a heavy unsure breath, Hikaru slowly nodded, "so what happens now? What are you going to do?"

"It's time for me to start what I came here for . . . I need to find my prince and it would probably be a good idea if I find where the Nzers are staying," Esal replied while strapping his sword's quiver to his belt.

"Nzers?"

"Oh," he smiled, "it's what they are, or what they are calling themselves. I suppose its fitting . . . it means dark malice."

"Yea," Hikaru cringed, "its fitting. So what should I do?"

Glancing around the shrine as a soft breath eased through his chest, Esal turned toward her with a pointed glare. "For now . . . I think it's best if you try to stay outta trouble. I wouldn't say anything drastic like leaving the country, it'd draw too much attention and it wouldn't really matter where you are. If those things want you badly enough they'll find you. The only thing veiling you at this moment is me and then this memorial . . . could come in quite handy if you're ever in a bad situation. Try to remember that."

With a soft nod, she watched Esal snap his feather brooch into place and pull down his hood when two gigantic blue eyes suddenly shot in front of her face. Screaming, Hikaru slapped Gobu against the shrine's floor where he laid flat, the top of his fin and his belly bulging out.

"There you are," Esal exclaimed to walk up and peel Gobu off the floor. "Where have you been huh?"

"Is that yours?" Hikaru inquired rubbing her hands against her shirt.

"Yeah, he's mine."

"What is it?"

"He's an Arinumian, a native of the Water Ruin planet in my universe," Esal explained setting Gobu on his shoulder.

"He looks like a blob!" Hikaru declared poking Gobu's tummy to get her finger whacked. "Ooh . . . he's squishy!"

"Their bodies are super pliable making them very agile in the air as well as in water."

"He flies?"

"Oh yeah, it's stopping he has problems with . . ." Esal smiled as Gobu started cursing in his own language. "Hey, none of that."

"He's actually kind of cute . . ." Hikaru declared once again poking Gobu to get whacked harder. "Well, I should get . . . I'm sure after last night and then this morning my brother's probably having a heart attack!"

"All right, I'll check on you later tonight," Esal called as Hikaru left the shrine.

Stepping off the revitalized steps, Hikaru walked around the corner of the house to get startled when her friends yelled out and confetti was thrown in the air. Placing her hand on her chest, Hikaru smiled brightly as Kimiko raced up and hugged her.

"Happy Birthday," Kimiko yelled then whispered, "We need to talk!"

"About what . . ."

"What's going on with you . . ."

Hikaru gazed at Kimiko in confusion when En bounced over and interrupted, "Okay, move over Kimiko . . . my turn to hug the birthday girl!"

She watched Hikaru as she was pulled away to be overwhelmed with hugs and congratulants, small knots forming on her thin brows as she let her thoughts rage.

"Yeah, I know how much you like these weird light up things, so I thought the bubble machine would entertain you . . . it did En!" Jeremy laughed.

"Ha ha, I forgot how to laugh . . ." En replied whacking Jeremy's head.

"Thank you, Jeremy. I have the perfect place for it . . ." Hikaru smiled.

She wasn't crazy, but she couldn't understand why no one else seemed to be concerned with everything that had recently happened. Kimiko's lips curled in frustration as she sat staring at them all from her spot on the lawn chair, her body tense and aching beyond words. Releasing a sigh, Kimiko stood to her feet and walked across the lawn toward Hikaru. It was apparent she wasn't going to get the opportunity to find out anything tonight.

"It's getting late, I have to head home . . ." she sighed while hugging the birthday girl, "I'll talk to you later. Happy birthday, cutie!"

"Thanks for coming over . . ." Hikaru stated.

"Bye, Kimiko . . ." En yelled.

"See you at school . . ." she yelled back while opening the gate.

"We should probably head home to . . . come on En," Jeremy called after hugging Hikaru, "Happy birthday Hikaru!"

"See ya tomorrow . . . love ya bunches . . . happy 16th!" En yelled.

"Come on, you better get to bed, you've got school tomorrow . . ." Masumi stated.

"So do you . . ." Hikaru giggled picking up all her stuff. "Thanks, Masumi, I had a great birthday party. I can't believe you did this to me again!"

"Yeah, you're my little sister, it's my prerogative to surprise you and spoil you when I want!" Masumi smiled putting his arm around her neck, "Happy Birthday kiddo."

Meanwhile

The moon slowly peeked around the night's evening clouds as Kimiko agitatedly walked home when the wind howled through the trees brushing along her figure, chilling her spinal cord. Her emerald eyes gazed nervously around the street when a large dog-like creature without an ear peered down at her from the building. It's torn fur hug loosely off its hide. Long talons curled over the roof's edge as it stepped closer. It's long scraggly mussel released large amounts of drool from its hungry wanting mouth.

Kimiko walked silently along the sidewalk when a shrilling howl pierced the peeking night. Gazing around the street, Kimiko broke off in a run and turned the corner of her street. On top the building the dog creature hung dead over the side of the building as a tall bronzed man whipped his gloves of the carcasses blood. His bright blue eyes watched Kimiko steadily while his bare bronzed chest rose and fell lightly. Dropping his hands at his sides the man turned and jumped into the air to disappear down a dark alley, light reflecting off the smooth surface of a golden cross.

At the Shiru house

Antony Shiru, the second eldest, lay sprawled on the couch watching a movie when Kimiko raced through the front door, quickly shutting it once inside. Glancing over the arm of the chair, Antony sat up to stare at Kimiko as she panted heavily.

"Dude, lil' sis you all right . . ." Antony asked stopping the movie.

"Yeah, I'm all right . . . I'm just going to bed . . ." Kimiko stated quickly racing up the stairs after locking the front door.

"How was the party . . . Kimiko? I swear that girl . . ." Antony declared lying back down on the sofa.

Upstairs, Kimiko pulled off her clothes and climbed into her pajamas while, she thought about Hikaru. Tying the drawstring to her shorts, Kimiko walked into the hall toward the bathroom.

"Hey, Anty," Kimiko called reaching the stair's bottom. "Where's everyone?"

"Louise, Izeus, and Esu are already in bed. Jaime's out with Kate, and Mom and Dad are upstairs doing only God knows what," Antony confirmed, "Why?"

"No reason . . ."

"Oh, while I remember . . . don't forget to take your running clothes tomorrow, we have track practice," Antony stated sitting up to look at Kimiko.

"Antony, I'm not on the track team . . ."

"I know that, but I'm tired of you running alone at night when something could happen to you, so you're going to run with me at the school!"

"Oh, for the love of pity . . . are we going to have to go through this again? Antony I've said it before and I'm saying it again: just because you're the captain doesn't mean you get to show me off to all you friends!"

"Kimiko the day I would show you off is the day a pig would fly . . . and there's no way in hell I would have you gawked at by the losers on the track team!"

"Well, I'm glad we got that understood, so you can go to your track practice alone!" Kimiko called.

"Kimiko, you know you're going so stop arguing and go to bed . . . I'll talk to you tomorrow," Antony stated as a pillow was whacked against his face. "Ow!"

10

As the nightlights rise

The gentle, swaying motion of the trees bordering the Neijo plantation was invisible through the darkness when Esal landed in front of the house. The white wings upon his back radiated when the moon's fingers extended to touch them as they slowly disappeared. Walking across the red bricked path, Esal strolled around the corner toward Hikaru's window when Gobu zipped quickly past him to slam into a tree beside the house. Placing his hands on his hips, Esal dropped his head and scowled in annoyance.

"If anyone was sleeping . . . I think you just blew it!" Esal yelled in a whisper.

"I no blow it . . . Esal-pu blow it!" Gobu gurgled.

"Shhhh . . ." Esal commanded bringing a finger to his lips.

"Yousa. Shhhh . . ." Gobu teased.

Inside her room, Hikaru sat on her bed holding her stuffed bear when she heard Gobu outside her window. Jumping up quickly, she raced up to the window, pulled up the mini-blinds, and quickly unlocked it. Shoving her head through the opening, Hikaru gazed out at Esal and his flying fish.

"Hi . . ." Hikaru called startling Esal.

"What are you still doing awake . . . did someone wake you?" Esal asked gazing at Gobu.

"No, no one woke me . . . I waited up for you, I wanted to talk to you about something very important!"

Pushing Gobu away, Esal laid his arms across the window pane, "What do you want to talk about?"

"It's my best friend, Kimiko. I think she knows somehow . . ."

Esal gazed at Hikaru stunned, "What do you mean . . . did you tell her?"

"No, I didn't tell her. I don't know how she knows, but she's going to corner me one of these days and force it out of me . . . I have classes with her tomorrow!"

"Okay, calm down . . . this may not be a bad thing, did you think maybe she's a Devilry Hunter?" Esal suggested.

"No . . . I didn't think about that . . . do you think she is?" Hikaru excitedly asked. "What's a Delivery Hunter?"

"Devilry Hunter!" Esal chuckled. "It's what this planet's protectors are called."

"Oh," Hikaru smiled, "so you think that Kimiko might be one as well? One of these Hunters?"

"I wouldn't doubt it . . . they say the leader's best friend should usually end up being the second in command," Esal smiled, "And besides I wiped all the memories remember. If your friend still remembers what happened the other night, it's a dead giveaway that she's one of your Hunters."

"Wow . . . that would be great . . . Kimiko and I being Devilry Hunters, protectors of our planet . . . oh, Masumi and Antony better watch out!" Hikaru giggled.

"Okay, yeah, can we get back to reality? So is everything all right, nothing happened while I was gone—no attempts on your life or anything like that?"

"Nope, see me . . . here . . . in front of you!" Hikaru smiled.

"Keep it going miss lippy . . . all right, there's going to be times that I can't always be watching you . . . give me that stuffed bear!" Esal ordered.

Turning Hikaru gazed back at her bed, "Cleo?"

"Yes, Cleo . . . give it here!"

Walking toward her bed, Hikaru lifted the stuffed bear from the mattress and handed her to Esal. She watched him curiously as he shot a tiny chip inside the stuffing and sprinkled dust over her head.

"Here . . ."

Taking the bear from Esal, Hikaru gazed at him, "That's it . . . now you're going to be able to track me, because you put a chip inside my stuffed bear?"

"WHO'S STUFFED . . . I'LL SHOW YOU STUFFED. WOULD YOU MIND LOOSENING YOUR GRIP A BIT? YOU'RE CHOKING ME!"

Slowly gazing down at her hands, Hikaru astonishingly watched her stuffed bear wiggling in her hands. Dropping Cleo, Hikaru let out a tiny scream and gazed at Esal. "You brought my stuffed animal to life!" Hikaru exasperated.

"OH, THAT HURT . . . ALL THE TIMES I'VE HIT THE GROUND YOU'D THINK I'D BE USED TO IT BY NOW . . . NOPE, NOT AT ALL. IT FEELS THE SAME EVERY TIME . . . IT HURTS PRETTY BAD!" The little stuffed talking bear, Cleo replied.

"Oh my . . . I've dreamed about this so many times, I can't believe what I'm actually seeing . . . my stuffed animal's alive!"

"YEAH, I'M ALIVE . . . SO I'D APPRECIATE IT IF YOU WOULD STOP SQUEEZING *ME TO DEATH!*" Cleo stated as Hikaru hugged her. "HELLO UP THERE . . . *HEY!*" Cleo bellowed getting Hikaru's attention. "I WOULD GREATLY APPRECIATE IT IF YOU WOULD PUT ME DOWN NOW . . . *PUT ME DOWN!*"

Dropping Cleo, Hikaru stepped over her and walked toward Esal at the window. "So why did you bring my bear to life?" Hikaru questioned.

"For the moments I can't be there . . ."

Hikaru stared at Esal doubtful, "The stuffed bear's going to protect me?"

"I'M NOT STUFFED!"

"That stuffed bear may be the difference between you being dead or staying alive!" Esal declared seriously.

"YEAH, SHOW SOME RESPECT SISTER . . . *HEY, WAIT* . . . I'M PROTECTING HER? OH, CLEO . . ." the bear whimpered.

"All right, I have searching to do . . . now that I know your OK. I'll see you later . . . shut and lock this window!"

"Oh, I thought I'd leave it open!" Hikaru sarcastically stated shutting it before Esal could say anything.

As Esal disappeared from the window, Hikaru gazed at Cleo as she sat on the floor staring up at her. Smiling, Hikaru crawled into her bed and pulled the covers up while; Cleo desperately tried to climb the sheets.

"THIS SEEMED SO MUCH EASIER WHEN SHE WAS MAKING ME DO IT . . . I ALWAYS THOUGHT TO MYSELF AND I QUOTE: 'OH, I CAN DO THAT . . . I CAN DO THIS WITH MY EYES CLOSED AND ALL PAWS TIED TOGETHER BEHIND MY BACK!' . . . *FUNNY HOW THINGS TURN OUT, HUH!*"

11

Earth—Monday, April 14, 2026

Leaves broke away from branches to blow along the gentle breeze that passed through Amin Mela Academy's foundation as the school day came to an end. Students were walking out to the parking lot to drive home while others were being picked up by parents, siblings, or friends. Sport practices were beginning shortly after school when Kimiko walked down a set of steps with En and Jeremy.

"So what have you guys got planned for the rest of the day?" Kimiko asked.

"Not sure, go home and mess around with Mamoru . . . take Riley for a walk . . . there are so many things to do," En declared.

"Like your homework Skilou!"

"Mr. Freché! I was going to get right on that . . ." En stated quickly walking away.

"Little punk, I'll get him one of these days!"

"How ya doing En?" Kimiko asked.

"Shut up, you aren't constantly hounded by that man!" En replied.

"That's because I don't fall asleep in his class!" Kimiko stated.

"Whatever . . . hey, my soccer game's on Wednesday at 4:45pm, you guys coming?" En questioned.

"Oh, jeez . . . I don't think I can En . . ." Kimiko stated then burst out laughing at En's stunned expression. "Guy, I'm joking . . . you know I'll be there, who else will explain it to Jeremy? Not Hikaru, she gets too into the game . . ."

"Did you actually ask that . . . of course I'm going!" Jeremy ventilated.

"Well, I'll see you guys later . . ." Kimiko called heading toward the locker rooms.

"Where you going?" Jeremy asked.

"I'm running on the track with Antony . . ." Kimiko replied opening the door.

"Oh, have fun . . ." En called walking outside.

The breeze felt cool and refreshing against Hikaru's hot sweaty body as she raced around the track. A white band wrapped around her head soaked sweat into it keeping her forehead cool as did the wrist bands. The white sports tank and pink shorts stretched over Hikaru's body moved leisurely in the wind when she raced by the bleachers where Gobu and Cleo sat watching.

"So, What's Your Bet . . . I Think She'll Collapse After Ten! What Do You Think Squishy, Flyer Thingy?"

"Mesa . . . tinks miybe . . . fifte!"

"Fifty . . . Are You Insane? She's Not The Flippin' Flash!"

"Yousa aska mesa . . . mesa anser yousa!"

Pulled up into a ponytail, Hikaru's long black hair blew through the wind hitting her back and shoulders as she once again raced by the bleachers. Gazing beneath, Hikaru spied a large ball of dust moving up and down the steps with Cleo and Gobu's arms erupting out. Rolling her eyes while continuing to run the track, Hikaru turned around when someone yelled her name to spy Kimiko racing toward her with a smile.

"Hey Kimiko, I thought you swore that Antony was never going to get you to run on the track with him," Hikaru wheezed.

"Yeah, well normally I wouldn't no matter how long he razed me, but I really wanted to talk to you!"

"How did you know I would be here?" Hikaru questioned.

"Are you joking . . . I always see you running on the track with your brother!" Kimiko giggled. "You actually enjoy being with your brother!"

"Oh, Kimiko Shiru you know you like your brother," Hikaru stated.

"Yeah, I like him a lot . . . when he's not hurting me!" Kimiko chuckled. "But seriously, Hikaru, we need to talk!" Kimiko demanded.

Hikaru stopped on the track and gazed at her best friend, "talk about what?"

"Hikaru Neijo, I know you're keeping something from me . . . I'm your best friend I can sense when there's something different . . . I know when you change your shampoo!" Kimiko declared.

Whipping sweat from her forehead, Hikaru strolled toward the bleachers where her water bottle stood and sat down. "Well, its evident you didn't come to run . . . and since I've done my five mile extension . . . OK, Kimiko, I'll tell you but I don't think your going to believe it!"

"Try me . . . I've been seeing a lot of weird things as of late," Kimiko declared walking up beside Hikaru and sitting on the bleachers.

Hikaru smiled and tossed her hair off her shoulder, "Do you remember the last day we had the fight with Clare Syatlaoi?"

"Of course, you know we should start cataloging all the times we fight with her," Kimiko giggled. "Sorry, go on . . ."

"Well, I went home and while, I was sitting on the putter millstone beside the fountain I heard someone's voice . . . I thought it was Masumi, so I got up and walked in front of the shrine . . ."

"I'm guessing it wasn't Masumi . . ." Kimiko assumed.

"No, because when I went before the shrine I was swallowed into something—something like a black abyss . . ."

"What happened?" Kimiko demanded.

"It was so bizarre—while I slid down a bright tunnel these bright rings shot past me as I came closer and closer to a tiny light flickering beyond my feet . . ." Hikaru explained pointing at her feet.

"Were the rays moving or were you . . ." Kimiko pondered.

"Good questioned . . . I don't know . . . I was in the tunnel at most six seconds when I fell through the other end . . ."

"And . . ." Kimiko pushed.

"After losing my stomach, I opened my eyes to see I was floating . . ."

"Oh, sweet . . . you were floating? In the air?"

She stared at her for a moment before shaking her head with a smile, "Yeah Kimiko, as if there's anywhere else to possibly float. I saw a person standing at the very top of the tower and last time I checked no one could get that high—not even mechanics!" Hikaru assumed.

"Was it that man in white I saw come get you at the party?" Kimiko asked.

"Yes, it was him. I'll explain him in a moment, but he was just standing there watching . . . then he turned to look at me, and it seemed he was as surprised to see me there as I was to be there!"

"Wow, this is really weird," Kimiko stated.

"I know, that's what I thought because right after that, I was back in front of the shrine—everything was back to normal . . ."

"But the guy's real. I saw him with you," Kimiko replied.

"Yeah, I'm getting there . . ."

"Oh, sorry," Kimiko smiled.

"It's OK. After the little flight I had, I came back to Earth and that's when that meteor struck and then while I was sleeping I had a really weird dream . . .

"I dreamed I was in the middle of a dark street and where a single moonbeam was pouring down on me, then as I stepped backward, these rays shot out and started bouncing around the street. I saw people concealed within the darkness, jumping around as if they were fighting something . . . and since that night at the party, I'm beginning to think the people are fighting those creatures . . . but then one of the dark figures spoke to me. He said that: 'The smoldering darkness quickly rides among the wind of deceit . . . desolate and unwavering, it devours the pure heart!'"

"Wow . . . that's really creepy!" Kimiko whispered.

"I think that the dream was a vision Kimiko . . ."

"What makes you think that," Kimiko asked.

"Because when I woke up I found the shrine was rejuvenated and that's where I met the man in white again . . . he told me that he was sent to here to protect me and that the meteor was actually a spacecraft that brought the creatures from the party to Earth . . ." Hikaru explained.

"Why . . ."

"Esal, the man in white, said that the creatures were here trying to kill me, because I may interfere with their search for the Prince of Esal's Universe!"

"Okay . . ." Kimiko urged.

"But the weirdest thing is that Esal believes I'm the leader of a band of Earthling protectors called the Devilry Hunters . . ." Hikaru smiled.

"Do you believe him," Kimiko giggled.

"At first no . . . but then the night of the party came and now . . ." Hikaru exasperated. "Esal told me that I have to find the rest of the Devilry Hunters because we may be able to help him!"

Kimiko gazed at Hikaru with a big smirk on her face when she suddenly burst out laughing hysterically.

Hikaru gazed at Kimiko confused, "What . . . what's so funny?"

"Oh, gosh I thought it was going to be something ridiculous, but I never thought it was going to be this ridiculous," Kimiko chuckled as a sour expression flowed over Hikaru's face. "Oh, come on Hikaru . . . admit it this is the worst story you've come up with—the meteor's a spaceship. The guy's an angel, and you're a protector of the Earth!"

"Gosh, you see . . . now this is exactly why I didn't want to tell you, I knew you weren't going to believe me . . . no one believes me anymore, but I'm not making this up!" Hikaru yelled as a high screech pierced the air.

Gazing at the far end of the track, Hikaru and Kimiko watched as the Nzers leapt over the fence to land on the track crushing it. Kimiko stared stunned at the grotesque creatures as they chased after several track members.

"Oh, my god . . . Antony and Masumi are over there!" Kimiko cried.

"You see . . . do you believe me now?" Hikaru asked jumping off the bleachers.

"Hikaru I've seen them before, it doesn't mean you're one of those hunter things . . ." Kimiko declared.

Shaking her head, Hikaru gazed around the track, "Gobu!" Shooting out from under one of the bleachers, Gobu zipped toward Hikaru and grabbed hold of her hair to stop. "Ow, that hurt!" Hikaru yelled lifting her hair to watch Gobu pull a humongous smile over his tiny face. "Go, distract them, I'll think of something to do!"

Kimiko watched Gobu zip toward the Nzers before turning toward Hikaru, "What do you think you're doing?"

"I already told you . . . you're the one that doesn't believe me!" Hikaru stated picking up a javelin and racing toward the Nzers.

Racing after Hikaru, Kimiko yelled, "Come back, you're insane . . . HIKARU!"

Then as Kimiko chased after Hikaru a large Nzer jumped down in front of the girls startling them causing Kimiko to scream. Lifting the javelin, Hikaru thrust it toward the Nzer and screamed. Dodging the thrust, the Nzer grabbed the javelin and pulling it out of Hikaru's hands broke it in two then smiled wickedly.

"Okay . . . new plan," Hikaru exasperated.

"Yeah, run!" Kimiko screamed.

"Kimiko wait," Hikaru yelled when the Nzer pushed past her knocking her to the ground.

"Wow," Kimiko yelled after noticing the Nzer was chasing her. "Go away you ugly thingy!"

Pulling herself off the ground, Hikaru stared after Kimiko as she raced around the track with the Nzer behind her to glance over at her brother and Antony. The boys were throwing track equipment at the Nzers with the rest of the track team cowered behind them while, Gobu zipped around several Nzers distracting them.

"Okay, I'm lost for thoughts . . . Esal, I need your help!" Hikaru whined.

"HE CAN'T HELP . . ." Cleo called at Hikaru's feet. "REMEMBER, HE WENT TO THE MOUNTAINS SUMMIT TODAY!"

"The summit right . . . what I wouldn't give for you to be a little bigger," Hikaru stated gazing down at Cleo.

"HEY, I'M A STUFFED ANIMAL COME TO LIFE. REMEMBER . . . I CAN BE ANYTHING YOUR IMAGINATION WANTS ME TO BE!"

Smiling, Hikaru lifted Cleo into the air, "I have an idea."

Running for her life around the track, Kimiko raced toward her brother as the Nzer quickly approached. She could feel its hot breath on her legs and heard its long talons scrapping up the track when someone pulled her to the side. Falling onto the school lawn, Kimiko rolled over her back to hear the Nzer screech in pain. Quickly rising to her hands and knees, Kimiko gazed surprisingly at Hikaru as she stabbed a javelin into the Nzer's thick hide.

"Hurry, get up I can't hold this thing down with a javelin pole!" Hikaru declared when the Nzer whacked her off.

As Kimiko stood up beside Hikaru, the Nzer lifted itself from the ground and gazed wickedly at the girls. Its large, empty, yellow eyes widened as it glared at Kimiko and Hikaru realizing at last who Hikaru was.

"Wars-sh . . ." it bellowed when a silver sword severed its head off its shoulders.

The head fell to the ground and rolled into the grass while, the large body crumbled to the track floor at Esal's feet.

"Esal . . ." Hikaru happily shouted.

Straightening to his full length, Esal lowered his blade and gazed at Hikaru and Kimiko, "Is that her?"

Hikaru shook her head while, Kimiko looked from one to the other, "What?"

Glancing back at the Nzers, Esal lifted his sword and swiped past a charging Nzer, "Find somewhere safe to hide!"

"Wait, I," Kimiko protested as Hikaru grabbed her hand and pulled her toward the school.

"Come on, you can argue with him another time," Hikaru stated pulling Kimiko as the Nzers charged toward Esal.

"What about Antony and Masumi . . . we have to help them!" Kimiko stated.

"Don't worry I got it covered," Hikaru replied running across the track.

"Got what covered," Kimiko asked gazing at the boys as an enlarged Cleo fought off the Nzers. "Hikaru isn't that your stuffed animal?"

"Yeah . . ."

Esal warded off the Nzers while, the girls raced into the building when the second dispatch of Nzers came to the school grounds. They charged into the area and bounded onto the side of the building to watch the others that had previously failed were being slaughtered by Esal.

"Come, the girl went ins-side this-s-s building . . . we mus-st find her and des-stroy her before s-she finds-s-s the other Hunters-s-s!" The leader ordered.

12

$\mathcal{I}$ nside, Hikaru sat slummed beside several lockers watching Kimiko pace back and forth while, she hysterically mumbling to herself. Hikaru released a breath and gazed back at Kimiko when her senses suddenly went off alerting her body. In the essence of Hikaru's mind—the door leading to the track slowly pushed open to let several leaves roll in as the wind stretched out into the hall. Light pushed inside the hall as far as the opening would allow when a shadow stretched across the top from the ceiling. Peeking into the hall, a large Nzer climbed through the open doorway onto the hall ceiling while, six others followed onto the walls and the floor. They crept leisurely along through the dark school looking down halls pausing briefly to venture on again 'til they came to the locker room. The Nzer upon the ceiling crept closer to the door and slowly brought its large face down to examine the doorknob. Its wet nose inhaled large breathes near the knob as its forked tongue slithered around the cool metal.

Quickly standing to her feet, Hikaru grabbed Kimiko's arm and pulled her to the back of the room and ducked behind an aisle of lockers. Slamming her hand over Kimiko's mouth, Hikaru listened quietly staining her senses to see what was happening.

The large Nzer reached its muscular arm out and pressed its long, razor talons against the knob to slowly curl its fat talons around it and push the door open. Hanging on the wall, a smaller Nzer caught the door with its head and pushing the door again crawled through the opening into the locker room. Sitting on the opposite side of the wall it had previously been on, the smaller Nzer held the door open with its leg allowing the others to enter.

Sitting quietly on the floor, Hikaru lurched over Kimiko while, she lifted her head and slowly peeked around the corner of the lockers. Gazing down at Kimiko, Hikaru glanced at the pool entrance when a large, muscular arm slammed through the lockers behind Hikaru's head. Pulling Kimiko up, Hikaru pushed her toward the door and stepping back raced toward the lockers to slam her weight into them. After knocking the lockers against the Nzer, Hikaru raced after Kimiko toward the pool with the rest of the Nzers in hot pursuit. Pushing through the locker room door, Kimiko slid across the pool's floor and quickly turned the corner when Hikaru raced through the closing door.

Crashing through the door, the large Nzer hammered into the pool floor and sliding across knocked Hikaru over before slamming into the corner. Quickly sitting up, Hikaru watched amused as the Nzer slipped on the tile floors 'til she heard the others rushing in across the walls and ceiling. Standing to her feet, Hikaru raced across the floor avoiding the large Nzer and ran along the opposite side Kimiko was on. Running along the pool as one of the Nzers dropped in front of her. Hikaru glanced behind at another and dove into the pool barely avoiding the swiping arms.

On the other side of the pool, Kimiko stopped and gazed at Hikaru as she pushed away from the pool walls avoiding the Nzers while, they crowded around the pool swiping at her. Glancing around the room for something to throw, Kimiko raced up to a basket and pulling up a water, polo ball turned quickly to thrown it to unfortunately gaze into a scaly, reptilian face.

"Ohhhh, crap . . ." Kimiko mumbled as the Nzer snarled up its drooling lips. Watching the Nzer drooling as it released an eerie hiss, Kimiko dropped to her knees avoiding a swiping arm and rolled away from the second blow. Standing to her feet, Kimiko gazed at the Nzer with disgust as it bellowed at her. "You are one ugly mother . . ." Kimiko uttered as the Nzer leapt at her again.

Drawing back her arm, Kimiko pitched the water, polo ball quickly and accurately square against the Nzer's large head. Quickly dodging the stunned Nzer, Kimiko watched it hammer into the floor and slid across toward the far wall. Jumping into the air, Kimiko triumphantly shouted her enthusiasm to get smacked across the back into the bleachers.

Sliding back as an arm instantly hammered into the bleachers, Kimiko let out a tiny squeak while, she stared at the large arm in front of her face. Rolling upon her back, Kimiko slammed her feet into the Nzer's stomach and quickly pulled them back to rub them when the Nzer angrily gazed down at her. Avoiding the arms, Kimiko pushed her feet into the Nzer's stomach again to attempt to lift it when her frustration began to erupt.

"You stupid ugly mother—" Kimiko screamed slamming her hands against the Nzer's stomach tossing it into the air to smash through the wall.

Sitting up to stare at the wall, Kimiko gazed around her at the black, blood splatters upon the bleachers, the floor, and her clothes to peer down at her hands. Slowly pulling up her hands, Kimiko gazed astonished at her hands to watch a mixture of red, pink, and purple energy sweeping along her hands to her forearms. Standing to her feet, Kimiko waved her hands through the air watching the energy surrounding her hands slice through the air following the movement of her arms. Gazing at Hikaru, Kimiko watched her ducking into the water as she avoided the Nzers while, they moved around the pool furiously attempting to catch her.

Scrunching up her nose, Kimiko gazed down at her hands. "OK, let's see what you can do . . . oh, come on, I know you're in there!"

Suddenly, Kimiko watched the energy around her hands heighten casting a rosy glow across her face then smiled wickedly as she gazed at the Nzers. Dropping her hands at her sides, Kimiko strolled toward the Nzers when a smug, little smirk spread across her tanned face.

Treading through the water, Hikaru avoided all the talons swiping at her when she saw Kimiko strolling up. Drowning for half a second, Hikaru pushed herself back over the water's surface and screamed at Kimiko.

The Nzers stared down at Hikaru while, she swam in the center of the pool away from their talons when the Nzer furthest away released a blood-curdling wail. Quickly turning in the direction of the scream, the others gazed at the Nzer as a hand encircled by energy burst through its scaly hide. The other Nzers watched stunned as their companion was sliced in half to fall to the ground dead at Kimiko's feet.

Enraged, several of the Nzers climbed onto the walls to charge toward Kimiko while, the largest continued to swipe at Hikaru.

Kimiko stood watching the approaching Nzers with a smile as they dove toward her. She effortlessly lifted her hand into their faces. The energy surrounding Kimiko's hand emitted on contact with the first Nzer's flesh and blew it into millions of pieces then sliced the second into a four quarter meat puzzle.

Turning away from Hikaru, the largest Nzer snarled its lips up at Kimiko angrily when Esal came charging through the doorway with sword drawn. Screeching to his companions, the Nzer quickly turned to the exit and hammered through the other door, avoiding another possible slaughter.

Racing up to the pool, Esal dropped his blade and quickly helped Hikaru out of the water as she choked on the mouthfuls of water she had consumed. His muscular arms pulsed through his sleeves as he pulled Hikaru over the side and dropped back with her in his arms when Kimiko raced up.

"She OK?"

Setting his hand to Hikaru's forehead as she choked on her breaths, he nodded with a soft smile. "Other than the lungfuls of water she swallowed I think she's fine."

"So . . . do you still not believe me . . ." Hikaru choked.

"You didn't believe her?" He frowned to pat Hikaru's back gently as she began to push to her feet.

"Well . . . no, not at first," Kimiko declared. "But what did you expect? It was too crazy to actually be real!"

"And now," Esal questioned.

A mischievous grin lifted to her cheeks as Kimiko lifting her arms. Clenching her fists to release a deep gasp as the swarms of energy burst up the edge of her arms to settle softly back around her wrists, Kimiko chuckled merrily as she swiped her arms through the air, her bright eyes following the flames.

"I hope I haven't lost my mind . . . cause this is possibly the coolest thing in the entire world!"

Helping Hikaru to her feet, Esal sheathed his blade and approached Kimiko with a stern look on his face. "Tell me your name."

"Kimiko . . . Kimiko Shiru."

"Honored to meet you Miss Shiru, I am called Esal," he bowed slightly to turn to Hikaru, "and I'm not from your world—"

"I kinda know already, Hikaru explained a bit about . . . everything. You're from another universe. So are those things," she nodded to the pile of sizzling flesh near the pool bleachers. "But how is it we can do these things? Are we from your world to?"

"No," he smiled with a soft shake of his head. "Whether it's my universe or this one, each planet had been ordained from its creation to have those that would be the ultimate defenders. Earth is young. She hasn't faced the devastating catastrophes that would warrant the awakening of Her defenders. Not til now. You are one of those such people Kimiko, the planet has blessed you with the power to help protect your leader. And it couldn't have come at a better time." He sighed while glancing toward Hikaru. "they've figured out who you are. And are now determined to kill you before you find anyone else that may stand with you and against them."

"How can that be? I thought I killed all of them when I dropped that building on top of them!" Hikaru hyperventilated.

"Wow wait there's not supposed to be a lot?" Kimiko frowned.

"There's supposed to be only one," Hikaru groaned.

"So what now then?" Kimiko shrugged.

"It's best if we leave . . . we cannot linger in one place too long after an encounter with the Nzers," Esal declared.

"Why . . ."

"The Nzers travel two to three at a time usually, but if enraged they could return in greater numbers!" He stated.

"Ha, they can bring it on!" Kimiko declared following Hikaru.

"I'm sure you think you can take on anything now, but you need to realize that the Nzers have been locked away for millenniums waiting for the moment to take a life . . . you have just now discovered what you're capable of. You're no match for an enraged Nzer born to kill!" Esal declared.

"Point taken," Kimiko replied.

Esal lead the girls safely yet quickly to their homes while, the large Nzer followed at a leisurely distance. Its piercing yellow eyes glared through the heat of the pavement surrounding him as he watched Kimiko run up her sidewalk to be grabbed and shook by Antony. Snarling its seeping lips, the large Nzer followed Esal and Hikaru to the Neijo plantation and sat outside the border before disappearing down an alley.

Hidden within the moon's shadows

The large Nzer with yellow streaks over its body stood at the control room door as it slid open allowing it to pass under the arch. Strolling around the display panel of Earth, it hovered over the technical chief as it processed the general layout of Earth's atmosphere. The planet was divided into quarters across the screen identifying every creature that walked on the surface and beneath. It studied and analyzed the technology of the planet and, most importantly, identified the vermin's' weakness'.

"Are all their s-sys-stems-s-s operational?" The yellow marked Nzer questioned retracting its long talon beneath its forearm.

"For the moment . . . a dis-spatch has-s-s been s-sent to knock out the aliens-s-s power s-sourc-ce it was-ss located at a weird building with needles-s-s pointing out of the top . . ."

"It's-s-s called a power planet you imbec-cile, and thos-se needles-s-s are the power couplings-s-s which dis-spers-se the electric-city into the c-city . . . their technology will be rendered us-seless-s-s . . ."

"What of the defens-sive equipment thes-se vermin are s-sure to have?" The technical chief questioned.

"That to will not be a problem . . . the s-strike team has-s-s already touched back with the bowel and informed us-s-s that the vermin s-shan't be able to defeat us-s-s that way . . ." the yellow marked Nzer informed.

Just then a small Nzer with a feather truffle behind its head strolled into the room and saluted the yellow marked Nzer.

"Commander Ras-sp, a transmis-ssion is-s-s being rec-ceived from the vermin's-s-s planet . . . he want's-s-s you to attend the mes-s-sage with him."

"Very good lieutenant, you may return to your s-station."

The yellow, marked Nzer walked into the Control Room and stopped before the throne bowing his head in respect before moving to the side. A large panel dispersed into a clear visualization of the largest Nzer on the planet Earth. It bowed its head and hammered its arm to its chest in respect to the great one.

"My lord, we regret to inform that the girl has-s-s uncovered another like her and is-s-s now looking for the res-st with her aids-s-s help."

A low hiss radiated from the shadows as the great one's large, snarling lips became visible. Large amounts of slobber streamed from its lips to the floor as its enraged, red eyes glared at the Nzer in the transmission.

"Your incompetenc-ce is-s-s mos-st tax-xing captain . . . I thought I was-s-s s-sending s-someone able to handle a tiny, little girl!"

"It's-s-s not s-so eas-sy with a s-second vermin bes-side the girl now, plus-s-s they have the aid of the White Guardian . . ."

The yellow marked Nzer hissed angrily, "the White Guardian is-ss on the planet?"

"Yes-s-s commander."

Turning toward the great one, the yellow marked Nzer bowed its head and dropped to its knee, "My lord let me go ex-xterminate thos-se who threaten us-s-s!"

"No, I need you here . . . the captain's-s-s companions-s-s will finis-sh the tas-sk! We will begin our invas-sion s-soon and all the loos-se ends-s-s mus-st be taut . . . as-s-s for you captain, I find your failure appalling and vex-xing to my nerves-s-s!"

Extending its arm toward the panel, the great one clenched its large fist breaking the captain's neck. He watched amused as the dead body fell from the transmissions view before it was shut down.

The yellow marked Nzer turned toward the great one with a confused look on its wicked face, "my lord you s-said s-so yours-self, we can't have any loos-se ends-s-s s-so clos-se to our triumph . . ."

"Yes-s-s, but I'm beginning to s-see that this-s-s girl is-s-s a worthy opponent and maybe if we watch her clos-sely s-she will lead us-s-s to the Latrinian! Then I will have what I came for and you may reap your revenge on the White Guardian . . ."

"Playing cat and mous-se . . . you're willing to wait that long . . . you're willing to allow her to rally more to her banner and have a bigger pos-ssibility to vanquis-sh us-s-s . . ." the yellow marked one asked.

"Not at all . . . we will meet her in battle. We will take the companions-s-s from her as-s-s s-she finds-s-s them leaving her alone in that retched world, and we will be triumphant when we des-stroy her . . ."

13

It was an early Tuesday morning on April the fifteenth when Hikaru and Kimiko strolled through the awakening city. They merrily greeted the baker as he brought freshly, baked, blueberry muffins out to the street for the passing customers. They assisted Mr. Elmer with finding his glasses and picking up the apples he had bumped into, but it was Hikaru who helped an elderly lady across the street sidewalk.

Once alone with Kimiko, Hikaru turned to her in frustration, "What was that for?"

"What for . . ."

"Don't play coy with me . . . you know perfectly well what I'm talking about!"

"Refresh my memory . . ." Kimiko demanded.

Hikaru turned away from Kimiko and stormed down the street with Kimiko close behind demanding she speak to her.

"Hikaru Neijo, don't be mad at me again . . . you now I have issues with old wrinkly people . . . I don't want to touch them they smell funny!" Kimiko called worsening the situation. *"Hikaru . . ."*

"Hush, Kimiko I have nothing to say to you . . . elderly folk are not bad . . ."

"You say that because you have an awesome Grandpa that whips the crap out of your brother at a hundred and sixty-eight years old!" Kimiko stated chasing after Hikaru.

"Would you mind being serious for once and help me find the street!" Hikaru yelled at Kimiko.

"Oh, yeah, why didn't you ask?" Growling angrily, Hikaru stomped down a street with Kimiko in hot pursuit.

Fifteen minutes later

The two girls walked quietly down a street shaded by large, towering trees to stop in front of a little, pale-yellow house. A small, white-picket fence with yellow-painted daisies bordered the tiny plantation the small, ranch house sat on. A brick sidewalk bordered by many colorful flowers of different varieties reached from the driveway to the front steps. The white porch held pots of flowers and a white rocking chair at the right corner beside a swinging seat. Children's toys were scattered about the yard—in the bushes by the driveway, mixed within the flower beds, stuck in trees around the front yard, and protecting the front porch from unwelcome guests.

"I think this is it . . ." Hikaru stated.

"Oh, look Hikaru . . . kids live here, I bet their sweet . . ." Kimiko sarcastically stated with a frown.

"Be nice . . ." Hikaru warned. "Remember, Esal sent us to find this person . . . it's important that we don't insult them before we find out about who we are exactly!"

"I get it, I get it. Be nice, find out who we are, yeah, yeah . . . let's go!" Kimiko smiled walking through the gate.

"How old you think the kids are?" Kimiko asked when an arrow hit her head. Bending over, Hikaru laughed hysterically at the annoyed expression on Kimiko's face as she pulled the suction cupped arrow off her forehead. "When I find who did this they are so dead . . ." Kimiko fumed.

"Halt who go's there . . ." a tiny voice yelled out from behind a lawn chair.

Hikaru stepped forward and raised her hands playfully.

"Yeah, good Hikaru . . . distract him so, I can sneak up and rip his arms out of socket!" Kimiko whispered.

"My name is Hikaru Neijo and I've been sent here by the White Guardian!"

Poking his head over the lawn chair, the little boy raced around the back of the house.

"Well, that went well . . . and you say I scare kids!" Kimiko declared pointing her finger accusingly at Hikaru. Walking onto the porch, Kimiko followed Hikaru and gazed around the porch as Hikaru rang the doorbell. Her bright emerald eyes searched through the toys when she spied something sparkly.

"Hey, Hikaru look at this, it's the rapid-fire-tumble cartoon cat, Noodles! Remember how Antony used to take him from me and burn him with dad's blowtorch!"

"What a nice childhood memory!"

"It's funny," Kimiko giggled as the front door opened. The girls turned toward the door to see Mrs. Tenko standing in front of them drying her wet hands. "Mrs. Tenko . . ." Kimiko pondered.

"Hello girls, what can I do for you?"

"Um, I think we must have the wrong house. Sorry . . ." Hikaru stated turning walking down the steps.

"Do you think its coincidence or fate, Miss Neijo . . . Miss Shiru? Meeting at the party I mean," Mrs. Tenko called out to the girls as they moved down the sidewalk.

Turning Hikaru gazed at Mrs. Tenko with wonder in her eyes, "I'm afraid I don't know what you're asking."

"Aren't you curious why I appeared before you as I did . . . why only you saw when there was a room full of guests," Mrs. Tenko suggested with a query look in her lavender eyes, "unless maybe you were supposed to . . . that maybe we were meant to meet again for a far more meaningful purpose!"

"See what," Kimiko asked puzzled.

Hikaru gazed at Mrs. Tenko before turning to Kimiko, "the first time I saw Mrs. Tenko, she was encircled in a bright light and cloaked in all white."

"So, are you the person he sent us to find?" Kimiko asked abruptly.

"He being," Mrs. Tenko acquiesced.

"The White Guardian," Kimiko suddenly blurted out getting a look of frustration from Hikaru. "Uh-oh!"

Mrs. Tenko gazed at both girls, "You're the new generation of Devilry Hunters?"

"How do you know about the Devilry Hunters?" Hikaru questioned.

"I think you better come in—make yourselves comfortable!" Mrs. Tenko replied opening the door wide and retreating back inside.

"Do you trust her?" Kimiko asked in a whisper before walking under the doorframe.

"I don't think we have a choice . . . she may know something."

"About the Devilry Hunters . . . you may say I do," Mrs. Tenko called as the girls walked in the house.

Hikaru gazed at Mrs. Tenko in surprise, "is that why you appeared before me like you did?"

"You can say that . . . to everyone else we appear normal, but to each other . . . we appear as who we really are, we're dignified, out of the ordinary . . ." Mrs. Tenko replied.

"So wait . . ." Kimiko ordered, "are you a Devilry Hunter to?"

"Oh heavens no, I'm not a Devilry Hunter!"

"Than who are you?" Kimiko demanded. "It's kind of obvious that you aren't just an elementary director!"

"Kimiko, do you mind?" Hikaru interrupted. "Stop badgering Mrs. Tenko!"

"It's quite all right, Hikaru, I haven't been asked this many questions in a long time . . . it's actually very refreshing!"

"See . . ." Kimiko sneered.

"All right then could you tell us about who we really are . . . it's become clear that we, like you said, are out of the ordinary!" Hikaru questioned sitting in a chair beside Kimiko as directed by Mrs. Tenko.

"You already know who you really are Hikaru . . . you haven't changed into a different person . . . you've just been added to." Mrs. Tenko declared.

"What do you mean," Kimiko asked.

"You girls will remain as you are . . . your figure, your appearance, your attitude . . . you've just simply discovered the concealed part of your lives that has been waiting for the right time to appear!" Mrs. Tenko stated.

"The way you explain things is beautiful Mrs. Tenko . . . but you are confusing the crap out of me," Kimiko giggled.

"So, you're saying that this power Kimiko has, has been slumbering within her . . . waiting 'til we needed it!" Hikaru suggested.

"Yes, but you both weren't just given this power. You weren't picked from a large group of people by a finger . . . it was passed down through the generations, through the genes," Mrs. Tenko declared.

"Mrs. Tenko, I don't understand what you're trying to say," Hikaru declared.

Mrs. Tenko set her china set down in between herself and the girls and sat into a wicker chair. Her lavender eyes stared steadily at the mantel over her fireplace where a rosy fire was kindling with Takkun sitting close beside it.

"When you girls came over you spoke of the White Guardian . . ."

"Yes . . ." Hikaru stated gazing at Kimiko.

"Yeah, and he's adorable . . ." Kimiko declared to get another look from Hikaru. "Hey, I can't help it . . . I call 'em as I see 'em!"

"It is a man?" Mrs. Tenko asked.

"He didn't want us to talk about him . . . he doesn't want too many people knowing . . ." Hikaru began.

"That he's here . . . I'm afraid its already to late for that . . . every Nzer is already alerted to his presence and if he's sworn to be your protector Hikaru, there's no way none of the Devilry Hunters won't know of him!" Mrs. Tenko declared.

"How do you know of the Nzers . . . we didn't mention them?" Hikaru asked with a scowl.

"Miss Neijo, don't flatter yourself . . . you're still young there's much you don't understand . . ." Mrs. Tenko stated coldly.

"Excuse me . . . you don't have to get rude. We're here for your help, not to get reprimanded!" Kimiko fumed, standing to her feet.

"I know I'm sorry, I mean no offense."

"Well, you did offend. You offended Hikaru, so therefore, you offended me!" Kimiko fumed.

Mrs. Tenko smiled brightly at Kimiko before gazing at Hikaru, "you have a truly remarkable friend . . . you two will go far with your new tasks!"

Sitting back down, Kimiko gazed at Hikaru as she leaned forward toward Mrs. Tenko, "you were the first generations White Guardian, weren't you?"

"What makes you think that?" Mrs. Tenko asked with a smile.

"The way you appeared was almost exact with my guardian . . ." Hikaru stated.

"It seems there's no way of fooling you Hikaru Neijo . . . yes, I was the first White Guardian . . . but I wasn't sent to find the Devilry Hunters or to tell them they were selected to fight for their planet against a threat that could possibly destroy it!"

"Then why?" Hikaru asked curiously.

"I can't tell you that Hikaru!"

"Who was the first Devilry Hunter, Mrs. Tenko . . ." Kimiko asked.

Mrs. Tenko gazed at the girls before turning toward the flames jumping behind the screen before her son. Laying her hands neatly over knees, Mrs. Tenko recalled the first day she came to this planet . . .

14

$\mathcal{I}$t was a sunny afternoon on the twelfth day of July in the year 2005 and Clyde Neijo was standing on the pitcher's mound preparing to give his best friend his legendary "heater." The heat from the sun beat down on Clyde's bare shoulders lightly tanning them as sweat rolled down his back. His clear hazel eyes gazed steadily ahead as he turned his ball cap to the back and fingered the ball between his hands.

Gripping the bat tightly, Terrence Skilou watched Clyde attentively waiting for the moment he released the ball. Sweat rolled down his cheeks as he slid his tongue along his teeth growing impatient for the collision he hoped the ball and bat would create.

Then the moment came. Clyde drew back and threw the ball toward Terrence as he waited at the home plate. The few second pause came before Terrence swung his bat at the ball, both boys watched the ball attentively hoping in their favor . . . the ball flew cleanly over the home plate a second before the bat swing.

"Yeah . . . that's right Skilou! I told you, you didn't want my "heater" but you wouldn't listen," Clyde yelled triumphantly jumping into the air throwing his hat from his head.

"Shut it, Neijo . . . you just got off lucky, the sun was in my eyes!" Terrence declared annoyed.

Chuckling, Clyde whirled around in place motioning with his arms, "what sun buddy . . . we've had 90% cloud coverage today . . . that's why we agreed to play!"

"Hey boys . . ." a soft voice called from behind the arguing boys.

Turning around, Terrence and Clyde watched as Missi Ling and Jocelyn Cody strolled toward them.

"Missi . . . hey sweet cheeks how's things going?" Terrence asked throwing his arm around her shoulders.

"Nothin much, we were watching and I wanted to let you know that you looked so professional out there!" Missi flirted.

"Professional . . ." Clyde stated surprised.

"Well of course, all you did was throw a tiny ball . . . Terrence had to swing that heavy bat . . ." Missi teased.

"Whatever, you two can bite me. No one can hit Clyde's 'heater' . . . I've been trying for years!" Terrence declared.

"I bet I could do it . . ." Jocelyn stated.

"No offense Jocelyn but you're a girl . . . everyone knows girls can't play baseball!" Terrence stated.

"What's wrong Terrence afraid I'll make you look like a retard?" Jocelyn asked pulling her long, raven hair into a ponytail.

"We're done for the day Jocelyn . . . its going to start to get humid!" Clyde replied as she shoved the ball into his chest.

"Just pitch the "heater" . . . I'll be done by the time you can raise your arm!" Jocelyn declared challengingly.

Clyde watched Jocelyn walk proudly toward the home plate with a fascinated glare in his hazel eyes. Picking up a handful of dirt, Clyde strolled toward the pitcher's mound and rubbing the dirt along his fingers drew the ball between his fingers waiting for Jocelyn to ready herself.

Shooting dirt over the home plate, Jocelyn thumped the bat against the plate vaulting the dirt into the slow moving wind. Casting her hair behind her shoulders, Jocelyn drew the bat up and waited for Clyde's action. Her dark, brown eyes watched Clyde's sweaty body steadily when he drew back and heaved the ball toward her. Pressing her lips together, Jocelyn swiftly cast the bat toward the ball and cleanly hammered it into the air. Lowering the bat, Jocelyn watched proudly as the ball dropped into the outfield before turning toward Missi and the boys.

"That's how girls play baseball Terrence . . ." Jocelyn stated walking past him toward Clyde.

"Well, I guess you won't underestimate us women again, huh?" Missi chuckled shutting Terrence's mouth.

Jocelyn held the bat between her hands as she stopped in front of Clyde. Her brown eyes gazed at him to where he thought she could almost see straight through him.

"I'll see you around Neijo . . ." Jocelyn stated handing the bat to Clyde, their hands briefly clasping each other's.

"Bye, Jocelyn." Clyde replied impishly as Missi chased after Jocelyn.

"Wow, who would've thought that a girl would hit your "heater" . . . see Clyde I give you permission to marry that girl!" Terrence stated gazing at Clyde before chuckling. "Dude, when are you going to tell Jocelyn you like her?"

"What, are you insane . . . girls make it impossible for a guy to confess their feelings!" Clyde stated walking toward the outfield.

"Take the chance man . . . you're going to lose her to another guy one of these days!" Terrence called to Clyde chasing after him.

"No, I don't think I could . . . I've attempt to do it every time I see her and I buckle under the pressure!" Clyde declared grabbing the ball from the grass. "I just can't Terrence!"

"Man, you know how long it took me to confess to Missi . . . I know it's not easy. Love isn't supposed to be easy . . . there wouldn't be any fun and than any idiot could have it. There wouldn't be any meaning to it. No magic left for those who really deserve it!"

"Thanks for that Preach!" Clyde chuckled before grabbing Terrence to put him in a headlock. "But Missi's far different from Jocelyn . . ."

"How," Terrence choked trying to get Clyde off him.

Releasing Terrence, Clyde shoved him into the grass. "Well, for one, Jocelyn's more outgoing then Missi is!"

Shaking his head, Terrence chuckled taking Clyde's offered arm. "And I can't picture Missi playing baseball . . ."

"That's for sure . . ." Clyde smiled. "I'll see you later buddy, I promised Gramps I would be back for his death dinner!"

"Ohhhh, good luck with that . . . I'll come to your rescue when I don't see you in a couple hours!" Terrence chuckled before heading off across the opposite end of the street than Clyde.

Fifteen minutes later

Clyde Neijo walked quietly down the street toward his grandfather's house carrying the bat over his shoulder while, he spun the ball across his fingers. He walked beside a small white, fence when he came to the stairwell leading to the Neijo plantation. Throwing the ball into the air, Clyde caught it before he raced up the steps past the budding Cherry Blossom trees bordering the stairwell. Reaching the top, he hopped over the gate and raced across the sidewalk to the front porch. Quietly sliding open the door, Clyde peeked inside for his grandfather before sneaking inside. Closing the door behind him, Clyde turned around to gaze into Grandpa Neijo's frustrated face.

"Clyde Li Neijo, I thought I told you to be back earlier . . ." Gramps yelled.

"I'm sorry Gramps . . . I was . . ."

"None of your excuses, I've heard just about all of 'em . . . now go clean up and come to dinner!" Gramps stated hobbling away.

"I think I'll shower first . . ." Clyde replied running down the hall avoiding Gramps stick.

"Dad-gum-it you lil' wop . . . I've been waiting for near thirty minutes for your sorry a . . ." Gramps yelled as Clyde shut the door.

The shower nozzle poured over Clyde's naked body as he tilted his head back allowing the water to rush down his tanned chest. The steam radiating from the heat of the water brushed up along Clyde's nude skin curling around his legs and stroking up his arms. The water trailed down along Clyde's body flowing were it pleased—slithering down along Clyde's tensed biceps as his hands combed through his short black hair, streaming down his raising, bronzed chest to brush along his sturdy abdomen, gliding over his slender hips to course down his muscular thighs.

His hazel eyes opened slowly blinking water out as he gazed up at the ceiling where the steam leisurely rose. Releasing a long held breath, Clyde laid his hands against the wall and slid down to his knees. Hunching over his knees, Clyde suddenly found himself feeling dizzy and one lung short when he fell back against the tub. His eyes trembled while, he stared up at the ceiling to hear Gramps yelling his name when darkness consumed him.

A tiny, dim light reached across the white, satin sheets that lay over Clyde's slender body when his hazel eyes slowly opened to gaze up at Gramps. A soft sigh escaped his lips followed by a groan and scowl when he slowly stretched out his legs.

"Steady son . . . you've had a bad case of some illness . . ."

"Some illness . . . do you not know what it was?" Clyde questioned.

"I'm afraid so . . . I've never seen anything like what had consumed your body!" Gramps declared.

"How long was I out?" Clyde asked straining to sit up to his elbows.

"Two weeks . . ." Gramps replied laying Clyde back down.

"Two Weeks . . ."

"Hush, hush . . . you're going to over work yourself son . . . and that's the last thing I need! For two weeks I've sat here worrying about you as you lay there murmuring something . . ." Gramps whimpered.

"Murmuring . . . you mean I was saying something?" Clyde asked sitting up on his arms.

"You might say that . . . but it was a language I've never heard before . . . and I know several!" Gramps declared happily.

"Yeah, I know you made me do the same thing. Only you made me learn all the others you didn't! What did it sound like?"

"Well, how should I know," Gramps reminded with a yell, "I told you Clyde, it was an unfamiliar language to me!"

Placing his hands over his ears, Clyde lay back against the bed, "Thanks Gramps, my ears are going to be ringing for hours now."

"Why you impudent lil' . . ." Gramps began as Jocelyn peeked open the door.

"Am I interrupting something?" She softly questioned.

"No, it's best if I leave before I put him in another coma!" Gramps stated hobbling out the door shutting it behind him.

Jocelyn watched Gramps with a smile before turning toward Clyde which is where a frown crept onto her face. Walking across the room, Jocelyn stopped before the bed and smacked her hand against Clyde's chest.

"Owwww, Jocelyn what was that for?" Clyde asked grabbing her hand stopping the second attempt.

"You are so reckless Clyde Neijo . . . did you even think about all the people you were going to leave behind, the people that care so much about you?" Jocelyn demanded trying to pull her hand away from Clyde's.

"Jocelyn, calm down I'm fine . . ."

"No, you weren't fine you were in a coma for two weeks . . ." Jocelyn yelled.

"What are you getting so worked up about?"

"You scared the crap out of me, Clyde!" Jocelyn stated.

Clyde gazed at Jocelyn stunned before she pulled her hand out of his. She stood holding a pot of flowers against her hip gazing at him infuriated. Turning away, Jocelyn set the pot on the stand beside Clyde's bed as he sat up to his elbows.

"I was really worried about you Clyde . . . I couldn't stop thinking that you were going to leave me without saying good-bye," Jocelyn quietly stated.

Clyde gazed upon Jocelyn with remorseful eyes desperately trying to find the words to soothe her pain to no avail.

"I'm sorry . . . I didn't come here to yell at you Clyde . . . I'm glad you're better . . . those flowers are for you!" Jocelyn stated to quickly flee the room.

"Jocelyn, wait . . ." Clyde yelled.

Lying back against the bed, Clyde stared at the ceiling as his thoughts strayed from his mind. What is going on here? Why did I go into a two-week coma? Why was I speaking some tongue unfamiliar to even grandfather? Why is Jocelyn so upset with me? What's happening to me?

* * * * * *

The soft rays of the night sun stretched leisurely down over The city as the clock tower chimed out into the prevailing silence. The wind softly howled through the trees escaping into the city—it breezed slowly down the streets, pushed up buildings to the roofs, crawled along lawns to slumbering houses. Sleeping lightly in his bed, the white satin sheets stretched lowly over Clyde's body. His shoulder blades pressed lightly up while his arms cradled his pillow beneath his head. His bronzed legs lay in view over the sheets while a sheet lay over his hips barely concealing it.

"Clyde . . ."

A soft voice echoed around the room when Clyde's sleepy, hazel eyes slowly peeked open to gaze at his dark walls. He slowly raised his head to glace around his empty room before lowering it once again to sleep when a bright, white light filled his room. Pinching his eyes tightly, Clyde slowly opened his eyes to quickly reseal them from the blinding light. Rolling onto his side, Clyde lifted himself to his arm and shielding his eyes slowly reopened them to stare at the light.

Giant rays of light pulsed through the room soon followed by a soft Angelician melody when a young woman suddenly appeared within the light. Her long, lavender hair blew through the air as she stepped from the light into Clyde's room. Her bright, innocent, lavender eyes lifted slowly to gaze at Clyde as two, giant, crystal wings folded behind her back. The sapphire gem in the center of her head shined brightly through the light radiating from her body. The white, pheasant dress blew lightly against her legs as the snowy, cotton robe draped over her bronzed arms lay piled at her feet.

"Who are you?" Clyde questioned pulling the covers closer.

The young lady smiled kindly when her voice echoed out like porcelain, wind chimes, "please don't fear me . . . I have not come to hurt you . . . I've come to grant you power beyond your wildest dreams."

"Why me?" Clyde questioned.

"You heard me when you were weak . . . you spoke to me when I was searching for the one to bestow this gift upon."

"My illness . . . you mean that was you who was speaking?" Clyde asked.

"No, it was you . . . you were speaking in my tongue proving you were the one the gift was going to come to!" The young lady explained.

"What gift?"

"You will know when the time comes."

Clyde stared at the lady stunned and confused, "Who are you?"

"I am Sinobu Selenia Daistasi Tenkako, Warrior Queen of Evalëantía, Warden of the Southern Plantír, the White Guardian sent to assemble the first clan of Earthling Warriors!"

"Earthling what?" Clyde asked.

"I've come to you because you've been chosen to lead the group."

"Me . . . no, there's no way . . ." Clyde exasperated, "I can't be some warrior leader, I'm only seventeen!"

"I was nine when I became a warrior and I'm a woman! You're age matters not when you have a will to defend the ones you love." Clyde sat staring at his covers when Sinobu walked up to the bed. "I can understand this is a major step for you . . . considering what kind of planet this is."

"What do you mean what kind of planet this is?" Clyde angrily questioned.

"I come from a universe of planets that have been infested with wars from the time it came into existence . . . your planet is young, naïve to the evils out in the universes . . . but that's why I've come to help you . . . my power will be your wings. Your weapon to fight off the ones who will soon threaten your very existence and those after you!"

Clyde stared at Sinobu with unbelieving eyes, "so I'm becoming the world's only hope?"

"No, there are people close to you in this world that are your companions in life . . . they are now your companions for this new era of heroes!"

15

There was a long silence throughout the Tenko house when Sinobu suddenly finished her tale. The rosy glow from the fire was the only motion within the house as Sinobu sat staring at it while, Kimiko gazed unbelievingly at Hikaru.

"My father was the very first Devilry Hunter!" Hikaru breathlessly stated.

"Yes," Sinobu replied gazing away from the fire at Hikaru. "He was the bravest man I've ever seen for a race that was not born warriors . . ."

Hikaru stared into the tea cup watching the liquid ripple slowly from the movement of her hands. Her brown eyes slowly gazed up at Sinobu when Kimiko suddenly broke the silence.

"Was my Aunt Missi a Devilry Hunter?"

Turning to gaze at Kimiko, Sinobu nodded slowly, "The closest friends to the leader always end up being Devilry Hunters!"

"Well, I can agree to that . . . I'm Hikaru's best friend and I'm a Devilry Hunter!" Kimiko mused.

Hikaru lifted her head and gazed at Kimiko, "what did you say?"

"I'm a Devilry Hunter . . ."

"No about being my best friend?" Hikaru demanded.

"Sinobu said that the closest people to the leader are always Devilry Hunters." Kimiko explained.

Smiling brightly, Hikaru exasperated, "Of course, it makes sense now!"

"What does . . . come on don't leave me in the dark!" Kimiko demanded.

"Sinobu is it possible that the Nzers are aware of that fact as well?" Hikaru asked.

"I don't think so . . . why Hikaru?"

Releasing a breath, Hikaru gazed at Kimiko and Sinobu, "I think I know who the next Devilry Hunter's going to be!"

"Well, fill us in!" Kimiko acquiesced.

"What time is En's soccer game at Kimiko?" Hikaru asked standing to her feet.

"At 4:45pm, why . . ." Kimiko asked.

Looking at her watch, Hikaru took Sinobu's hand, "thank you, you don't know how much I needed that."

"You are welcome here anytime Hikaru, all of you!" Mrs. Tenko replied.

"Hikaru . . ." Kimiko yelled chasing after her. "Where are we going?"

"To En's game . . ."

"Why . . . I wanted to hear more!" Kimiko whined.

"Kimiko stop thinking about yourself, I think En may be the next Devilry Hunter!" Hikaru declared walking down the sidewalk to the street.

"You think what . . ."

Nearby

A cold currant of air blew down from the mountains to the forests bordering the city, passing gently through the towering trees as the afternoon rose to its peek. Small snowflake particles rolled down from the mountain's peek to float leisurely down onto the forests canopy bringing forth the first sign of a rising storm. Breezing quietly along a beaten path, the wind broke weatherworn leaves off branches to spiral through the air to fall leisurely around Esal's concealed figure. The wind swept beneath his snowy cloak lifting it into the air while his bangs breezed before his crystal blue eyes.

"Magnificent isn't it . . ." Esal stated gazing at a waterfall as Gobu dropped beside him. "The simplicity of this planet is astounding . . . I hate to think of the possible destruction that may come to it."

Agreeing with a gurgle, Gobu floated toward the waterfall with Esal following close behind him. The sweet smell of the water drifted along the wind to their nostrils as the roaring from the falls grew louder. Stopping beside the riverbank, Gobu playfully sliced his tiny sponge arms through the fog emitting from the water impact.

"Come on Gobu, we don't have time to waste!" Esal declared walking along the riverbank when a snap echoed through the forest.

Gazing into the thicket, Esal watched the breeze lightly lift the branches while, others shook violently as Gobu slowly floated up to him. He started to chirp 'til Esal silenced him with a look when an eleven-foot Nzer suddenly burst out of the thicket landing three feet away. It scraped its talons through the forest floor casting dirt into the air as it charged furiously toward Esal.

Dropping into a fighting stance, Esal waited patiently as the Nzer approached when he spied a second one suddenly lunge from behind. Springing into the air at the last moment, Esal watched amused as the two Nzers collided when another leapt at him from the trees' canopy. The Nzer landed upon Esal's back tearing into his crystal wings sending them plummeting toward the ground.

Zipping in front of the Nzers, Gobu distracted the two on the ground when Esal and the other hammered into the river. The tall Nzer pushed Esal beneath the river attempting to drown him when a blue ball of energy blasted through the water into the

Nzer. Gasping as he surfaced, Esal slowly dragged himself unto the bank when the same Nzer ripped him out by his hair.

Held in place by several muscle tissues, the Nzer's arm lay limp beside its weeping body as it pulled Esal toward its snarling fangs. Drawing Esal near its mouth, the Nzer lashed its forked tongue out to lick up the blood which was slowly running down Esal's face. Hammering Esal into the ground, the Nzer took his hands within its one larger hand and lifted him into the air.

16

Earth—Wednesday, April 16, 2026

The cool breeze passed through the ballpark sweeping along the walkways to the fifth field where En Skilou lead his team through the before game practices. The refreshing feel of the cool breeze on the boys already sweating bodies limited the torture En was putting them through. Trotting up the fifth field walkway, Hikaru came within view of the bleachers where Jeremy sat with his little sister Mamoru. Followed closely by Kimiko, Hikaru leapt up the metal stairs to stroll casually toward Jeremy when Mamoru noticed her.

"Hikaru . . ." Mamoru happily yelled jumping off the bleachers.

Dropping to her knees, Hikaru returned Mamoru's big hug, "hey, Mamoru . . . how are you?"

"I'm great, can't wait to see En destroy another team . . ." Mamoru smiled brightly.

"Yeah, same here . . ." Hikaru giggled.

"Come sit next to me . . ." Mamoru ordered pulling Hikaru with her.

Jeremy watched Mamoru drag Hikaru past him before turning toward Kimiko with a smile, "Looks like I won't have Mamoru's attention now!"

"Yeah, Hikaru gets that honor now . . ." Kimiko chuckled.

"Where've you guys been . . . En and I tried to call both of you earlier to go to the arcade before his game, but we couldn't get a hold of you!" Jeremy questioned.

"Oh, yeah Hikaru and I went to visit a friend . . . it was a pretty interesting visit!" Kimiko declared thinking back on the visit with Sinobu.

"What happened . . ." Jeremy questioned.

"To be perfectly honest . . . I have no idea. I got very confused!" Kimiko declared.

"Why doesn't that surprise me?" Jeremy stated with a smile.

"So, how do you think En's teams going to do?" Kimiko asked.

"Well, the team their playing is the second best team in the league . . . it's going to be a good game, the number one team against the second . . . I can't wait to see En face off against the other team's captain!" Jeremy laughed.

"Why . . ."

"Everyone's been telling me that Duke's better than En . . . I begda differ with that . . ." Jeremy stated.

Kimiko smiled at Jeremy before turning to watch En stretch himself before the ref signaled the game was to begin. The excitement began to erupt across the bleachers as friends and family began to cheer as the ball was put into play. Cheering loudly, Mamoru bounced up and down on the bleachers beside Hikaru while, she carefully watched En's every move vigilantly observing his movements and expressions. For once, Hikaru's attention had drifted away from the actual game to En, whether he was on or off the field.

Watching En as well, Kimiko was dumbfounded as to what she was looking for when Maya Fui came walking up the steps. Her shoulder-length, strawberry-blonde hair breezed lightly through the wind as she walked up beside Kimiko and sat down. Her bright, denim-blue eyes gazed steadily at En watching him race up and down the field challenging every player that came toward him.

"How's he doing?" Maya questioned turning to Kimiko.

"How En always does when it comes to soccer—total domination . . . he's scored two of the three goals already!" Smiling brightly, Maya bit her lower lip and turned her attention back to the field as Kimiko gazed at her. "So, Maya . . . are you and En getting serious?" Kimiko asked with a grin.

Turning away from the game, Maya looked at Kimiko with a stunned expression, "No, Kimiko Shiru . . . En and I are strictly friends!"

"For now . . . I look forward to the day you two tie the knot!" Kimiko mumbled.

"What did you say . . ." Maya questioned grabbing Kimiko as she tried to scoot closer to Jeremy.

Halftime came too soon for the viewers that were becoming enthralled with the game while, for most of the players it hadn't come soon enough. The coach of Duke's team could be heard yelling from down the field where En stood listening to Coach O'Ryan. After talking with the coach, En strolled over to the fence line where Hikaru patiently stood with an impatient Mamoru. He smiled brightly at the girls while, he whipped sweat from his forehead with a towel as he stopped by the fence.

"En, you're destroying the other team . . . keep it up big brother, soon their going to be eating your dust!" Mamoru sinisterly laughed.

"Mamoru, I told you this is a friendly game . . ." En stated.

"Yeah, you can make it friendly . . . after you annihilate them!" Mamoru declared with an impish grin.

"Okay, munchkin . . . I hear Jeremy calling you!" Hikaru replied pushing Mamoru toward the bleachers.

"How you doing Hikaru," En asked after Mamoru left.

"What do you mean," Hikaru asked turning back to En.

"You've seemed really tense lately . . . just checking to make sure you're OK!" En relayed.

"I'm fine . . . considering what's been happening this past week!" Hikaru replied.

"Yeah, what is going on Hikaru . . . I didn't want to ask earlier, because I wasn't sure if you were up to par yet . . ." En acquiesced. "I'm really worried about you . . . you know you can tell me anything!"

"I know, I just . . . weird things have been happening to me that you may not understand just yet!" Hikaru replied.

"You don't want to talk about it," En asked as the whistle blew.

"We'll talk," Hikaru assured before En ran back onto the field. "Real soon . . ."

The next five minutes of the thirty minute half went smoothly. En led his teammates brilliantly down the field toward the opponents' side. He continually set up addition goals. He assisted his defense with keeping the ball on the opposite side of their field, and he alone successfully challenged Duke.

Watching her best friend proudly, a chill crept up Hikaru's spine when the cool breeze shot past her. Diverting her attention from the game, Hikaru slowly searched the area for what she feared was coming. Once again straining her senses, Hikaru's brown eyes steadily searched the trees surrounding the field. She gazed through the concrete building around the area, and she looked beyond the point where she could nearly search through the whole city.

The wind followed the opponents' players as they raced down the field when a shrilling howl pierced through the ruckus of the game. Standing to her feet, Kimiko walked across the bleachers toward the fence line where Hikaru stood. Jumping off the stairs, Kimiko trotted up to Hikaru and stopped as the ball rolled out of bounds.

"That was them wasn't it," Kimiko questioned to get a nod from Hikaru. "What are they coming here for . . . you think they followed you?" Kimiko questioned as En's friend, Regan, came to claim the ball.

"Regan, you're going to want to delay that pass . . ." Hikaru called to Regan as he picked up the ball.

"I can't Hikaru . . . the ref will give it to the other team!" Regan stated before throwing the ball back into play.

"Why did you want him to hold the ball . . ." Kimiko asked quite confused.

"I think Sinobu was wrong . . . I think the Nzers do know who the other Devilry Hunters are going to be . . . I think the Nzers are trying to stop me from finding the rest of the Devilry Hunters by beating me to them with extended talons!"

The wind pushed violently past Hikaru and Kimiko extending out across the field, hammering into the bleachers and pushing over the players on the grass when the second, shrilling scream rang throughout the park. Pulling her hair away from Kimiko's face and her own, Hikaru stared out over the field watching the breeze aggressively lift what it wished into the air.

Hikaru and Kimiko gazed at each other when a young man on the opponents' team, whom was racing down the field with the ball, suddenly got leapt onto by a large Nzer. The Nzer sat crushing the boy beneath it when it lifted the ball into the air and growling threateningly burst the ball with its talons. Streams of slobber streaking through the Nzer's teeth hung loosely from its large mouth as it sadistically gazed at the players in front of it.

Overcome by their growing fear, several people in the stands dashed down the metal steps toward the walkway. Abandoning their concealment, three Nzers leapt out to claim their newest victims. Blood-curdling screams pierced the air causing a panic throughout the entire field—players, coaches, friends, and families bolted across the park trying to escape the fate they didn't wish to have.

Lifting Mamoru into his arms, Jeremy jumped down the metal steps to get pushed beneath the bleachers by Hikaru. "Stay hidden . . . these creatures are driven by movement," Hikaru yelled ready to turn when Jeremy grabbed her wrist.

"Then why are you going back out there," Jeremy asked cradling Mamoru.

"Because I have to," Hikaru stated as Kimiko ran up behind her.

Jeremy gazed at Hikaru confused as Mamoru took Hikaru's arm and whimpered, "I'm scared. I don't want you to go."

"Mamoru listen to me," Hikaru stated kneeling. "I'm going to be fine. Those things aren't going to hurt me . . . Jeremy stay hidden . . . for Mamoru's sake!" Pulling from both Jeremy and Mamoru's arms, Hikaru took off toward the field with Kimiko leaving Mamoru sobbing in Jeremy's arms.

"So, what's the plan . . ." Kimiko questioned running along Hikaru's side.

"I think we're going to have to wing it . . . I really don't have a set plan other than getting En!" Hikaru smiled.

"Oh, OK . . ."

"You up to this . . ." Hikaru questioned gazing at Kimiko. Looking at Hikaru, Kimiko smiled wickedly approving the decision as they hopped over the fence surrounding the field.

Hunched upon his knees, En held several of his teammates including Regan back trying to control their peeking fears while, they watched the Nzers descend upon the people around them. Grabbing a nearby soccer ball, En stood to his feet when one of the smaller Nzers spied him with his teammates. Waiting several seconds, En pitched the ball at the last possible moment as the Nzer charged toward them. Laughing as the ball hit the Nzer square in the head. En quickly pushed his teammates away from the area where the Nzer landed.

Lashing out its long, muscular arm, the Nzer caught hold of En's leg and pulled him to the ground while, several of his teammates continued to move away. Taking hold of En's arm, Regan tried to pull En away while Taylor, another one of En's friends, kicked the Nzer's arm to get pulled beneath the Nzer's waiting talons. Pulling a screaming En away from the Nzer, Regan clumsily fell backward accidentally avoiding an attack by another Nzer. Landing upon the ground, Regan and En both flinched as the Nzer leapt at them missing the large bolt of energy spray out from Kimiko's hands.

Watching proudly as the Nzer particles fell to the ground, Kimiko turned toward En and Regan as Hikaru dropped beside them. Smacking her hands together in order to remove the dust upon them, Kimiko walked toward the boys noticing a piece of Nzer on her shoulder.

"What are those things," Regan whimpered.

"Not your buddies, for one," Kimiko sarcastically answered.

"Kimiko," Hikaru stated in an ordering tone. "You guys all right?" Hikaru asked as Kimiko whacked the piece of Nzer off her shoulder.

"Yeah, we're OK . . . what about Taylor . . ." En questioned.

Looking over at Taylor's lifeless body, Kimiko turned back toward the boys, "which half?"

"Oh my god," Regan exasperated.

"He's dead," En asked stunned.

Scoffing, Kimiko nodded, "yeah, I'd think so!"

"We'll deal with that later, right now we have to get you outta here," Hikaru stated.

"Why," En questioned.

"Because they came for you," Hikaru whispered to En while, Kimiko pulled Regan to his feet.

"For me . . . why?" En asked with a half raised voice.

"You remember asking me what has been bothering me lately . . ." Hikaru whispered.

"Yeah . . . is this what's been going on?" En asked gazing at the Nzers.

"I don't have time to explain everything," Hikaru stated gazing at the Nzers. "But the short version is that I've become a leader of an Earthling Warrior group called the Devilry Hunters and my closest friends are part of the group!"

En gazed at Hikaru when he realized the look in her eyes, "Me . . . you think I'm one of your . . . those people?"

"I know you are, because these creatures are trying to kill my followers before I can find them . . ." Hikaru stated pulling En up.

"Is Kimiko one of them," En questioned.

"Yep, and it's awesome," Kimiko stated enthralled.

17

Strolling out of the forest onto the field, a large red-faced Nzer gazed past the frantic people and their attackers to En standing with Hikaru. Its long, muscular legs plowed through the ground as it started racing toward Hikaru and her friends. Throwing itself over the fence line, the red-faced Nzer charged across the field knocking people and its companions from its path as it leapt at the friends.

Turning around as the red-faced Nzer came down toward them, Hikaru pushed En to the ground just as Kimiko did the same with Regan. Lifting her arms to guard her face, Hikaru braced herself against the weight of the Nzer as it slammed into her. Opening her eyes, Hikaru gazed at the Nzer as it slashed its long talons across some barrier between itself and Hikaru. Pulling a small smirk across her face, Hikaru pushed her head forward slamming the barrier into the Nzer sending it through the air to skid across the field. Pulling her whipping hair from her face, Hikaru walked away from En and Regan with Kimiko close behind her.

"What just happened . . ." Regan asked En looking after Hikaru and Kimiko.

"I'm not sure," En replied.

Dodging the large, swinging talons, Hikaru and Kimiko battled against the very, irritated Nzer. Successfully distracting the Nzer, Hikaru gave Kimiko the time she needed to slip behind the creature as the swarms of energy engulfed her arms. Enraged, the red-faced Nzer watched Hikaru and Kimiko diverting its attention from its primary goal when it quickly jumped into the air avoiding Kimiko's attack. Landing in front of En and Regan, the Nzer bellowed out causing his companions to surround Hikaru and Kimiko. Dropping to the ground, the red-faced Nzer slowly approached En and Regan with a menacing smirk creeping over its scaly face.

"Oh, my god . . . we're going to die!" Regan whimpered jumping behind En.

"Regan, calm down," En yelled backing away from the Nzer.

"I'm too young to die!" Regan exasperated.

Lunging forward, the red-faced Nzer slammed into En and Regan, throwing them across the field. Landing on the ground, the red-faced Nzer charged toward En with its talons raised. Sitting up, En gazed over at Regan assuring himself that he was OK before turning his growing anger toward the charging Nzer. The cool wind breezed through En's damp hair lifting it away from his sweaty forehead as he gripped several grass blades in his hands. The approaching Nzer reflected in En's bright, brown eyes carried a sadistic look across its face as it leapt at En.

Dropping back onto the grass, En raised his arm protecting himself when the breeze shot past him and hammered into the Nzer pushing it into the air to drop it twenty feet away. Rising to his hands and knees, En gazed at the Nzers attacking Hikaru and Kimiko to be filled with some stream of energy while, annoyance took hold of En coursing through his body to escape into the air.

The wind stretched across the field breezing past En toward Hikaru and Kimiko as the ground began to shake ferociously. Staggering back against Kimiko, Hikaru fell back onto the quaking ground to watch it suddenly open to effortlessly swallow every Nzer throughout the park. Scooting closer to the gap in the soil, Hikaru gazed down into the interior of the planet before it resealed. Gazing at Kimiko, Hikaru looked up to watch En come running up with Regan close behind.

"You guys all right?" En questioned, grabbing Hikaru and pulling her up.

"Thanks very much," Kimiko sarcastically stated pulling herself up.

"We're OK . . . you?" Hikaru asked gazing at En then at the ground.

Pulling a little smirk onto his face, En whispered into Hikaru's ear, "I think we need to talk!" Nodding, Hikaru turned toward a frightened Regan when Jeremy quickly racing up with Mamoru and Maya.

"En . . ." Mamoru whimpered.

"Hey, it's OK . . . they're gone now, nothing's going to hurt you!" En stated.

"And what about you mister . . ." Maya questioned punching En's arm. "What did you think you were doing, huh?"

Rubbing his arm, En turned toward Maya, "What're you talking about . . . I was minding my own business when those big, ugly creatures attacked everyone!"

"What did they want," Jeremy questioned.

Taking hold of En's hand, Hikaru squeezed it, silencing him. "It's hard to tell . . . considering they were swallowed by the planet. I would say we won't be able to find out, Jeremy!"

Scratching the top of his head, Jeremy gazed at En. "You OK?"

Pulling a smirk across his face, En replied, "I'm all right!"

Regan gazed back and forth at the friends before blurting out, "Well, I'm not all right . . . we were attacked by something no one's ever seen on this planet . . . and they killed Taylor . . . oh god!" Regan exasperated turning toward Taylor.

"No, Regan . . ." Hikaru demanded, grabbing his arm.

"Let go, he may not be dead . . . we may be able to help him . . . maybe he's just mostly dead!" Regan cracked.

"No, Regan . . . he's gone you can't help him!" Hikaru stated. Looking at the grass, Kimiko smirked reaching down to lift a large stick. "Regan . . . calm down!" Hikaru yelled as Kimiko whacked him in the head.

Stepping back to watch Hikaru drop Regan onto the grass, Kimiko gazed up at her and smiled, "Problem solved!"

Scrunching her nose, Hikaru gazed at Kimiko, "thanks!"

"You're welcome," Kimiko stated.

"We should probably call an ambulance," Maya stated.

"Yeah, he's probably got a concussion now," Hikaru replied.

"How, he's already dead!" Kimiko stated looking at Hikaru.

Gazing at Kimiko confused, Hikaru pressed her lips together, "I'm talking about Regan . . . I know Taylor's dead, you moron!"

"Oh, well, why didn't you say so," Kimiko chuckled.

"Kimiko, you better call an ambulance, because you're going to need it in a few seconds," Hikaru threatened.

Thirty minutes later

Flashing across the blood streaked grass, the red and blue lights on top the patrol cars highlighted the park as the dusk rays began to cascade down upon the city. Scattered across the scene of the attack, police officers were busily collecting evidence while, Hikaru stood with Kimiko beside an ambulance car.

While a paramedic was tenderly dressing Regan's head, another one was cleaning a cut across En's arm as Maya raved at him with Jeremy and Mamoru joining in. A look of frustration was painted over En's face while, he sat and listened to the three scold him for something he hadn't intended.

Standing silently beside Hikaru, Kimiko soon felt herself becoming overwhelmed by the large, amount of curiosity bouncing around within her. Turning her attention away from the lights flashing across the park, the officers busily collecting evidence to what she already knew, and the sounds of crying friends and families. Kimiko gazed at Hikaru.

"Do you think it's going to get worse?" Kimiko questioned.

"I don't know," Hikaru quietly answered.

"Do you think more people are going to die?"

"I hope not." Hikaru softly breathed, walking toward En. Smiling brightly as she approached the others, Hikaru laid her hand on Maya calming her for a second. "En, Kimiko and I are going to head home . . . we'll talk to you later!"

"Bye, Hikaru," En stated to whisper in her ear, "thank you!"

Patting En's shoulder, Hikaru turned and hugged Mamoru, Jeremy, and Maya before walking toward the walkway with Kimiko beside her.

"What are you thinking?" Kimiko asked once they were alone again.

"I am lost with who the next hunter's going to be," Hikaru stated

"Don't worry, you'll know when you need to, you won't lose to the Nzers," Kimiko confidently stated.

"I wish that could be true . . ."

"Hikaru tell me what's bothering you . . . please, you know I can tell when something's up!" Kimiko declared.

Turning toward Kimiko, Hikaru softly released a long held breathe, "I don't know where Esal is!"

Kimiko stared at Hikaru stunned, "what do you mean?"

"I mean, I don't know where he is . . . up until today, every attack I've been involved in with the Nzers, Esal's always been there, but he wasn't this time!" Hikaru heavily breathed.

"Do you think he's in trouble . . ." Kimiko asked following Hikaru down the street leading to their houses.

"I'm still lost with all that's been happening. I'm not sure if he's just so consumed with finding the Latrinian that he didn't pick up the attack this time!"

"What should we do . . ." Kimiko asked stopping at her front gate.

Turning to look at Kimiko, Hikaru sighed, "I'm not sure what I'm doing Kimiko . . . a few days ago, I was an ordinary sixteen-year-old teenager. Now I'm a struggling leader dumbfounded to what I'm doing with this new identity!"

"You are going to be terrific Hikaru . . . we'll figure this out, even Batman had to start out rusty!" Kimiko declared.

Smiling brightly, Hikaru hugged Kimiko, "night Kimiko, I'll see you at school!"

"Don't worry Hikaru . . . I'm sure Esal's just busy with his errands or what ever he's supposed to do!"

"Yeah," Hikaru stated walking down the street. "Why do I still feel so insecure?"

The evening had given in to the growing darkness as the later hours of the night stretched further into a restless, unsure state. The cool, mountain breeze howled lightly through the prolonging night. The creatures of the night prowled throughout the streets. The chirping of restless insects echoed into the soft melody of the rustling bushes and the wind pushing through leaves.

The wind softly blew through the open window of En's bedroom lightly lifting the gray curtains away from the sandy walls. Stretching out to blow over his desk, the breeze trailed toward his cracked closet door slightly pushing it open as it continued creeping through the dark room. Reaching up the night stand beside En's bed, the wind pressed gently around the lamp and pictures of En with Jeremy and Mamoru.

Slowly feeling its way across the cotton sheets laying over En's slender body, the wind blew over his bare, tanned chest. Lightly lifting his brown bangs away from his face, the wind blew past En's restless brown eyes while, they stared at the dark ceiling.

Lying outstretched upon his bed, En stared up at his ceiling thinking of the day when his door slowly creaked open. Lifting his head, En gazed over his chest to see Jeremy standing in the doorway.

"Why are you still awake?" Jeremy asked in a whisper.

Rising to his elbows, En gazed at Jeremy with a disbelieving expression, "Why are you still awake?"

Scoffing, Jeremy walked into the room and sat on the edge of the bed, "same reason you are!"

Quietly chuckling, En shook his head, "no, I think we're probably awake for different reasons!"

Dropping his head, Jeremy nodded as he gazed back at En. "You know, if there's ever anything bothering you . . . I'm here!"

Smoothing his hands over his sheets, En softly sighed, "I know, Jeremy, I . . ."

"You can tell me, En."

Gazing long upon Jeremy's serious expression, En slowly nodded. "Something's happening to me Jeremy!"

"What . . . are you hurt . . . did that creature make you ill. Do I need to take you to the hospital?" Jeremy quickly began to panic.

"No," En stated, covering Jeremy's mouth, "I'm fine . . . do you remember when the creatures suddenly disappeared today at my game?"

"You mean the earth splitting open?" Jeremy questioned.

En stared at Jeremy before finding the words to utter. "I don't know how, but I did that, Jeremy!"

Jeremy stared at En with a curious look in his eyes. "What?"

"Please don't think I'm insane. I'm being serious!"

"I think that wound is making you crazy . . . get dressed. I'm taking you to the hospital!" Jeremy stated standing to his feet.

"Jeremy, wait . . ." En whispered in a louder tone.

"Now, En . . ." Jeremy commanded continuing to walk toward the door.

"No . . ." En finished as the wind blew the door shut in Jeremy's face.

After pulling on the door for a while, Jeremy turned toward En, puzzled. "Why won't the door open?"

En gazed at Jeremy and sadly shook his head. "Because I didn't want you to leave thinking I was insane!"

Shifting his weight, Jeremy walked toward En. "So you had the wind push the door shut for you?"

"I don't know, but it happened to one of the creatures at the park earlier . . . and when I saw them attacking Hikaru and Kimiko the ground broke open!" En explained.

"How is this happening," Jeremy questioned sitting beside En.

"Hikaru told me that I'm a Devilry Hunter, an Earthling Warrior."

"How does Hikaru know?" Jeremy asked. En looked at Jeremy as he pressed him further, "En how does she know?"

"Hikaru's the leader and Kimiko's one too . . ."

Jeremy gazed at En and scoffed. "Now it's beginning to make sense . . . I didn't understand why Hikaru and Kimiko went back into the park with those things today. Now I do . . . and the party incident that makes a little sense now to!"

"So you don't think less of me?" En asked.

Jeremy gazed at En stunned, "En, you're my little brother . . . there will never be anything to make me think ill of you!"

"Thanks, I feel better now."

"Is that why you were still up, you were unsure of me still liking you?" Jeremy asked.

"Well, you were beginning to think I was insane," En declared.

"No, I was afraid you were becoming ill, I didn't know if the creatures had something infectious inside them!" Jeremy stated walking toward the door. Lying back onto his bed, En watched Jeremy open his door and walk into the hall to turn and grab the knob to reseal it. "Oh, and En . . ."

"What Jeremy . . ."

"I already knew you were insane," Jeremy smiled shutting the door.

18

The wind softly blew through the quiet, halls of the Latrinian palace as Jeannee raced into the LDCR, Latira's Database Control Room. Bounding up the steps to the CPU's mainframe, Jeannee trotted up to the master computer where Doc sat sleeping. Smiling brightly, Jeannee gently lifted him off the desk and pushed the chair toward the stairs. Pulling a nearby chair beneath her, Jeannee rebooted the master computer as she heard Doc's chair stubble down the steps. Scowling as she heard Doc wail on contact with the floor, Jeannee chuckled as the CPU came on line.

"Jeannee you little bi . . ." Doc fumed.

"GOOD MORNING JEANNEE!" The CPU greeted.

"Good morning CPU, I need you to check the central COM link and see if there's a glitch in it!" Jeannee acquiesced.

"Why do you need the CPU to check the COM link?" Doc questioned stopping behind Jeannee's chair.

"We can't get any response from the solar system planet."

"Could we before . . ."

Jeannee gazed away from the CPU at Doc, "Doc, we're the ruling planet of the Solari of course we can pick up anything from the other universe . . . we would know if someone was ordering a pizza!"

"COM LINK FILES READY FOR OBSERVATION . . ."

"Thank you CPU, please check if the communication has been disrupted!" Jeannee ordered.

"SCANNING . . ." the CPU flashed as it processed for a few minutes. *"NO DETECTION OF INFECTION . . ."*

"See if Earth's communications have been disrupted," Doc suggested.

"ONE MOMENT . . ." the CPU flashed before answering, *"ACCESS DENIED!"*

"What," Jeannee and Doc both exasperated.

"How is that possible . . . CPU see who posted that command!" Jeannee ordered.

"SEARCHING . . . COMMAND SENT FROM LATRINIAN WARSHIP G-731"

"That's the ship in the solar system . . . they've knocked out Earth's communication . . . they must be preparing to invade!" Jeannee exclaimed. "CPU, bring up a visual of the planet Earth!"

"ACCESS DENIED!"

"Can you bring up any visual of the solar system?" Jeannee asked.

"CHECKING . . ." the CPU brought a large visual of the solar system's nine planets to the master computer's screen when it suddenly disappeared. *"ACCESS DENIED!"*

"Damn it . . ." Jeannee fumed.

"Try something else . . ." Doc suggested.

"I'm trying, Doc, but the **Warship G-731** is somehow blocking us out of the solar system!"

"Try to override it," Doc suggested. "Send a **Model F-98** out to confront the **Warship G-731**, force them to surrender to our command!"

"The **Warship G-731** is the most advanced warship we built, Doc . . . we modeled every other ship after it, we can't force it to surrender . . . it could blast any ship we send toward it into particles of dust!" Jeannee stated.

"Then what do we do," Doc exasperated.

"I don't know Doc . . ." yelled Jeannee.

"We have to think of something . . ." Doc exclaimed.

"CPU, I need you to do one last thing for me and let's pray that it's not being blocked . . . set up a COM link with the **Warship G-731** and send this message: 'Commander of the **Warship G-731**, this is the first-rank petty officer, Jeannee Nova, of the Latira Command . . .'"

19

Earth—Thursday, April 17, 2026

The wind blew gently through Hikaru's hair while she sat alone on a school bench in the garden lunch area. She stared up at the sky watching the white clouds floating overhead leisurely roll by when Kimon walked up. Stopping behind the bench, Kimon gazed down at Hikaru while, she continued to stare up at the clouds. His indigo eyes trailed away from Hikaru toward the sky when Hikaru dropped her head to the side to look at him.

"Did you want something Mr. Chairman?"

Gazing at Hikaru somewhat offended, Kimon sat beside her on the bench, "What's with this Mr. Chairman stuff? I've told you, you don't have to call me that!" Looking away with a smug expression, Hikaru continued to watch the passing clouds while, Kimon stared at her. "Are you going to be mad at me forever?" Kimon questioned.

"For the moment 'til I decide I'm done!" Hikaru stated staring up at the clouds.

"I'm sorry that you're so infuriated with me, but . . ."

"Infuriated doesn't cover it!"

"Hikaru . . ." Kimiko yelled from across the yard.

"Excuse me, Mr. Youitan. I have to go!" Hikaru stated walking away toward Kimiko. Standing on the opposite end of the garden, Kimiko watched Hikaru walk toward her with a frustrated expression. Following her down the trellis, Kimiko came alongside Hikaru when she burst out. "Kimiko this is driving me insane!"

"What is . . ."

"I want to be mad at him . . . but then I don't!" Hikaru declared.

"And what's wrong with that . . . I can stay mad at Antony for days." Kimiko proudly stated.

"Kimiko, Antony is your brother. It's completely different!"

"Oh, Hikaru . . . that's it. I'm putting my foot down, when you see him again tell him how you feel."

"I'm supposed to be mad at him!"

"Don't hold a grudge over that argument we had with Claire. I heard he only puts up with her 'cause he's so focused on making sure that Yuri gets the best education possible!"

"What are you talking about?" Hikaru questioned.

"Claire's father is the principal of the academy Hikaru, if Kimon did something to upset his daughter he'd probably expel Yuri to get at Kimon!"

"Really . . ."

"I wouldn't doubt it . . . and besides I still think Kimon likes you!"

"Shut up Kimiko, you say that because you're my best friend."

"Yeah, and I also see the way he looks at you. It's completely different from the way he looks at other girls . . . it almost looks like he blushes like you do, just not as red!" Kimiko giggled.

"Stop teasing me or I'm going to ignore you!"

"Okay, I'll stop . . . by the way En told me in third block that he was going to be all by himself at Jeremy's fencing practice today, so I think we should show up and surprise him!" Kimiko suggested.

"Kimiko I don't have time to mess around, I have to find the rest of my Devilry Hunters . . ." Hikaru finished in a whisper.

"Come on Hikaru, it's for En . . . he looked pretty shook up still!"

"How long does Jeremy's fencing practice last?" Hikaru questioned.

"Shoot if I know . . ."

"Stop trying to talk like Antony . . . he sounds like an idiot when he does it, I don't need you to as well!" Hikaru ordered.

"Antony only does it because it annoys dad," Kimiko smiled.

"I can see why!" Hikaru laughed walking down a sidewalk.

"So are we going?"

"Of course, but I'm not going to stay for hours!"

"Okay, yeah . . ." Kimiko sarcastically stated.

"I'm serious, Kimiko. I need to find the others!" Hikaru yelled chasing after Kimiko.

20

Twenty Thousand Light-Years Away

Jeannea raced down the palace halls looking in and out of corridors followed by a wheezing Doc. Pushing through a pair of large doors, Jeannee found the Holy Priest centering the Grand Hall. Running through the doors, Jeannee approached the Holy Priest accidentally allowing the doors to shut on Doc's face. Sweeping across the porcelain, granite floors laid across the Grand Hall. The Holy Priest's dark maroon eyes gazed steadily upon his large staff while, he swiped it through the air. Giving off a multitude of dazzling lights, the large orb sitting on top the staff flashed across the Grand Hall's extensive, crystal walls to push through the walls beyond. Racing up behind the Holy Priest, Jeannee watched the lights flash around and through her when she ran in front of his path.

"Priest we are in serious trouble!"

"You're in trouble," the Holy Priest chuckled. "Think of the trouble Esal is going through right now . . . constantly in a predicament with the creatures, trying to handle a rambunctious, sixteen-year-old girl constantly on the move, and now the loss of communication with the Solari. Esal's the one we need to be worrying about!"

"What do you think I'm so frantic about, Doc's health . . ." Jeannee exclaimed. "Esal is completely by himself on that planet with those ruthless creatures!"

"He has Gobu with him . . ." Doc stated rubbing his nose as he approached.

"Yeah, that's got to be worth something . . . no offence to Gobu, but he'll be like a feather hitting the Under Dwellers, Doc! Their heads are like stone, their scales are tough like leather, and they can battle in any terrain!"

"Not true . . . water. They are very vulnerable in water. Since they live beneath the ground they never really had to deal with its wet, controlling power. Since they are so tall; their very heavy and would sink!" The Holy Priest stated gazing at the two.

"Well, I'm glad you told us this now, considering we have no way to tell Esal!" Jeannee yelled.

"Oh, ye of little faith . . . Esal is a very bright, young man. He survives through the roughest ordeals. Besides, I've already seen that he has figured out their weakness!" the Holy Priest stated.

"What, how . . ." Jeannee questioned.

"The Under Dweller isn't as smart as it thinks . . . he's unaware that I have the ability to see what I please when I please . . . I was given that power by the Soul Star so that no one person or thing could rule over the two worlds!"

"The Soul Star . . ." Jeannee repeated. "I always believed that to be another one of our many fairy tales!"

"The Under Dwellers were once a fairy tale and look what's happening . . . some things we tried to make only appear to be fairy tales, as you put it, to protect the innocent existence of our future generations! Some tales are really our past . . ." the Holy Priest declared, "Nightmares!"

"Since you can see anything can you see Esal on the planet?" Jeannee asked.

"Yeah," Doc added excitedly.

"I'm trying to find him again . . . that boy never stays in one place too long, but it has never taken me this long to locate him!" The Holy Priest replied.

"Do you think he's in trouble?" Jeannee exasperated.

"Or worse, dead," Doc stated to get smacked by Jeannee.

"Don't say that . . ." Jeannee yelled.

"It's possible . . . why else would he be so hard to find?" Doc whimpered.

"No, no, I would know if Esal was hurt or dying . . . he's simply hidden himself from me; probably doing something he doesn't want anyone knowing about. He knows I can see him and probably figured that Jeannee would sooner or later come to discover it as well!" The Holy Priest chuckled.

"Da, gods, you're probably right . . . Esal you retched, little pain in the . . ."

"Yes, well, if you plan to stick around I would appreciate it if you would be silent!" The Holy Priest ordered gazing at Jeannee.

"Sorry . . ."

21

Pushing the gym doors open, Kimiko briskly walked into Amin Mela Academy's Gymnasium with Hikaru close behind her. The two girls trotted down the stairs toward the gym floor where En sat on the bottom bleacher. Dropping onto the plastic bench beside En, Kimiko shook the entire row of bleachers as Hikaru walked past the two to sit on En's other side.

"What are you guys doing here . . ." En asked surprised.

"We were in the neighborhood . . ." Kimiko chuckled.

"Kimiko said you were going to be all by yourself, so we came to be with you," Hikaru explained.

"Checking up on me . . ." En asked.

"No," Hikaru replied. "But now that you mention it, are you OK?"

Shaking his head, En smiled, "I'm fine Hikaru . . . I'm a big boy, I can take care of myself!"

"I never doubted that En, but these creatures are ruthless, bloodthirsty vermin; they don't feel anything like we do!" Hikaru declared.

"How are Taylor's parents doing?" Kimiko asked.

"All right considering . . . his funeral's April 24!" Gazing at the floor, En quietly confessed, "Hikaru, I told Jeremy . . ."

"What . . ." Kimiko exasperated.

Hikaru gazed at Kimiko back to En, "what did he say?"

"He didn't believe me at first, but then when I didn't want him to leave the wind blew the door shut and wouldn't let him out!" En replied.

"So you control the wind? That is so cool . . ." Kimiko exclaimed.

"I think it's more than that, remember the ground splitting . . . I think En can manipulate the elements of Earth to do his will!" Hikaru stated.

"The elements of Earth . . ." En and Kimiko both questioned.

"Yes, the actual earth, fire, water, wind, and probably other things as well like weather!" Hikaru smiled.

"Wow, En that's awesome . . ." Kimiko smirked.

"What can you do . . ." En asked Kimiko.

"Well, I'm not really sure what it is, but I can blow the creatures apart . . . I've done it before, it was awesome!" Kimiko smiled.

"What about you Hikaru . . ." En questioned.

"Yeah, what do you do, I haven't seen your power!" Kimiko declared.

"I really don't know; at points I don't think I have any abilities . . ." Hikaru stated.

"What about when that thing came at us . . . you were in front of us all and then when it came down upon us it hit some barrier before you and shot backward!" En recalled.

"Yeah, and you told me about acid bubbles!" Kimiko added.

"Yeah, but it's possible that it's only Esal protecting me!" Hikaru stated.

"Who's Esal . . ." En asked.

"Hikaru's hot Guardian Angel, he came from another world hidden inside ours!" Kimiko replied.

"Another world . . ." En puzzled.

"Yeah, I know I almost didn't believe it either 'til he played some trick on me, so don't ever bring it up in front of him or he'll probably do something to you to!" Kimiko declared.

"Thanks . . ." Hikaru stated gazing at Kimiko.

"You're welcome . . ."

While the three sat talking on the benches, Jeremy swept across the gym mats practicing with his younger peers when several Nzers crashed through the ceiling. Quickly moving himself and his classmates out of the way, Jeremy fell against the mats as the Nzers gazed around the gym. Pulling the netted mask off his head, Jeremy gazed at the same creatures that had attacked En yesterday when the nearest one grabbed hold of his foot and pulled him into the air.

"Target identified one les-ss worthless-ss vermin!" The Nzer hissed raising its talons toward Jeremy's face.

Jeremy gazed at the large claws coming toward his face with widen eyes when the creature was suddenly severed in half by a bright swarm of energy. Jeremy dropped onto the mats where En pulled him to his feet with Hikaru along his side. He watched the Nzer's body crumble to the floor in pieces to see Kimiko standing proudly behind it with swarms of energy around her arms.

"See En that's what the Kimiko does . . ." she chuckled.

Pushing En and Jeremy out of the way, Hikaru dodged the leaping Nzer, "En, get Jeremy and the others out of here now!"

"Hikaru that creature . . ."

"I see it Jeremy . . . get out of here!" Hikaru yelled kicking the Nzer in the head.

Grabbing Jeremy's arm, En started pulling him and the others to safety when a chunky Nzer dropped in front of them. Quickly stopping in front of the Nzer, the nervous emotions in En's body began to erupt causing the floor to quiver. Standing in front of the others, En watched the Nzer struggle to keep its footing when every window in the gymnasium shot open unleashing a strong currant of air into the room to hammer into the Nzer blocking En's path.

Astonished, Jeremy smiled brightly at his younger brother releasing a chuckle from his throat when another Nzer tackled En. Watching the Nzer hammer across the ground with En beneath it, Jeremy's fury entwined with his nerves and as he raced toward the creature he sped across the floor and hammered into it. Quickly stepping backward, Jeremy pulled En to his feet and watched the Nzer stumble across the ground.

"What just happened . . ." En questioned gazing at Jeremy.

"I knocked it off you!"

"You came out of nowhere . . ." En exasperated.

"Oh, I did not . . ." Jeremy stated as the Nzer jumped at him. "Stop!" Jeremy ordered lifting his hand in front of the descending Nzer freezing it in midair.

Jeremy and En gazed at the frozen Nzer puzzled. Looking at the Nzer then at his hand, Jeremy pointed at the creature and moving his finger toward the right then the left; smiled wickedly as he watched the Nzer move in the direction his finger did.

"Well, would you look at that . . ." Jeremy chuckled.

"Magic . . . Jeremy you're a Devilry Hunter . . . Hikaru!" En yelled.

"I think I'm going to like this!" Jeremy stated with a smile as he moved his finger continually in a circle. Standing beside En while, he waited for Hikaru, Jeremy threw the Nzer across the gymnasium as it began to get heavy. "I'll be back . . ." Jeremy chuckled.

"Jeremy . . ." En yelled as Hikaru came running up.

"I thought I told you to get out of here . . ." Hikaru stated.

En gazed at her before turning her head toward Jeremy. Gazing in disbelief, Hikaru watched Jeremy disappear and reappear around the remaining Nzers when a large smile crept toward her ears.

"I have a Devilry Hunter Magician!" Hikaru giggled as Kimiko walked up.

"This isn't fair; Jeremy's hogging all the smelly, creepy things!" Kimiko whined.

"By all means Kimiko go join him . . ." Hikaru stated.

Watching from twenty thousand light-years, the Holy Priest smiled brightly as he watched Jeremy teasing the Nzers when Kimiko raced up to join in the fun. Swiping his staff through the visual, the Holy Priest expanded the scene scanning the room 'til his eyes befell En and Hikaru.

"Well, there's our little Hunter . . . young, naïve child of the innocent, walk your new path carefully . . . the trials are about to reach toward the flames!"

22

As the twilight began to descend upon the city, Hikaru sat on her bed with Kimiko stroking Cleo's fluffy body. The wind blew the curtains covering Hikaru's bedroom window slightly as the girls contemplated over the past few days.

"Wow this is great . . . I bet the Nzers weren't expecting so many of us in so little time!" Kimiko mused.

"I still can't believe that there are already four of us and that my three Hunters are in fact my best friends!" Hikaru declared.

"I know, ain't it cool!"

"Something's still bothering me Kimiko . . ."

"You're worried about Esal; aren't you?"

"It's been three days now since I heard from him! Do you think something happened?"

"To that guy; no way . . . I bet he's probably stumbled onto something major and just got occupied!"

"For nearly three days . . ."

"Maybe; I don't know . . . I'm newer at this than you are!" Kimiko declared.

"You're right . . . I'm probably worrying over nothing, but I can't help it!"

Kimiko looked at Hikaru and smiled mischievously, "Are you crushing on him Hikaru?"

"No," a surprised Hikaru replied. "He's my White Guardian Kimiko; and besides, you already know who I'm in love with!"

"Oh, yeah; like that's real hard to figure out . . . but you aren't a littlest bit?"

Shrugging, Hikaru blushed slightly, "well, I admit that I've certainly found myself staring at him . . . but I don't think it's as serious as when I am around Kimon!"

"I admit it; I've looked to . . . Hikaru that man is adorable!"

"Yeah, but I've been thinking about all that's been going on and I've decided that I don't need anymore distractions."

"What do you mean Hikaru?"

"I'm going to bury the controversies I end up in when I'm around Kimon . . . I'm going to do everything in my power to avoid him!" Hikaru sternly stated.

Bursting out laughing, Kimiko stared at Hikaru, "You're joking right . . . Hikaru he's Yuri's brother how are you going to avoid him?"

"Make sure that Yuri isn't with him . . ."

"What about the school, he's the acting chairman, it's going to be pretty hard to avoid him in class if he comes in looking for you!"

"I'll figure something out . . . I need to be focused; I don't know how many more Hunters are out there . . . I need to spend all my time working on finding them!"

"Okay, but don't forget that you have three Hunters available to help you now . . . don't ever go by yourself!" Kimiko stated standing to her feet.

"I won't," Hikaru replied hugging Kimiko.

"Bye, I'll see you at school tomorrow . . ." Kimiko yelled after Hikaru walked her to the front door.

"Good night . . ." Hikaru called after her.

Floating beneath the Moon

Lights radiating from the spacecraft, floating beneath the moon, sparked throughout the universe's darkness as Rasp, the yellow marked Nzer, moved toward the core. His clear, yellow eyes stared coldly ahead of him while; his long, muscular legs took three feet strides quickly carrying him through the dark halls. Strolling through the large archway leading into the spacecraft's Control Room, Rasp pushed smaller Nzers out of its path and dropping to its knee in front of the dark seat overlooking Earth.

"My Lord, we've rec-ceived a mes-s-sage from the Command Force of Latira," the yellow marked Nzer hissed.

"I've no des-sire to trans-svers-se with the vermin rulers-s-s!" The hidden Nzer hissed menacingly.

"As-s-s you wis-sh my Lord," the yellow marked Nzer replied standing to its feet preparing to walk away.

"Wait Ras-sp; what did the vermin want?"

"S-shall I play the trans-smis-sion for you?"

"I would like to s-see what they reques-sted of us-s-s!"

Turning toward the control deck, Rasp rebooted the last transmission received and brought it up to the viewing deck screen. The hidden Nzer's red eyes narrowed as Jeannee's face came over the screen.

"Commander of the **Warship G-731** this is the First Rank Petty Officer, Jeannee Nova, of the Latira Command. I humbly ask that you allow us to continue to survey the solar system in order to keep things in order. I also ask for you to surrender the planet Earth to us and return to the Solari without a cause of action that could lead to war; we would like to send a **Model F-98** out to bring you home! We wish to commune with you in a respectful manner; please send us a reply answering our terms."

A thunderous laughter rang out from the darkness within the Control Room as the hidden Nzer pointed its large, ivory talons at Earth.

"Hear my reply dec-ceitful vermin—Ras-sp, s-send the barracks-s-s down to the planet Earth; begin the invas-sion and have the remaining Nzers-s-s on Earth bring me that girl's-s-s head!"

"My Lord," turning in its seat a smaller Nzer bowed to the larger Nzer. "We're rec-ceiving a mes-s-sage from our forces-s-s on the planet!"

"Proc-ceed . . ."

Once again the view screen highlighted only this time with a large; Nzer's face covering the screen. "My Lord, I regret to inform you that the fourth Hunter has-s-s been awakened!"

"You're not one of my intelligent followers-s-s are you . . . ins-stead of fleeing to the furthes-st end of the planet to hide; you dec-cided to tell me that you **have failed AGAIN!"**

"Yes-s-s, I regret that I have again failed with the Hunters-s-s, but I proudly inform you that we have captured the White Guardian!"

23

Earth—Saturday, April 19, 2026

The dark hours of the early morning stretched across the Neijo plantation where Hikaru stood alone before the crumbling shrine. Her weary eyes sadly gazed at the broken shrine as long, raven strands blew silently past her bronzed face. Turning toward the forest bordering the city, Hikaru walked toward the back fence and quietly hoping over it ran down the hill toward the streets below.

The occasional dim beams of light that escaped the musky skies flashed across the desolate streets that lead Hikaru to the border of the city. Taking one last look over her shoulder, Hikaru disappeared into the dark forest and followed the thin path highlighted by the few beams that escaped the canopy.

Running through the winding forest, Hikaru made her way over jutting roots, vine nets, low branches, and large; spider webs. Clearing several miles of trees, Hikaru walked out onto a shadowed meadow within the forest. Stepping through the grassy floor, Hikaru trotted up to a hill and gazed down at the waterfall where Esal had previously been attacked. Gazing down at the dark waterfall, Hikaru's senses strained to pick up someone approaching to late. Turning her head as she got smacked into, Hikaru fell forward down into the dark waters below.

Submerging, Hikaru frantically gazed around confused by her senses not picking up her attacker when Kimiko surfaced beside her. Stunned, Hikaru nearly drowned again as she angrily vaulted water at Kimiko.

"What is the matter with you . . . why did you tackle me?" Hikaru fumed choking on water.

"First of all, I didn't tackle you I tripped on a root and fell into you . . . it's not my fault that you didn't keep us from falling!" Kimiko declared.

"Why are you out here?"

"Because I told you that I didn't want you going anywhere without one of us three and somehow I knew that you weren't at home, so I came to find you!" Kimiko declared swimming toward the bank.

"That explains a lot," Hikaru sarcastically stated lying against the bank.

"My turn, why are you out here?"

"He woke me up."

"He . . ."

"Esal, I think he's in trouble; major trouble . . . I almost sensed a feeling of pain coursing through him as he reached out to me!" Hikaru stated sitting up. "I think it has something to do with the Nzers!"

"Well, what are we going to do?"

"We . . ."

"Whether you like it or not; I'm a Hunter also, one of the first ones you discovered, so that basically makes me your general! I've had a little more experience than En and Jeremy put together with these creatures and I know how much they hate you! I'm not about to leave my best friend all by herself as she attempts to take them on; not when I can be there to help!" Kimiko declared standing to her feet.

"General," Hikaru stated gazing up at Kimiko.

"Yeah, you found me first . . . there's got to be some symbolism there!" Kimiko smiled offering Hikaru her hand.

Shaking her head, Hikaru grabbed Kimiko's hand, "You're wishing aren't you?"

"Me, no . . . I've been your right hand since we were three, it's not so unbelievable!" Kimiko replied pulling Hikaru up.

"I suppose you're right . . ." Hikaru giggled.

"I know . . ." Kimiko chuckled walking across the meadow. "So where do we go?"

"I'm not sure . . ." Hikaru replied as Gobu shot through some branches.

"Look out Hikaru!" Kimiko yelled charging her hands at a frightened Gobu.

"No Kimiko wait," Hikaru yelled pushing Kimiko's arms down deflecting the shot into a branch above Gobu.

"Hikaru what are you doing . . ." Kimiko questioned.

"That's Esal's Flying Fish . . ." Hikaru stated walking toward a quivering bush containing Gobu. "He may know where Esal is!"

Parting the tiny branches before her eyes, Hikaru gazed into the bush at Gobu's quivering, shrunk body. His large eyes covered the rest of his body while, he stared ahead of him watching Kimiko as Hikaru pulled him out of the bush. His tiny lips quivered as he pointed his chubby, sponge arm accusing at Kimiko.

"I know; she scared you . . ." Hikaru smiled.

"She shot at mesa . . . mesa not scared; mesa freaked!" Gobu exasperated.

"Focus Gobu; where were you . . ." Hikaru asked.

"Uglies . . ."

"You were where the Nzers were?" She questioned as Kimiko walked up beside her.

"Oh, mesa forgot zee uglies . . ."

"Forgot what . . ." Kimiko questioned when several Nzers burst out of the trees.

"Oh, boy . . ." Kimiko bellowed as a Nzer leapt at the girls.

Dropping back onto the grass, Hikaru and Kimiko avoided the leaping Nzer when the second charged toward them. Quickly springing up, Kimiko leapt out of the way as Hikaru rolled away with Gobu in her arms. Clinching her fists, the swarms of energy ignited around Kimiko's arms as she walked toward one of the Nzers. Dodging the swinging blow, Kimiko thrust her charged hand through the Nzer's arm severing it. Dropping back to avoid the next attempt, Kimiko sprayed a ball of pulsing energy from her hands through the Nzer's abdomen. Shielding her face, Kimiko smiled as the Nzer melted before her eyes when she turned toward Hikaru.

Throwing Gobu from her arms, Hikaru lurched back avoiding a blow to flip her legs over her head barely missing the next attack. Straightening her body, Hikaru lifted her hands shielding herself against the leaping Nzer. Grunting as the Nzer hammered into a barrier between her hands and its mouth, Hikaru skidded backward unearthing the ground as the Nzer pushed against the barrier. Closing her eyes as she struggled with the weight of the Nzer, Hikaru heard Kimiko suddenly yell her name. Straightening her arms, Hikaru flung open her brown eyes surrounded by a ring of fire and blew the Nzer backward to crumble into pieces as it sailed through the air.

Quickly stopping, Kimiko watched the pieces of the Nzer drop before her when she gazed up at Hikaru then back at the meat heap. Stepping around the pile, Kimiko ran up to a stunned Hikaru as she breathed heavily.

"Kimiko, did you see that . . . how did I do that?" Hikaru asked pointing at the pile of Nzer.

"I'm not sure, but it was awesome!" Kimiko exclaimed.

Hikaru gazed at Kimiko with a smile, "it was wasn't it . . ."

"And you thought you didn't have any power . . . I begda differ!" Kimiko stated gazing at the dead Nzer.

"I guess it comes and goes . . . it only happens when I start thinking that the Nzers may decide to forget me and will hurt one of you guys. It happened when they came for En and just now when I heard you coming toward me!" Hikaru softly breathed as Gobu floated toward the girls.

"Hikaru . . . Esal-pu needs help!" Gobu whimpered.

"Oh yeah, Gobu where is he . . ." Hikaru questioned grabbing Gobu's tiny arms.

24

Briefly peeking around the dark, dense clouds crawling through the condensed, eerie skies; the moon shimmered down upon a patch in the depths of the forest. The wind silently crawled along the forest floor suddenly becoming motionless to join the dead aura set within the forest this night.

Dropping down onto a branch, Hikaru watched two Nzers almost float through the forest when Kimiko dropped beside her followed by Gobu. Quietly dropping onto the forest floor, Hikaru and Kimiko cautiously followed the Nzers with Gobu floating beside them. Straining her senses to make them oblivious to the Nzers, Hikaru jumped into a tree overlooking the clearing.

Sweeping like shadows through the trees, the Nzers dashed toward the forest clearing carrying numerous, motionless bodies into their encampment. Sweeping around a couple pods; the Nzers trotted up toward the red marked Nzer and dropped the people at its large feet.

Turning around to face the smaller Nzers, the red marked Nzer gazed down at the people to move them around with the large talons upon its feet. Tilting its head as it noticed a male; the Nzer dropped down and pulled the male cautiously toward it. Carefully cutting the fabric covering his chest, the Nzer peeled back the cloth and inspected the man's flesh.

Sitting safely within the tree's shelter, Hikaru gazed confusingly at the red marked Nzer as it inspected the men lying before it. Gazing at Kimiko, Hikaru questioningly mouthed 'what's it doing' to get shrugging shoulders in reply.

An infuriated expression flared across the red marked Nzer's face as it finished inspecting the male victims. Gripping the shirts upon every man, the Nzer threw them across the forest into the tree Hikaru and Kimiko were hiding in.

Dropping backward onto the branch as the bodies flew toward them, Hikaru took Kimiko's hand as she flew toward the ground after getting smacked off by a body. Struggling to keep Kimiko from hitting the ground and drawing attention, Hikaru desperately tried to hold her best friend within the air while, she heard the Nzer start to bellow angrily. Slowly lifting her trembling arm, Hikaru brought Kimiko toward her where she grabbed the branch and helped pull herself back into the veil of the tree.

"What just happened," Kimiko whispered.

Shrugging her shoulders, Hikaru lifted a finger to her lips and standing in the tree started climbing closer to the Nzers. Cautiously moving closer to the enraged Nzer, Hikaru and Kimiko watched as it beat on the smaller Nzers and cast unearthed dirt into the air. Halting over head, the girls watched as the Nzer threw a smaller Nzer from its path and charged angrily into the encampment.

Gazing back at Kimiko, Hikaru nodded her head in the direction the Nzer was moving before she started back across the branches. Pushing past many smaller Nzers, the red marked Nzer swept around pods within the encampment toward the east end of the patch with Hikaru and Kimiko following it unknowingly. Watching it brush past the last pod; the girls followed the Nzer as it pushed past several trees to disappear around the next bend.

Gazing around in disbelief, Hikaru moved closer to the bend when her senses ignited. Tightening her grip around the branch, Hikaru gazed beyond an invisible barrier while, her eyes followed the red marker Nzer as it charged toward several trees. Her nostrils flared of the strong musky smell of decaying flesh as the Nzer brushed past dead bodies and the puddles of blood they sat in.

Gazing back at Kimiko, Hikaru quietly whispered, "Follow me!"

"Where . . ."

"Trust me . . ."

Reaching toward another tree, Hikaru carefully stepped off the branch on which she was perched and climbed over to the tree to head toward the invisible barrier. Passing through the barrier, Hikaru lead Kimiko and Gobu past the decaying bodies in the direction Hikaru had last seen the Nzer.

Striding down a beaten path, the red marked Nzer swiftly moved around the bend and quickly approached a large branch entwined between two trees. Clinching its talons, the red marked Nzer threw its hand diagonally over Esal's chest ripping across the armor plate. Hammering its fist into Esal's stomach, the red marked Nzer gripped Esal's neck in between two talons on its hands.

"I'm growing impat-tient White Guardian; I know you've found your vermin princ-ce, now tell me where he is-s-s!" the red-marked Nzer bellowed.

The wire wrapped around Esal's hands binding him to the branch cut into the gloves staining them with his blood as he hung three feet away from the ground. The talons sliced through the cloth upon Esal's neck cutting into his flesh as the Nzer ripped him toward its hissing mouth. Growing impatient with Esal's deepening silence, the red marked Nzer ripped its talons away from his neck to cut along his cheeks.

"S-speak vermin . . ."

Annoyance flowed over Esal's face as he opened his crystal, blue eyes to stare coldly at the Nzer, "even if I knew where my prince was . . . there's no way I would tell such a worthless creature that draws breath!"

Watching Esal spit across the Nzer's face, Kimiko smiled brightly as she watched the Nzer frantically scratch it from its face. A look of disgust covered Kimiko's face as she watched the Nzer scrape layers of flesh from its face in order to remove the spit.

Gazing angrily at Esal, the red marked Nzer pulled him forward by the front of his cape and snapped its teeth in front of his face. "Fight as-s-s much as-s-s you want . . . when we find the male vermin with the mark, your princ-ce will be no more!"

Gazing confused at the Nzer for a moment, a look of realization flowed across Esal's bronzed face, "Oh my god . . ."

"It's-s-s too late for you and your vermin kind!"

Esal stared at the Nzer before him when a bright smile spread across his bronzed face, "you should really stop underestimating us vermin!"

Raising his legs toward his chest, Esal hammered his feet into the Nzer casting across the forest floor. Gripping the wire around his hands, Esal's arms shook as he pulled himself toward the branch when the Nzer stood to its feet. Gazing at the Nzer as it charged toward him with extended talons, Esal released his grip and dropped down to once again hammer his feet into the Nzer. Grimacing as the wire cut into his hands, Esal swayed in the air as the Nzer stared at him with malicious contempt within its eyes.

"Wars-sh," The Nzer bellowed out echoing through the forest to the encampment.

Casting the Nzer away again, Esal lifted his legs toward his chest and raised himself toward the branch when a smaller Nzer leapt onto his back. Unable to hold the massive weight of the Nzer, Esal dropped down causing the wire to cut deeper into his hands as the Nzer bit into his shoulder trying to tear the armor. Wailing as the Nzer speared its talons through his arms, Esal swung through the air as the red marked Nzer shot toward him. In an attempt to protect himself, Esal raised his legs before him as the Nzer came toward his face with its teeth. Pulling his head away from the slowly declining teeth, Esal suddenly spied something moving within the trees.

Spearing out of the leaves upon the tree branches, Gobu zipped down to Esal and hammered into the red marked Nzer. Whapping his tiny sponge arms against the Nzer's hard scaly face, Gobu zipped around its body when it slammed its hip into a tree squishing Gobu.

"Is-s-s this-s-s what was-s-s going to res-scue you," The Nzer chuckled as it pealed Gobu off its hip.

Throwing Gobu across the forest floor, the red marked Nzer slowly extracted the long claw beneath its forearm.

"I'm not allowed to kill you, but I was-s-s never told I couldn't torture you!" The Nzer chuckled attempting to spear the long claw through the armor on Esal's hip.

Running across the branch above the Nzer, Hikaru leapt from the tree to land upon the Nzer as Kimiko leapt onto the one upon Esal. Bouncing off the Nzer's large body, Hikaru rolled across the ground and flipped onto her feet. Hammering her fist into the Nzer beneath her, Kimiko blew the creature to a million tiny bits as the energy ignited around her hands. Gazing toward Hikaru, Kimiko watched as she struggled against the large Nzer to lift herself off the ground and race toward her leader.

Falling backward as the Nzer hammered into her, Hikaru separated her legs avoiding the large muscular arm as it speared through the ground. Staring wide-eyed at the large arm before her eyes, Hikaru lifted her foot and hammered it into the Nzer cracking the arm. Rolling away as the Nzer lurched back, Hikaru stood to her feet and blew a purple ray through its face. Staring amazed at her hands, Hikaru watched the Nzer crumble to the ground before racing toward Esal.

Flipping the white, cerulean hair out of his face, Esal gazed angrily at Hikaru as she raced toward him. Gripping the wire in his hands, Esal attempt to lift himself toward the branch when Hikaru leapt into the tree to crawl across the branch. Sliding out toward Esal, Hikaru grabbed his hands and helped him to the branch where she carefully assisted on removing the wire from his hands.

"What were you thinking," Esal demanded as Hikaru threw the wire to the ground. "They could've killed you!"

"Me . . . what were you doing?" Hikaru questioned as Esal dropped down from the branch. "The Nzer's were killing you!"

Pulling Hikaru down from the tree, Esal shook his head, "No, they weren't . . . they can't!"

"Well, I'm glad you're so sure . . . I've been so worried; I thought something bad happened to you!" Hikaru whimpered.

Gazing at Hikaru when his stern expression faded to a compassionate one, Esal took her hands into his own, "Nothing's going to happen to me Hikaru . . . I'll always be there to protect you; I swear."

Once again encouraged by his strong words, Hikaru smiled brightly at Esal as Kimiko yelled out to them. Quickly turning to see the Nzer encampment racing toward them, Hikaru suddenly felt a strong compulsion take hold of her. Lifting her hands to block the Nzers, a large veil of light burst out of Hikaru's body to spear through the Nzers' bodies. Falling backward into Esal's arms, Hikaru shook a sudden weariness from her body as she watched the Nzers crumble into piles. Regaining her footing, Hikaru walked out into the encampment staring at the dead bodies as Kimiko raced up to her.

"How did you do that?"

"I'm still trying to figure that out," Hikaru declared.

Walking out into the clearing, Esal gazed around before turning toward Hikaru with a smile, "You certainly know how to leave a mark!"

25

A soft echo of a nearby bird slowly rang out into the forest as the three wandered around the encampment. The girls walked around the pods searching through the crates while, Esal searched inside each pod for any chance of contacting the other universe. Stepping away from the others, Hikaru lifted a small box off the ground to examine it when a tiny light flickered across her eyes. Turning to curiously gaze at the source of the light, Hikaru gazed at a dark mirror planted into the ground beside the largest pod. Setting the box back onto the ground, Hikaru stepped over many broken fragments and body pieces of creatures and human as she approached the mirror.

"Hey guys, I think I found something!" Hikaru called whipping dust off the screen making the flickering light more visible.

Gazing harder at the dark mirror, Hikaru stared curiously at the object when a bright ray sprayed out momentarily blinding her. Stepping back, Hikaru lifted her arms to shield her eyes when Esal raced up to her with Kimiko close behind. Finally as the light died down, Hikaru gazed at the dark mirror when a visual of a Control Room filled with Nzers suddenly appeared before her eyes. Stepping closer to the mirror, Hikaru gazed closer into the craft when another red marked Nzer lifted its head and gazed at her.

"That's the Control Room of the Latrinian **Warship G-731**!" Esal exclaimed.

Up in the **Warship G-731**, the red marked Nzer jumped from its seat and dropped before the Mighty One's seat.

Lifting its trembling head, the Nzer pointed toward the view screen, "S-sire, we're rec-ceiving a trans-smis-s-sion . . . from the vermin girl!"

Leaning forward in the darkness surrounding it, the large Nzer blared it white fangs at the view screen, "well, finally a fac-ce to the vex-xation that has-s-s been regularly defeating my war trained minions-s-s . . . tell me what I'm s-suppos-s-sed to do to kill you!"

A stern look crossed over Hikaru's face as she took a step toward the mirror, "You won't kill me, nor will you kill anyone else like me . . . I'm going to find every last Devilry Hunter and when I'm done with that . . . I'm going to find the prince of the other universe, and I'm going to do everything in my power to help him kill you!"

A low hiss escaped through the darkness as the Nzer widened its blood-red eyes, "S-strong words-s-s for s-such a tiny vermin! I will make you eat your word-s-s, you little alien!"

"We will see . . . and another thing; you may want to spend more time training your "War Trained Minions" 'cause their doing a good job," Hikaru sarcastically stated moving from the screen to show the dead carcasses.

The large Nzer's eyes shook violently through the shadows as it glared at Hikaru, "you better be prepared for the time we meet little girl, caus-se not even the White Guardian will be able to protect you from me!"

"I was going to say the same thing," Hikaru stated as the mirror grew dark.

Up in space

The large Nzer's roar echoed throughout the spacecraft as Rasp walked into the Control Room. Pushing past several smaller Nzers, he dropped to his knee before the darkness.

"What is-s-s thy bidding my Lord?"

"How many battalions-s-s have been s-sent to the Earth?"

"Five full ones-s-s."

"S-send them all!" The large one bellowed. "I want that planet brought to its-s-s knees-s-s, I want to s-see the little vermin girl s-struggle to keep peac-ce on her beloved planet and Ras-sp . . ."

"S-sire . . ."

"I want you on the nex-xt battalion. Kill them all, but I want the pleas-sure of the girl and the princ-ce's death!"

"Unders-stood S-sire . . ." Rasp confirmed as he stood to disappear from the Control Room.

26

At the Neijo Plantation

The growing hours of dusk loomed over the quiet house when the sudden sound of running water filled the air. Locked behind a shut door, Hikaru turned the knobs turning the shower on as she climbed into the tub. Pulling the curtain around her, Hikaru walked beneath the shower nozzle allowing the water to pour over her naked, bronzed body. Tilting her head back allowing the water to rush down her tanned chest, Hikaru watched the steam gradually grow as the water began to heat up. The steam radiated around the water to brush along Hikaru's nude skin as she began to lather soap through her long hair.

Slowly opening her brown eyes, Hikaru blinked through the water as she suddenly realized someone else was in the bathroom with her. Glancing to her side, Hikaru stared through the curtain at a figure standing in front of the tube. Closing her fingers around the curtain, Hikaru slowly pulled it back to peer at Esal as he sat on the bathroom sink.

"What are you doing in here?" Hikaru exasperated pulling the curtains closer to her body.

"Calm down . . . I'm not doing what you think!" Esal assured dropping off the sink. "I thought you may need this."

Gazing down into Esal's hand, Hikaru pulled a wet hand out and slapped his chest. "I know I need to wash with soap you big . . ."

"Before you finish, you should know that this is a special soap that will wash away any trace the Nzers may have left on you!"

"Oh," taking the soap from Esal, Hikaru gazed at him before disappearing behind the curtain. "How are you . . . did you use that water to heal your wounds again?"

"No actually, I didn't need to . . ."

"Why . . ." Hikaru questioned poking her head back out.

"My body can heal rapidly if given the time."

"Why didn't you do that the first time?" Hikaru questioned.

"I didn't have the time . . . I wanted to try to find the prince!"

149

"Have you found him yet?" Hikaru questioned once back inside the shower.

"No, not yet, but now I know what to look for."

"What . . ."

"A birthmark; the Royal Mark of a Latrinian child—two crescent moons entwined together with a small star to the side of it!"

"So if you find the person with this mark, it'll be your prince!" Hikaru stated.

"Yes, but we have to hurry . . . the Nzers know what to look for as well!"

"We have some time now . . . we just destroyed every Nzer on Earth!"

"You mean you destroyed every Nzer on Earth," Esal chuckled gazing at Hikaru as she poked her head out of the curtain.

"I'm working on it OK," Hikaru replied. "I can't seem to control the source of my power!"

"Don't worry; you will," Esal reassured.

"Esal I'm not sure who the next Hunter is going to be."

Gazing at the curtain as Hikaru poked her head out, Esal smiled brightly, "that hasn't stopped you yet."

"Esal I'm serious."

"I know Hikaru but all you need to remember is that the Hunters are always the closest people to you, besides the other three who else is your friend or theirs?"

Staring at the floor, Hikaru suddenly looked up at Esal with a smile, "Maya . . . Maya is close to all of us!"

"There you go . . . go see her tomorrow!"

"All right," Hikaru nodded disappearing behind the curtain. "I hate to be rude, but would it be possible for you to leave so I can get out!"

"Yeah, and Hikaru . . ."

Sticking her head out from behind the curtain, "what?"

"Be careful tomorrow."

"I will, you to."

"Good night Hikaru," Esal replied kissing her forehead before leaving.

Lifting her hand to her head, Hikaru blushed slightly before turning the shower off and wrapping a towel around her body, stepped out of the tub. Combing a brush through her hair, Hikaru thought over the possibility of Maya being a Hunter and who the others were going to be.

27

$\mathcal{T}$he morning rays had yet to rise when large, pod ships descended into the forest outside the city. The black, metal surface reflected the appearance of the trees off its body duplicating the color and alignment making the ships appear to be more forestry. Large pockets of steam blew out the rear of the pod ships as large, landing gears dropped out onto the forest floor. Cargo doors opening from the base of the ships released multitudes of Nzers as they crept out into the towering trees.

Using the shadows for cover a dozen Nzers raced toward the city to begin the search for the rest of the Hunters and the prince. Leaping majestically off branches, the Nzers swept through the forest onto the city roofs when the city began to come to life. Moving through the shadows to conceal themselves, the Nzers studied and analyzed every person they past.

Earth—Sunday, April 20, 2026

The wind lightly blew through the park where En sat watching his little sister, Mamoru, playfully running around with other children. His light, brown eyes steadily watched his little sister's movements as his mind wondered over the past few days in which he had unexplainably neutralized some kind of alien creatures. Leaning against the bench, En dropped his head back closing his eyes when Maya quietly walked up and sat down beside him.

Tilting her head as she stared at his worn out face, Maya frowned in annoyance as she folded her arms across her chest waiting for En to catch wind of her. Staring for a few minutes when her annoyance burst into frustration, Maya smacked her hand across En's chest finally drawing his attention.

"Are you trying to avoid me En Skilou?" Maya questioned as En shot up.

"What . . . no, of course not; why would you think that?"

"Well, let me think . . . maybe because you haven't returned any of my calls, you haven't said anything to me since your game on Wednesday; which was four days ago, and you seem like you're in a completely different world Skilou! Come back to Earth En . . . if you're in trouble or something's disturbing you; tell me! I'm getting tired of being ignored and put aside when I may be able to help you!"

"Gosh, I'm sorry Maya; I never meant to push myself away from you, but now I'm beginning to think it might be best if you stay away from me for a while!"

"You see; that's what I'm talking about!" Maya fumed standing to her feet.

"Maya wait," En yelled chasing after her.

"Get away from me En before I hurt you!" Maya warned pulling out of his hand.

Racing in front of Maya, En quickly avoided a swing, "Maya it's not what you think . . . all I've ever wanted was to be close to you, but strange things are happening to me and I'm not sure if it's going to be OK for you to be around me!"

"I know where this is going!"

"It's true Maya . . . those creatures are after Hikaru, Kimiko and now Jeremy and I for some reason that I can't figure out . . . I don't want you getting hurt if they find out about us!" En exclaimed.

"There is no us, you're too scared to take that step!" Maya fumed.

"This is new to me to Maya, do you think I want to live like this . . . to push myself away from everyone, and not get to close to anyone 'cause they may get hurt?"

"I've had it Skilou, I'm sick of you doing this to me! First you say you aren't trying to stay away, but then you instantly change your mind 'cause you get scared! I know you're still the same person inside En, but I can't wait for him anymore . . . I'm tired of waiting for you!" Maya stated walking around En.

Quickly turning toward Maya, En stared after her speechless as she walked down a sidewalk to disappear around a corner. Walking back toward the bench as Mamoru raced up, En leisurely dropped onto the seat and stared up at the sky as his sister gulped down water from the fountain.

"What's the matter En?"

Pulling his head off the bench back, En looked at Mamoru, "nothing kiddo, are you done?"

"Not yet, can we stay a little longer?"

"Yeah, go 'head . . ." En replied pushing her toward the playground.

"Thanks En . . ."

"Yeah . . ."

A few hours later

"No Kaho, I don't want to annoy her more I . . . Kaho, please put Maya on the phone! Yes, I know she's mad at me . . . yes I know she probably . . . all right I know she hates me Kaho, but I really need to speak to her!" En declared walking back and forth through the den.

Lying on the floor, Mamoru leaned to her side as she played on Jeremy's game system while, En talked to Maya's little sister on the phone. Glancing toward En after she paused the game, Mamoru watched En lean against the wall quickly growing frustrated as Kaho refused to take the phone to her sister and Maya refusing to speak to him.

"Yeah I know, but . . . all right; fine Kaho, you win!" En yelled hanging up the phone to drop his head against the wall.

Walking into the den, Jeremy walked up to En and dropped his hand on his brother's shoulder.

"Guess she isn't talking to you!" Jeremy stated with a chuckle.

"Whatever Jeremy, shut up!" En yelled storming into his room.

Waiting in the hall for a few minutes, Jeremy declared he had waited long enough when he walked into En's room. Shutting the door behind him, Jeremy walked up to the bed and pulled En's head off his pillow. Pulling a chair beside En's bed, Jeremy sat down and gazed at En for a long time before saying anything.

"What's up little bro . . ."

Sitting up to stare at Jeremy, En shook his head in annoyance, "Maya hates me 'cause I'm unintentionally shying away since I've become a Devilry Hunter! Jeremy I can't do this . . . I don't know what to do! All I've ever wanted was Maya and now that seems to be impossible!"

"Wow, wow; calm down En!" Jeremy ordered whacking him. "Things are never supposed to be easy, but you have to understand we were given these powers for a reason! What we want has to come last; with great power comes great responsibility . . . no one else can do what we have been given; Hikaru needs our help!"

Gazing down at the bed, En stared at his hands as the wind blew through his hair before looking back at Jeremy, "what about Maya?"

"Well, you can tell the truth and if she truly loves you; she's going to have to realize that all she can do is wait!"

Pulling a smile onto his face, En shook his head at Jeremy, "I hate it when you do that . . . make everything sound so simple and logically right!"

"Yeah, years of listening to dad did that to me!"

"En," Mamoru yelled from the den.

"What Mamoru . . ."

"Someone's wants to speak to you!"

"Who is it?" En questioned.

"I don't know . . ."

Sighing, En leisurely slid off his bed to stand up and walking from his room into the den took the phone from Mamoru.

"Thank you Mamoru . . ." En stated as she dropped back onto the floor to finish playing the game.

"You're welcome . . ."

Smiling, En placed the phone to his ear, "Hello!"

"Is this En Skilou?" A deep, scruffy voice called into the phone.

"Speaking . . ."

"Is your mother's name, Becky?"

"Who is this?" En questioned when the dial tone suddenly buzzed into his ear.

"Who was it?" Jeremy questioned leaning against the door jam.

Gazing questioningly at the phone, En dropped it onto the receiver before turning toward Jeremy with a curious look on his face.

"I don't know, hung up . . ."

Walking through the hall, Becky Aino turned toward the boys fingering her keys as she slipped on her slipper shoes.

"Boys I have to run to the store to get a few things for dinner; I'll be right back don't wreck the house!" She warned kissing Mamoru before opening the door.

"We won't mom . . ." En declared.

"All right, be good I'll be back soon."

28

April 21, 2026

The dread and annoyance of actually staying attentive in Freché's government class began to crawl down En's back as he gazed across the room at Kimiko, who was making faces at him. Releasing a tiny chuckle, En smiled at Kimiko when Freché slammed his yard stick down on En's desk hitting his arms. Quickly pulling his arms away from his desk, En stared at Freché stunned as his arms began to throb.

"What was that for?"

"You just can't help yourself can you Skilou?" Freché yelled.

"I wasn't doing anything wrong!" En proclaimed as the bell rang.

"En stay after; I have a few things to ask you!" Freché ordered as half the class ran out the door.

"You've got to be kidding me?" En exasperated as Kimiko, Hikaru, and Jeremy walked up beside En.

"It wasn't En, Mr. Freché; I made a face at him!" Kimiko confessed.

"Yes, well, don't next time," Freché ordered, "And he's still staying after!"

Grabbing En's shoulder, Jeremy pulled his little brother behind him.

"I don't know who you think you are, but you have no jurisdiction over my brother! You are here for the students, Mr. Freché, En doesn't owe you anything!"

"Bold words, I'd like to see what the principle has to say about this!"

Stepping in front of Freché as he grabbed En's arm, Hikaru laid her briefcase over her legs, "if you want to proceed with this type of action Mr. Freché; I'm sure the Acting Chairman would be quite interested to know that you mishandle your students and abuse them . . . you'd probably lose your job."

"Do you think the Chairman would listen to you for a second . . . you're nothing but an ignorant girl?" Freché spat.

"How did you get this job?" Kimiko asked pulling En beside her.

"He probably knocked off the real professor!" En chuckled.

"That's it Skilou!" Freché stated pushing through the others toward En.

Pushing En against the corner of a desk, Freché raised his yard stick slamming it down toward En's face when someone grabbed his arm.

"Professor Freché, what do you think you are doing?" Kimon questioned pulling En behind him.

"Chairman Youitan that punk needs to be put in his place!"

"And why do you think you have that right sir . . . I want an answer!" Kimon yelled stepping in front of Freché's face.

"His mother obviously doesn't do a good enough job!" Freché declared.

"I think I've seen all I need to see, Mr. Freché clean out your desks and cubicles immediately; I want you off the campus now."

"Chairman Youitan!"

"Mr. Freché you're fired!" Kimon stated leading the four friends out into the hall.

Rubbing his side, En leaned against Jeremy as he helped him into the hall with Kimiko and Hikaru close behind with all their things.

"Come on, we'll get you to the nurse!" Kimon stated leading the friends down the halls to the nurse's station.

"Thank you so much," Jeremy thanked walking into the nurse's office.

"Don't mention it, you guys try to have a nice rest of the day and I'm extremely sorry about what happened!" Kimon stated before turning down the hall.

"Kimon wait," Hikaru called as Jeremy disappeared into the room with En.

Turning toward Hikaru as she approached him, Kimon gazed down into her brown eyes, "What is it Hikaru?"

"Listen I've been really rude to you lately and I wanted to . . ."

"You don't need to explain anything to me Hikaru, I know that you are having a difficult time right now and I also know that I haven't been what I should be for you . . . that I'm really sorry about, but I can't talk right now! I have to make sure Freché leaves without trying anything and I have Yuri waiting for me, but I promise we will talk! There's something very important I need to discuss with you!" Kimon stated before respectfully dismissing himself.

Watching Kimon disappear around a corner, Hikaru turned to see a smiling Kimiko standing in the nurse's office doorway.

"Don't say a word!" Hikaru stated whacking at Kimiko as she giggled.

Sitting quietly in the nurse's office as she examined En; Kimiko, Hikaru, and Jeremy sat patiently waiting when Touko Keig walked in with Maya. Dropping her bag on a chair, Maya walked up to the examining table and slugged En's arm.

"Darn you Skilou, why are you constantly hurting yourself?" Maya yelled.

"Oh, honey, he's not hurt!"

"Excuse me," Maya replied looking at the nurse.

"I thought you weren't speaking to me?" En questioned.

"I'm not; I'm yelling!" Maya stated.

"It's the same thing," En replied.

"No it's not; yelling is a louder form of speaking!" Maya argued.

Shaking his head, En looked away from Maya waiting for the nurse to finish while; he desperately tried to ignore her yelling at him. Finally to his relief, the nurse declared he was OK and ready to leave, En jumped down from the examining table and walking up to his brother lifted his backpack off the floor. Walking out the door, En started walking down the hall when Maya ran out the door with the others.

"I'm not done yelling at you En!" Maya screamed.

"Well, that's nice to know!" En stated.

"En, listen to me!" Maya yelled.

"No, you listen!" En yelled back to Maya's surprise. "I haven't hurt you in anyway Maya, but you have me! You yell and scream at me when I get attacked by one of my professors like it was my fault! I know you're real upset with me but I'm sorry; I can't change what happened! Either you take me for what I am, or you don't!"

"What's going on guys?" Touko questioned walking up to Maya and En.

"Nothing . . ." En replied.

"Yeah, there is . . . hey here's an idea; tell Touko about what's happened to you En and we'll see what she thinks about this!" Maya suggested.

"What happened . . . En did you get hurt?" Touko started panicking.

Dropping his backpack off his shoulder, En lifted his arms and looked at Maya. "What do you want from me?"

"Tell Touko; that's what I want!" Maya declared.

"I can't believe you're acting this way to him, Maya! All En's ever done was tell you the truth and do everything he could to please you . . . and you treat him like this?" Hikaru questioned stepping in front of Maya.

"You don't understand how hard this is for me Hikaru!"

"Hard for you . . ." Hikaru questioned. "You haven't been through as much as you think Maya!"

"Okay will someone please explain to me what's going on?" Touko demanded.

Glancing toward Touko, Hikaru nodded, "Yes, I'll explain everything only because I should be the one to do it; after all I'm the one that started it! As unbelievable as this is going to sound every bit of it is true . . . the day before my birthday, I was visited by a man that proclaimed he was from another world. Shortly after alien creatures arrived on Earth and ever since they've been trying to kill me and everyone I find to be a Devilry Hunter; like myself!"

Touko and Maya stared at Hikaru for a while, before Maya questioned, "You're kidding right . . . aliens coming here to kill you and now all of you are protectors of the Earth?"

"Yeah, you might say that!" Kimiko replied.

"Are you guys feeling all right?" Touko questioned worriedly.

"I'm glad I got to see what kind of person you are before my brother asked you out Maya!" Jeremy angrily stated.

"Look I'm sorry, but this is ridiculous . . . Earthling Protectors called what?" Maya giggled.

Shaking her head in frustration, Kimiko walked in front of Maya and Touko.

"You guys don't want to believe us . . . you think we're insane?"

"I'm sorry Kimiko; I don't know what to believe . . . do you have any proof?" Touko politely questioned.

"Proof . . . yeah, I think I do!" Kimiko stated lifting her hands as the energy ignited around them.

Stepping back, Touko and Maya gazed at the swarms of energy wrapping around Kimiko's arms.

"Is that burning your hands?" Touko panicked.

"No Touko, I'm fine!"

"How are you doing that?" Maya questioned staring at her hands.

"I'm not sure how I'm doing it, but I do know that it's triggered by my emotions, so it's kind of difficult to hind when I start getting upset with Antony!" Kimiko declared to get a laugh out of everyone. "Why are you laughing, I'm serious?"

"What can you do En?" Maya questioned.

"So know you believe me?"

"I'm sorry . . . you had to have done the same thing in the beginning!" Maya replied.

"Yeah, Hikaru thinks I control elemental things like the wind and the ground!"

"What about you Jeremy?" Touko questioned.

"Magician!" Jeremy smiled.

"And you?" Maya asked Hikaru.

"I really don't know what I can do . . . my power comes and goes; it's always something different!"

"I have a question . . . shouldn't you be trying to keep this a secret? You know like secret identities!" Touko asked.

"Well, to be perfectly honest there's a chance that you guys may be Hunters as well . . . my Guardian Angel told me that the other Hunters will be someone close to me and the other Hunters!" Hikaru explained.

"Us . . . Devilry Hunters?" Touko and Maya questioned.

"It's possible . . ." Hikaru nodded.

29

Later

Dropping onto the roof of Amin Mela Academy, several Nzers scratched their talons through the glass windows above the school gymnasium where a gymnastics meet was in progress. Quietly lifting the piece of glass from the window, the red marked Nzer leading the others nodded toward the hole as it dropped the cut glass onto the roof. Dropping through the hole onto the rafters, the Nzers crawled through the shadows watching the people below as they sniffed the rising air of odors.

Standing beside her teams' circlet, Maya bounced up and down nervously as she watched Touko beautifully perform her routine on the double bars. Cheering joyfully as Touko landed the end of her routine, Maya gazed over toward the bleachers to smile at En and the others as they waved at her. Retreating into the circlet as Touko walked in, Maya dropped onto the floor to stretch herself before her turn came up.

"Touko you were magnificent!" Maya congratulated.

"Thank you Maya, are you ready for your routine?"

"Yes, I just wish it was now!"

"Why, do you want to show off for a certain brown haired boy?" Touko smiled teasingly.

"Maybe," Maya giggled gazing over at En. "I was so awful . . . I can't believe I did that to him!"

"I know a way you can make it up to him!"

"Touko Keig!"

"See you in a little bit Maya," Touko called walking toward the fountain.

Watching Touko walk away, Maya gazed over toward the bleachers shaking her head when her name was called to begin her routine. Watching the meet from the bleachers, the four friends shouted loudly as Maya walked out onto the large blue mat to perform her dance routine. Smiling from ear to ear, En watched enchanted as Maya elegantly swept across the mat perfectly landing every flip, spin, and jazz move.

Watching En proudly watch Maya's every move, Hikaru released a happy sigh when her little purse strapped to her back started moving. Glancing back, Hikaru quickly pulled her bag in front of her prohibiting anyone else from seeing. Unzipping the bag, Hikaru gazed down as Cleo popped her head out whacking Hikaru in the head.

"Ow, it's a good thing you're stuffed!"

"FOR YOU MAYBE . . . ARE YOU TRYING TO SUFFOCATE ME OR SOMETHING? CAUSE YOU'RE DOING A GOOD JOB!"

"No, why are you coming out; what if someone sees you?"

"THEN THEY'RE GOING TO SEE ME; ESAL PUT ME IN CHARGE OF PROTECTING YOU IF HE WASN'T AROUND; SO I'M TAKING CHARGE!"

"What are you talking about . . . why would you need to protect . . ."

Gazing up at the ceiling rafters to see particles of dust falling from the beams, Hikaru leapt to her feet and jumping down the bleachers raced across the floor toward the meet director. Taking his eyes off Maya for a second, En stared after Hikaru curiously pondering why she had become so frantic when he suddenly felt the wind calling to him from the broken window.

"Hey, space cadet . . . Maya just finished her routine; aren't you going to cheer for her or something . . . En, hello; are you there?" Kimiko giggled.

"Yeah, I'm here . . ." En replied pushing Kimiko's waving hand out of his face.

"Then what's wrong?" Kimiko questioned.

"I think they're here!" En replied.

"They can't be; Hikaru obliterated the entire camp a few days ago!" Kimiko stated watching En stand to his feet.

"Then explain the shattered window above us and Hikaru trying to stop the meet!" En declared.

Crawling across the rafters, the red marked Nzer followed Hikaru's movement as she protested with the meet director to stop the meet.

"No you don't understand; you need to stop the meet and get everyone out of here immediately!" Hikaru informed.

"Listen, I'm not stopping the meet on one person's accusation that something may happen; I'm sorry!" The meet director declared.

"You're the one that doesn't understand I'm trying to save lives here, you need to cancel the meet now!" Hikaru stated raising her voice.

Walking to the edge of her teams' circlet, Maya whipped the sweat off her neck with a towel as she gazed at Hikaru confusingly when the red marked Nzer dropped down onto the blue mat. Dropping the towel, Maya gazed unbelievingly at the Nzer as it rose to its full height and shrieked.

"What the hell is that?" the director asked petrified.

"What I was warning you about!" Hikaru stated running toward the Nzer.

"Wait," the director yelled grabbing Hikaru's hand. "Where do you think you are going?"

"Sir, let go of me; since you wouldn't listen to me I have to stop it before it hurts anyone!" Hikaru stated pulling her hand out of the man's.

"But it will kill you!"

Watching everyone dart around, the red marked Nzer scanned the room when the others dropped down beside it.

"Find the ones-s-s the Hunters-s-s cheered loudes-st for . . . thos-se are their friends-s-s which may make them other Hunters-s-s." The red marked Nzer commanded.

Pushing through frantic people, Maya raced up to where Touko was hiding and grabbing her hand pulled her to her feet.

"What are you doing those things are out there!" Touko resisted.

"Yeah, and their also going to kill people trying to find us, so come on Touko!"

"Why do you think they're after us . . . maybe they came looking for the others!"

"Touko, come one . . . this isn't up for discussion!" Maya yelled.

"If you get me killed Maya; I'm going to injure you!"

Racing around several people, a small Nzer leapt at Maya and Touko as they ran out of the circlet. Screaming in Maya's ear, Touko dropped to her knees as the Nzer came down upon them to get frozen in place. Opening her blue eyes, Maya stared at the Nzer's hideous face as it glared menacingly at her in mid-air. Peering around the Nzer's body, Maya spied Jeremy standing behind it with his arm raised.

"I don't think it's a big fan!" Jeremy laughed.

Picking up a pole, Touko whacked the Nzer across the face making it twitch in the air before Jeremy threw it across the room. Dropping behind Jeremy as several Nzer's leapt at them, Touko screamed out as a strong gust hammered into the creatures. Pushing past Touko and Jeremy, Maya raced up and took hold of En as he approached. Holding Maya in his arms, En sent the wind toward the attacking Nzers prolonging them as Kimiko attempted to charge her arms.

"Anytime would be great Kimiko!" En exasperated.

"They won't charge, I'm not emotional at the moment."

"Well get emotional fast!" Jeremy ordered.

"Too late," Touko screamed.

Sailing through the friends, the Nzers hammered across the ground to stand up and charge again. Scraping its talons through the wood floor, the Nzer leapt at the friends.

"All right now I'm mad!" Kimiko declared as the energy flared out around her arms. Lifting her arms at the last moment, Kimiko slammed her hands through the Nzer burning through its hide to slice it in half. Standing to her feet, Kimiko shot a burning ball toward the nearest Nzer as another Nzer raced up from behind.

Lifting the pole Touko dropped; Maya hammered the pole across the charging Nzer's face sending it flying through the air. "How did I?" Maya pondered gazing down at the warped pole.

Standing up, En gazed at the pole in Maya's hands when his legs got ripped out from under him. Dropping the pole, Maya took hold of En's arms as the Nzer started pulling them across the floor to throw them through the air. After smacking into the floor, En sat up with Maya when the Nzer grabbed their necks and lifted them into the air. Once the Nzer inhaled Maya and En's scent, it threw them toward the wall and slowly approached. Descending toward the floor, En hammered against some equipment as Maya crashed through the cement wall.

Pulling herself out of the wall, Maya gazed at En's motionless body as the Nzer slowly approached him. Gritting her teeth while holding her side, Maya jumped out of the wall and raced up to grab the Nzers swigging talons as they came toward En. Struggling to hold the Nzer's massive weight, Maya stepped back toward En while she continued to hold the talons and avoid the snapping mouth. Gazing at the Nzer's hideous scaly face; frustration began to overwhelm Maya as she stepped back against En's motionless body.

"En, please wake up!" Maya yelled as the Nzer pushed its hands down.

Growling through her teeth, Maya closed her hands tightly around the Nzer's thick arms causing it to start to shift uneasily. Taking a few steps away from En, Maya started pushing the Nzer backward as her hands suddenly started crushing the bones in the Nzer's arms. Twisting her arms, Maya shattered several muscles and bones in the Nzer's arms as she effortlessly lifted it above her head.

Quickly stopping as he came toward En and Maya, Jeremy stared at the Nzer hanging above Maya's head astonished when Kimiko and Touko slammed into him. Falling on top of Jeremy, Kimiko and Touko stared at Maya as she leaned back and threw the Nzer across the gym to smash through the opposite wall. Gazing from the Nzer to Maya back to the Nzer, Kimiko and Touko burst out yelling as they jumped off Jeremy.

Dropping down beside En, Maya pulled him onto his back and shook him trying to rouse him as Kimiko, Touko, and Jeremy raced up to her. Distracted by En finally coming to; Jeremy, Maya, Kimiko, and Touko didn't notice the red marked Nzer until it was nearly landing on them. Taking Jeremy's arm, a screaming Touko pulled Kimiko to the floor as the red marked Nzer suddenly blew past them to explode against the wall.

Black strands of hair flew leisurely around Hikaru's face as she dropped her lifted hand and raced up to her friends. Individually helping each one of her friends to their feet, Hikaru stopped as Maya grabbed her arm.

"Hikaru you were right . . . I must be one of your Hunters!"

"Wow, calm down Maya . . . this isn't something you need to get overworked about, OK!" Hikaru stated pulling Maya to her feet.

"Hikaru, I lifted one of those creatures above my head!"

"Wow, superhuman strength . . . that's awesome!" Kimiko exclaimed.

"Okay, what about Touko?" Hikaru questioned.

"Does screaming really loud count?" Kimiko giggled dodging a swing.

"Let's get out of here before any reporters arrive . . ." Hikaru suggested heading toward the gym doors.

"I thought you killed all the Nzers Hikaru . . ." Kimiko replied.

"More must have been sent to stop us!" Hikaru declared.

"How many more are we talking about?" Maya questioned.

"Tons," Jeremy suggested.

"Oh this is horrible, what are you guys going to do?" Touko questioned.

"Don't worry, Touko, I'll get you answers soon, OK. I don't have them right now, but I will!" Hikaru encouraged.

"All right, one more thing . . . you really think I'm a . . ."

"Devilry Hunter . . ."

"Yeah that!" Touko replied.

"Yes, Touko, and don't worry about it so much, you'll be OK!" Hikaru declared.

Once walking down their street alone, Kimiko looked at Hikaru.

"What are you going to do?"

"I'm not sure; I've never found two at one time, its possible that Touko may not be a Hunter!" Hikaru replied.

"Uh-huh, well; just don't forget about tomorrow," Kimiko stated walking up her sidewalk.

"Wait Kimiko, what's tomorrow?"

"That dinner we're having for Jaime and Kate, you didn't forget did you?" Kimiko asked to get silence from Hikaru. "Hikaru, you're still coming right; you can't leave me stranded through this all by myself!"

"Okay, I won't; all that's been going on it just slipped my mind . . . I'll be there!"

"Thank you!" Kimiko smiled as Hikaru continued to walk down toward Gramps plantation at the top of the hill.

30

The sun slowly rose over the trees bordering the Neijo plantation when Hikaru woke to something slamming into the wall above her face. Quickly opening her startled brown eyes; Hikaru sat up and scanned the room when she heard something moaning behind her. Slowly glancing behind her, Hikaru saw Gobu sliding down the wall to lay as flat as the sheets when Cleo jumped onto the bed from her desk.

Tromping across the ruffled sheets, Cleo stopped beside Gobu's flat body and taking his tail in her mouth walked to the edge of the bed and opened. Scowling as she heard Gobu splat against the floor, Hikaru smiled as she watched Cleo vault herself down to the floor as Gobu flew into the air. Giggling as Cleo laid spread across the floor; Hikaru threw the covers off her legs and walked toward her dresser.

Removing a clean white shirt from the drawer, Hikaru climbed into the Amin Mela Academy attire when her brother knocked on the door. Hooking the last button on the jacket, Hikaru looked toward the door as Masumi poked his head into her room.

"What do you want?" Hikaru asked pulling on her white thigh-high socks.

"Came to see if you were up."

"It's a school day of course I'm up." Hikaru stated.

"Yeah, well; there's some lady at the front door asking for you!"

"Who . . ."

"I think she said Tenko . . ." Masumi stated as Hikaru stepped into her black slipper shoes and walked past him.

"Thank you Masumi . . ."

Striding down the hall, Hikaru stepped into the den to find Mrs. Tenko looking at a painting above the fireplace. Walking across the beige carpet, Hikaru stopped beside Mrs. Tenko as she looked down at her.

"I saw what happened at the school last night on the news . . . your friends Maya and Touko are now Hunters!"

Glancing around, Hikaru looked up at Mrs. Tenko, "can we go somewhere private to talk about this?"

"Of course, I have the perfect place . . ." Mrs. Tenko stated walking to the door.

"Oh, well; I meant somewhere my brother couldn't hear, but OK . . ." Hikaru stated grabbing her book bag.

"You won't need that . . ." Mrs. Tenko stated looking down at the bag.

"Okay, Masumi I'm leaving; I'll see you later!" Hikaru yelled running out the door after Mrs. Tenko.

"But school doesn't start for an hour . . ."

Earth—Tuesday, April 22, 2026

The wind whistled lightly through the trees while Hikaru followed Mrs. Tenko as she lead the way down the street to turn the corner. Glancing up at Mrs. Tenko, Hikaru gazed ahead of her again watching people as they began to emerge out of their houses or apartments.

"So who broke the concrete walls?" Mrs. Tenko giggled in a half whisper.

"That was Maya . . . I'm guessing that she has acquired superhuman strength!"

"What about Touko?"

"Nothing, she didn't equip any power last night," Hikaru stated gazing curiously at Mrs. Tenko. "How do you know my friends names, I didn't mention them!"

Turning a corner, Mrs. Tenko glanced down at Hikaru then back at the street. Staring confusingly at Mrs. Tenko, Hikaru suddenly realized . . .

"You've known all along whom the other Hunters were haven't you . . . of course you have, you're the first White Guardian that that Holy Priest sent down to watch the . . . oh my, that means you know who the prince is too!" Hikaru exasperated as Mrs. Tenko stopped to look at her.

"Of course I knew Hikaru, but it's not my place to tell you these things . . . you have to discover it on your own!" Mrs. Tenko declared.

"But what if I never find all the Devilry Hunters and the prince . . . the Nzers aren't going to stop and this won't ever be over!"

"I know and though I shouldn't be doing this; I'm taking you to meet a very special boy," Mrs. Tenko stated pressing a button on a mansion gate.

"What," Hikaru asked as someone came on the intercom.

"Hello, my name is Sinobu Tenko and I have an appointment with Mr. Vorin!"

"Inan Vorin . . . as in the multi-billionaire; why are we here?" Hikaru asked following Mrs. Tenko after the gate opened.

"I happen to know that Mr. Vorin's son is a very bright student, he has a college GPA of 12.46. The highest anyone has ever gotten is a 6.01."

"What is he some super genius," Hikaru smiled, "or a Devilry Hunter."

"Now Mr. Vorin is very possessive of his son Manabu, so I need you to try to find a way to get up to the second floor without being seen."

"How do you expect me to do that . . . I can't turn myself invisible, can I?"

Mrs. Tenko gazed down at Hikaru, "when the door opens stay behind me, I'll hide you; but then you need to discreetly make your way up to Manabu."

"How am I going to find him?" Hikaru asked stepping behind Mrs. Tenko as the door opened.

"Mrs. Tenko, what a splendid surprise; come in . . . Mr. Vorin is waiting for you in the Grand Hall!" The butler exclaimed.

"Hello again, who's playing the piano?" Mrs. Tenko questioned, waving her hands behind her back at Hikaru.

"The young master, amazing isn't he?" The butler replied as Hikaru dropped behind a large pot.

"Yes, indeed," Mrs. Tenko stated following the butler.

Once Mrs. Tenko and the butler were out of sight, Hikaru cautiously stepped out of her hiding spot and snuck toward the giant stairwell leading toward the second floor. Slowly moving up the steps, Hikaru peeked around the corners of the stairs as she followed the sound of the piano. While the music grew louder, Hikaru gazed at the large windows reaching from the ceiling to the floor and the maroon curtains that hide them during dusk hours. Peering into the large mirror she passed, Hikaru traced her eyes over the golden embroideries upon the walls and stared at the gold trimmings surrounding every door and window. Stopping in front of the large door she identified the music to be coming from, Hikaru wrapped her hand around the golden handle and leisurely opened the large door.

Peeking into the room, Hikaru spied a tall young man sitting on a red oak piano stool entranced with his practicing. Stepping into the room, Hikaru quietly shut the door behind her and watched Manabu's fingers elegantly dance across the black and white keys. His lavender-gray hair fell loosely upon his shoulders as he leaned into every key he majestically played. Lifting his head, Manabu closed his bright violet eyes hidden behind his clear rounded glasses as he sophisticatedly finished. Releasing a breath, Manabu nodded his head in approval to open his eyes and put his music notes neatly inside his white pine desk. Sitting upon the stool for a few seconds, Manabu stood to his feet and turned toward Hikaru.

"Did you like it? I know you didn't hear all of it, but did the ending please you?" Manabu questioned walking toward his large bed.

"Uh, yeah. It was beautiful . . . I'm sorry, but aren't you the least bit concerned, who I am and how I got in here?" Hikaru asked puzzled.

"No, I know that father was meeting with the director of the elementary school, and I'm guessing you must have come in with her!" Manabu stated glancing at Hikaru.

"Yeah, how did you know that," Hikaru questioned.

"I just knew . . . I hate to sound rude but could you lower your voice; my sister is ill and I just found a way to help her sleep?" Manabu questioned pulling the covers closer to a violet haired girl.

"That's who you were playing for," Hikaru asked stepping up to the bed to look down at Manabu's little sister.

"Yes, I wrote that song for her." Manabu declared.

"What's it called?"

"Maron . . . I named it after her!" Manabu replied.

"Okay, I know that not many girls come up here asking you this but . . ."

"No one comes up here to see me."

"No one," Hikaru questioned.

Shaking his head, Manabu spied a small stain on Hikaru's jacket. Walking around the bed, Manabu took Hikaru's arm and pulled her away from the bed. Once safely out of earshot, Manabu pointed to the stain.

"What is that?"

Gazing down at the jacket, Hikaru scowled, "Ohhhh, it's something I missed!"

"It's those creatures blood isn't it?" Manabu questioned.

"How do you know about them?" Hikaru asked.

"Reporters are having a field day with these attacks; they can't get any leads on them . . . plus I know that there's no creature on this planet that leaves black blood stains!" Manabu declared.

"Yep, you're a genius . . ."

"You need to take that off so I can analyze that blood!" Manabu stated.

"I'm sorry what?" Hikaru questioned stepping back.

"I may be able to help you find some weakness!"

"What makes you think I'm going to strip my clothes for you?" Hikaru demanded.

"Because unlike other men, I see things as they are and because you want my help anyway, so take off your clothes or do I have to?"

"Who said I wanted your help?"

"You did when you snuck into my room . . . and besides I've talked with the Director for years; I know who she really is and she told me that a beautiful girl with long black hair would eventually come see me!"

"All right, fine; but I want something else to put on and you need to turn around!" Hikaru ordered.

"I've studied everything on the human bodies, under garments are not going to make me go local!"

"Yeah, nice to know; you aren't stripping in front of the opposite sex!" Hikaru nervously declared.

"You've got two seconds." Manabu warned.

* * * * * *

Scrapping a small metal file across Hikaru's jacket, Manabu carefully pulled it away and dropped the fragments onto a small examining dish. Placing the dish beneath a microscope, Manabu gazed fascinated at the cells as they slowly moved around beneath his violet eyes.

"This is wonderful!" Manabu exclaimed.

"For you maybe," Hikaru stated buttoning a white shirt.

"Oh, I'm sorry I didn't mean it in either of those ways . . . I simply meant that given the time I can possibly find any weakness these creatures have by studying them! Do you have anything else from them?"

"Well the police may have certain things, but I'm not going to steal something from a police station!" Hikaru declared.

"I didn't expect that . . . how about this, next time you guys kill one bring it to me so I can analyze it and find weaknesses or make them!" Manabu stated handing Hikaru back her jacket. "Thank you."

"No, thank you . . . you don't know how much this is going to help me!" Hikaru stated when she heard someone approaching Manabu's door. "Someone's coming!"

"Quick; get under the bed!" Manabu suggested when the door started opening.

Diving under the bed, Hikaru watched as the butler walked into Manabu's room, "young master, your father wishes for you to come and visit with the Director!"

"Very well Maurice, tell my father I will be right down when I'm properly dressed!" Manabu replied.

"Yes, young master . . ."

Watching as the door shut, Hikaru started inching out as Manabu dropped down onto his knees to peer under the bed.

"That was close," Hikaru exclaimed.

"I'm sorry, but I better go . . . he'll get really upset if I don't come down!"

"Don't worry; I need to be somewhere anyway!" Hikaru stated walking toward his window.

Watching Hikaru sadly, Manabu lowered his head, "will I ever see you again?"

Turning around to look at Manabu, Hikaru smiled brightly, "of course you will, I never forget a friend . . . and besides I promised you one of those smelly carcasses!" Hikaru giggled. "I'll come back soon!"

Walking up to the open window, Manabu gazed down at Hikaru as she carefully climbed down the lattice.

"Father's normally gone from 8:00am to 5:00pm Monday thru Friday and he's in bed by ten every night!"

"What about weekends?"

"He has to be a father some time . . ." Manabu smiled. "Good bye Hikaru!"

"Bye Manabu . . . I shall return!"

* * * * * *

Dropping onto the sidewalk, Hikaru stared back through the gate at the Vorin mansion before trotting down the street. *I'm late; she's going to kill me!* Hikaru thought to herself as she headed toward Kimiko's house.

31

Kimiko sat on the steps of her front porch frantically searching the street for Hikaru when Antony walked out to join her. Dropping onto the steps beside her, Antony laid his arms over his broad thighs and glanced at his little sister. His ratty dark brown hair fell loosely over his bright red-violet eyes that gazed curiously at Kimiko. Leaning back onto his hands, Antony dropped his head back and closed his eyes.

"So . . . why are you sitting out here searching the streets when everyone else is enjoying themselves inside?"

"I'm waiting for Hikaru," Kimiko declared.

"Yeah, I could've guessed that . . . you know she's going to be here so stop fretting!" Antony ordered.

"But . . ."

"Uh-huh, no buts . . . now come inside with me, so I won't be the only one that gets the honor of telling Kate all of Jaime's embarrassing moments!"

Taking Kimiko's hand, Antony pulled his little sister to her feet and walked into the house. Strolling through the foyer, Antony led Kimiko into the kitchen and pulled a soda out of the refrigerator. Popping the lid off using the side of the counter, Antony handed his sister the bottle and leaned against the cabinet.

"Sis, if you were in trouble you'd tell me wouldn't you?"

"What do you mean Antony?"

"Don't think I've forgotten about that attack at the school when you suddenly disappeared and then those creatures did and then several of them were found disintegrated inside the school!"

Taking a sip of the soda, Kimiko gazed at the floor as Antony stared at her.

"You are hiding something aren't you . . . Kimiko nothing you do would ever make me shun you! Anyone that loves you for that matter . . . and even if they wouldn't stand by you, I would!"

"I know Antony I just . . ."

"Remember when you told me that you thought Hikaru was hiding something from you . . . it really bothered you didn't it? Well, that's how I feel Kimiko; please don't hide it from me, I beg you!"

"All right, I know that this is going to seem impossible, but on the day of that meteor shower an alien race came to Earth. They're searching for a prince from another universe hidden in our own because he's the only one that can ultimately destroy them! Because of this certain people have been given powers to stop these creatures while a Guardian Angel searches for the prince. Hikaru's the leader and En, Jeremy, Maya and I are also these Devilry Hunters!" Kimiko reluctantly explained.

Staring at his sister with a long gaze, Antony shifted his weight against the cabinet and folded his arms neatly across his chest. Perching his lips, he dropped his eyes toward the floor then back at Kimiko.

"That's what you've been hiding?" Antony cheerfully questioned.

"That doesn't sound bizarre to you?"

"Yeah, it does, but it's you Kimiko . . . you've done worse things before!"

"Do you believe me or do you think I'm crazy?"

"I already knew you were crazy Kimiko . . . and no I'm not entirely sure if I believe it, but if you say its true then I'll believe you!"

"Really," Kimiko enthusiastically questioned hugging Antony when Touko walked into the kitchen.

"Yeah guys, I was wondering where you two had disappeared to; come on, I think its time to share our future couples' embarrassing moments!" Touko giggled taking their hands and pulling them into the living room.

Racing down the street she and Kimiko lived on, Hikaru stopped in front of the white fence surrounding the Shiru house to momentarily catch her breath. Dropping her hands onto her knees, Hikaru leaned over taking in a few deep breathes when Gobu shot by her face to grab her hair to stop himself again.

"Owwww," Hikaru yelled lifting her hair to glare angrily at Gobu as he pulled a massive smile across his tiny face. "Dang it Gobu stop doing that . . . my hair is attached! If you need to stop yourself quickly aim for my clothes!"

"But, Hika-pu; mesa come to warn yousa . . . the uglies comin thesa way!"

"The Nzers are coming . . . Gobu what did you do?"

"Mesa . . . uh uh, mesa not do aneting!"

"Well they're following you . . ."

"Mesa not a Huntar . . ." Gobu squeaked.

Glancing down the street, Hikaru spied several Nzers land upon nearby roofs and hiss menacingly at her. Pushing the fence gate open, Hikaru raced down the sidewalk toward the house and leaping onto the porch hammered his fist rapidly against the door. Once the door opened, Hikaru pushed her way to the living room and lifting Izeus ran up to Kimiko.

"The Nzers are coming we need to get your family out of here now!"

Taking Izeus, Kimiko turned toward her parents, "Mom; Dad, those creatures that have been attacking people lately are coming this way . . . we need to get out of here!"

"How do you know they're coming here?" Louise questioned.

"Because I'm here . . ." Hikaru stated.

"Because we're here . . ." Kimiko stated as Touko walked up beside her.

"What are you talking about?" Mr. Shiru questioned.

"I know this sounds crazy but Touko, Kimiko and I have been given powers to ward off these creatures so they don't dominate the planet!" Hikaru replied.

"What does that mean?" Kate Keig questioned looking at Touko.

"That means that you guys need to get somewhere safe while, we ward of the creatures!" Hikaru stated running outside to whack the red marked Nzer away as it nearly broke down the door.

Shutting the door as Kimiko raced out after Hikaru, Touko gazed at the Nzers as they charged toward the house.

"They will kill everyone in that house, even little Izeus!" Touko whimpered as the lamps on the porch flickered. Gazing at the lamps, Touko stared curiously upon the flickering lights when they suddenly blew. Shielding her eyes as the tiny pieces of glass flew toward her; Touko felt a warm spark course through her body. Opening her eyes, Touko looked down at her arms as a dim white light started to surge around her hands. Lifting her hands inches away from her face, Touko gazed out to watch every light across the street flicker. "I can manipulate electricity," Touko giggled.

Dropping to her knees as Kimiko blew her large ball of energy over her head, Hikaru watched the ball burst through the Nzer. Glancing to her side at an approaching Nzer, Hikaru watched as a surge of light pierce through its scaly hide. Watching the body fall to the ground, Hikaru stood to her feet to watch the light spear through every Nzer that remained to fight. While Hikaru stared at the dying Nzers, Kimiko turned around to watch the white light return to Touko's hands as she approached.

"Then there were six . . ." Kimiko giggled as her family raced out to the yard.

Tackled by Louise, Kimiko fell backward as Kate grabbed Touko.

"What were you thinking?" Kate questioned Touko.

"What are they?" Louise asked poking the dead body closest to him before getting pulled back by his father.

"They're creatures from another universe hidden within our own!" Hikaru stated as the rest of the Shiru family came up.

"Another universe . . . are you girls feeling all right?" Mrs. Shiru questioned putting her hand to Kimiko's forehead.

"Yes, Mom . . ." Kimiko stated fidgeting out of her mom's arms.

"I know this is crazy but what else are you going to believe?" Hikaru asked.

"So these aliens have come to invade Earth . . . why?" Mr. Shiru questioned.

"They're here for revenge. The prince of the other universe destroyed their race almost a millennium ago . . ."

"Then how are there so many?" Jaime questioned.

"Let her explain Jaime . . ." Kimiko yelled.

"Don't panic, everything's OK . . . the prince died during the battle and he was sent here to be reborn, the creature that survived the battle knows this and its come to kill the prince before he awakens to his old identity!" Hikaru explained.

"So how do you guys fit into this?" Kimiko's twin brother, Esu questioned.

"Since the prince is here unaware of his past life, he needed someone to protect him 'til he reawakened . . . Earthling Protectors called Devilry Hunters!"

"Here's the cool part . . . Hikaru's the leader and since she found me first that makes me her general!" Kimiko proudly stated.

"No, you can't go out there again . . . what if those creatures kill you?" Mrs. Shiru questioned looking at Kimiko.

"It's been Kimiko that's been protecting me Mrs. Shiru . . . Kimiko is a very strong warrior!" Hikaru smiled at Kimiko.

"Yeah, we saw that . . ." Antony smiled.

"Oh, thanks Antony!"

"I don't want Kimiko getting hurt!" Mrs. Shiru declared.

"Same here," Kate agreed. "There is no way that I'm going to let Touko go fight monsters! I was left in charge of her well being and its not going to happen!" Kate stated grabbing Touko's hand. "Come on Touko we're going home!"

Glancing back at Kimiko and Hikaru, Touko snarled her nose. Forcefully snapping her hand out of Kate's hold, Touko took a step back toward the younger Hunter girls. "No Kate!"

"Touko . . ." Kate gasped stunned.

"I understand how you think this is possibly another one of our jokes . . . well it isn't!" Touko stated. "And that is our proof!" She declared pointing at a Nzer carcass. "Do you think that we wanted this?"

"Your teenagers . . . why wouldn't you?" Jaime added.

"Oh, so because we're teenagers you think that we would like this?" Kimiko quickly snapped.

"Come on Kimiko . . . I grew up with you and I know just how much this would enthrall my little sister!"

Hikaru gazed at everyone and shook her head sadly, "Whether you want us to do this task or not, we have no choice. The creatures know that we have been given the power to protect the planet . . . they won't stop trying to kill us and they may come harder once they find out one of us quit! We are the only ones that can stop these creatures . . . either you let us continue to do our mission or we as a race become extinct!"

"Wait you said that they are here to kill a prince, not the planet!" Mr. Shiru recalled.

"Yes, they are but out of spite they'll destroy the entire planet! They've already killed many people searching for the prince . . ." Hikaru stated. "It would horrify you to know what we've seen these aliens do to innocent people! It's almost as if they are harvesting us . . . the bodies we found were completely drained of blood. And the faces were beyond identification!" Hikaru breathed regretfully. "Do you really want us, those who are able to stop them; just let them move around our city freely? What if they came to your house next . . . do you want that death for your young boys?"

"How do you know that . . . the police haven't found any bodies?" Jaime replied.

"Then explain Taylor Kane's death?" Kimiko stated. "The police haven't released anything because they don't know what to release!"

"Kimiko's right . . . I'm trying to prevent that but I won't be able to if you take away my Hunters . . . I cannot do this by myself that's why they've been given powers; to help me!"

Hikaru watched the reluctant faces upon Kate and the Shiru's faces when she heard several sirens with her acute senses.

"One more thing . . . you can't tell anyone about this! We won't be able to do our jobs if we have reporters and officers hounding us for information!" Hikaru informed.

"As much as I hate this, I suppose you're right . . ." Mr. Shiru stated. "Watch over my little girl Hikaru!"

"I will, don't worry this will all be over soon!" Hikaru stated.

"You guys better go," Mrs. Shiru stated.

Running down the street; Hikaru, Kimiko, and Touko raced toward the Neijo plantation at the top of Cendlock Hill. Resettling the gate in its station, Hikaru stared down at the flashing lights upon the squad cars as they pulled up to the Shiru house.

When is this going to end? Hikaru thought quietly to herself as she turned to walk toward her house.

32

Earth—Thursday, April 24, 2026

The afternoon sun slowly restricted its rays as dark clouds pushed leisurely before it as the funeral for Taylor Kane persisted. The agony of Taylor's loss weighed heavily upon everyone's shoulders as they sat within the church listening to the Pastor pray for Taylor's soul. His mother and father wept bitterly as they gazed at the oak coffin before their sunken teary eyes.

Sitting four rows behind the Kanes; Hikaru, Masumi, Gramps, and Hagane respectfully wept for Taylor when a soft voice whispered in Hagane's ear. Opening his light brown eyes; Hagane peered around looking for the body to the voice to reseal his eyes and resume praying. With his hands folded neatly over his knees, a soft satin hand brushed by Hagane's cheek followed by a cool cotton ribbon.

Quickly opening his eyes, Hagane found himself floating in a crystalline world captivated within a sphere. Small bubbles floated around his body as he peered around the sphere when a tall young woman turned to face him. Enchanted, Hagane stared spellbound upon the young woman as she smiled brightly at him.

Her long ginger hair spread out behind her back as she floated around several crystal stakes toward Hagane. Her majestic blue eyes stared through the long bangs hanging loosely over her bronzed skin. The golden-black armor plates strapped to her arms and hips shimmered across the sphere as she reached her hand out to Hagane. The golden cross engraved to the white breast plate shimmered through Hagane's eyes as she closed her hand around his.

Floating alongside the young woman, Hagane found he couldn't take his eyes off her for a second as she landed beside a long river forking across the sphere to flow toward a magnificent palace in the horizon. Its large crystalline towers magnified the sun as it pushed through the walls to fall upon Hagane's skin warming him with a sweet essence unlike he had ever felt.

There are many things within your world that need your healing Child of Grace! The young woman's voice echoed across the crystals lining the river.

"What do you mean?"

You are Hagane Rouse, the adapted son of the most skilled teacher in the healing arts on Earth! You are also the Hunter of life and death; through your hands ignites the power God gave to sustain life!

"A Hunter . . . what is that?"

Smiling brightly at Hagane, the young woman kissed him on the cheek, *An inhabitant of Earth chosen to assist the youngest Neijo on her journey of peace! You are the Hunter of Existence.*

"Hikaru . . ."

"What . . ."

Opening his eyes, Hagane found himself sitting in the church seat by the aisle with Hikaru leaning toward him.

"I'm sorry . . ."

"You called my name Hagane; what do you want?" Hikaru asked.

"I . . ." glancing around the church, Hagane searched for the young woman he had previously been with.

"Hagane are you OK?" Hikaru questioned takin his hand.

"You don't look so good buddy!" Masumi stated looking at Hagane.

"I'm fine; I . . ." Hagane stuttered looking at the Kanes.

Yes, Hunter; . . . look to your hands and sustain the body before the real affect of the creatures curse takes over the boy's body! The woman's voice echoed in Hagane's head.

"Hagane . . . hello!" Masumi whispered.

Gazing at Masumi, Hagane slid to the aisle and stood to his feet as Masumi and Hikaru called to him. Striding down the aisle, Hagane approached the Kanes and dropping to his knee before them bowed his head respectfully.

"I'm deeply sorry for your loss Mr. and Mrs. Kane; Taylor was a bright positive young man." Hagane declared.

"Thank you for your kindness . . ." Mrs. Kane whimpered through tears.

"Hagane what are you doing?" Masumi questioned grabbing his arm.

Pulling his arm out of Masumi's hand, Hagane stood to his feet and gazed away from Masumi to the Kanes. With a whispered encouragement from the young woman, Hagane gazed at the coffin back to the Kanes.

"Mr. and Mrs. Kane, I don't wish to offend you or Taylor in anyway but I ask you for permission to inspect your son's body?" Hagane breathed not believing he just asked the questioned.

Pulling Hagane around as Mr. Kane's anger began to flow to his body; Masumi looked at his older brother. "Hagane, what on Earth are you doing?"

"What do you want to look at Taylor's body for?" Mrs. Kane questioned as Hikaru walked up.

"I understand that this is disrespectful, but it's for Taylor that I'm doing this for . . . those alien creatures that have recently disturbed the city are killing anyone they can because those they kill will come back to live and be their malevolent minions . . ."

Standing to his feet, Mr. Kane gazed angrily at Hagane and cruelly spat, "I knew your parents well Hagane Rouse and I say you have shamed them to the lowest point anyone could shame their parents!"

Pierced through his heart by those words, Hagane sadly looked away from the Kanes to walk down the aisle when something groaned behind him. Turning back around, Hagane stared at the coffin as Taylor's body rose when several Nzers burst through the roof. Raising their scaly bodies, the Nzers shrieked out breaking the windows and glasses throughout the church. Glancing toward her friends, Hikaru pushed Masumi and Hagane down as the red marked Nzer leapt toward them. Rising to hammer her leg into the leaping Nzer, Hikaru walked toward the red marked Nzer to be joined by Kimiko, En, Jeremy, Maya, and Touko.

"Hikaru . . ." Masumi yelled.

Glancing back at her brother, Hikaru looked at Kimiko, "will you?"

"Go we got this!" Kimiko smiled blasting her energy ball through a small Nzer.

Jumping over a dead Nzer's body, Hikaru raced up to Masumi and Hagane when a chubby Nzer jumped in front of her. Stopping quickly, Hikaru's long hair blew past her irritated face as she glared at the Nzer.

Falling backward, Masumi scooted behind Hagane as the Nzer shot a side long glance at them and hissed. Yelling as the Nzer leapt at them, Masumi grimaced as the Nzer hit into Hagane. Opening his eyes to see Hagane holding the Nzer's massive arms as the talons came down toward his face, Masumi squirmed to his feet and lifting a pot smashed it across the Nzer's head.

Gazing at Masumi angrily, the chubby Nzer raised its large foot and slammed it down where Masumi had been before leaping out of the way. Shooting its face back to look down at Hagane, the chubby Nzer pushed its face down to snap at Hagane. Pulling his face away, Hagane pushed his hands forward attempting to move the Nzer when a young boy's voice called out to him.

Looking up at the Nzer, Hagane watched the scaly face dissolve into a young bright eyed boy's weeping face. Losing his breath, Hagane stared at the boy's face with sorrowful eyes. Gritting his teeth, Hagane shifted his weight throwing the Nzer to the ground and dropping onto it slammed his hands through its chest.

Sitting up from falling into the rows of benches, Mrs. Kane nudged her husband, "Thomas . . . look!"

A blinding ray shot out from the Nzer's body to fall back over Hagane as a pale pink aura emerged around his hands. Leaning into the Nzer, Hagane pulled his feet under him and pulled the young boy out of the scaly hide causing it to flatten against the floor. Carrying the boy over to the Kanes, Hagane laid him down on the bench as he released a tiny moan.

"How did you do that?" Masumi questioned looking at Hagane.

"I told you that the Nzers were beginning to use their slain victims . . . you wouldn't listen!" Hagane replied looking at Mr. Kane.

"Yeah, but how did you rip that kid out of that thing?" Masumi questioned.

Gazing at Masumi with a smile, Hagane shook his head when the red marked Nzer dropped behind them. Turning around as Mrs. Kane screamed, Hagane and Masumi stared into the Nzer's face as it speared its talons through Hagane's abdomen.

"I can ans-swer that . . ."

Hearing the wails from Masumi and Mrs. Kane, Hikaru pitched her hair over her shoulders as she threw her head back to stare at the Nzer arm piercing through Hagane's body as it lifted him into the air. Staring horrified, Hikaru yelled at the Nzer as it threw Hagane toward the back of the church.

"He was-s-s going to be a Hunter!" The red marked Nzer hissed with a chuckle.

Standing to her feet, Hikaru raced toward the Nzer with tears streaming away from her eyes. Knocking a Nzer out of her way, Kimiko blasted her ball of energy through a Nzer leaping at Hikaru's back as she raced up to the red marked Nzer.

33

Standing in front of Mr. and Mrs. Kane, Masumi stared across the church where Hagane had been thrown when the Nzer whipped around to face him. Stepping back to fall against the bench, Masumi stared at the Nzer as it bent down toward him.

"What are you vermin?"

"Not your friend!" Masumi fumed punching the Nzer in the face, "Owwww!"

Grabbing the front of Masumi's shirt, the Nzer lifted him into the air as Hikaru blasted a ray through its abdomen. Dropping onto the floor, Masumi gazed up to see Hikaru blast another ray through the Nzer as tears raced down her cheeks. Sitting up to his knees, Masumi glared angrily at the Nzer Hikaru had blown something through as it continued to attack her.

Looking over at Mr. Kane, Masumi angrily yelled, "Do you think he still shames his parents . . . well I guess he'll find out since he's **dead!**"

Turning toward the Nzer, Masumi suddenly found he could stare through its thick hide at its blood veins. Shaking his head, Masumi stared closely as he suddenly felt drawn toward the Nzer. Reaching his hand out toward the Nzer, Masumi tried to distinguish what he was feeling when he lifted the Nzer into the air.

"There it is . . ." Masumi softly breathed closing his eyes, "You have far too much iron in your blood!"

Clenching his fist, Masumi started sucking the iron out of the Nzers body piercing it through its hide to slowly swirl above his hand. Watching his face slowly reflect back across the growing sphere, Masumi gazed at Hikaru as she stared at him and smiled.

"How am I doing this?"

"Don't ask just go with it!" Hikaru stated whacking a Nzer in the eyes.

"All right . . ."

Staring at several Nzers charging toward him, Masumi opened his palm causing the sphere to sail through the air throughout the Nzers hide. Smiling, Masumi watched the ball of metal fly in any direction his mind thought of. Crossing his arms over his chest, Masumi proudly watched the ball flew across the church when a Nzer jumped on him from behind. Smashed beneath the massive body, Masumi lost his grip on the sphere as he attempted to lift the Nzer off him when a field of energy slammed into the Nzer. Sitting up, Masumi gazed unbelievingly at Hagane as he offered him his hand. Pulled to his feet, Masumi grabbed Hagane's arm and pressed his hands against his solid chest.

"But I saw it pierce through you!"

"As I heal others I guess my body will rejuvenate as well!" Hagane smiled.

"So you aren't a ghost?"

"Do I look like a ghost?"

"I don't know; you look different!" Masumi declared squinting at Hagane to get pushed backward.

"So do you; it's called getting dumber!" Hagane stated.

Gazing toward the church pew, Hagane raced up to Taylor's coffin and peered down to stare at Taylor's body as small scales began to form over his skin. Shaking his head in disgust, Hagane laid his hand upon Taylor's forehead.

"Not this child . . ."

The pale pink aura surrounded Hagane's hands once again as he swept them across Taylor's forehead causing his body to arch toward him. Standing in front of Hagane as the remaining Nzers attempted to get to the reviving body, the Hunters new and old fed off the creatures when the doors blew open.

White feathers blew into the church to brush past the Hunters toward the church roof to leisurely descend back to the floor. A sweet smell of candy and flower nectar pushed around the Nzers to fill everyone's nostrils as the wind began to lift the bells from their stationary posts. Clanging loudly through the church, the bells rang out streams of holy voices to sing along the walls and shattered windows.

Cowering back the living Nzers shot quick glances around the church when they spied a figure land on the statue of Jesus Christ towering over them. The sudden realization of his shadow falling over them sparked panic through the Nzers as they turned to race out the doors. Spearing through the cloth upon the figures back, crystalline wings shot feather dust out into the church to fall down upon every spectator still inside. Dropping down onto the church floor, Esal walked toward Hikaru and the rest of the Hunters as everyone else in the church passed out.

"What's going on . . . what did you do?"

"Never mind what he did, who are you?" Masumi questioned.

"No, I was right the first time . . . what did you do?" Hikaru questioned looking at Esal.

"They didn't need to know any of this . . . so I erased it from their memories!"

"But you can't do that . . . it's horrible that it happened like this but you shouldn't undo something that's already taken place . . . its changing a short history!" Hikaru replied.

"Hikaru . . . you can't deal with any other matter but the one you're at the moment dealing with; we don't have time for distractions!"

"Okay now can I know who he is?" Masumi questioned.

Glancing at Masumi, Esal smiled, "so your brothers' are Hunters after all!"

"Yeah, whatever; Hunter sure, now your name . . ." Masumi demanded.

"Guardian Esal, an Archangel of the Universe hidden in yours!" Esal smiled.

"Oh no, I've found why Hikaru's been so loony!" Masumi stated.

"Well you must be crazy as well, because you're the one who ripped iron out of the Nzers blood!" Esal reminded.

"All right, OK. Point taken . . . one more thing, can someone explain to me what's going on!" Masumi questioned.

"What more can we explain . . . you've been given powers because those creatures are here to invade Earth! They're here to kill the prince of my universe, because he ultimately wiped them out last time! In other words I need your help the ones Hikaru discovers to be her Hunters to help me find the prince and save your planet from destruction, understand?" Esal questioned.

"Yeah, I guess . . ." Masumi stated continuing to think as the others started walking away.

As the Devilry Hunters and Esal disappeared the church reverted back to the way it had once been and everyone woke up to see Taylor lift his mother to her feet. Crying hysterically, Mrs. Kane held her son as she thanked God for bringing him back to her.

34

$\mathcal{T}$he Holy Priest shook his large staff through the air as he walked around the Grand Hall with his eyes closed. Kicking his thick beige boots across the ceramic tile floors, the Holy Priest bobbed his head casting his aqua-green tinted baby-blue hair before his tanned face. Waving his free hand through the air, the Holy Priest sliced his white glove through the red-violet smoke dispersing out of the large dark rainbow orb at the top of his staff. While continuing to walk in his circular path, the Holy Priest occasionally spun lifting his large blue-green cloak to flare around his smaller body.

Ridding inside a crystalline cerulean sphere-shaped carriage; a hooded figure gazed out over the large kingdom bordering the Latrinian palace. The tall trees to the small streams glistened in the bright amber eyes hidden beneath the white hood as the purple Pegasus landed the carriage in front of the courtyard gate. Gazing at the large river stretching around the towering wall, the figure peered at all the curious onlookers the carriage passed 'til it stopped before the steps leading to the front entrance of the palace.

Opening the white feather-shaped door; the concealed figure stepped down onto the porcelain leaf steps to lay two blue-gray boots onto the silver stones lying across the courtyard. Shutting the carriage door, the figure turned toward the large engraved doors hiding the elegant majesty of the palace's inside chambers. Pulling the white cloak tightly around its frame, the figure stepped down on the silver stone steps leading to the castle entrance. Extending a brown glove; a bright blue orb centering the figure's hand reflected the orange rays of Latira's afternoon moon across the courtyard. Pushing the doors open, the figure walked inside the palace to gaze down at the Holy Priest as he danced in the Grand Hall. Lifting the hood to reveal a young woman's face, the figure tilted her head to the side as she stared at the Holy Priest while he pranced around the Grand Hall.

"I'm pleased to see you so gleeful Priest!" The young woman stated approaching the Holy Priest.

Stopping in the center of the Grand Hall, the Holy Priest turned toward the entrance and smiled, "well, I haven't seen you in ages, young Lle . . . who are you?"

Stepping toward the Holy Priest with an annoyed look on her face as the doors closed, the young woman approached the Holy Priest, "tell me Priest, why are you dancing around the center of the Grand Hall?"

"No particular reason . . . why?"

"Who know perfectly well why, Priest! I'm missing a young crystal blue-eyed Prince of Evalëantía!"

"Oh, that matter . . . he's gone to earth!"

"What . . . why has he gone to a planet in the other universe?"

35

The hours of the evening shortly began to diminish as the moon began to rise as Hikaru slowly walked up the Neijo plantation steps after visiting with Kimiko's family for several hours. Opening the gate, Hikaru started across the sidewalk when she spotted Kimon sitting on the front steps to the house. Gazing at him as the gate resettled in the lock, Hikaru started back across the sidewalk and stopped in front of the porch as he stood to his feet.

Folding her hands before her, Hikaru gazed questioning at Kimon, "What are you doing here?"

"Well I tried to come by yesterday, but you weren't here, so I came by earlier today you weren't here then either . . ." Smiling nervously, Hikaru gazed at Kimon as he moved closer to her. "However, I knew that even you had to come home sooner or later so I came later and waited."

"How long have you been waiting?" Hikaru asked astonished.

"Not long, even though it seemed like an eternity."

Dropping down onto the front step Hikaru looked at Kimon as he sat beside her, "What do you need Kimon . . . nothing's wrong is it?"

"No nothing's wrong, I just came by to invite you to Yuri's recital this Saturday . . . she's playing at a concert finally and I wanted her best friends to be there, it would mean the world to her!" Kimon stated.

"Oh, well of course I'll be there!" Hikaru replied enthusiastically.

Staring into Kimon's deep indigo eyes; Hikaru could fell that he was arching toward her as much as she was toward him. She nearly felt his lips touch hers when she gazed out over the city.

"I've never seen such a large moon or so bright!"

Gazing at Hikaru before turning toward the moon, Kimon dropped his eyes toward the softly blowing blades of grass. Standing to his feet, Kimon started across the lawn when he turned back toward Hikaru.

"Some call it Hunter's Moon!"

Watching Kimon disappear down the hill, Hikaru whimpered as she pulled herself to her feet and walked into the house. Strolling down the hall, Hikaru walked into her bedroom to drop onto her bed where Esal sat waiting on her dresser.

"What was that about?"

Shooting up to see Esal, Hikaru dropped back down onto her bed, "nothing, he invited me to go see his little sister Yuri, play at a concert this weekend!"

"That's what you're so worked up about?"

Sitting up Hikaru gazed at Esal as tears came to her eyes, "no, I'm so in love with him and the first time he shows a little interest in me I shun away!"

Dropping off the dresser, Esal sat beside Hikaru, "why did you do that?"

"Because you said that I can't have any distractions!"

Gazing down at the floor, Esal pushed tears off Hikaru's cheeks, "Yes, but I didn't say you couldn't love someone or allow him to love you! In this line of work you need to share passionate feelings with someone!"

"Oh, I wish I had known that I few minutes ago!" Hikaru chuckled as Esal stood to look out her window.

After a few minutes Hikaru looked at Esal.

"Is there anyone back home waiting for you?" Hikaru questioned.

Dropping the curtain over the window, Esal gazed down at the floor and grew very silent.

"Esal . . ."

Turning to gaze at Hikaru, Esal released a breath and approached the bed, "Yes, there's a young woman that has captivated my heart . . . though she doesn't realize it I've numerous times given my life to protect her; forfeiting my life for hers!"

"Who is she?" Hikaru questioned gazing at Esal's sad face.

"I'm not at liberty to say!" Esal stated.

"Esal it's me . . . who am I going to tell!"

Gazing at Hikaru as she smiled brightly at him, Esal's face brightened, "She isn't like anyone else in the world; she stands out in a crowd and smiles as brightly as the sun's rays!"

"And yet I still haven't heard her name!" Hikaru smirked.

Leaning against Hikaru's desk, Esal gazed up at the ceiling, "She's the prince's little sister . . ."

"The prince . . . wow, and does she like you back?" Hikaru questioned.

"Sometimes I wonder if she knows I exist . . ."

"Really . . . Esal that's terrible!"

"But then there are times when I find her staring at me and I get knots in my stomach so tight that I can't breath!"

"I know the feeling," Hikaru stated as she thought of Kimon. "How do you stay calm when you're around the person you like though . . . and how do you finally work up the courage to tell them you like them very much?"

"Well first you better hope they actually listen to you and don't ignore you like every other soldier around the palace . . . and then you have to make sure you get it out because they have a very short attention span," Esal stated.

Looking at each other realizing they were just referring to previous incidents, Esal and Hikaru smiled brightly at one another when Gobu slammed into the window. Turning toward the window, Esal cautiously approached the window and drawing back the curtain watched Gobu slowly start to fall. Shaking his head, Esal opened the window and pulled Gobu inside resealing the window before sitting beside Hikaru on the bed.

"What else can I possibly do to utter the words?" Hikaru questioned looking at Esal. "I've tried so many times and failed; how can I be sure that I won't again?"

"Because failing isn't part of you any more Hikaru, you are the strongest person I've ever seen for a starting warrior . . . you have power within you I haven't seen in some of our oldest strongest warriors back home! I have no doubt that you will come out triumphant on the challenge you speak of."

Raising Gobu so he stared into his large eyes, Esal smiled brightly "now what is wrong with you?"

"Esal-pu mesa thinks mesa may've found yousa prince!"

"What . . ."

"Uh-huh . . . yousa come with mesa quickly!"

"Do you want me to come?" Hikaru asked as Esal pulled his white cloak over his shoulder to pull it over his head.

"Not this time Hikaru . . . I think you've had enough excitement for one day! Try to get some rest I'll see you in a little bit!"

Watching Esal disappear into the dark skies, Hikaru walked toward her door and quietly opening it walked out into the hall. Sneaking down the hall, Hikaru stopped in front of Masumi's door and pushing it open peeked in to see her brother spread across his bed. Rolling her eyes, Hikaru resealed the door and strolled down to Hagane's room. Quietly opening the door, Hikaru peered in at his far more peaceful position than Masumi's and smiled as her mind wondered.

To think I almost lost you . . . Hagane I couldn't live without you; or Masumi for that matter! I swear as long as I live I won't let anyone close to me get hurt ever again!

36

$\mathcal{T}$he planets rotated slowly around the atmosphere as the Latrinian **Warship G-731** sat quietly beneath the moon. The stars continued to reflect off its glossy surface as large puffs of smoke blew out the back of the ship. Lights flickered off and on in the front of the **Warship G-731** as it slowly began to descend.

In the Other Universe

Racing up the stairs toward the Grand Hall, Jeannee and Doc found the Holy Priest continuing to prance around the room waving his large staff through the air. Cautiously stepping behind him, Jeannee avoided the swinging staff while Doc got it smacked into his face once again. Cutting in front of the Holy Priest, Jeannee watched him as he stared at the ceiling mumbling something under his breath.

"Priest I hate to be rude, but the **Warship G-731** is moving!" Jeannee yelled.

Dropping his head and staff in perfect unison, the Holy Priest stared at Jeannee with wide eyes, "Moving where?"

Releasing a breath, Jeannee looked at the Holy Priest, "To Earth!"

Earth—Friday, April 25, 2026

A soft breeze blew in through Hikaru's window as she lay sleeping upon her warm cotton sheets. Her long raven hair lifted leisurely against the wind to lay back over her while Cleo slept at the foot of her bed swinging her paws through the air swiping at the nightmare she was having. The prolonging hours of the night stretched out through the deep darkness throughout Hikaru's room when a bronzed hand gently shook Hikaru from her slumber. Slowly peeking her brown eyes open, Hikaru gazed up into her brother's face and grimaced with frustration. Whacking the hand away, Hikaru turned her head toward the wall and mumbled for Masumi to go away.

Gazing at Hikaru curiously, he bent down to her head and whispered in her ear, *The sun will rise without you my little Soul Star!*

Quickly opening her eyes, Hikaru sprang up right in her bed, "Dad!"

Sliding a finger over her mouth the young Clyde Neijo, wrapped his arms around Hikaru, *You've grown to be such a beautiful young woman, Hikaru!*

"Oh my god, dad; how are you here?" Hikaru sobbed holding her father.

The White Guardian brought me back, because I believe you are now old enough to hear the entire story! Clyde stated.

"Mrs. Tenko already told me that you were what I am now!"

Yes, but I wanted to tell you everything else—I wanted to tell you about the betrayal, how we one by one began to diminish; how the Devilry Hunters vanished!

"Vanished . . . what do you mean?"

Holding out his hand, Clyde looked into Hikaru's eyes, *Let me show you!*

Gazing upon the young face of her father, Hikaru saw so much of him in Masumi when he offered his hand to her. Carefully laying her hand in his, Hikaru stood to her feet as her father pulled gently on her hand. Following him as he walked toward the window, Hikaru stared entranced into her father's bright hazel eyes as his ragged short black hair swept slowly before them.

Roused from her slumber when Hikaru pulled her legs out from under her, Cleo looked up into the darkness with wiry eyes and mumbled she was innocent; she didn't do it. Blinking her sleepy eyes, Cleo stared around the room 'til she saw Hikaru following, in her opinion, a better looking Masumi. Extending her front paws, Cleo stretched her fluffy when she was suddenly blinding by a bright white light. Quickly jumping off the bed, Cleo raced after Hikaru as she and "Masumi's twin" disappeared into the bright light to slam into the wall.

Taking a look around as her bedroom walls melted into sky, Hikaru watched the scenery rapidly shot about her. Lights flashed throughout the area Hikaru was standing when she looked up at her father.

"Dad, what was mom like?"

Gazing at Hikaru as the lights continued to flash brightly past them; Clyde drew in a deep breath as he thought about his wife Jocelyn.

Your mother was the most wonderful person in my life, she had a spirit as wild as the wind yet as tame as still water . . . she had bright brown eyes and raven hair that shone of the morning sun when it struck it! She wasn't afraid of anything; not even death . . .

The sky grew dark red when the buildings throughout The city where surrounded by raging flames. Walking out onto the wet grass upon Cendlock Hill, Hikaru stood with her father as she looked out over the dying city.

"Is this what happened or is it going to happen?" Hikaru questioned looking at her father.

Turning to look at Hikaru, Clyde gazed back out over the city, *This will be what happens if you fail as I did!*

"What happened daddy?" Hikaru asked finally.

Gazing at the burning city, Clyde looked down at his daughter and pointed toward a flickering light. Staring closely at the light, Hikaru suddenly found herself warped nearly twenty years in the past . . .

* * * * * *

The skies were dark with the smoke from the burning city as Clyde hammered into the street inhabiting Cendlock Hill. His clothes were stained from large cuts across his skin as he rolled to his back to inch away from a tall man that landed a few feet away from him. Staring remorsefully at the man through his hazel eyes, Clyde pulled himself backward with his arms as blood seeped out of his side.

The man watched Clyde through his blank eyes with a sorrowful smirk on his face as he watched him slowly inch away. Tightening his grip around a silver blade within his left hand, the man lengthened his strides 'til he was looming right over Clyde. Pausing for a moment the man prolonged his slaughter to gaze down at Clyde as he stopped pulling himself away.

"I don't understand why you're doing this . . . we're supposed to destroy evil not become it Terrence!" Clyde yelled.

"Yeah, but I can't help it!" Terrence Skilou's blank eyes stated.

"Terrence, you've got to snap out of it . . . it's me Clyde, your best friend!"

Tears began to pass down Terrence's face as he lifted the sword above his head, "I'm sorry Clyde . . ."

Thrusting the blade down, Terrence speared the sword through his own abdomen shooting his blood over Clyde's face. Quickly pulling himself toward Terrence as he fell to the street, Clyde lifted his dead friend's body into his arms and wept. Tears flowed across Clyde's filthy cheeks streaking clean paths as he tenderly held Terrence's body in his arms crying out for help. Looking toward the sky, Clyde yelled in anger as the dark clouds overhead burst open to let the rain fall over the two bodies. Gazing down at the street, Clyde watched blood stream out from under Terrence's body toward the sewers when Sinobu landed in the street.

Gazing angrily at Sinobu, Clyde screamed out through the rain, *"Is this what I became the leader for . . . to hold the dying bodies of all my friends in my arms!"*

"Clyde," Sinobu sadly stated. "This was not your fault; Terrence did the last thing he could to protect you! Make his sacrifice honorable . . . don't question his actions!" Sinobu cried. "He preferably to die for you than to let anything happen to his best friend; the one that stood by him through all his hard times and pains!"

Gazing away from Sinobu to the once again peaceful expression upon Terrence's face, Clyde dropped his head onto Terrence's neck and sobbed. "He suffered so much . . ." Clyde stated gazing into the rain with vengeful eyes.

"But he's at peace now Clyde!"

Watching the rain as it fell against his face and into his eyes, Clyde looked up at Sinobu as she walked up and laid her hand on his shoulder.

37

It was coming up to our third year of being Devilry Hunters when Terrence sacrificed himself for me! Clyde recalled as Hikaru watched how Terrence died. Whipping tears from her eyes Hikaru gazed at her father "why daddy; why did he do that?"

Once we came together as a group the Devilry Hunters spent over a year equipping ourselves and gaining the trust of the city. We trained ourselves in every technique known to man and even after that Sinobu trained most of us in the art of battle from her planet. Where we were unaware of the real danger Sinobu had felt it from the beginning. She told us that a long silence comes before the storm just like a deep breath comes before the plunge . . .

"I don't understand daddy . . ."

As we came closer to becoming ready in Sinobu's eyes relationships began to form . . . after two years of the labor we were going through I found certain things were still missing in my life; your mother and I were married when she came!

"She . . ."

In the beginning we fought off simple things the police should have taken control of but then a Queen from Sinobu's Universe came to Earth . . . she had a look your mother didn't trust from the beginning; Jocelyn had never been so serious about one of her feelings before which made the rest of us wiry! Jocelyn's best friend Missy said that she was just overreacting; Missy went to see the queen to negotiate. We wanted to see what she had come to Earth for because Sinobu said she was of the Dark Moon planet within her universe . . .

"Go on daddy . . ." Hikaru pushed.

They sent Missy's body back to us in a box . . . later Sinobu told us that Missy's mind had exploded as well as her heart . . . at that point we realized that the queen had come for us but we couldn't figure out why! One by one she dismantled us all . . . Gary and Karla Rouse died when they went to disrupt the power feeding into her ship! Shortly after the Rouses died the queen began to grow inpatient and sent her hardhearted son out to finish the rest of us off . . . he burned Filipe Fui and Mira Li alive inside a nuclear building; Ondrea Keig died taking a blast meant for your mother and Terrence died fighting an infection caused by a Seira Moudeian blade!

Tears streamed from Hikaru's eyes as she sat upon the wet grass "how could someone do this?"

Sinobu saved your mother and I from the bloodthirsty son and took us to a sacred place where the Dark Queen couldn't enter; there Sinobu began to explain what she thought was happening . . . Sinobu told us why she really assembled us to protect the planet . . .

Hikaru gazed at her father as he inhaled a deep breath "well?"

Gazing down at Hikaru Clyde pointed at the flickering light as it expanded . . .

* * * * * *

A dense cloud swept over a crystalline valley setting the remorseful mood the planet Earth was currently exposing to the rest of the Universes. A small clear creek dribbled through the valley to fall leisurely down several falls while a cotton breeze pushed gently along the snowy blades of grass. Tiny dwarf rabbits darted across the valley playing when Sinobu appeared with Clyde and Jocelyn.

Holding Clyde's arm over her shoulder Sinobu carried him toward the small creek desperately trying to get him into its healing waters before the infection set in. Following closely behind Sinobu and her husband Jocelyn tenderly held a tiny baby boy in her arms when she spied the destruction of Earth reflecting off the crystals around the valley. Sitting beside the creek as Sinobu dropped to her knees Jocelyn watched as the garments came off Clyde to see the large gash through his side. Scowling as she watched him grimace at the water burning into the gash Jocelyn rocked little Masumi in her arms as Sinobu walked up to a large crystal.

Swiping her hand through the crystal Sinobu watched the planet Earth came over the surface and revert to the large black ship of the Dark Queen of Seria Moudei hovering over the city. Sliding her hand back across the crystal Sinobu watched as it stretched toward the sky and drop a large dagger onto the snowy blades. Lifting the dagger Sinobu walked up to Jocelyn and laid it beside her before racing up to help Clyde.

Lifting the blade in her hand Jocelyn stared at her reflection in the crystal as it cast different colors across her tanned face. Looking down at Masumi as he squeaked Jocelyn smiled brightly at him before turning back toward Sinobu and Clyde.

"What are we going to do . . . hide here while that witch destroys the planet?"

Looking at Jocelyn as Masumi giggled Sinobu helped Clyde to the bank and laid him on his back allowing the snowy blades to seal the gash. Straightening her body as she turned toward Jocelyn Sinobu released a breath before dropping onto the snowy blades.

"For right now yes . . . neither of you are ready to face the Dark Queen at the moment besides your unborn child must come to this world Jocelyn!"

"You have been telling me that since Masumi was born . . . you knew I was going to have this child before I did!" Jocelyn replied.

"Yes, and here's why" Sinobu stated looking at Jocelyn and Clyde.

"Our universe is a war-plagued world, full of menacing creatures and evil people as you have discovered . . . during a recent war the young prince of my world was killed along with many other princes and princesses! As a result the Holy Priest and I took it upon ourselves to give them a new life; the Priest used his power to bring the children back to life to be reborn and I came to guard over them!"

"So you're trying to tell us that we're going to give birth to a royal child of your universe?" Jocelyn questioned.

"Clyde and you were chosen because you both were seen as noble worthy beings to take on this responsibility . . . but you're going to bring the prince and his subjects' protector to this world! I just don't know if it's your unborn child or young Masumi . . ."

Glancing down at Masumi's tiny little face Jocelyn looked up at Sinobu "what about the Dark Queen?"

"I'm guessing that somehow she knows what I'm here for and now she's trying to take the unborn children for herself or . . ."

"What Sinobu; trying to what?"

"It only makes sense why she's killing the Devilry Hunters; once she has all of you out of the way she could freely search the planet . . . I don't know what she plans to do!" Sinobu stated looking around her sanctuary.

38

$\mathcal{H}$eat from the leaping flames tore at Hikaru's tearstained face. Her raven hair reflected the rosy glow of the fire washing over the city. Hikaru looked at her father as he gazed out over the burning city, "So who is the prince's protector?"

Sinobu never figured it out . . . we stayed in her sanctuary for months trying to figure out everything—why the Dark Queen wanted the royal children; why if she was so strong, why then did she need to get rid of the Hunters . . .

Hikaru watched her father as he grew silent, "what happened daddy?"

We thought we would be safe to figure certain things out before we had to go face the Dark Queen again, but we were wrong . . . it was April 13, 2010, a few days before your mother was due to bring you into this world; when a tall man entered the sanctuary's barrier . . . he had power that I had never seen before!

"So what happened?"

That man destroyed any hope we had for any kind of safety zone; he could get through anything . . . he even destroyed Jocelyn's hope of raising a family in peace . . . so we attempted to try our luck on Earth again! Sinobu managed to help us escape again, but we didn't see her again until your mother died bringing you to this world.

Gazing at the grass, Hikaru quietly questioned, "Did mom feel any pain?"

Turning to look at Hikaru, Clyde bent down and lifted her chin. *Knowing she wasn't going to be able to see you grow up was the only pain your mother felt! Your mother wished that you would grow into a beautiful strong child Hikaru and you have . . . I have no doubt that your mother smiles down from heaven on you!*

"Thank you daddy . . ." Hikaru smiled hugging Clyde.

After releasing her father, Hikaru stood to her feet and walking to look out over the city turned back to Clyde.

"So why have you told me all this . . . what am I supposed to do with it; the Nzers and the Dark Queen are completely different in the mind and species for that matter! I'm dealing with an alien race that's trying to come to kill the Prince of Sinobu's Universe!" Hikaru stated.

Yes, but do you know where those alien creatures came from?

"All I know is they came from the other universe . . ."

That ship came from the Dark Moon before entering our solar system.

"Isn't that where the Dark Queen's planet was?" Hikaru questioned to see her father nod his head. "Do you think she has something to do with this?"

I can't begin to tell what she is currently doing; all I know is that she is a very deadly person and shouldn't be underestimated . . . trust no one that's new to the city Hikaru! And keep the innocent Hunters under your eyes . . . the Dark Queen feeds off your anger by doing things to the vulnerable!

"'*Things are never as they seem. The world isn't as innocent as we deem, trust only as far as you can dream!*' That's what you always told me before tucking me in at night . . . now I slowly begin to understand!" Hikaru replied gazing at the smoking city.

I wish I could help you Hikaru, but I did all I could to make sure you could get to this point in your life . . . there are evils in this world that I wish weren't . . . but since they are; people like you are born to vanquish them!

Turning away from the burning city, Hikaru gazed at her father as the rosy glow of the flames below shone through her raven hair.

"Daddy, why did you have to leave me?"

I didn't leave you Hikaru . . ." Clyde stated as the city began to diminish back to Hikaru's bedroom. *I've always been with you and still I remain! I love you very much my little growing woman . . . you have made me and your mother so proud!* Clyde stated kissing Hikaru's forehead.

"Aren't you going to tell me how you died?" Hikaru questioned as Clyde began to lift into the sky.

I'm not allowed to tell you anything concerning my death; Hikaru, but you will discover the truth yourself in time! Clyde stated as his hand slipped out of hers.

"Daddy, don't leave me alone again!" Hikaru cried as Clyde started to fade away. "I don't what to be alone!"

You're never alone Hikaru, you have so many people that love you within arms length . . . don't be afraid to reach out to them! Clyde replied with a smile.

Staring at her father as a smile crossed over her face, Hikaru whipped tears from her eyes as she watched her father disappear into the night. Peering around as the city, trees, buildings, and grass reverted back to her room; Hikaru released a small breath when she spied Cleo against the wall. Smiling brightly, Hikaru stared at Cleo as her face was flat against the wall and her body spread across her carpet. Shaking her head, Hikaru walked up and lifted Cleo from the floor.

"What were you doing?" Hikaru giggled at Cleo.

"YOU'RE NOT SUPPOSED TO GO ANYWHERE WITHOUT ME . . . SO WHAT DO YOU THINK I WAS DOING; I ATTEMPTED TO GO AFTER YOU AND I GOT A WALL IN MY FACE!" Cleo whimpered rubbing her paw over her nose.

"Ohhhh, I'm sorry Cleo . . . I promise I won't go anywhere without you anymore!" Hikaru chuckled.

"NOW YOU'RE MOCKING ME! JUST GREAT; NO ONE SHOWS ANY RESPECT TO A TINY BEAR ANYMORE . . . *I HAVE FEELINGS TO YOU KNOW!*" Cleo whimpered with a few snivels.

"Okay, Shhhh . . . I'm sorry, but you need to be quiet before you wake the entire household!" Hikaru smiled.

Whipping her paw across her nose, Cleo snorted her nose, "OKAY!"

Smiling at the tiny, little bear in her hands, Hikaru gazed at her window as the morning sun began to rise.

"Good Morning Cleo . . ." Hikaru smiled setting her on the bed to open her door and walk down the hall.

"OH WONDERFUL, YOU'RE ONE OF THOSE CHEERFUL MORNING PEOPLE THAT EVERY OTHER SENSIBLE PERSON WANTS TO SHOOT!" Cleo chuckled jumping off Hikaru's bed to follow her out into the hall.

Walking into Hagane's room, Hikaru gently shook his shoulder, "Hagane its morning time to wake up!"

"YOU'RE NOT SERIOUSLY GOING TO CONTINUE DOING THIS ARE YOU?" Cleo asked as Hikaru walked out of Hagane's room to head back down the hall.

"Cleo, there's nothing wrong with what I'm doing; I'm simply getting everyone up so we can get the day started!" Hikaru stated walking into Masumi's room. Walking up to her brother's bed, Hikaru slid her hands under the mattress and flipped it over throwing Masumi onto the floor followed by his pillows, sheets, and mattress. "Good morning Masumi!" Hikaru chuckled walking out his door.

"Hikaru . . ."

Chuckling as she walked outside to be followed closely by Cleo, Hikaru gazed up into the sky at the sun as it slowly rose into the sky. Lifting a hand to shield her eyes from the blinding light, Hikaru stared into the sky when a shadow slowly began to creep over the lawn. Gazing down at the shadow, Hikaru stared curiously 'til she raised her eyes to the sky to see the Latrinian **Warship G-731** slowly descended before the sun's bright rays. The radiant smile upon Hikaru's face slowly diminished as she watched the spaceship slowly pass over her house toward The Tower.

"Masumi . . . Hagane!" Hikaru yelled as Cleo cowered at her feet.

Racing onto the porch, Hagane and Masumi stared up into the sky after watching the large shadow to gaze breathless at the spacecraft. Staring at the ship with determined eyes, Hikaru turned toward her brothers as a foggy cloud began to shoot out of the top of the ship. Turning her attention back toward the ship, Hikaru watched the cloud quickly disperse across the sky hiding the sun's light from the city.

Across Town

Sinobu raced out of her house to her white picket fence with Takkun following close behind her to gaze at the large Latrinian warship. Her lavender eyes stared appalled as she watched the bright lights within the ship reflect within the growing shadows as Takkun pretended to shoot his water pistol at the ship.

"My Lord, help us . . ."

* * * * * *

Pushing his large French doors open, Manabu walked out onto his balcony to stare into the expanding cloud as volts of electricity sparked out the back end of the spaceship. Quickly catching his glasses as they fell off his nose, Manabu replaced them and pushed them up to his eyes to gaze at the ship when Maron walked up beside him.

"What is that Manabu?"

"I'm not sure Maron!"

* * * * * *

Falling to his knees as his dog, Riley tripped him racing away from her ball; En gazed up into the sky as Jeremy raced into the yard. Watching the spaceship loom above the tower from across the city; En stood to his feet as Jeremy and Maya walked up to him while Mamoru raced inside with Kaho.

"This is not good!" En stated looking at the others.

"What are we going to do?" Maya questioned looking at both boys.

"We'll see what Hikaru has to say!" Jeremy stated glaring at the ship.

* * * * * *

Racing around the back of the house, Kimiko jumped up onto the jungle gym to stare at the **Warship G-731**. Staring curiously at the ship as Touko yelled at her from the porch, Kimiko fell backward off the jungle gym as several small ships ejected from the bottom of the mother ship.

"Oh crap!" Kimiko mumbled watching the tons of little ships enter the skies. "This is going to be most unpleasant!"

* * * * * *

Jumping over the gate of the fence bordering his house, Kimon grabbed Yuri's arm pulling her from the street as a car slammed into the light pole that was directly behind her. Holding his little sister in his arms, Kimon stared at the ship as people throughout The city started panicking.

"I sense something terrible is about to happen!"

"What do you mean?" Yuri asked pulling on Kimon's shirt.

* * * * * *

Standing in front of the rejuvenated shrine upon her grandfather's plantation, Hikaru stared at the Latrinian **Warship G-731** while her long raven hair swept wildly before her narrowed brown eyes. "They're ready to begin their invasion!" Hikaru stated looking over at Hagane and Masumi as the entire city was veiled in darkness.

39

Earth—Saturday, April 26, 2026

Climbing up the towering stone wall surrounding the Vorin Mansion, Hikaru peeked her eyes over the top to wait for the guard to walk around the other side of the mansion with his dog. Climbing over the wall, Hikaru dropped down into the lush green grass and raced toward Manabu's window. Jumping onto the lattice, Hikaru quickly climbed up to Manabu's balcony when another guard walked around the house. Dropping onto the balcony floor, Hikaru peered over the side at the guard when Manabu opened the French doors.

"It sure took you long enough to get here!" Manabu stated taking her arm to pull her inside his room. "What did you do; stop and have a conversation with the guard at the front gate?"

"No, I had to crawl over the fence and then I had to race across the yard to climb up your lattice before the other guard and his dog spied me!" Hikaru stated breathless.

"Why didn't you just go to the front gate . . . I told them I was expecting someone?" Manabu questioned with a chuckle.

"Why, didn't you tell me that over the phone . . . speaking of which, how did you get my number?"

"I asked the White Guardian at her last visit what your last name was and I looked it up in the phone book . . . did you know that your family is the only Neijos in the city?" Manabu questioned.

"Yes, Manabu I knew that!"

"Good, now did you bring me anything?"

"Yeah," Hikaru stated pulling a tiny cylinder out of her pocket.

Manabu stared at the cylinder before lifting his eyes to look at Hikaru, "What is that . . . I thought you were going to bring me an intact body not a tooth!"

Perching her lips in annoyance, Hikaru looked at Manabu, "Do you have somewhere you were going to put the body?"

"Yes, in that air locked room," Manabu stated pointing toward a door. "But I don't need to air lock a tooth!" Manabu replied following Hikaru.

Opening the door, Hikaru walked into the rectangular room connected to Manabu's bedroom and set the tiny cylinder upon a large examining table. Pulling the blinds over the windows between the bedroom and this room, Hikaru shut the door behind Manabu as he walked up to the table.

"What are you doing?"

Glancing at Manabu, Hikaru walked up to the examining table and taking the cylinder between her fingers twisted it 'til the colors on both ends matched. Replacing the cylinder on the table, Hikaru watched as it quickly expanded into a clear box to drop a large Nzer on the table. Smiling as Manabu dropped back onto the floor, Hikaru chuckled at the astonished expression on his face.

"Wow, I've never seen such I shocked face . . . are you all right Manabu?" Hikaru questioned helping Manabu to his feet.

"Yes, I'm fine . . . is that one of the creatures?"

Holding Manabu's arm, Hikaru looked at the Nzer before turning back to him.

"Yeah, that's one of them . . . do you think you can find anything that may help us?" Hikaru questioned as Manabu raced up to the table.

"Wow, this is amazing . . . it has to be at least thirteen feet tall," Manabu stated running from one end to the other. "Is this the smallest one you've seen?"

"No actually that's one of the average sizes; of what's attacked us!" Hikaru stated as Manabu raced to a table to pull certain scientific equipment out. "If you plan to cut the hide you're going to need something thick and unbreakable!"

Gazing up at Hikaru as he put goggles over his glasses, Manabu's eyes expanded to the point where all you could see was the violet color.

"Why do you say that?"

"Because the only thing that's been able to cut through their skin is Kimiko's burning energy balls," Hikaru smiled leaning against the wall.

Nodding his head, Manabu raced up to the table and carefully laid his utensils onto a tall standing plate. Gazing at the Nzer to his utensils, Manabu looked up at Hikaru and smiled nervously.

"Now you are sure that it is dead?"

"Yeah, Manabu . . . I think Kimiko blasting her hand through it would kill it!"

Quickly nodding his head, Manabu stared back down at the Nzer, "Okay!"

Leisurely dropping his hand onto the Nzer's scaly chest, Manabu cut into its side with a long knife. After several minutes of trying to puncture the flesh, Manabu finally sliced the body open once he laid his weight into the knife. Pulling his head away as the putrid smell of the creature's insides smacked him in the face; Manabu drew closer to the body to start cutting the organs out to examine them.

Standing at the far wall, Hikaru held her hand over her mouth as the smell filled her nostrils. Grimacing at the creature on the table as Manabu quickly pulled its insides out, Hikaru motioned to him that she was leaving before running out the door. Once inside Manabu's room, Hikaru hunched over her knees sucking in deep breathes of the fresh sweet smelling air. Laying her hand over her upset stomach, Hikaru gazed over at Manabu's piano where Maron sat staring at her. Holding her breath as her eyes widened, Hikaru froze in place as Maron sat smiling at her.

"Are you my brother's girlfriend?"

Mouth dropping, Hikaru raised her hands and quickly shook her head, "Ohhhh, no, no, no; you're a funny, little girl . . ." Hikaru chuckled. "No, Manabu and I are just friends!"

"People always say that so they will not feel embarrassed, but you do not need to worry . . . I won't tell anyone!" Maron smiled.

Smiling brightly at Maron, Hikaru walked up and sat beside her on the bench, "does your brother tell you everything?"

"Of course, we keep no secrets from each other!"

"Wow, well soon you'll find reasons to!" Hikaru mumbled shifting her weight. "Well, did he tell you that he is the Hunter of Intelligence?"

"He did not say it in that way, but he told me that he was a follower of a tall beautiful girl with long raven hair!" Maron stated smiling at Hikaru as she looked away from her hair.

"Uh-huh, great well; your brother is in the other room dissecting one of the creatures on that spaceship above the tower, because I need to find some weaknesses so I can whip out the race and bring peace back to the planet!" Hikaru explained quickly.

"What . . ."

"I'm getting good at explaining this!" Hikaru chuckled in a mumble.

* * * * * *

After a few minutes alone with the Nzer, Manabu sat upon a stool inspecting different parts of the body under the microscope. His eyes gazed entranced upon the blood cells as they moved around under the glass sheets lying in the microscope view panel. Removing that plate, Manabu carefully set the skin cells down on the view panel to increase the magnification to get a better look. Sliding off his seat, Manabu pulled off his gloves and walking toward the door strolled into his room to find Hikaru dancing with Maron. Shutting the door behind him, Manabu leaned his hand against his desk and looked at Hikaru as she noticed she was being watched.

Quickly freezing in place and dropping her hands to her sides, Hikaru cleared her throat seriously, "So what did you find?"

Waving his gloves through the air while he pointed at the two, "were you having fun . . . playing with my little sister?"

"Actually yeah, but seriously what did you find out?"

Smiling, Manabu walked toward Hikaru throwing his hands into the air wildly gesturing his excitement, "it is outstanding; they have to be the most interesting creatures I have ever seen . . . I have so much to tell you, but it might be good to have all the Hunters come here to hear it! It may be helpful to say this once." Manabu smiled at Hikaru.

"That sounds like a perfect idea!" Hikaru smiled.

40

&very Hunter sat within Manabu's room while Hikaru held Maron in her lap when Manabu walked in whipping his hands. Dropping the wet towel into a whicker basket, Manabu leaned against his desk and smiled brightly at everyone.

"Hello everyone . . . first I would like to say thank you for coming; second, my name is Manabu Lí . . . most of you do not know me and I you . . . though we do not have the time I wished to properly get to know one another, considering a spacecraft from another universe is less than five miles away," Manabu smiled before growing serious. "We do not have time for formal introductions!"

Setting Maron on the bench, Hikaru stood to her feet and walked up beside Manabu, "we've gathered together guys, because Manabu has found some interesting things dealing with our loveable friends the Nzers . . ."

"That's great . . . what!" Kimiko excitedly questioned.

"Well, when I analyzed the capacity of their hearts I found that they have some enzyme within the tissue caused by a lack of sunlight, suggesting they are cave dwellers or live somewhere it is very dark!"

"We already knew that . . . Hikaru's Guardian Angel told us that!" Maya stated.

"Yes, but because of the extra enzyme within their hearts for the lack of light it causes them to grow very big . . ."

"How big . . ." Jeremy asked Manabu.

"I cannot say how tall, but I say at least close to fifteen feet would possibly be the average! Also since they grow so big, their skin stretches causing a need for more scales to rejuvenate and cover the exposed areas . . . so every time they grow an inch, more scales grow over the others to protect their bodies . . ."

"How does that help us; it only explains why their hide is so thick . . . did you find a way for us to penetrate it?" Masumi questioned.

"Guys calm down," Hikaru stated. "Even if there is no way for us to penetrate their hide we can find ways around it . . . Kimiko can burn through it, she has no problem; Maya only has to punch them to get her hand through their hide; Masumi, you somehow are able to pull the iron from their blood through the hide; Hagane can pierce it easily enough; Jeremy doesn't need to worry about it, all he has to do is throw the Nzers around a little bit to find something to pierce their bodies with; Touko's electrifying abilities splits the hide; I think the only ones who have to worry about it is En and I!" Hikaru stated looking at everyone.

"And even then you may not have to worry . . . with their height and the weight of all the scales and body fat, the creatures would be extremely heavy! They would sink in water, break through anything thin, and other things like that . . . you can find ways to defeat them like Hikaru said! I'm working on creating weakness by finding certain items on Earth that may have a negative effect on them!"

"Could we get acid to throw on their scales?" Kimiko questioned.

"Make it yourself . . ."

"What . . ."

"Hikaru said that you can burn through the hide anyway so you can create some kind of substance strong enough to eat through things just like acid!" Manabu smiled.

"What do we do about the people that can't defend themselves . . . we can't be all over the town at the same time!" Maya asked.

"That's another point I wanted to talk about . . . what if you guys separated into groups and went out across the city that way, if you double up you could cover all four corners of the city and work it that way!" Manabu suggested.

"You've thought a lot about this haven't you?" Masumi questioned.

"He has double your brain power Masumi, of course he's going to come up with brilliant ideas . . ." En chuckled.

"En I will still hurt you!"

"There's a shocker there . . ."

"What if we run into trouble and one of us gets hurt . . . what do we do then?" Maya questioned Manabu as Masumi struggled with En behind her.

"I have that taken care of also . . ." standing up, Manabu pulled eight little COM boxes out of his desk drawer. "After I met Hikaru I figured I could put my brain to work and I built a communication device for us to signal each other with!"

"Wow, you have thought of everything!" Maya giggled while Masumi held En in a headlock behind her.

"First, if you press your thumb against this little gray square it will conform to your fingerprint and automatically open . . . then no other person will ever be able to use the COM box but you! So go ahead and get your COM box to recognize you . . .

Once it opens, you will see several buttons; the red button will bring up a satellite picture of the city you are currently in . . . if you press the red button again it will bring up color markings of all the Devilry Hunters, so you can see where everyone is. To clear the city grid press the red button twice and hold four seconds on the third . . ." Waiting for everyone to try it several times, Manabu started to continue when Touko drew his attention.

"How do we know who's what color?"

"Good question; I forgot to say . . . Hikaru happened to tell me everyone's favorite colors so I marked you all according to your favorite color; Hikaru is light pink, Kimiko is green, Masumi is red, Hagane is brown, Touko is sky blue, Jeremy is lavender, En is orange, Maya is fuchsia; bright pink, and I am yellow! If you can't remember a certain color or it escapes your memory, you can press the yellow button when the grid is up to see a small chart of the colors with the Hunters next to it!"

"How did you make this?" Jeremy questioned playing with his COM box.

"Very easily; next if you are doing undercover work and you need to track someone; you can point the COM box, discreetly, at the target and press the red button; it will mark them with a very bright blinking white light! To use that you will need to use the grid . . .

"Now as for being able to communicate with each other, do you all see the large black button at the bottom of the box . . . I certainly hope so; you use it like a wocky talkie! To choose a person to talk to press one of the miniature colored buttons in the center that coincides with the person. After hitting the miniature colored button matching the certain Hunter; press the large black button to speak to the chosen person and let up to receive messages.

"Also if you missed any messages; press the blue button; it holds every message sent to you with color markings telling you which Hunter it was!"

"You are a genius!" Kimiko chuckled. "I'm going to like this thing!"

"Also this is very important; if your box vibrates it means someone is trying to signal you, so don't ignore it ever! A blinking mark will be a Hunter in distress; to send out a distress call you press the clear white button at the very top of the COM box!

"To quickly locate any Hunter or talk to them press the miniature color necessary and hit the large black button or the red button . . . depending on what you want to do!" Manabu stated when Kimiko called his attention.

"What are these miniature gray buttons for . . . there so many of them?"

"Oh those are for when Hikaru finds more Hunters if she hasn't found them all already . . . I can easily add them to all our COM boxes without making new ones!"

"Wow, you made these cleverly!" Hagane stated.

"Thank you, so does everyone understand?" Manabu questioned while everyone played with their COM boxes.

"I guess so!" Hikaru chuckled looking at Manabu.

41

Hikaru walked home with Kimiko while she played on the COM box sending little messages back and forth with En and Jeremy. "Ya, the streets are bare over on this side of the block to; over . . ." Kimiko playfully transmitted.

Listening to En as he sent over a message, Kimiko and Hikaru smiled at the sound of him playing military boy: "The battalions are closing in on us from the right flank it's a, no wait . . ."

Laughing as En made the sound of a bomb exploding as a dog barked into the COM box, Kimiko smiled brightly while Hikaru shook her head.

"Riley, get off . . . oh, the sky is falling red commander, Ahhhh . . . it was a nuclear bomb!" En faked dying as his dog, Riley barked wildly in the background. "No Riley, get off me . . ." came En's voice over the COM box. "Yeah, well I got to go in now, this is Hunter three signing off, over!" En stated as static filled the COM box.

"Good night En, over . . ." Hikaru and Kimiko called as Kimiko shut off her COM box. "So what you doing the rest of the night . . . you can come over to my house!"

"Thanks Kimiko . . . I don't think I'm; oh my gush!"

"What, what's wrong?" Kimiko questioned as Hikaru gasped.

"Tonight is Yuri's concert . . . Kimon wanted me to go with him to Yuri's concert!" Hikaru cried.

Gasping, Kimiko smiled menacingly at Hikaru, "Kimon asked you on a date . . . oh Hikaru, hurry up and get home; get ready . . . doll yourself up and get a kiss tonight!"

"Kimiko, I'm not going to the concert with the intention of getting a kiss from Kimon!"

"You've thought about it haven't you?"

Biting her lower lip, Hikaru smiled at Kimiko, "yeah, I thought about it!"

"Get your butt home!" Kimiko stated kicking her foot at Hikaru as she ran toward her house.

Racing up the steps to the Neijo plantation, Hikaru hopped over the fence and sprinted across the sidewalk to the front porch. Quickly running inside, Hikaru raced down the hall to her bedroom and racing back out with clothes shut herself in the bathroom.

A few minutes later

As the darkness created by the spaceship made the evening appear to be eerie, the street lamps bordering the streets highlighted the city leaving a gentle feeling throughout the air. The wind lightly blew through the streets, stirring wind chimes from their motionless slumber as Kimon walked up the steps to the Neijo plantation.

The cherry blossoms fell slowly around him as he unlatched the gate and proceeded toward the front door. The black tuxedo fitting perfectly around his frame brought out the bronzed color of his skin. His indigo eyes stared ahead of him patiently when Masumi opened the door.

"Yeah, buddy . . . how you doing? I think Hikaru nearly forgot, because she raced in frantic and plowed through me to get into the bathroom first!" Masumi chuckled.

"I know what you go through . . . Yuri took six hours to get ready for this concert . . . she's doing a duet with a boy before her solo and I think she likes him!"

"Speaking of liking . . . are you ever?" Masumi questioned in a whisper.

"I'm working on it . . . your sister doesn't make it an easy task!"

"Yeah, try living with her!" Masumi replied as Hikaru's bedroom door opened.

Stepping into the hall onto a white pair of slipper shoes, Hikaru walked to the foyer entrance where Masumi stood with Kimon. Dressed in a slender white spaghetti strap dress lying loosely at her knees; Hikaru dropped her hands at her sides as Masumi stared at her with his mouth hanging open. Her long raven hair was wound tightly in a pin at the top of her head with several strands hanging leisurely at the sides of her face.

"What are you staring at?" Hikaru asked Masumi.

"Nothin . . . you look nice!" Masumi stated in a daze.

Closing Masumi's mouth, Kimon walked past him to Hikaru and lifted her hand to kiss it, "you look dazzling!"

Smiling with embarrassment, Hikaru could feel her cheeks start to flush, "thank you Kimon!"

Hooking his arm in hers, Kimon led Hikaru past a dazed Masumi, "I'll have her back no later then eleven!"

"Okay . . . have a good time!" Masumi stated in a dazed voice.

The darkness seemed to separate as Hikaru stared upon Kimon as he led her down the steps to his car. As if in a trance, Hikaru felt herself drawn to him more than ever as he tenderly, yet securely held her hand within his. Never taking her eyes from his as he opened and set her inside his car, Hikaru shook herself to steady her nerves as he drove toward the Concert Hall. Besides the sound of the whipping wind and the hum of the car, the silence between the two was beginning to make Hikaru very uncomfortable.

"Yuri never said it directly, but I knew she wanted you to be there . . ." Kimon finally broke the silence to look over at Hikaru and smile. "She would hint at it, but never asked!"

"Why does she do that . . . she knows I would love to come!"

"My little sister, a bright student but the shyest person in this city . . . she will never ask something of someone!"

"It's not like she asking a favor, it's an invitation to see one of her many talents!"

"That also makes her nervous . . . because she knows if she knows her friends are watching she tries so hard to be another Beethoven!" Kimon smiled as they finally pulled into the concert lot.

"Yuri just needs to learn that being herself is enough for anyone that cares for her!" Hikaru declared.

"Yes, exactly!" Kimon replied looking at Hikaru.

The bright decorative walls of the Concert Hall enchanted Hikaru as Kimon led her through the multitude of people. Carefully surveying every detail of her surroundings, Hikaru soon found everyone they passed was staring at her. Taking Kimon's arm that carefully held her other hand, Hikaru drew his attention.

"Why is everyone staring at me?"

"I never come with anyone but Yuri . . . they're just curious! Or they may be thinking the same thing I am, that you are the most spectacular piece of art throughout the entire hall!" Kimon smiled making Hikaru blush.

42

A bright ray of white light speared through the darkness as Esal landed on top the tower with Gobu. The black ship reflected off Esal's crystal blue eyes as he stared up at the tiny spaceships floating along side the mother ship. Glancing out over the city, Esal released a breath as he saw tiny ships setting on top large buildings throughout the city. Walking to the edge of the platform, Esal pulled his large wings out as Gobu flew up to his face.

"Go find her . . . we don't have anymore time to waste; he's fortifying the city so that no one leaves and nothing comes in! I'm going to inspect those ships at the city's border, we'll meet up later!" Esal commanded before Gobu zipped across the city in search of Hikaru.

Setting eleven rows back, Hikaru watched the elegant performances of both women and men when Yuri came on to do her duet with a skinny boy. Smiling, Hikaru giggled under her breath as she looked at the tuxedo that did a poor job of filling out the boy's body. Proudly watching Yuri as she began to string her bow across the violin resting on her shoulder, Hikaru listened to the tender melody. Gazing down at Kimon's hand as he closed his around hers, Hikaru could feel her heart leap as he looked down into her brown eyes. The elegance captivated within his majestic eyes entranced Hikaru once more as the duet ended. Turning away as he arched toward her, Hikaru stood to her feet to clap for Yuri as she began to feel very nervous. Taking several glances around, Hikaru spied an open window lightly blowing a curtain away from the far wall.

Come on Hikaru, you are trying to find reasons to make yourself panic so you can't enjoy the fact that he keeps trying to kiss you! Hikaru thought when Gobu zipped into the Concert Hall and plowed through a large ice sculpture of a whale.

Gasping, Hikaru brought her hands to her mouth as she sat down with Kimon. Drawing Gobu's attention, Hikaru gazed around the Concert Hall when Yuri started to play her solo.

Floating over to Hikaru, Gobu gurgled his distress, "Hika-pu, Esal-pu zent mesa to find yousa!"

"Why what's wrong . . . no don't tell me the . . ."

Shaking his head quickly, Gobu gurgled, "Uh huh!"

Looking toward the stage as a red marked Nzer crashed through the roof; Hikaru stood to her feet and started pushing people toward the aisle. Upon the stage, the Nzer looked around the hall leisurely inhaling deep breathes while; it watched people dart toward the exits. Tilting its head to the side, the Nzer turned toward Yuri as Hikaru yelled out over the screaming. Whipping around to search the crowd, the Nzer spied Hikaru as she jumped up onto a chair in the center row. Snarling its lips to screech at her, the red marked Nzer leapt down onto people to start jumping upon chairs toward Hikaru.

Quickly turning, Hikaru started bouncing across rows of chairs to the balconies above. Jumping to grip the railing, Hikaru pulled herself into the booth as the Nzer quickly raced up beneath it. Running out the booth door, Hikaru raced down the top hall toward the grand stairwell in the concert's entrance. Jumping onto the stair railing, Hikaru slid down the stairwell to the bottom to jump behind the clergy booth to bump heads with the clergy.

"Girl, go hide somewhere else!"

Smacking her hand over the clergy's mouth, Hikaru hushed him as the Nzer jumped to the bottom of the stairs to race back into the hall. Gazing over the top, Hikaru jumped up onto it and snuck into the hall. Senses straining, Hikaru ducked as the Nzer arm hammered into the door behind Hikaru's head. Diving down the aisle, Hikaru pushed through several people to drop down in the center of the middle row. Releasing a breath when Yuri suddenly screamed, Hikaru peeked over a chair back to see Kimon racing up to the stage where a large Nzer was cornering Yuri. Springing to her feet, Hikaru raced down the aisle toward the stage with the Nzer following a few seconds after her.

Attempting to make his way toward the stage, Kimon tried pushing through people as they raced toward the exit. Turning into a row, Kimon started leaping over rows of seats toward the stage. Bouncing off a seat to pull himself onto the stage, Kimon raced up to his little sister and pulled her away from the leaping Nzer to get slammed into by another Nzer.

Sitting up as Kimon sat upon his arms, Yuri stared horrified as the Nzer dropped over her brother. Inching forward on her hands and knees, Yuri stood to her feet and screamed out to Kimon as the Nzer snapped its fangs in front of his face. The fear in Yuri's emotions erupted when she screamed causing the many stained-glass windows throughout the Concert Hall to shatter. The stage curtain blew into the air reaching toward the ceiling as several seats in the thousands of rows busted out of the seam to flip into the air. A strong gust blew up into the hall knocking over frantic people and Nzers as it wrapped around Yuri.

Staring confusingly at his sister as the Nzer on top of him started creeping toward her, Kimon reached toward a broken piece of the stage. Lifting it off the stage, Kimon hammered the broken wooden pedestal into the Nzer's lower leg. Rolling away from the Nzer, Kimon raced up to Yuri and pulled her toward the stage stairs when the red marked Nzer jumped in front of them. Stepping in front of Yuri, Kimon lifted a metal stage prop and swung it at the Nzer as it approached.

Crawling in through a shattered window at the top of the Concert Hall, a large Nzer hidden by shadows crept over the ceiling rafters until it was sitting directly over the front of the stage. Directing its clear yellow eyes down at Hikaru to Kimon standing before Yuri, the Nzer lifted its snarling lips to flash its razor sharp fangs.

Dodging flying seats, Hikaru made her way through the rows of seats as she watched the Nzers start to surround Kimon and Yuri. Hiking her skirt up, Hikaru leapt up onto the seats back and started jumping over rows. Long strands of Hikaru's raven hair fell down to whip around her body to be followed by the rest as she jumped onto the stage and tackled the Nzer in front of Kimon.

Looking after Hikaru, Kimon spied a second Nzer racing toward them from the side stage. Pushing Yuri down at the last second, Kimon took the full throttle of the blow as he and the Nzer hammered through the stage wall. Sitting up, Yuri whimpered out to Kimon as the red marked Nzer crawled toward her. Staring appalled at the hideousness of the creature, Yuri screamed at it before a gust of wind hammered into it.

Watching the Nzer fly off the stage, Yuri watched black ooze drop down onto the stage in front of her. Dropping her fingers into the black liquid, Yuri gazed at it as she brought it close to her eyes when draperies and flags throughout the Concert Hall began to lift away from the wall once again. Turning her attention to the moving objects, Yuri started curiously when a violet light started to blow around her hands. Lifting her hands before her face, Yuri stood to her feet as the draperies and flags started to pull toward her.

Turning toward several Nzers as they leapt onto the stage, Yuri lifted her arms to shield her eyes unknowingly ripping flags from the wall to wrap around the Nzers. Peeking through her arms as every Nzer that leapt at her got wrapped within a flag or drapery, Yuri stared around the stage to see every creature bound while the Concert Hall started to fill of police officers. Jumping as someone grabbed her arm, Yuri turned around to stare at Kimon as he pulled her into his arms.

Kicking the dead Nzer body off her, Hikaru crawled out of a stage prop and gazed at Kimon and Yuri as police officers raced up to them. Raising her hand to rub her head, Hikaru's long raven hair blew across her face as dust fell from the rafters. Glancing toward the ceiling rafters, Hikaru spied a large Nzer jumping out of a broken window when an officer walked up and gently called to her. Staring at the window as the officer led her toward a paramedic, the sound of screaming people, squad cars sirens, and voices in general drowned out of Hikaru's mind as she released a long breath. Looking to her shoulder, Hikaru wirily smiled as Gobu dropped onto her shoulder.

Sitting outside the Concert Hall on the back of a paramedic van, Hikaru stared at all the reporters as they went around trying to get something from someone. Leisurely blinking her eyes, Hikaru released another long breath as Gobu rubbed his cold body across her achy forehead. Pulling the blanket over her shoulders closer to her body, Hikaru pulled Gobu into her hands and stroked her fingers across his plump little body while she listened to the Concert clergy talk to the reporter.

"Yes, I'm telling those creatures came after me, but I was lucky and got away . . . I think they've come for us all, they must be meat eaters because I saw them cutting into several men's chests!"

Rolling her eyes, Hikaru shook her head in disgust, "when did you see that . . . before you hid behind your desk and left everyone else to die?"

Gazing at Hikaru, the clergy fell silent as the reporters looked from Hikaru back to the clergy with disgust in their eyes. Dropping her microphone, the reporter walked away from the clergy and ran up to Hikaru.

"You're the girl that Mr. Youitan told us saved both his and his sister's life aren't you?"

Swallowing, Hikaru nodded her head as she looked at Gobu, "yes, what do you want . . . something to air for the next hour news?"

"I just have a few questions . . . it won't hurt anything and maybe they will help me help the public!"

Shaking her head, Hikaru glared at the reporter, "You want to help the public . . . stop filming these attacks and starting more panic than there already is!"

"Do you have some harsh feeling you wish to share about these matters?"

"These creatures can smell our fear and you're creating more and more of it . . . if you want to help; stop!" Hikaru stated.

"How do you know what these creatures can or can't do?"

"If you want to know things to help the public, tell them that the creatures don't like water being so tall and heavy they sink in deep water and an important fact is they are drawn to quick movement, so don't run!"

"How could you possibly know that?"

"What does it matter . . ." Esal questioned walking up with his white cape draped around him concealing him. "She gave you something to help, so make yourself helpful and go inform the public!"

After the reporters disappeared, Hikaru turned toward Esal, "What are you doing I thought you wanted to remain anonymous!"

"Yeah, and you weren't supposed to be cornered by reporters or tell them anything, so I had to step in and stop anything else from being told and forfeit my cover!"

"I'm sorry . . ."

Laying his hand on Hikaru's shoulder, Esal pulled her into the security of his arms. "You're OK, Hikaru, you've done nothing wrong!"

A few feet away, Kimon looked up from the paramedic bandaging his arm to look at Yuri as she stood in front of him with trembling eyes. Folded neatly over her chest, Yuri's arms pressed her shoulders to her ears as she looked over at Hikaru to stare at Esal curiously. Relaxing her arms, Yuri gazed at Esal entranced when he looked past Hikaru directly at her. Staring back at Yuri, Esal gazed at her long raven hair and bright indigo eyes when Hikaru called his attention. Gazing away from Esal as Kimon stood to his feet, Yuri took his arm balancing him. Walking toward his car, Yuri took one last glance toward Esal as he walked with Hikaru.

Why does he look familiar? Yuri thought to herself as Kimon drove home.

43

$\mathcal{T}$he darkness radiating from the spacecraft veiled the city as the only Nzer to escape the Concert Hall leapt up the tower. The massive muscles in its legs restricted as it raced up the miles of metal to the platform below the Latrinian **Warship G-731**. Gazing up at the millions of tiny flashing lights below the deck of the spacecraft, the large Nzer crouched down to spring up into the mother ship as it opened an access hole. Quickly racing up to the Control Room, the Nzer swept under the arch leading into the room to drop down before the Mighty One.

"S-sire, the Hunter leader located another one of her pathetic followers-s-s and I regret to inform you that the battalion s-sent to des-story them failed . . ."

Slamming its fist onto the arm of its chair, the Nzer hidden within the shadows of the room hissed angrily to echo throughout the craft. "S-she's-s-ss a tiny little girl half our s-siz-ze; why can my minions-s-s not manage to s-stop one girl?"

"I wis-sh you would allow me to put an end to all this-s-s trouble, S-sir!"

"No Ras-sp, I need you to help me with the more important matters-s-s . . . do you have anything els-se to tell me?"

Standing onto its large thick legs; Rasp extended his talon toward the shadows around the Mighty One. Lying upon the Nzers talons were dried streaks of blood which brought the Mighty One leaning toward the light. Its red eyes widened as is glared at the blood upon Rasp's talons before it hissed out across the craft again.

"Is-s-s that?"

"Yes-s-s, sire, he was-s-s at the place where the girl found the other Hunter . . . he was-s-s protecting the other Hunter who res-sembled one of the princes-s-ses-s-s you've told me about!"

"No doubt it's-s-s he's-s-s vex-xing little s-sis-ster . . . go now and quickly get rid of the one to stand in our way!"

"Of cours-se, s-sire . . . S-sire, what about the girl; do you think s-she will caus-se any problems-s-s?"

"That little wars-sh rat has-s-s already caus-sed me more than enough annoyance-ce . . . whack her around a bit if s-she gets-s-s in the way, but do not kill her! I want that pleas-sure before I finally take my revenge on the princ-ce."

"Very good, s-sire, I will go back to the vermin planet and dis-spos-se of our threat with much joy!" Rasp sneered before disappearing from the control room to once again drop down onto the tower.

"After s-so long of dreaming and waiting for this-s-s moment; it has-s-s finally come within reach of my waiting talons-s-s! The S-Solari will be los-st without their prec-cious-s-s princ-ce and will not be ready for my attack and triumph! Have a pleas-sant res-st of your lives-s-s, both you worthles-s-s vermin and the S-Solari s-scum!"

Earth—Sunday, April 27, 2026

The flames dancing with the hold of the Shrine cast a rosy glow over Esal's white appearance as he stared into the depths of the burning element. His crystal blue eyes captivated the jumping flames as they still held the face of Yuri within their memory. The flashing lights of the squad cars occasional highlights through her long raven hair didn't compare to the bright deepness of Yuri's eyes. Tilting his head back, Esal closed his eyes thinking back to the last time he saw Princess Yurianne when she was dancing in the ballroom. Everything was the same—the innocence on her face, the tanned complexion, the long raven hair, and the bright indigo eyes. Gazing back into the flames, Esal pushed his hood back and turning toward the front of the shrine stepped across the granite stones into Hikaru's yard.

Racing around the front of the house, Hikaru stopped as she finally found Esal walking toward her. Stepping to the side as he walked past her, Hikaru chased after Esal while he approached the front gate. "Esal, I know you're still upset with how careless I was last night, but I have something extremely important to tell you!"

"I don't have time Hikaru . . . I need to find someone quickly!"

"But a giant Nzer escaped last night . . . it was in the rafters and left when the officers came!"

"How is that important?" Esal questioned looking at her. "Hikaru you need to gather your Hunters and start trying to find a way to destroy that mother ship . . . they will use the destructive weapons on her when they find the prince!"

"But I thought we were going to find him first!"

"I'm trying to Hikaru," Esal yelled. "This isn't an easy task!"

"And you think being what I am is . . . constantly being attacked by those creatures; having to try to protect myself never knowing if some kind of power is going to come to me so I'll be able to keep myself from dying! Plus I have the entire city, my friends and their families to consider; I never know if they're being attacked or hurt! You've been gone for I don't know how long and then you finally come back and start getting upset with me . . . all you've had to do is try to find your prince 'cause you've been doing a poor job of protecting me!" Hikaru yelled.

Esal stood before her with a stunned look upon his face when Hikaru realized what she had done. Bringing her hand to her mouth, Hikaru watched Esal start to walk away again before chasing back after him.

"Esal wait, I . . ."

"I didn't intentionally neglect you Hikaru . . . do you think I've been having an enjoyable time coming here to sacrifice myself for your planet! Every time I've been there to help you, I've always put you before my own safety!"

"I know I'm sorry . . . I shouldn't of said that I didn't mean it!"

"Seventy-five percent of what we say is the truth Hikaru . . . you feel like that or you wouldn't have thought it!" Esal stated as his wings expanded.

"Esal please forgive me!" Hikaru yelled as Esal flew into the air. "Ahhhh, what's the matter with me?" Hikaru growled stomping her foot.

Looking after Esal as he flew through the dark skies, Hikaru shook her head in disgust about what she had done. Leaning against the fence, Hikaru stared out over the eerie city when someone touched her arm. Looking to her side, Hikaru stared at Yuri as she stood in front of the gate smiling.

"Yuri . . . what are you doing here?"

"Something's happening to me Hikaru . . . I keep having these nightmares and they started when that ship came here!" Yuri stated pointing toward the Latrinian **Warship G-731**. "Then last night when I started to get scared, I . . . well I did something I can't explain!"

Unlatching the gate, Hikaru took Yuri's arm and pulled her inside the yard, "I can explain it for you . . ." The wind blew gently past Hikaru as she sat Yuri down on the front porch. Whipping her hands down her sides, Hikaru released a long breath before smiling wirily. "This attack has been going on for several weeks; it started the morning before my birthday . . ."

Then all the new memories Hikaru had within her mind unfolded as she retold the tail to Yuri. She recalled the dream where she had seen many dancing shadows and the warning before the first glimpse of the Nzers. Of the rejuvenation of the shrine and her first meeting with Esal, how mysteriously strong he appeared. She told her how she had seen Mrs. Tenko as a completely different person when she first meet her and went on to tell Yuri that Sinobu was actually the first White Guardian. Then she spoke of her first confrontation with the Nzers and how she somehow created acid spheres and killed one. Then she told of Kimiko becoming the Hunter of Energy when she hammered her arm through the Nzer at the school pool. Of En splitting the ground and calling upon the wind to do his biding. How Jeremy could use a source of magic to do whatever he thought. The superhuman strength Maya had enabling her to lift the heavy creatures above her. She spoke of Touko's electrifying debut, where she drew an entire blocks' power to her and pierced it through every Nzer that had come to attack.

And of the intelligence Manabu had enabling him to find weaknesses the Nzers had and making the COM boxes.

"We're called Devilry Hunters and after what happened last night, I would say that you're one to!" Hikaru finished.

Yuri stared at Hikaru for a while before turning away, "For some reason I already knew everything you told me . . ." looking up into Hikaru's face, Yuri quickly assured, "I don't know how I know these things but there's so much more . . . like your White Guardian, I swear I've seen him somewhere before . . . but I don't now where!"

"What do you mean?" Hikaru questioned.

"I recognize him from somewhere . . . and I keep seeing this large castle with porcelain walls and vibrant parties with exquisite gowns dancing across a floor that looks almost like a river!"

"That's how Esal described the royal palace of Latira!"

"How could I know what that looks like . . . and since the concert last night I keep seeing these horrible images, I am so scared that I'll see them again in my dreams I haven't falling asleep for several days!"

"It's all right, Yuri, but if I'm going to help you I need you to tell me these dreams!" Hikaru assured patting Yuri's hand.

Shaking her head, Yuri released a tiny breath and proceeded to tell Hikaru what she was seeing. "I see many different images, but they are never complete or in order! I'll see a tall man sitting on a beautiful throne, then I see the same man fighting in a war, but then I see him inside the palace again talking to I'm guessing an aid . . ."

Hikaru listened patiently to Yuri as she told her many different images from her dreams when she started to become confused. Tilting her head in frustrated annoyance, Hikaru continued to listen 'til Yuri finished. Looking out over the darkness veiling the city, Hikaru shook her head as she gazed back at Yuri.

"I don't know what to say . . . none of this makes sense! Maybe if you tell Esal he can explain some of it . . . after all he lives in the other universe, he may know!"

"Wait Hikaru, I don't think I can!" Yuri stated as she jumped off the porch.

Turning to look back at Yuri, Hikaru shrugged her shoulders, "Why not?"

"Because for some reason I feel drawn to him and I know I won't be able to say anything!" Yuri embarrassingly stated.

Looking at Yuri puzzled, Hikaru shook her head, "but you've never . . ." tilting her head, Hikaru dropped her mouth open as she realized, "met him!"

"Hikaru I just told you that . . ." Yuri stated walking down the steps.

"I know but if you've never met him how can you recognize him or feel . . . like I do around Kimon!"

"Hikaru what are you talking about?" Yuri questioned as she watched Hikaru start to pace back and forth across the lawn.

"You said that you've been having nightmares since the spacecraft came to Earth, well what if they aren't nightmares . . . what if they're visions of things that are going to happen!" Hikaru thought stopping in the middle of sidewalk.

"Visions . . ." Yuri questioned.

"No they can't be visions, because you told me you say a tall man inside the Latrinian palace . . . Yuri do you remember what the man looked like?"

"He looked like . . ." gazing at Hikaru, Yuri softly stated, "now that I think about it, the man looked a lot like my brother! He had black hair and bright indigo eyes; he wore a purple tunic and red cape with a golden band above his eyes."

"I think that's supposed to be the prince, but that would make the visions you're having really memories!"

"How can I be having these memories Hikaru?" Yuri questioned as Hikaru paced before her.

"I don't know," Hikaru pondered when she stopped pacing, "unless they're someone else's memories . . . Yuri who have you been around lately?"

"Since the spacecraft came . . . only my brother, you, and the boy at my concert!"

Standing with her hands on her hips, Hikaru gazed at the ground to stare up at Yuri with wide eyes. Raising her hands to comb them roughly through her hair, Hikaru yelled out in frustration as Yuri raced up to her.

"Hikaru what are you doing?"

"It's beginning to make sense, why you're having these memories and mental powers!"

"It is . . ." Yuri questioned looking at Hikaru questioningly.

"Yeah, it's your brother Yuri . . . and that's why you're having these dreadful dreams because like your brother you were there to!"

"Hikaru you aren't making a littlest bit of sense, now would you please explain to me what you're rambling on about!" Yuri stated placing her hands on her hips.

"Yuri I don't have time to explain . . . you need to tell me where your brother is!"

"He's at the park with the injured children from the hospital; he takes them every Sunday afternoon, why?" Yuri questioned as Hikaru turned to race toward the gate.

"Because I need to talk to him; it's urgent!" Hikaru yelled opening the gate.

"Hikaru . . . wait for me!" Yuri yelled chasing after her.

44

The streetlamps lit up the park as Kimon helped several nurses set up lights around the playground while the children eagerly waited in the hospital van. The bright smiles upon their faces reached past their ears while they bounced excitedly in their seats as Kimon finally approached the van. Cheering happily as Kimon opened the van door, they grew quiet as he put his finger to his lips. Smiling brightly at all the joyous faces before him, Kimon leaned down 'til he was eyelevel with all the children. Perching his lips, Kimon gazed seriously at every last child when he straightened back up and hooked up the ramp to the van.

"Now before I let you off this van what did we agree to?" Kimon questioned turning back to the children.

"No wondering off and stay where we can be seen!" All the children stated.

"Very good," Kimon smiled before stepping into the van to carefully bring a wheelchair down to the park path. "Now, go play nicely!" Kimon stated turning back toward the van.

Delightfully filing out of the van, the children slowly ran across the park to the playground as Kimon quickly pushed the child in the wheel chair around the path. The sound of the children's laughter brought joy to the heavy hearts of the nurses that carefully watched each child. The fear of the spacecraft's appearance to take over the world was bringing the ladies spirits down and Kimon could see it, which is why he made sure that they didn't cancel this trip.

The wind gently blew through the dim lights from the many lamps across the park when Hikaru raced up to the street entrance leading to the park. Racing by the park gates, Hikaru moved along the path to stop at the next bend to stare at all the children from the hospital happily playing. Walking down the path, Hikaru looked around the children and nurses for Kimon when Yuri grabbed her arm.

"Hikaru Neijo what are you doing?" Yuri angrily questioned.

"What's the matter with you; I'm looking for your brother!"

"Hikaru, you can't be here when the hospital children are here playing!"

"Yes, I can; they don't own it . . . and besides, if I'm right, which I think I am, they will be glad that we are here!"

"We . . . Hikaru what do you think you're going to do?" Yuri questioned grabbing her arm.

"All right, you know what I'm getting sick of you grabbing me!" Hikaru stated pulling out of Yuri's hand. "I'm in charge!"

"What are you doing here?"

Quickly turning around, Hikaru looked up into Kimon's stern face. Looking past his upset face, Hikaru looked at the tiny boy with an arm sling before smiling at Kimon. "I came to see you!"

"You need to leave Hikaru; you're not supposed to be here!" Kimon stated turning to walk back toward the playground.

Staring stunned after Kimon, Hikaru started to follow him when a nurse pushed her back. "Miss, you need to leave!"

"What are you the park police . . . this is a public place I can stay if I want!" Hikaru stated gazing back at Kimon. "Kimon are you upset with me about something and as a result you're giving me the cold shoulder?"

"You disappeared at the concert last night Hikaru . . . you think I'm not going to be upset about that?"

"I disappeared . . . I was there the whole time!" Hikaru stated.

"Then explain the man you left with?" Yuri stated looking at Hikaru.

"What is this gang up on Hikaru day . . . he's a friend of mine; he took me home!"

"You didn't come with him!" Kimon replied.

"Is that what this is about . . . gosh, I'm sorry Kimon, I didn't think it was going to be a big deal . . . Yuri had a rough night and I thought she came before anyone else!" Hikaru stated with a frustrated look crossing over her face.

Kimon gazed at Hikaru for a while before turning to walk back toward the playground, "Hikaru go home!"

Staring at Kimon as her anger rose to its peak; Hikaru snarled up her nose and released a long breath.

"Do you know about the dreams Yuri's having?"

"Yes, Hikaru I know, now go home!"

Pushing the nurse off her, Hikaru placed her hands on her hips, "Yeah well, did you know they are the same dreams you're having!"

Stopping to look back at Hikaru, Kimon stared at her serious face before turning toward Yuri.

Gazing at Kimon, Yuri dropped her mouth open, "You're having dreams to?"

Hikaru gazed seriously at Kimon, "you've been having these dreams since the spacecraft arrived haven't you?"

Setting the little boy down, Kimon pushed him toward the playground before walking up to Hikaru, "how did you know that?"

216

"I know more than you think . . . I know that since Yuri is so close to you, she's seeing the dreams you're having at the same time. Yuri has a mental control over everything; she can read someone's thoughts or their memories!"

"But these aren't memories!" Kimon replied.

"Yes, they are . . . of a past life you had! Kimon you are the ruling prince of another universe!" Hikaru stated.

Kimon gazed at Hikaru like she was a lunatic, "Hikaru are you feeling well, because Nurse Patterson can look at you!"

"Kimon, listen to me!" Hikaru yelled grabbing his hand, "I know this is beyond reason, but believe me when I tell you that the creatures have come to Earth to kill you! They remember you as you once were and will not wait for you to regain that memory, because you're the person that destroyed them the first time!"

"If I destroyed them Hikaru, how are they still alive?" Kimon questioned.

"One was left alive . . . but Esal hasn't discovered how the others are drawing breath!" Hikaru stated as several lights on the eastside of the park went out. Gazing past Kimon, Hikaru stared at the darkness as it reached up to the lamps and retracted the light. Looking around at all the children, Hikaru grabbed the nurse's arm and pulled her toward a child. "You need to get all the children back into the van quickly!"

"Why what's going on?" The nurse questioned as another red marked Nzer leapt out of the darkness and charged toward the playground. "Oh my god, we're all going to die!"

"Nurse, get the children in the van!" Hikaru yelled pushing her toward the child before running toward the border of the playground.

45

Racing across the sawdust chips, Hikaru sprinted up to a child playing in the sandbox and pulling him to his feet pushed him toward the van. Gazing toward the Nzer, Hikaru saw it quickly racing up to the little boy in an arm sling she had seen earlier. Jumping out of the sandbox, Hikaru raced up to the boy and moving in front of him stared angrily at the Nzer. Pushing the child in the wheelchair into the van, Kimon turned around as Hikaru moved in front of the leaping Nzer. Jumping off the van, Kimon charged toward Hikaru screaming out her name.

Gazing sternly at the Nzer; Hikaru shut her eyes while her nose wrinkled as her hair slowly lifted off her back. Racing her hands out to her sides, Hikaru's hair flared out into the air as the Nzer slammed into an invisible barrier. Opening her eyes, a strong currant blew past Hikaru's frame to hammer into the Nzer casting back onto the ground. Glancing back to the front of the park, Hikaru smiled brightly at her seven Hunters.

Blowing roughly around his annoyance filled brown eyes; the short brown strands of hair whipped wildly around En's face as he stood in front of the other Hunters. Closing his eyes, En released a heavy breath as he lifted his arms above his head. A strong breeze lifted up along his body to push away from his hands toward the Nzer as it stood back up to hammer into its head snapping it back. Swaying as his eyes reopened, En stared at the Nzer at it lay dead on the park floor.

Smiling as a mischievous expression burned through her emerald eyes, Kimiko threw her arms out to her sides igniting the energy to turn around and spear her arm through a leaping Nzer. Growling as the Nzer dropped to her feet, Kimiko's eyes widened as she stared at all the Nzers racing out of the shadows.

"Set up a perimeter!" Hikaru yelled up to her Hunters.

Lifting his hand to freeze the leaping Nzers, Jeremy allowed his friends to position themselves around the playground before throwing the Nzers backward. Moving his long blond bangs from his eyes, Jeremy released a nervous sigh as an army of Nzers raced toward them.

"What's going on Hikaru?" Maya yelled slamming her fist through a red marked Nzer's hide.

"They know who the prince is!" Hikaru yelled holding her barrier in front of Kimiko as she blasted her energy ball into several Nzers.

"What are we going to do?" Masumi questioned.

"There's too many Nzers, Hikaru . . . more and more keep coming; we're not going to be able to hold them off for long!" Touko screamed sparking her volts of electricity through the park highlighting it as they speared through Nzers.

"What ever we do we can't leave Kimon!" Hikaru stated.

"Why?" Kimiko yelled questioningly as hundreds of Nzers slammed into the barriers.

"Guys I can't hold this forever!" Hikaru stated.

"Me neither . . ." Jeremy declared.

With Jeremy's help, Hikaru struggled to hold the hundreds of Nzers back as they hammered into the barrier while the rest of the Hunters killed the Nzers in the front the line. Digging her heels into the dirt as she slid back across the ground, Hikaru looked up into the sky to see a bright white light spear through the darkness above and hammer into the ground to sweep throughout the park disintegrating every Nzer within a thirty mile radius. Falling back from the force of the blow, Hikaru and her friends sat up to watch the Nzers glowing bodies explode into a million flashing lights before fading away.

A bright white light dispersed through the clouds above causing onlookers to shield their night worn eyes. As if descending from the golden gates of heaven cotton feathers began to leisurely fall around the park when a sweet scent of rivers and blossoming flowers blew through the wind. Zipping around Esal's crystal wings, Gobu shot down to circle around Hikaru before grabbing the bottom of her skirt and yanking it forward with him as he attempted to stop.

Pushing her skirt down as it started to fly above her thighs, Hikaru took hold of Gobu's tail and pulling him in front of her face glared at the humongous upside down smile. Shaking her head, Hikaru smiled as she looked toward the sky to see Esal floating down from the dark clouds to land on the ground.

The crystalline sword cast a prism glow throughout the park as the glow from his body reflected off it. Opening his crystal blue eyes; Esal gazed past his sword held in front of his face and looked individually upon everyone standing staring at him when his eyes befell Kimon. Lowering his sword, Esal strolled across the grass and stepping over the wooden boards surrounding the playground walked up to Hikaru. Dropping his hand on Hikaru's head, Esal laid his head against hers and quietly whispered.

"You've done well; just as I knew you would!"

A bright smile crossed over Hikaru's face, "Then you aren't mad at me anymore?"

Tilting his head, a smirk crossed over his face, "Hikaru."

Shaking her head, Hikaru released an embarrassed sigh, "you did all that on purpose didn't you?"

"Of course I did, I needed to see if you were going to be able to rely on yourself through anything!"

"Why?" Hikaru questioned as Esal pulled his head off hers.

"To give you confidence in yourself."

Taking Hikaru's hand, Esal pulled back her sleeve and gently kissed it. Stepping back, Esal bowed to her with a tiny smile crossing his lips.

"You're teasing me now," Hikaru chuckled.

Straightening his body, Esal nodded his head before turning toward Kimon. Lifting his sword from the grass, Esal walked toward Kimon and Yuri to drop to his right knee in front of them. Slicing his sword through the ground, Esal bowed his head causing it to touch the hilt of the blade.

"My prince; I have traveled many light years to offer my sword to your hands. I wish to fight alongside you once again and restore peace to the Universes!"

Kimon gazed at Esal puzzled when he looked at Hikaru, "there's been a mistake . . . you have the wrong guy, I'm not a prince of another universe!"

Pulling his sword from the ground as he stood to his feet, Esal laid the tip to the ground and pushed Kimon's shirt down to look above the left side of his chest. Moving the white fabric, Esal stared at the entwined crescent moons and the star to the side.

"You bear the royal mark of the Latrinian prince."

"That's impossible . . . I can't be a prince!"

Shaking her head, Hikaru looked at Esal, "isn't there someway you can help him remember?"

Looking up at Kimon, Esal stated, "No, the memories of a royal child must come back to the individual on their own will . . ."

Looking toward the Latrinian **Warship G-731**, Maya softly stated, "Uh, guys . . . the ship's doing something!"

Turning toward the tower, Esal and the Hunters stared at the **Warship G-731** as a translucent light surrounded the entire whole. Gazing in disbelief, the onlookers watched as the **Warship G-731** lowered a large needle down toward the tower.

"What is that?" Kimiko questioned taking a step toward the tower.

Staring at the large needle descending toward the city, Esal unhooked his long white cloak and walked out in front of the Hunters. Removing the white glove from his left hand, Esal lifted his sword and sliced it across his palm 'til blood streamed from the cut. Clinching his fist so that his blood streamed off his hand to dribble onto the ground; a bright blue aura surrounded Esal's body as the wind lifted his hair off his neck.

Up in the Warship G-731

Staring down at Earth from above the tower; the Mighty One clinched his large hand as it hissed out the command, *"Fire!"*

Watching the needle suddenly engulfed by swarms of violet energy, Yuri screamed out as the **Warship G-731** shot a ray toward Earth. Upon hearing Yuri scream, Esal opened his crystal blue eyes and raising his crystalline blade into the air shot a white light out to meet the Latrinian missile. Piercing his crystalline blade through the ground, Esal dropped to his knee as he dispersed a translucent barrier around himself, his prince, and the hunters.

Watching the two lights collide with one another, Kimon shielded his eyes as a plasma cloud shot throughout the park into the city dismantling everything it touched. Falling backward with his sister as the cloud slammed forcefully into Esal's barrier, Kimon suddenly felt as if he had been struck by lightning. Lights flashed around him sweeping the universe back thousands of years through space and time until Kimon saw the bright glowing rays of Earth's sun surpassed by the dim fluorescent glow of three other moons. The air felt easier to breathe while; long grass swayed gently amid the grasping wind that breezed along a wide piercing blue river that stretched out toward a large towering castle surrounded by the cotton candy clouds.

Standing to his feet to peer around the kingdom of Latira, his home, Kimon slowly began to relive his past life as the prince of a conflicting universe and the war that had taken place nearly twenty-eight millenniums ago . . .

46

It was a cold morning when the wind slowly pushed the balcony door open to breeze through the prince's bedroom. The morning's first light had yet to rise and the young thirteen-year-old prince sat at his desk with his head dropped in his hands. The wiry look upon his face indicated that he hadn't slept the previous night from his unending worrying thoughts. Then as the first drop of light peeked across the porcelain tile floors toward the maroon velvet carpet, Prince Kimiochen lifted his head from his hands to stare at his balcony window as a distant roar trailed up to his ears.

Gazing curiously at the window, Prince Kimiochen rose to his feet and strolled toward the blowing glass door. The light violet tunic draping on his shoulders dropped down to his knees covering the cream shirt lying over his bronzed skin. The white sash wrapped around his small waist dangled behind his back as the small ray of light slowly stretched over his gray boots. His short raven hair fell loosely upon his neck over the white collar of his light violet tunic. The long raven bangs draping over his bright indigo eyes blew slowly uncovering the golden band wrapped around his forehead.

Stepping up to the glass door, Prince Kimiochen wrapped his fingers around the handle and pushing it open walked slowly out onto the balcony. Stepping out to the railing, the young prince gazed out at his slumbering kingdom with tired eyes when a loud hum caught his attention. Staring out toward the rising blue sun, the young prince gazed at a fiery arrow that was quickly descending toward him. Gazing curiously at the arrow, Prince Kimiochen stepped back once he realized what it was and jumped back into this room as the missile exploded on his balcony.

The entire castle shook as the missile blew up on the young, prince's bedroom balcony. The wall to the outside of the palace crumbled into rubble as it fell to the castle courtyard with the entire balcony. Large pieces of debris shot through the prince's bedroom to hammer into the walls and other furniture. Smoke dispersed into the bedroom as fire radiated across the side of the palace when the Holy Priest raced into the chamber. Lifting his staff into the spreading smoke, the giant orb sparkled blindingly as it pushed the suffocating air outside the chamber.

Racing into the royal chamber, the White Guardian watched the Holy Priest lift large pieces of debris from the large hole in the wall to cast them outside to the courtyard below. Running up to the Holy Priest, the White Guardian extended her hand toward a large pile and released a short breath. Staring sternly at the pile of debris, the White Guardian's long white lavender hair lifted away from her shoulders as a blue aura surrounded her body. Her lavender eyes grew cross when the debris rose into the air and floated toward the hole where the White Guardian released her hold.

"I found him!" the Holy Priest yelled.

Jumping over pieces of debris, the White Guardian raced up to the Holy Priest and lifted the large pile of debris off the young prince. Casting the pile out the hole as the Holy Priest gently lifted the unconscious prince into his arms, the White Guardian quickly followed him toward the prince's bed. Laying the prince on the bed, the Holy Priest worriedly gazed at him as he searched his neck for a pulse. Releasing a breath once he found a steady beat radiating from the young prince, the Holy Priest looked toward the door. Turning around, the White Guardian looked at the prince's tiny little sister; Yurianne, standing in the doorway holding her hand over her mouth. Trotting toward the doorway, the White Guardian lifted the tiny princess into her strong arms and walked into the hall assuring her that her brother has all right.

The Holy Priest whipped the dried blood and dirt from the young prince's face as he wheezed in his unconscious slumber. His innocent bronzed face lay against the feathered pillow as the White Guardian threw the rest of the debris through the hole. Sitting on the edge of the bed, the Holy Priest gazed at the young face before him when he turned toward the White Guardian as she patched the wall. Standing to his feet, the Holy Priest walked toward the White Guardian as she replaced the balcony on the newly repaired wall.

"We need to find who ordered this attack!"

"There's no need for that . . ."

Looking toward the chamber doorway, the Holy Priest and the White Guardian stared at Doc as he pointed toward the southeast window.

"Take a look outside!" Doc wirily breathed.

Turning away from Doc, the Holy Priest and the White Guardian walked up to the large window stretching from the floor to the ceiling. Pulling the dark violet curtains away; the Holy Priest and the White Guardian gazed out toward Latira's southeast valley to see it covered in darkness. Standing in large sectors of two hundred, the Under Dwellers of Latira's catacombs towered over the lush green valley. Their large bodies where covered in a mossy coating as they stood before the castle walls growling war cries to the guards standing on the wall.

"They wish to talk to the person in charge . . ." Doc stated.

"Do they now, those doubtless . . ." turning toward the Priest the White Guardian stated, "They must think that they've killed the young prince!"

"Should we allow them to continue to think that?" the Holy Priest questioned looking toward the prince.

"I don't know . . . I would like to know what they think they're doing though!"

47

*D*rops of the nightlights of the blue sun cast a dull color across Latira as the Under Dwellers continued to roar and bellow at the castle walls. The sweet fragrance of Lillian flowers and Rose Blossoms blowing along the wind had yet to improve the foul smell of the Under Dwellers' putrid hides. Floating above the kingdom of Latira, the candy clouds leisurely let their tears fall upon the massive army of Under Dwellers when the castle gate opened.

The large thick wooden door slowly restricted as the drawbridge lowered over the moat allowing four magnificent purebred horses to cross over to the southeastern valley. Pushing through his fellow comrades, a large Nzer with a blue frill extending down its back walked to the front of the barracks as the Latrinians approached. His clear yellow eyes glared at the Latrinians with a smug smirk on his face as they stopped ten feet away. Watching them dismount from their horses, the Under Dwellers smug smile disappeared as he saw the young prince emerge before the Holy Priest and White Guardian. Staring stunned at him as he walked up with the Holy Priest close to his side and the White Guardian a few steps behind, the Nzer snorted a long breath from his nostrils.

Cautiously approaching the giant creature before him, Prince Kimiochen stopped three feet away from the mound the Nzer was standing. His bright indigo eyes gazed upon the creature valiantly with contempt for its actions that could possibly lead to a revolution. The golden band lying beneath his raven bangs reflected the glow of the blue sun as Prince Kimiochen laid his hand upon the hilt of his sword. His indigo eyes trailed away from the Nzer to overlook the large treacherous army that had gathered before his peaceful kingdom.

Catching wind of the young prince's growing fear, the large Nzer curled its long talons against its scales upon its chest. Shifting its weight to rouse the young prince's uncomfortable state, the large Nzer snarled its white fangs as it snapped them together.

"I as-sked for the pers-son in charge, not a s-sniveling weakling proclaimed to be the ruling princ-ce!" the Nzer disrespectfully spat.

"Hold your tongue you worthless piece of creation," the White Guardian yelled back to be silenced by the prince.

"I am the man in charge Under Dweller; state your business and leave!"

Chuckling as Prince Kimiochen finished, the Nzer arched toward him, "S-see here little princ-ce . . . my bus-siness-s-s is-s-s s-simple, I don't believe you are worthy to govern over this-s-s planet! S-so we've come to forc-ce you to hand over your birthright and no harm will come of the innoc-cenc-ce you claim to be in charge of."

Prince Kimiochen stared at the Nzer before smirking as he slowly shook his head in disgust. Reopening his indigo eyes, Prince Kimiochen gazed at the Nzer with an annoyed expression upon his face. "You think that I am unworthy . . . well, what makes you think that you are better fit for this title . . . tell me what you have done in your lifetime, Under Dweller; to qualify you for the honor of this title . . . because I cannot think of the answer!"

"We are s-stronger . . ."

"Oh, you're stronger . . . is that why the first Under Dweller came to this planet begging for a home, somewhere to call its own so it could feed itself and its possible offspring? Or is it that you have thought you shouldn't have to take orders from a weaker species that allowed you to make a home here or are you just power hungry?"

Leaning closer toward the young prince, the Nzer hissed its forked tongue out at his face, "you s-speak big for s-such a s-small pers-son!"

"It's my duty to do so to whoever decides that they should rule in my stead . . . and know this, Under Dweller; I will not hand over my birthright to such an alienating species . . . I owe my people that much not to leave them with a creature that looks to his own comfort but not to his subjects!"

"What is-s-s your meaning, young vermin princ-ce?"

"You are doing this for yourself, Under Dweller; you didn't stop to think what your companions wanted . . . you shame your ancestor!" Prince Kimiochen declared.

Glaring vengefully at the young prince, the large Nzer leapt from its mound and extended it thick talons toward the prince's face. It's clear yellow eyes were filled with merciless hatred as it descended through the air toward the prince. Raising his arm to shield himself from the Nzer, a translucent violet aura burst out of Prince Kimiochen's body to hammer into the Nzer's face casting it backward to land in between its barracks. Lowering his arm to gaze past the large rainbow orb on his glove, Prince Kimiochen stared at the tiny hole in the barrack where the Nzer had landed. He watched the Under Dwellers surrounding the hole lifting the Nzer up while; others gazed angrily at the prince and started snapping their fangs together.

Releasing a chuckle, the White Guardian watched the Nzer push its companions away to fall back down into the tiny hole while the Holy Priest quickly took the prince's arm. Turning to follow the Holy Priest the White Guardian pushed the old Captain of the Guard toward his horse as several Under Dwellers charged after them on command from the blue frilled Nzer. Swinging up into his saddle, Prince Kimiochen watched the Under Dwellers approaching when the Holy Priest moved in front of his sight urging him to get inside the castle courtyard.

Turning his muscular white stallion toward the castle gate; Prince Kimiochen quickly charged across the lush green valley with the Holy Priest along his side. Quickly mounting her horse, the White Guardian rode toward the slow moving Captain of the Guard and gripping his shirt pulled him onto her lap as an angry Nzer leapt for him. Whistling to the other steed, the White Guardian raced after the Holy Priest as Prince Kimiochen's stallion galloped across the drawbridge into the courtyard. Turning around in his saddle, Prince Kimiochen gazed up to the gate keeper as the Holy Priest and the White Guardian crossed beneath the courtyard wall's gate.

"Close the gate!"

Taking hold of the handle connected to the gate crane, the gatekeeper turned the wheel counterclockwise pulling the gate against the castle barricade as the Under Dwellers raced onto the drawbridge. Peering over the stone rail, the gatekeeper stared terrified at the Under Dwellers as they started hammering into the gateway. Turning away as one of the Under Dwellers gazed up at him with its fangs snarling, the gatekeeper raced to the courtyard railing and gazed down at Prince Kimiochen.

"Sire, the creatures are trying to come through the gate!"

Gazing at the pulsing door, Prince Kimiochen turned toward the castle keep, "Archers to your posts!"

Drawing their bows, guards standing upon the castle wall fitted their arrows and released them to watch disappointedly as the arrows deflected off the Under Dwellers hides. Firing continually, the guards released arrow after arrow but couldn't manage to pierce the Under Dwellers' thick hides.

"Sire, we can't pierce the hides; our arrows slid straight over their scales!"

"Aim for the frill at the Under Dwellers' necks!"

Gazing down at the Under Dwellers as they hammered into the wooden gate while another started to climb up the stone wall; a young guard drew an arrow close to his chin and aiming for the frill at the top of the Nzer's neck, released. Lowering his bow, the guard watched the arrow zip down to the Nzer crawling up the wall to spear through the frill. Smiling brightly as he watched the Nzer drop off the wall screaming angrily, the young guard fit a second arrow to his bow and pulling it toward his chin, released it to spear through the second Nzer's frill.

"Sire, it's working," the young guard yelled.

"Excellent," Prince Kimiochen yelled as he turned toward the gatekeeper, "gatekeeper, raise the drawbridge!"

"But, Sire; the Under Dwellers are standing on it!"

"I said raise the drawbridge!" Prince Kimiochen bellowed restating his orders.

"Yes, sire," the gatekeeper stated pulling on the crane.

Watching on the courtyard wall, the young guard stared down at the Under Dwellers as the drawbridge slowly started rising preventing another Nzer from coming close to the castle gateway. He watched confused while the Under Dwellers standing on the drawbridge frantically raced around as they quickly realized they had no chance of escaping. Then to his amazement, the young guard watched as the Under Dwellers jumped from the drawbridge trying to land on the bank of the moat to land in the water where they disappeared from his site.

"Sire, they're gone!"

Gazing up at the young guard, Prince Kimiochen pulled his horse toward the castle entrance, "Did they land in the moat?"

"Yes, sire . . . but where did they go; is there a waterway entrance?"

"No, the Under Dwellers are too heavy; they sink in deep water and drown in about six seconds!" Prince Kimiochen stated demounting from his horse.

Trotting up the steps to the palace, Prince Kimiochen pushed open the large ceramic doors and smiled brightly as his little sister raced toward him. Taking hold of her, Prince Kimiochen lifted her into his arms and walked with the Holy Priest toward the throne room. Shutting the doors behind him, the Holy Priest walked up to the prince as he stared out the window with Princess Yurianne in his arms.

"What am I going to do, Priest? I just started a war!" Prince Kimiochen sadly stated wrapping his arms tightly around Yurianne's legs.

"You've done nothing wrong, young prince . . . you were right to refuse that creatures demands!"

"Yes, but maybe I should've tried something other than what I did!"

"Prince Kimiochen, you are the Ruler of this Planet and Keeper of the Solari; everything you did had justification! Do not be ashamed of the way things turned out . . . that Under Dweller wouldn't have settled for anything other than your title!" The Holy Priest declared.

The young innocence upon Prince Kimiochen's face reflected off the large window he stared out of across the valley where the Under Dwellers were angrily bellowing up at the castle walls. Lowering his head, Prince Kimiochen turned toward the Holy Priest and released a heavy sigh. "I'm afraid of what's going to happen, Priest; I don't want to see Latira plagued by a long unending war!"

48

Three years later

The wiry expression upon the face of sixteen-year-old Prince Kimiochen was concealed by the anger he felt as he nearly dragged his Captain of the Guard across the drawbridge. The weight of the older man pulled Prince Kimiochen closer to the ground as he tightened his grip around the Captain's arm hanging over the prince's shoulder. Pushing the Captain onto his feet before he got them both killed, Prince Kimiochen fell against the drawbridge as a large Nzer leapt over their heads. Staring at the Nzer as it stumbled onto its feet, Prince Kimiochen pushed the Captain off his shoulder as he staggered to his feet.

Avoiding the first swinging talons, Prince Kimiochen unsheathed his silver blade and severed it through the Under Dwellers neck cutting its head clean off its body. Watching the head roll across the drawbridge, Prince Kimiochen gazed up at a dozen fast approaching Under Dwellers. Sheathing his sword, Prince Kimiochen raced up to the Captain of the Guard and grabbing his arms started pulling him toward the gate. Dropping the Captain's arms, the prince turned toward the castle wall and yelled up to the guard at the top of the wall.

"Shut the gate and get a rope!"

Dropping onto the drawbridge, Prince Kimiochen kicked the captain toward the edge of the bridge and jumped to his feet avoiding a leaping Nzer. Racing up to the Captain, Prince Kimiochen jumped onto his plump body knocking both himself and the Captain into the moat as a large Nzer hammered across the drawbridge following them into the water. Submerging over the water's edge, Prince Kimiochen grabbed the Captain's shirt before he sank into the moat.

Halfway drowning as he pulled the Captain through the water, Prince Kimiochen swam toward the castle wall when a rope dropped down on his head. Quickly grabbing the rope as another Nzer leapt toward them, Prince Kimiochen scowled as it came down onto them right as he and the Captain rose out of the water. Gazing toward the castle wall, Prince Kimiochen looked back at the Under Dwellers upon the drawbridge as they leapt toward him. Lifting his legs avoiding the extended talons, Prince Kimiochen's arms trembled as he tightly gripped the wet shirt of the plump Captain.

Growling as he started losing grip on the Captain's shirt, Prince Kimiochen felt many hands grab hold of him and hoist him over the railing. Releasing the captain, Prince Kimiochen dropped onto the wall floor spitting water out of his lungs as he collapsed on the castle wall. Rolled onto his back, Prince Kimiochen gazed up at the frustrated expression on the Holy Priest's face.

"Prince Kimiochen, please explain to me what you think you were doing?"

"Not now Priest . . ." Prince Kimiochen ordered sitting up to stand to his feet, "Guards, get the Captain down to the medical wing immediately!"

"Prince Kimiochen!"

"I know Priest, I'm not supposed to be down there . . . but guess what; you're not going to stop me! I started this and I'm going to find a way to end it!" Prince Kimiochen stated before dropping to his knees.

Quickly catching the prince before he fell against the floor, the Holy Priest lifted him into his arms and headed toward the stairs.

"Of all the stubborn teenagers . . . you are the worst!"

"Save the unpleasantries Priest!" Prince Kimiochen stated lifting his hand to his chest.

"Send for the White Guardian, inform her that we need some space for our armies . . . then send her up to me!" The Holy Priest ordered.

"Right away sir . . ."

A few minutes later

"Priest, I can't breathe!" Prince Kimiochen gasped.

"Well what do you expect; the Under Dwellers will do anything to massacre you young prince! If you just listened to me you would be able to breathe!"

Dropping onto his bed, Prince Kimiochen coughed wildly as the Holy Priest unhooked the plate of armor lying over the prince's chest. Laying the breastplate beside the bed, the Holy Priest spied a small hole stained with the prince's blood off to his side. Lifting the breastplate up to examine it, the Holy Priest spied a tiny hole along the armor's side. Dropping the armor, the Holy Priest pushed the prince further onto his bed as he started to remove the cream undershirt. Pushing the undergarment away from the prince's body, the Holy Priest gently inspected his side to find a tiny wound surrounded by a yellow powder. Jumping to his feet, the Holy Priest raced out into the hall and pushed down a small blue handle triggering the parasite alert.

"Get the White Guardian up here now; the prince has been infected!"

The lush green valley outside Latira's castle was ravaged by the acidy black blood from the Under Dwellers thick hides. The many vibrant flowers were dried to the root while the wind howled angrily as more victims fell to the parched dirt to slowly die.

Many old and freshly killed bodies lying over the valley rotted under the intense heat of the blue sun without the shelter of the towering trees that once stood.

Making her way out the castle gateway, the White Guardian gazed appalled at the sight of blood being spilled for four and a half millenniums. Bringing her legs together, the White Guardian closed her eyes as she straightened her stature. Raising her arms half way into the air, the White Guardian's long lavender hair slowly rose into the air as a bright blue aura surrounded her body. Bowing her head, the White Guardian brought her soft hands before her chest to fold them neatly as she began to pray. Silently mouthing a prayer in her native tongue; the blue aura expanded as two small crystal wings appeared upon her back. Quickly springing her lavender eyes open, the White Guardian threw her arms above her head as the wings blew out into massive cotton feathered crystal wings. Lowering her hands to her eye level, the White Guardian closed her eyes again as feather dust began to blow across her face to swirl around her slender frame.

Flaring out around her body, the White Guardian's wings shot a strong gust of air against the drawbridge elegantly lifting her into the air. Extending her arms as her sealed eyes peered around the war-stained valley; the White Guardian rolled her arms around the air as she circled above the castle's fortress. Guards on the wall's trellis gazed up at the White Guardian entranced as the light of the blue sun reflected off her to descend upon the Under Dwellers blinding them allowing Latira's forces to retreat.

Punching her arms out across her body to extend away from her sides, the White Guardian quickly descended toward the southeastern valley. Unsheathing a crystalline blade, the White Guardian swiftly speared through the front of the Under Dwellers barracks. Slamming her sword into the ground, the White Guardian shot a white ray out across the Under Dwellers frontline disintegrating them to dust. Standing to her feet as her wings folded neatly behind her, the White Guardian smiled triumphantly as the young guard raced up to her.

"White Guardian, the prince has fallen ill . . . the Holy Priest requests your presence immediately!"

Staring after the White Guardian and the young guard as they raced toward the castle, the large Nzer with the blue frilled neck snarled its fangs wickedly.

"Who's-s-s s-smiling now vermin?"

Leaping up the winding stairwell leading to the prince's floor, the White Guardian rushed down the hall past many handmaidens into the royal chamber. Trotting up to the bedside, the White Guardian gazed past the Holy Priest at Prince Kimiochen's placid face.

Large droplets of sweat were steaming off the prince's wheezing body as his body temperature quickly rose. His raven bangs fell over his sweaty forehead soaking in the large amount of sweat lying upon his heated bronzed skin. Violent cough fits emerged every ten minutes producing more blood after each final cough. Prince Kimiochen's muscles restricted trying to fight the immense pain surging through his body when the Holy Priest laid his hand upon his head. Turning toward the White Guardian, the Holy

Priest nodded toward the door. Rising to her feet, the White Guardian quickly directed everyone out of the chamber as the Holy Priest rose to his feet.

Gripping his staff, the Holy Priest shook it over the prince dropping the satin streamers over his body to pull it away as the large orb started to glow. Stepping back away from the bed, the Holy Priest slammed the bottom of the staff onto the ceramic tiles causing a bright white light to disperse from the orb. Shielding her eyes, the White Guardian gazed at the white light as it shot many tiny rays across the room. Watching as his staff released a small thread of smoke; the Holy Priest dropped the staff bottom against the floor again releasing a violet fog. Gazing curiously, the White Guardian stared at the fog as it streamed out of the orb to flow across the carpet toward the bed to curl over the prince's sweaty body.

Later

Running down the palace hall, thirteen-year-old Princess Yurianne turned the corner with her attendant trying to pursue. Moving around handmaidens waiting outside her brother's chamber, Princess Yurianne quickly disappeared into her brother's room as the attendant passed the last handmaid. Quietly walking up to the White Guardian, Princess Yurianne stepped up to the side of the bed to gaze at the peaceful expression upon her brother's face as he slept. Combing her smaller hand through his damp, raven hair, Princess Yurianne crawled beside Kimiochen and lay against his cool body. Quietly entering the chamber, the princess's attendant raced up to the bed to be stopped by both the White Guardian and the Holy Priest.

"Let her be . . . this has been a long day; she could use a good rest!" The Holy Priest ordered with a smile.

"Nothing will happen; we'll be here the whole time . . . go rest yourself!" The White Guardian insisted.

Folding her hands before her legs, the princess's attendant smiled at the simple expression young Princess Yurianne had on her face. Respectfully making her leave, the princess's attendant quietly left the chamber while Princess Yurianne pulled her brother's arm up to hold his hand.

49

$\mathcal{I}$t was an early morning when the blue frilled Nzer climbed onto its mound and roared at the castle walls bellowing for the prince. The bloodstained dirt lifted leisurely to the failing wind as the sixth year of the Under Dwellers war waged on. The fear of the Under Dwellers raiding the villages caused the prince to have his subjects brought to the safety of the palace to live in its comforts 'til he could vanquish this enemy and give them their lives back . . .

Racing down the palace hall leading to her brother's room, the young woman that had taken control of Princess Yurianne's body frantically dodged around handmaidens as they stood outside the prince's chamber. Pushing the large cream colored door open, Princess Yurianne raced into her brother's bedroom searching the room. Finally her bright indigo eyes befell her brother beside his large desk fastening his violet tunic over his cream undergarment. Racing up to her brother as he lifted the white sash off the back of a chair, Princess Yurianne raced up and grabbed her brother's breastplate.

"Kimiochen, what do you think you're going to do?"

"I'm going to fix things!"

"You can't fix this, Kimiochen. The Under Dwellers will gun for you mercilessly . . . Kimiochen!"

"Yurianne, listen to me . . ." Prince Kimiochen commanded grasping her cheeks, "we have been waging war with these blood thirsty creatures for twenty-five long years . . . I'm tired of seeing my people hiding inside these walls when they should be out playing in the fields of flowers! But they can't with the fear of an Under Dweller attacking them . . . I have to end all of this for them!"

"But what if you don't come back . . ." Princess Yurianne sobbed as he took his breastplate from her hands before leaping into his arms grasping his sides, "Kimiochen, I won't live without you!"

"Yurianne you are a strong woman . . . I need you to be strong for our people!" Prince Kimiochen stated gazing down at her.

Looking up at her brother's steady face, Princess Yurianne stepped back shaking her head, "there's nothing I can do to talk you out of this; is there?"

"What other purpose do we have, but to live for our people; their happiness makes me strong and I know I will not fail, because I will not leave them or the most important person in my life to live with those creatures . . ." Prince Kimiochen stated sheathing his sword before walking up and pulling Princess Yurianne into his arms, "Be strong for them Yurianne!"

Standing on the mound the blue frilled Nzer bellowed continually at the wall with vengeful eyes when the drawbridge lowered. Extending its darkening eyes toward the castle gate, the Nzer smiled wickedly as Prince Kimiochen rode over the horizon on his mighty snowy stallion. Crouching to his knees, the Nzer watched patiently for the prince to pull his horse near the mound. Snarling its lips to release pockets of slobber, the Nzer hissed its white fangs at the horse making it nervously paw at the dirt.

"S-someone could die waiting for you!" The blue-frilled Nzer stated with a wicked chuckle.

"You mean something . . . but even that is pushing it!" Prince Kimiochen spat.

"Oh, princ-ce, you've cut deep into my heart!" the Nzer chuckled.

"I think you have no heart, Under Dweller; and you are a fool to think you do . . . creatures of flesh and blood containing hearts feel remorse for those they must kill, they feel pain and pity for others and will try to make it better, and they will not wage a war for twenty-five years for a pointless position that was never within their demeanor! So I ask; what are you?" Prince Kimiochen declared questioningly.

The blue frilled Nzer's dark eyes flashed a dark red as it gazed angrily at Prince Kimiochen, "I am the des-scendent of that worthless-s-s Under Dweller that had to beg your pathetic vermin for its-s-s right to live. I am Kler, vermin princ-ce. Hear my name and know fear . . . for when I kill you, which I will s-surly enjoy; I will mas-s-sacre every las-st vermin that holds-s-s allegianc-ce to you! The Revolution has-s-s come!"

Springing from its mound, Kler hammered into Prince Kimiochen pushing him off his stead to smash into the ground beneath the Nzer. Raising its talons, Kler sliced across the prince's breastplate before extending the long talon under its forearm. Piercing the razor sharp talon through the prince's armor, Kler speared through Kimiochen's side straight through the backside of the armor.

Yelling from the pain, Prince Kimiochen gazed at Kler's wicked smile, "aim for a fatal spot alien!"

Snarling his lips to drop slobber on Prince Kimiochen's face, Kler hissed happily, "who's-s-s to s-say it is-sn't fatal?"

Prince Kimiochen gazed at Kler's wicked face confused as it went on.

"You s-see, this-s-s talon here is-s-s lined by venom that immediately tightens-s-s mus-scles-s-s and eventually rips-s-s blood veins-s-s apart! Jus-st as-sking; what did you think you were going to do?" Kler questioned with a chuckle.

Snarling his lips, Prince Kimiochen hammered his fist into Kler's face distracting it allowing him to throw it off him. Pulling himself to his feet, Prince Kimiochen unsheathed his sword slicing it past Kler's stomach making it retreat. Breathing heavily,

Prince Kimiochen held his ground as Kler charged toward him as the rest of the Under Dwellers came toward them.

Racing up the fortress wall, Princess Yurianne dropped her hands onto the railing to gaze down at her brother as he fed off a dozen Under Dwellers while Kler watched with a wicked smile. Slamming her fist on the castle wall, Princess Yurianne turned toward the young guard.

"Petty Officer Zek . . . where are the archers?"

"The prince didn't want anyone to interfere!"

Gazing back down at her brother, Princess Yurianne watched with frightened eyes as Kimiochen fought off the attacking Under Dwellers, "Kimiochen, be careful!"

Spearing his sword through the last attacking Nzer, Prince Kimiochen turned toward Kler as it slammed its foot into his neck. Falling backward, Prince Kimiochen pulled himself off his side as Kler walked around him. Gazing at Kler's long skinny legs; Prince Kimiochen released a painful breath before spitting blood out of his mouth.

"What could've pas-s-sed through your brain vermin . . . what makes-s-s you think you could des-story a s-strong forc-ce of creatures-s-s hidden deep in the darkness-s-s for s-so many years-s-s? I admit, figuring out that we drown in deep water was-s-s intelligent, but s-serious-sly; what were you going to do, drop an ocean on us-s-s!" Kler chuckled. "Well, I'm glad we had that chat . . ." Kler stated extending his talon, "oh, before you die vermin, I thought you would like to know that for the years-s-s I've had to put up with your annoyance-ce; I plan to tear your s-sis-ster's-s-s organs-s-s out one by one, then eat them s-slowly while, s-she dies-s-s in agony!"

Gazing angrily up at Kler's wicked face as it chuckled at him, a surge of controlled abhorrence gripped the prince's weakening body. Piercing his blade through Kler's legs, Prince Kimiochen stood to his feet and blasted a violet ray against Kler's face. Flying through the air, Kler's face shot its acidy blood across the valley as Prince Kimiochen speared his sword through the ground sending the ray shooting across the valley blowing every last Nzer to ashes. Hammering into its mound, Kler rolled down to slam into several dead bodies as Prince Kimiochen walked toward him.

"Who's revolution were you speaking of?"

Gazing down at the beaten face of the last Under Dweller, Prince Kimiochen heard his sister screaming out to him. Turning around, Prince Kimiochen gazed at Princess Yurianne, the Holy Priest, and the White Guardian racing toward him with a great deal of his guards. Lowering his sword as Petty Officer Zek raced up to his side to lift Kler from the mound with help from other officers, Prince Kimiochen turned toward his approaching sister. Strolling across the blood-stained dirt, Prince Kimiochen gazed at all the fallen bodies of his men as Princess Yurianne ran up to his side.

Gazing at the broken armor and torn garments, Princess Yurianne took hold of her brother's arm as the Under Dweller was bound in chains. Stroking her fingers over the hole in Kimiochen's armor, Princess Yurianne gazed up at Prince Kimiochen with worry as Kler growled at them. Stepping closer to her brother, Princess Yurianne stared at the large gash crossing over the Under Dwellers left eye.

"You got lucky, vermin princ-ce . . . you won't be s-so lucky nex-xt time!"

"There won't be a next time, Kler; you are here with banished from the string of planets to the Dark Moon . . ." Prince Kimiochen ordered. "By the next full blue moon, you will be confined within an illuminated glass jar!"

"I'll out live you then!" Kler chuckled.

"Death is too good for something like you!" Prince Kimiochen spat, turning toward Latira's palace.

Watching Prince Kimiochen walk away with his little sister, Kler smiled wickedly before it was pulled toward the Gallo beneath the castle. Walking across the drawbridge into his courtyard, Prince Kimiochen lifted his deep indigo eyes to gaze at all his people as they started cheering when he passed beneath the gateway. Smiling brightly at a small girl, Prince Kimiochen collapsed to his knees causing a hush to fall over the crowd as Princess Yurianne helped her brother back to his feet.

"Sire, are you ill?" The child questioned walking up to Prince Kimiochen.

Gazing into the little girl's light orange eyes, Prince Kimiochen took her small soft hand. "What's your name?"

"Jeannee . . . I want to become one of your guards!"

Smiling brightly at Jeannee, Prince Kimiochen pulled himself to his feet; "well, I'll look forward to seeing you again!"

The brightest drops of the blue moon's fullness radiated down upon the last model of a Latrinian **Warship G-731** while, Petty Officer Zek loaded Kler into the Restricted Cargo bay. Pushing it inside the slender jar, Petty Officer Zek sealed the prison and activated the power beams radiating down on Kler.

Watching from his balcony, Prince Kimiochen leaned against the wall connecting his room to the balcony doors. Lifting his hand to grip the cloth over his chest, Prince Kimiochen released a heavy breath as he watched Petty Officer Zek walk out of the **Warship G-731**. Turning away from the landing bridge, Prince Kimiochen walked up to his bed and lowered himself down onto the soft satin sheets. Laying his hand over his chest, Prince Kimiochen released a last breath as he slowly sealed his deep indigo eyes.

Racing down the hall with a gleeful smile, Princess Yurianne pushed open her brother's door to see him lying on the bed. Slowly approaching the bed, Princess Yurianne's happy smile disappeared from her face as she saw Kimiochen's motionless body. Dropping next to the bed, Princess Yurianne pulled Kimiochen's body into her arms as tears started to stream down her rosy cheeks.

Hearing the princess's cries, the Holy Priest rushed into the room to find her crying over her brother's lifeless body. Losing his breath, the Holy Priest fell against the chamber wall as the White Guardian raced up beside him. Stepping into the room, the White Guardian walked up to the bedside and laid her hand over the prince's forehead. Dropping her head, the White Guardian's lavender eyes released small tears as the Holy Priest walked up and pulled the princess off her brother.

* * * * * *

The first echo of thunder passing through the candy clouds overheard disrupted the silence of the crowd that had gathered for Prince Kimiochen's funeral. Princess Yurianne's pale face was veiled by a black sheer cloth while her simple black dress blew lightly through the wind as she followed the guards carrying her brother. Tears ran continually down Princess Yurianne's rosy cheeks as she gazed at the peaceful expression upon her brother's face. Raising her handkerchief to her face, Princess Yurianne whipped the tears from her chin before laying it over her trembling mouth.

Lying upon a long porcelain table trimmed in gold, Prince Kimiochen's hands lay neatly over the black tunic stretched over the violet undergarment. The lavender orbs upon the prince's gloves glistened as several raindrops fell upon them to slid down to the white strings lying over his chest. The golden band wrapped around his forehead reflected the occasional flashing bolts of lightning across the thousands of sunken hearts.

Carrying the table up to the alter, the guards stepped back respectfully as Princess Yurianne walked up to stand beside her brother's side. Sucking in a deep breath, Princess Yurianne laid the violet rose she was holding in between Kimiochen's hands. Stepping back, Princess Yurianne bowed her head to her brother as she started to sing the song of Latira in their native tongue. Tears swelled up around the bottom of Yurianne's bright indigo eyes as she finished the final note to watch the Holy Priest approach and begin the final prayer to be prayed for their fallen prince while the **Warship G-731** entered the Dark Moon atmosphere.

50

Earth—Sunday, April 27, 2026

Quickly reopening his indigo eyes, Kimon gazed around to find he was still in the park with a translucent barrier around him. Breathing heavily, Kimon realized every past memory he had up to the battle with Kler were coming back to him; the memories of the Prince of Latira. Watching the park around him being blown to bits, Kimon gazed over at Esal as he stood before everyone else creating the barrier which the missile ray of the **Warship G-731** had slammed into.

Holding the handle of his crystalline blade, Esal's white fabric slowly started ripping as the force of the explosion beat against his body. Dropping to his right knee, Esal leaned his head against the hilt of his sword as blood started to stream out of his nose. Opening his crystal blue eyes; Esal tightly held his sword's handle as the **Warship G-731** shot a second missile ray. Sealing his eyes preparing for the second collision, Esal felt a strong hand take hold of his shoulder. Glancing up as the ray descended toward them, Esal stared up at Kimon as he blasted a violet ray through the missile ray back to the **Warship G-731**. Watching with disbelieving eyes, Esal smiled brightly as Kimon's ray destroyed the needle connected to the **Warship G-731** creating an explosion inside the spacecraft.

Jumping into the air, Hikaru screamed triumphantly as Yuri raced up to jump into her brother's arms. Hopping around the park, Hikaru grabbed Kimiko's hands forcing her to join her enthusiasm. Jumping into En's arms, Maya kissed his cheek happily as they watched the lower section of the spacecraft in flames. Grabbing Touko, Masumi whirled her around in the air while Hagane and Jeremy cheered happily.

Taking Kimon's offered hand, Esal pulled himself to his feet when Hikaru came leaping toward him. Grimacing as she wrapped her arms around him to tightly squeeze him, Esal patted Hikaru's shoulder as she released him. Turning toward Kimon, Esal lowered his sword and smiled brightly at him.

"It's my job to save you!"

Looking toward the ship, Kimon gazed back into Esal's crystal blue eyes and smiled, "I realize that . . . but you told Hikaru that she had to find confidence in herself!"

Walking up to Kimon, Yuri tenderly slid her hand into his to look puzzled up at his face, "what are you saying Kimon?"

Tightening his fingers around Yuri's, Kimon looked at Esal, "I don't know how it happened, but I just saw the battle that took place a century ago in the Solari!"

"What battle Kimon?" Masumi questioned.

"The battle that wiped out this species . . ."

"If they were wiped out; how are there so many of them?" Touko questioned.

"I don't know!" Kimon stated raising his voice. "I was the one that wiped them out Touko; I don't know how there are so many again!"

Standing off to the side as the Hunters interrogated his prince, Esal turned his head to gaze back into a large Nzer's face as it came down toward him. Throwing his crystalline blade through the Nzer's face, Esal watched it slice in half to fall dead to the park floor. Turning toward the dismantled forest lining the park, Esal watched a multitude of enraged Nzers racing toward them.

"Hunters, we've got company!" Esal yelled blasting a white ray out of his blade to spear through a dozen Nzers.

Turning around as a chubby Nzer swiped at her face, Kimiko dropped back onto her rear to blow her energy ball through the Nzer's legs. Freaking out as she watched the bone splinter across the park, Kimiko scowled at the Nzer's ugly face before blasting it again. Standing to her feet as the Nzer's acidy blood started eating the ground around her, Kimiko stepped back to admire her handy work when En slammed into her. Rolling across the saw chips, En and Kimiko flew half way up the slide to come back down to plow through the Nzer. Sitting up, Kimiko stared at En for a few minutes before bursting out in frustration.

"What's the big idea, Skilou?"

"What, you think I meant for that to happen?" En questioned as an orange marked Nzer flew above their heads.

Dropping onto the ground at the same time, En and Kimiko stared at Masumi as he slapped his hands together.

"What's the big idea, Masumi?" Kimiko questioned as En rolled his eyes.

"What, I didn't hit you!" Masumi stated.

"Guys focus . . ." Hikaru yelled at them as she blocked several leaping Nzers.

"Right . . ." Masumi, Kimiko, and En stated running opposite directions to get hammered back into each other, "This is not good!"

Shielding their faces from the leaping Nzers as Maya jumped in front of them; Masumi, Kimiko, and En watched her slam her fist into the Nzers' faces. Jumping up cheering after watching the Nzers hammer across the park; Masumi, Kimiko, and En raced to opposite ends of the park to confront the approaching Nzers. Ripping the large amounts of iron out of several Nzers' blood, Masumi shot the small balls of metal he morphed together across the park. Racing across the saw chips, Kimiko quickly climbed up to the top of the jungle gym to spray her energy balls through Nzers that leapt toward her. Shifting the weight of his body from side to side, En sent the wind like a tornado on a garden against the Nzers that charged toward him.

Ripping his crystalline blade out of several Nzers, Esal watched the acidy blood fall across the park floor to immediately start eating it. Peering up at a regiment of fast approaching Nzers, Esal pointed his sword at them and dispersed a large cerulean ray to spear through their hides. Glancing up as Gobu zipped above his head; Esal lifted one of his wings to stop him from slamming into a tree. Glancing at him with annoyance, Esal threw him toward Hikaru to help her keep the Nzers off her.

Whizzing around Nzers, Gobu shot through the park to breeze past Hikaru's head and slammed into a large Nzer's face. Floating off the Nzer's face to giggle anxiously, Gobu climbed through the air to fall upon Hikaru's shoulder. Giggling in her ear, Gobu glanced toward Hikaru's side to see a fat Nzer leaping at them. Screaming in Hikaru's ear, Gobu's eyes shot out of his head as the Nzer came toward them. Throwing his arms through the air, Gobu shot off Hikaru's shoulder and poked the Nzer in the eyes as Hikaru leapt out of the way.

Standing on the opposite side of the park, Yuri stood behind Kimon while he fought off the charging Nzers as best as he could. Gazing around the park, Yuri strained her mind trying to determine what was going on when she saw Touko blast a Nzer through the jungle gym. Staring at the long metal poles as they fell to the ground; Yuri tilted her head as she approached the wrecked playground. Reaching her arm out toward the wreckage, Yuri powerfully strained her mind to slowly lift several poles from the ground. Releasing an anxious breath, Yuri chuckled enthusiastically as she stared at the floating poles. Glancing over at her brother, Yuri extended her arm in his direction to watch excitedly as the poles flew past Kimon through the Nzers hides.

Lifting himself off the ground after several poles breezed past his head, Kimon turned around to see Yuri jumping around the park hysterically. Gazing confusedly at his little sister, Kimon curiously approached Yuri as she looked toward him. Smiling awkwardly at Yuri, Kimon looked toward the Nzers with poles sticking out of them back to his little sister. Widening his questioning eyes, Kimon dropped his arms to his sides as Yuri smiled brightly at him.

"Isn't this weird . . . you're starting to slowly remember a past life as a prince, and I'm starting to unleash strong mental capabilities—I can see someone's memories or dreams and now I can bend things to my will!"

Quickly grabbing Yuri's arms, Kimon shook her, "Yuri slow down . . . you're hyperventilating!"

"Sorry . . ." Yuri replied nodding quickly to see an orange marked Nzer leap at them, "Kimon behind you!"

Turning around too late, Kimon fell backward against Yuri as the orange marked Nzer hammered into him. Falling against the ground with Yuri directly behind him, Kimon caught the large mouth filled with razor sharp teeth. Constricting his muscles as the Nzer attempted to close its mouth, Kimon dodged the Nzer's large arms as it hammered them inches away. Snapping the Nzers mouth open, Kimon moved out from underneath it as it fell to his feet. Releasing a long breath, Kimon looked up into another orange marked Nzer's face to see it severed by Esal's crystalline blade. Glancing up at

Esal's serious face, Kimon spied an orange marked Nzer leaping at his back when he heard Yuri's voice call out over the ruckus.

"Esal, look out!"

Slightly turning his head, Esal spun around to spear his sword through the Nzer's hide to blow the white ray cleanly out its back. Snarling his lips, Esal kicked the massive body off his sword as the rest fell to the ground. Looking toward Yuri, Esal nodded his head respectfully before taking Kimon's arm and lifting him to his feet.

"Get everyone around Hikaru and tell her to put up her barrier or else you all will be very sore tomorrow!"

"All right . . ." Kimon replied walking toward Yuri as she raced up to Esal.

"What are you going to do?"

Gazing at Yuri with wide crystal blue eyes; Esal pulled a small smile across his bronzed face, "Don't worry about me . . . I've done this many times, I know what I'm doing! The Under Dwellers are going to feel a brief moment of intense pain before they feel nothing ever again! Help protect your brother!"

Gazing at Esal with a reluctant expression, Yuri stared at him as Kimon pulled her beside him to race toward the other Hunters. Her bright indigo eyes stared at Esal as he turned toward the thousands of Nzers racing out toward the park. Coming alongside Hikaru, Yuri gazed at Esal as all the Devilry Hunters gathered together when the clear barrier dropped down around them.

Watching the barrier start to radiate around the Devilry Hunters, Esal lifted the tip of his crystalline sword off the ground and turned toward the Nzers. Bringing his body tightly together like a beam, Esal gripped the hilt of his sword in between his hands and pulled it in front of his chest. Staring through the crystalline blade covering half his bronzed face, Esal stared at the approaching Nzers before closing his crystal blue eyes. Releasing a long breath, Esal stood motionless as a bright blue aura surrounded his body when the Nzers leapt at him. Softly murmuring a prayer in the tongue of his planet, the large crystal wings on Esal's back spread out around his body. Quickly opening his eyes as the Nzers hammered into the bright blue aura, Esal swiped his wings across his sides throwing the beasts into the air. Springing off the ground, Esal drew his crystalline sword tightly against his body before he sliced it through the air toward the park to blow a white ray through the thousands of quickly approaching Nzers.

Watching the ray hammer into the ground, the Devilry Hunters watched as it vaulted a large wave of ground in every direction. Bracing themselves as the wave crashed into Hikaru's barrier, the Devilry Hunters watched amazed as the ray concealed by the waves speared through all the Nzers. Gazing around the motionless park, the Hunters cheered hysterically as Hikaru dropped her barrier.

Releasing a relieved chuckle, Hikaru glanced over at Esal as he landed where his ray had struck. Glancing at the small circlet bordered by hundreds of Nzer bodies, Esal gazed toward Hikaru when a small snap echoed behind him. Turning his head, Esal stared around the woods to see a small white rabbit race out of a bush to dart across the park before he gazed back at Hikaru. Standing thirty feet away from each other, Hikaru gazed at Esal with a gleeful smile when the branches above cracked. Lifting her head, Hikaru glanced toward the branches to see the biggest Nzer she had seen hovering above her.

Hanging onto the side of the branch; a fifteen foot Nzer with blue markings staining the top of its head, its shoulder blades, and the jutting spinal cord, stared down at Hikaru and her Hunters with evasive yellow eyes. Restricting the massive muscles on its legs, the Nzer sprung toward the ground snapping the branch in half as the talons on its feet cut through the bark. Hammering into the ground, the Nzer plowed through Hikaru and the Hunters before Esal could react.

Hammering across the saw chips as her Hunters flew in different directions across the park, Hikaru slammed into the broken jungle gym. Laying her hand over her torn chest, Hikaru released an agonizing breath as she rolled off the metal poles to stare up at the Nzer's gruesome face. Grimacing at the snarling fangs before her eyes, Hikaru watched Esal's crystalline blade severe through the Nzers' hide before he dropped to a knee in front of her.

"Are you all right?" Esal quickly asked grabbing her face lifting it to look into her brown eyes.

"Yes . . . I'm OK, but the others!" Hikaru stuttered through long breathes.

"They're OK, you took the frontal assault . . . come on, let's get you to your feet!" Esal stated slicing his sword into the ground.

Gently gripping Hikaru's arms, Esal prepared to slowly lift her to her feet when something speared through his chest. Gasping as Esal's blood sprayed across her face, Hikaru started to rapidly ventilate as she stared at a long ivory talon piercing through Esal's chest.

51

*G*lancing up at the painful expression across Esal's face, Hikaru lost her breath as her spellbound eyes followed another movement. Gazing at two talons as they wrapped around Esal's neck, Hikaru's eyes quickly darted toward a raising Nzer head. Staring at the wickedness captivated within the Nzer's yellow eyes, Hikaru neglected to notice the large yellow marks marring Rasp's skin. Staring menacingly at Hikaru, Rasp took the back of Esal's hair and pressing its long talon further into Esal's chest chuckled at the wail that escaped his throat. Stepping away from Hikaru, Rasp raised its talon lifting Esal above the yellow marks on its head.

"No . . ." Hikaru yelled lunging for Esal, "give him back!"

Releasing a chuckle, Rasp stared at Hikaru, "give him back?"

Pulling herself to her hands and knees, Hikaru stared at Rasp as tears began to sting her eyes, "Give him back!"

"Or you'll what . . . is-s-s that not what you vermin normally s-say to each other? Or what . . ." Rasp chuckled gazing down at Hikaru as Esal hung limply in the air.

"I'll rip your head off!" Hikaru angrily cursed gritting her teeth.

"Fac-ce it vermin child . . . you've los-st! Your helpers-s-s are lying s-scattered across-s-s the area and like the White Guardian, you've failed to keep the princ-ce from us-s-s!" Rasp smiled nodding in the direction behind Hikaru.

Turning around to gaze at several small Nzers, Hikaru watched regretfully as they lifted Kimon of the ground. Grimacing through her pain, Hikaru watched helplessly as the Nzers started to walk away when Yuri jumped on the one carrying Kimon.

"Yuri . . ." Hikaru yelled as two Nzers ripped her off the other to get kicked by her feet.

Growling at the others, Rasp snapped its fangs at the smaller Nzers, "idiots-s-s get the vermin princ-ce to the s-ship now, take the girl with you if you mus-st!"

Turning angrily back toward Rasp, Hikaru stared at the long talon from its other arm as it extracted it in front of her face.

"You are a worthless-s-cs vermin that cannot manage a s-simple tas-sk of protecting one weak princ-ce!" Rasp chuckled.

Gazing past the long talon, Hikaru stared at Rasp with bold eyes, "if he is so weak . . . why then are you all so afraid of him?"

Snarling its lips to flash its large fangs, Rasp hissed at Hikaru, "killing your White Guardian and your pathetic friends-s-s will bring me great pleas-sure!"

Staring into the dark skies hovering above him, Esal's crystal blue eyes sparkled of the tears emerging from the agonizing pain coursing from the talon piercing into his flesh. With every movement Rasp made, the talon sliced further into Esal's body doubling the pain with every new cut. Pinching his eyes shut, Esal released a groan when a warm light touched his cheeks.

Opening his crystal blue eyes bordered by agonized tears, Esal stared up at white cotton clouds parting to release yellow sparkling beams from the sun reflecting off the golden gates of his planet, Evaleäntia. The white cotton valleys stretching across Evaleäntia sparkled like snow as the golden sun radiated its cool rays down onto the majestic villages surrounding the palace. The large walls surrounding the palace came together to form an elegant golden gate that captivated the unicorns prancing within the courtyard while; Pegasus babies flew through the clouds concealing the many large towers.

The sight of the crystalline walls of his planet's grand palace brought sad tears to Esal's eyes as his strength began to leave his body. Struggling to regain air for his lungs, Esal stared up at a young girl as she magically appeared before him. Gazing at the azure bangs lying over her tanned face that captivated her sapphire eyes, Esal stared at the smile that crossed over her face as she extended her hand to him.

Come back with me . . . there's nothing else you can do for them!

The immense pain coursing through Esal's body gave him the desire to lift his hand toward the young woman's extended hand. But hearing her last statement shot Esal back to a small string of awareness. Through the illusive reality before his eyes, Esal could hear the pleading cries of Hikaru below him. Staring sternly at the young woman, Esal slowly retracted his hand to her dismay.

Please, take my hand so I can take you home!

I am not finished here!

Rapidly blinking his eyes at the dark skies hovering above him, Esal could hear the Nzer beneath him hissing at Hikaru. Narrowing his crystal blue eyes as his nose pressed together; Esal gritted his teeth while a small white light emerged where the talon was piercing his chest. Growing bigger through the surrounding darkness; the small white light wiped away the coursing pain within Esal's body. Inhaling a long breath as the small white light shot into the dark clouds above, Esal allowed the air within his lungs to escape while he sealed his eyes when the light descended back over himself and Rasp.

Watching the white light conceal Esal and the Nzer, Hikaru shielded her face as ground blew into the air pushing her backward across the park. Landing on a dead Nzer carcass, Hikaru rolled off to raise her head and stare at the dirt leisurely falling to the ground. Quickly pulling herself to her feet, Hikaru raced toward where Esal and the Nzer had been to drop to her knees three feet from which. Crawling closer, Hikaru took hold of the large Nzer's heavy body and pushed him off Esal. Laying her hand on the blood streamed armor; Hikaru pulled the broken talon fragment out of Esal's chest when Rasp's hand shot out and took hold of her wrist. Yelping as the Nzer tightened its grip around her wrist, Hikaru turned the fragment in her hand and releasing an angry cry thrust it in its right eye. Prying the hand off her wrist, Hikaru collected Esal and pulled him safely away from Rasp as it fell to the ground to die.

Dropping onto her hip, Hikaru sat up to loom over Esal as he started to release hefty rasping coughs. Allowing a whimper to escape her throat, Hikaru frantically searched for the point to remove Esal's armor. Large tears coursed to her eyes as she gazed at his chest rising, fighting for one gentle breath to easily pass through his constricting lungs. Gently pushing her arms beneath him, Hikaru pulled Esal against her chest as he started to choke on his blood.

"Can't find it, I can't remove your armor . . . Esal, tell me how . . . I can't take off your armor . . . I can't take it off . . . I won't be able to stop all the blood!" Hikaru cried losing her grip on Esal's armor.

"Hikaru . . ." Esal softly called, "I don't . . . you don't need to remove my armor, Hikaru . . . I—"

"You're going to die if I don't stop the bleeding!" Hikaru sobbed hysterically.

Slowly opening his crystal blue eyes to peer at Hikaru; Esal softly breathed, "My body is broken Hikaru."

"No, no it isn't I just have to . . ."

"I can see the end of this war . . ." Esal softly replied shutting his eyes as blood streamed off his lips, "light is beginning to shine down on the planet once more."

Shaking her head, Hikaru looked behind her at the motionless bodies of her Hunters, "I-I'll, I'll get Hagane . . . Hagane will heal you!"

Opening his eyes, Esal gazed at Hikaru as brutal choughs filled his lungs. Sucking in his tormenting fits, Esal's now sparkling eyes gazed hopefully at Hikaru.

"I . . . will you take care of Gobu for me? He's not strong enough . . . he can't look out for himself." Esal gasped as Gobu floated down to press his sponge arms against Esal's blood splattered cheeks.

Shaking her head, Hikaru lowered herself closer to Esal, "you're going to stick around and do that yourself . . . you're going to pull through this Esal!"

Lifting his white and red glove to touch Hikaru's cheek, Esal fought back another choking fit before reopening his glistening eyes. "I don't have the air left within my lungs to sustain my body. My muscles have lost the strength to raise a finger . . . I can feel my heart slowing."

"Don't speak like that . . . you cannot leave me here alone! I need you; I need you Esal . . . you cannot leave me here!" Hikaru cried dropping her face against Esal's neck.

"Hikaru you've found the strength to master your fears, you . . ."

"Everything I am is because of you . . ." Hikaru sobbed looking into Esal's crystal blue eyes, "Every power that has come to my hands is your doing; I am not a strong person Esal . . . I've failed just like the Nzers knew I would, they've taken Kimon!"

Sucking in a final deep breath, Esal peered steadily at Hikaru, "all my life I've searched for the meanings of the unexplainable . . . of how if we are left in the dark, we will seek out the light; why if we are in a state of fear, we group together rather than stand alone; or why with the last bit of strength left to them someone would take the weapon that killed them to protect their wounded friend . . . its our subconscious that tells us to do so! It's the principles of one's soul . . . and of all the things I've seen in these worlds, I have never seen a person fight so strongly for a greater purpose than their life itself . . . then when I meet you Hikaru Neijo!"

Gazing down at the pure honesty across Esal's face, Hikaru could feel her tears start to swell within her eyes.

"You've shown me so many things about the purities in life Hikaru . . . you are the most remarkable woman I have ever meant; you show no fear to stand for what you believe in or the people you love! You're something special Hikaru; you're going to rattle the stars!"

Shuddering through her tears as Esal finished, Hikaru wrapped her arms around him while her head dropped back to lie against his neck. Crying hysterically against Esal's neck, Hikaru felt the strength within his body disappear. Slowly lifting her head, Hikaru gazed at the still expression across Esal's face. Shaking her head at the realization, Hikaru scooped Esal's body into her arms letting her tears freely fall over his face. Once again pulling him tightly against her chest, Hikaru suddenly lost grip on him to see his body slowly grow transparent. Watching his body begin to fade away, Hikaru screamed out across the park as she reached for Esal when he disappeared entirely.

"No . . . Esal!" Hikaru bellowed dropping against the patch of dismantled grass where he had laid.

* * * * * *

A sudden intoxication of acidy air slowly began to fill the Hunters lungs as they began to regain consciousness. Pushing slender poles off her body, Kimiko crawled out from underneath a broken jungle gym while not to far away En lifted himself out of a caved in playhouse. Within the center of the playground, Hagane rose to his knees as Touko took hold of his arm to assist him to his feet. Pushing a large stone wall off of her; Maya stumbled to her feet as Masumi pushed Jeremy off him.

Quickly standing to his feet, Masumi felt a rush of pain slap him in the face from rising to soon. Laying his hand on his side, Masumi searched through the dead carcasses until he spied Hikaru lying on a yellow patch of torn grass. Limping over the smelly Nzers' carcasses; Masumi slowly yet quickly dragged himself toward Hikaru when her soft whimpers trailed to the air.

Stumbling toward Hikaru, Masumi slowly leaned down to touch her shoulder, "Hikaru?"

Jumping as her brother softly touched her shoulder, Hikaru spun her head around to look at him. Tears were streaming down her dirty cheeks; her brown eyes were all red from a continual flow of tears; her lips trembled uncontrollably, and her torn chest was beginning to weep. Narrowing her eyes in sorrow, Hikaru lunged forward into her brother's arms pushing him to the ground.

Lifting to his elbows, Masumi slid his hands over Hikaru's shoulders, "Hikaru, what's wrong?"

She burrowing her face into his chest as she cried against Masumi, *"he's gone . . . Esal's gone!"*

"What, what do you mean he's gone?"

"He sacrificed himself for me!" Hikaru cried uncontrollably.

"Oh, man . . ." Masumi breathed quietly wrapping his arms tightly around Hikaru, "It's all right little sis' . . . I'm here!"

Sliding his hands tenderly over Hikaru's back, Masumi looked up at the others as they approached with questioning eyes. Shaking his head, Masumi lowered his head against Hikaru's as she continued to cry into his chest.

A soft crackling of thunder echoed above the still bodies of the Devilry Hunters as the clouds released a blinding rain. The smell of the corpses and the blood staining the ground slowly began to wash away while; Gobu sat beside Esal's crystalline sword watching the Hunters. His heavy heart sank as he leaned against the strong blade as the sound of the rain hitting it trailed to Hikaru's ears. Lifting her eyes, Hikaru stared painfully at Esal's sword as the crystalline blade unknowing slowly faded into a soft dazzling silver.

The soft ring of rain falling against crystal faded to a soft sound of a pure metal being dribbled upon. The sound disheartened Hikaru as she clung to her brother while the darkness began to radiate around them, cornering them with the realization that the White Guardian had fallen and the prince had been stolen by the enemy.

52

$\mathcal{D}$arkness continued to blow out of the Latrinian **Warship G-731** when the several Nzers that escaped Esal's final assault crawled up the tower. The leading blue marked Nzer held Kimon's motionless body over its right shoulder while the one below it followed closely with Yuri. Pulling themselves over the peak of the tower, the Nzers waited patiently below the **Warship G-731**. The loud ruckus of the hatchway releasing echoed across the bottom whole as the metal doors lowered allowing access into the **Warship G-731**.

Taking hold of the bottom grate; the blue marked Nzers climbed into the ship as sparking volts of electricity flashed above their heads. Walking through the dark halls following the flashing electrical surges as they quickly shot past their scaly hides; the blue marked Nzers long strides brought them in front of a massive iron door. Lowering its talons through the door handle; the blue marked Nzer bearing Kimon pushed the massive door wide to pass leisurely through. Occasional flashes of blue lights temporarily light up the dark room highlighting the Nzer as it strapped Kimon to the wall before walking back out. Resealing the door, the Nzer turned to the smaller one holding Yuri and hissed demandingly.

"The Mighty One did not want that one, s-so plac-ce it in the lower regiment quarters-s-s. I will inform that it came along when we attempted to take the vermin princ-ce . . . the Mighty One may want it for s-something!"

"Unders-stood commander, I will return in no time!"

Turning to walk briskly down the dark hall, the smaller Nzer carried Yuri toward the lower regiments within the spacecraft while the other Nzer headed toward the Control Room. The surges of electricity followed the Nzer's quick movement highlighting the evil expression upon its grotesque face as it passed under the Control Room arch to kneel before the Mighty One's shadowed body.

"S-Sire, I bear good news-s-s . . . we have obtained the vermin princ-ce, it is-s-s in the s-ship's-s-s obs-servation deck . . . I regret to inform you that Ras-sp has-s-s fallen . . . the White Guardian s-sacrificed its-self to des-stroy Ras-sp!"

Leaning forward in the shadows, the Mighty One's eyes widened angrily, "Ras-sp has-s-s fallen . . . yet the White Guardian fell with him."

Releasing a chuckle, the Mighty One lifted itself from its seat to walk into the dim lights within the Control Room. A large yellow scar lying over the Mighty One's right eye marred its massive scaly head as it stared coldly down at the city. Flexing its long talons, the Mighty One folded its arms behind its back over a long blue frill. Cocking its head to the side, the Mighty One turned to the blue marked Nzer.

"Commander, I want you to prepare a regiment . . . then you will go invite the young, vermin girl to join us-s-s for the princ-ce's-s-s ex-xecution!"

"On your command Mighty One . . ."

Bowing its head in respect; the blue marked Nzer retreated to begin its task as the Mighty One snarled its large fangs triumphantly down at the city. Dragging its long talons down the glass window before it, the Mighty One released a wicked chuckle to echo throughout the **Warship G-731**.

Earth—Monday, April 28, 2026

The rain showered down over the dark city quickly filling the gutters with erosion while the roaring thunder echoed through the empty silence that had consumed the city. Citizens across town refused to leave their homes out of fear of what the spacecraft was doing while others frantically rushed to the city exits to find them blocked off. Large towering trees lay in the center of the roads; bridges were caving in; train rails were deactivated, and airports were grounded.

The countries military was brutally attacked destroying the weapons of defense leaving the countryside completely open for attack. Tokyo's power plant had recently undergone a crippling power surge so now the city was blanketed in utter darkness. Other than the occasional flashing bolts of lightning that escaped the darkness lying throughout the skies, Tokyo was imprisoned within a Dark Age.

Flipping a flashlight on, Masumi unpacked several candles from the closet while; Hagane addressed everyone's physical wounds. The grave expression upon his face reflected across the entire dark room while Hagane moved about it making everyone as comfortable as he could. Glancing over at Masumi, Hagane watched him light several candles to limp around the room setting them in certain areas.

"Have you checked on Hikaru recently?" Hagane whispered as Masumi slowly sat down beside him.

"No . . . I think she needs to be alone for a little bit. She's taking Esal's death really hard!"

Nodding, Hagane took hold of Masumi's injured leg, "now let me look at that!"

The silence in Hikaru's room held no comfort for her as she repeatedly saw Esal dying—the long talon piercing through his body; him lying over it while he hung over eighteen feet in the air; the cries and pained expressions that crossed over his face, and the final attack he made to save her from death.

Hikaru's brown eyes sparkled of the tears that continued to flow across her cheeks to her pillow held tightly against her face. The rawness within her eyes showed her unending mourning through the long night to the morning. The quick shuddering echoed into her pillow every five minutes as Hikaru started to cry over and over again.

Sitting on the floor beside her bed, Cleo gazed sadly up at Hikaru before looking at Gobu squeezed into a ball over Esal's silver sword. Looking from Hikaru to Gobu, Cleo released a disappointed sigh before she approached Gobu's sniveling body. Walking up to stare at the quivering tail sticking out of Gobu's miniaturized body, Cleo pulled a tiny claw out and stuck it into Gobu's butt as she sank her teeth into his tail. Stepping back to sit down as Gobu sprang up into the air, Cleo watched him zip around the room mumbling before he slammed into the east wall. Scowling at his splattered body, Cleo started chuckling when Gobu floated up to her with a frustrated look across his face.

"Whadt was dat foar?"

"You Guys Are Beginning To Depress Me . . . I'm Tired Of Seeing You Two Crying, If You Guys Keep It Up; I'm Going To Start Crying!"

Walking up to the front door, Hagane slid back the screen to stare at Manabu's smiling face. Staring at him in surprise, Hagane nearly forgot to have him come inside.

"What are you doing here?" Hagane asked as he showed Manabu into the den.

"I was seeing that steps toward an invasion were finally put into action so I thought it was better if I came to speak with all of you!"

"Manabu this isn't a good time!" Masumi stated.

"I can see that Masumi, but I think you need to know certain things . . . before all the power went out last night I was watching the news broadcast and saw that the city has been closed in! Then when I did a little research with father's satellites I saw that the Nzers have blocked off the roads with massive trees or pieces of buildings! Also the bridges leading out of the city have been dismantled by the Nzers . . . they have sealed us inside the city! Not just us, but everyone . . . they don't want anyone to leave!"

"Why would they do that . . . I thought they were here for Kimon alone?" Masumi questioned.

"I'm not sure why, but I can tell you that it isn't for a good reason . . . I think they're going to try to wipe out the city!" Manabu stated.

"But everyone else hasn't done anything!" Touko replied.

"They see us all as vermin . . ."

Turning toward the hall, everyone stared at Hikaru as she held Esal's sword protectively before her chest while she approached the den with Cleo close behind.

"To them we are the aliens . . . and we shouldn't be allowed to sustain a state of life!" Hikaru stated as Gobu dropped onto her shoulder to gurgle his agreement. "The life of a good person means nothing to the Nzers; they have no sense of feeling for another!" Hikaru stated as tears slowly began to come to her eyes, "I want to end this . . . I don't ask for any of you to come with me, I know you all are hurting badly and I will not ask you to lay yourselves on the line!"

Standing to her feet with a look of frustration, Kimiko approached Hikaru with her arms crossed, "Hikaru Neijo, you know perfectly well that where ever you go I'm sure to be close by . . . I'm going to make a stand with you at the end of all things!"

"We will all make a stand with you Hikaru . . . we are all your Hunters and we proudly follow you down whatever path you choose!" En replied.

"I don't know what's going to happen guys . . . I promised Esal that I would save Kimon and Yuri as well!" Hikaru said seriously, "we cannot let the Nzers win or everything on this planet will die!"

With her last remark, Hikaru watched every one of her Hunters stand to their feet and nod their heads in agreement to her decision. A satisfying feeling filled Hikaru's soul momentarily whipping the sorrowful emptiness that had consumed her since Esal's death. The loneliness that still remained within Hikaru's soul was joined by a determination of freedom as she moved through her Hunters toward the front door. Pushing the door open, Hikaru walked out into the darkness when a large blue marked Nzer dropped down in the front lawn. Stopping on the front porch, Hikaru stared at the grotesque creature with vengeful eyes as Kimiko raced up alongside her. The anger she felt within her soul reflected through Hikaru's brown eyes as the blue marked Nzer hissed out into the darkness.

"The Mighty One wis-shes-s-s to invite you vermin girl to the ex-xecution of your beloved princ-ce and hopes-s-s you won't make him wait too long!"

Staring at its hideous face as it started to chuckle, Hikaru gazed at Kimiko and smiled encouragingly. Nodding her head, Kimiko ignited the energy around her hands and blew her energy ball through the Nzer. Smiling as the Nzer exploded into a thousand pieces, Hikaru stepped down from the porch with her Hunters following.

"I accept your invitation!" Hikaru replied with a smirk stepping over the meat pieces scattered across her yard.

"I think Hikaru's mad!" Jeremy whispered to Touko, who quickly nodded her agreement with a smile.

God give me strength to do what is right and not what my anger wants! Hikaru quietly thought to herself as she trotted down the steps to the street.

53

$\mathcal{L}$arge volts of blue light highlighted the dark chamber Kimon was trapped in when his head slowly lifted off his sweaty chest. Releasing a soft moan, Kimon opened his deep indigo eyes to peer around the darkness surrounding him. Glancing up at his wrists, Kimon moved his hands around the chains fastening him to the wall when the second volt of light highlighted a large Nzer face staring at Kimon. Gasping in surprise, Kimon stared at the Nzer as it remained motionless in the center of the chamber when the light turned off. Gazing around the darkness, Kimon's heart began to race as he searched for the Nzer when he heard its deep breathes echoing through the chamber. Trying to make out the position of the Nzer as the volt of light highlighted the room again, Kimon gasped as the Nzer slammed its fist inches above his head.

Opening his eyes, Kimon stared at the Nzer that was inches away from his own face as it blew its hot breath across his skin. Coughing as the Nzers breath filled his nostrils, Kimon shifted uneasily before the Nzer as it stared at him with its flaming red eyes when the room fell dark again. Releasing nervous breathes; Kimon stared into the darkness as he continued to feel the Nzer's hot breath blowing in his face. Coughing again as the volt of light brightened the room once again; Kimon stared at the long yellow scar running over the Nzer's right eye. Pressing his head back against the wall as the Nzer snarled up its lips to reveal its sharp fangs, Kimon gazed at the Nzer as it pierced its talons through his shirt pulling him toward its drooling face.

"You vermin dis-sgus-st me . . . because-se of you my beautiful face is-s-s marred with your brand!" The Mighty One hissed.

"My brand . . ." Kimon questioned coughing the putrid smell of the Nzer out of his lungs.

"You s-see what I had to do because-se you touched me!"

Kimon gazed at the Nzer in confusion when it released his shirt to go on.

"It is-s-s unholy to be touched by unworthy creatures-s-s s-such as-s-s yours-self . . . s-so I had to s-scrap every las-st s-scale off my face jus-st s-so I wouldn't be pois-soned by you!"

Gasping, Kimon stared at the Nzer, "Kler . . . how can you be . . ."

"Alive . . . I told you I would out live you, pathetic princ-ce . . . you thought that you were doing a s-smart thing by s-sending me to the Dark Moon!" Kler chuckled, "You were wrong, vermin princ-ce . . . for a c-century, I remained s-sealed within that god awful cage . . . but then an Angel of Darknes-s-s came to my res-scue!"

* * * * * *

The dark shadows of the Dark Moon realm passed over the spacecraft's silvery oval surface when it suddenly started to be pulled to the planet Seira Moudei. The stars disappeared from the atmosphere as the spacecraft came closer to the planet where it suddenly froze within the shadow of the fourth moon. Large gusts of air blew out of the ship as the outer wall opened for a dark lady as she stepped into the bright halls.

Lifting her hand to the lights, the lady's extended fingers curled shattering the lights as she walked down toward the Restricted Cargo bay. Moving her hand before the door, the dark lady ripped the door from its frame and cast it across the hall before walking into the chamber. Stepping up to the illuminated, glass jar Kler was floating in; the dark lady shattered the side of the jar as she coiled her fingers into a fist. Watching the water pour out of the jar, the dark lady approached the Kler as it sat up to stare up at the blinding light. Stopping in front of the jar as the water flowed around her body; the dark lady extended her hand and darkened the lights.

"Who are you vermin?"

"Show some respect for this 'vermin' that just rescued you Under Dweller!" The dark lady stated.

"Forgive me . . . what s-species-s-s are you?"

"All you need to know is that I'm the one that rescued you and when the time comes you will repay me!" The lady stated walking away.

"Repay you?"

* * * * * *

Kler stared at Kimon with a malicious smile across its face. "What's-s-s wrong, vermin princ-ce . . . afraid?" Kler questioned, raising Kimon's chin with its talon.

"Nothing you do can make me fear you, Kler . . . you are a pitiful creature that seeks power for unjust reasons!" Kimon stated, pulling his face off Kler's talon.

"You s-should learn to s-speak to me with more res-spect vermin princ-ce or els-se, I may take s-something that means-s-s more to you than life!"

"You don't frighten me, Kler . . . and leave everyone out of this, you try to gain ground by threatening me with people I care dearly about; but it only shows what a coward you are! You have to use other tactics to improve your chances of winning, rather than fight honorably!" Kimon replied.

"I have no honor, vermin princ-ce . . . you s-said s-so yours-self, a long time ago! Or have you not regained thos-se memories-s-s yet . . . after all you did die!" Kler chuckled.

Kimon stared at Kler with honor in his eyes as he leaned toward it, "I may have died Kler, but the point is that I lived; a far better and more honorable life than you did! I gained the respect of over thirty planets in the honorable steps I took, how did you gain your respect . . . by starting a war where you lost every last minion?"

Snarling his lips at Kimon, Kler grabbed hold of his hair and ripped Kimon forward, "I've invited your pathetic friends-s-s here to watch you die, vermin princ-ce . . . but I want you to know that I intend to let you live long enough to s-see every las-st one of them die, including your s-sis-ster, before you! And as-s-s for that leader which I can s-see you've taken a liking to . . . I will s-slowly kill her jus-st s-so I can s-see you s-squirm! Then I will kill you joyfully!"

Down on Earth

The rain showered through the darkness to fall over Hikaru and her Hunters as they made their way through the dark streets. The wind had suddenly picked up and the trees bent toward them in an attempt to catch them to delay their journey. Dropping into a large puddle setting around the street, Hikaru walked into the center of the street to stare at a long line of Nzers standing at the end of the street. Releasing a long breath, Hikaru gazed back at her Hunters one by one before turning her attention back on the Nzers. Pulling her whipping hair out of her face, Hikaru stretched her fingers through her soaking raven hair as the Nzers charged down the street.

"Fan out!" Hikaru yelled through the rain at her Hunters as the Nzers came down upon them.

Flashing across the darkness, the lightning danced above the Hunters as they combated the regiment of blue marked Nzers. Taller in height and quicker paced; the blue marked Nzers brought a vicious assault upon the Devilry Hunters. Their long talons sliced through the air hitting thighs, arms, abdomens, and chests as the darkness started to consume the battle.

Stepping back as her arm got cut; Kimiko grabbed the Nzers swiping arms as they came toward her face. Growling in frustration as annoyance quickly flooded her face, Kimiko scrunched up her nose and gritting her teeth ignited her hands with the energy burning the Nzers hands off its body. Dropping the chard hands, Kimiko slapped her hands together and blew an enormous energy ball through the Nzers chest. Stepping back with her lips perched, Kimiko gazed at the dying Nzer as it grabbed her leg with a last hiss escaping its throat. Kicking the hand off her leg, Kimiko turned and began to deal with the next Nzer that charged toward her signing its death certificate.

Racing around several Nzers, En dropped back onto his back and lifting his hands in front of the leaping Nzers mouth blasted it into the air as the wind swept over his body. Rolling over as another Nzer slammed its fist into the ground; En blinked his eye sealing the hole around the Nzers hand trapping it as a second jumped for him. Leaping into the air, En avoided the Nzer making it slam into the Nzer trapped in the ground. Landing back where he was, En gazed down at the hole to see the Nzer's hand still within the ground. Crossing his arms over his chest, En closed his eyes focusing all his attention on the wind that slowly began to whip around his body. Gazing at an approaching Nzer, En shot his hands away from his body directing the wind across the street to hammer into the Nzer's scaly face. Jumping up and down, En crossed his legs one over the other and spun around laughing triumphantly.

Holding his arms away from his body, Jeremy held this large sphere around himself as the Nzers charged toward him. Extending his hand toward one Nzer, Jeremy lifted it into the air and clenching his fist crushed all its muscles and bones together killing it. Throwing that one into a nearby Nzer, Jeremy lifted every other Nzer around him into the air and again crushed them before casting them aside. Crossing his arms over his chest, Jeremy smirked at a charging Nzer as it leapt toward him. Disappearing as the Nzer landed where he was, Jeremy reappeared behind it and kicking it in the butt disappeared to reappear once again behind it. Continually repeating this charade, Jeremy finally appeared in front of the Nzer and blasted a ball of sparking lights into its face. Snapping his fingers, Jeremy stepped backward and spun around to confront the next Nzer charging toward him.

Blocking a large Nzer's swinging talons, Maya drew back her arm and releasing an angry cry hammered her fist through the Nzer's face. Pulling her hand back out of the Nzer, Maya turned and throwing her leg up smashed her knee into the Nzers' leaping at her. Dropping her leg, Maya stared at the Nzer as they hammered across the street before she gazed to her left to see another coming toward her. Turning toward the Nzer, Maya spied another approaching from the other side and at the last minute ducked allowing both Nzers to slam into each other. Quickly jumping back up, Maya punched the Nzers casting them across the street before following them. Flipping over the Nzers, Maya landed on her hands and hammered her feet into the Nzers throwing them into the air to land on a jagged fence line to slowly die.

Standing with her legs and arms extended, Touko shot enormous volts of electricity throughout the darkness spearing through Nzers and highlighting the area for the other Hunters. Gazing over at a quickly approaching Nzer, Touko stared at the soaking tree five feet away from it and smiled. Pressing her hands into a circle, Touko charged an enormous bolt of electricity and cast it toward the tree. Watching as the bolt hammered into the wet tree, Touko smiled as everything fifteen feet away was electrified to a cinder. Sucking in a deep breath as the bolt touched her toes; Touko soaked up the electricity and threw it toward another charging Nzer as a big smile crossed over her face.

Swinging his baton through the showering curtain, Hagane hammered it against several charging Nzer's shattering their ribs. Turning around to push it beneath a smaller Nzer, Hagane lifted his baton into the air throwing the Nzer backward into a building wall. Twirling the large thick baton in front of his body; Hagane hammered it across one Nzer's face, another one's shoulder, and through one's abdomen. Pulling out his baton, Hagane stepped back to watch the Nzer fall to his feet before quickly turning to smash another Nzer away from his face. Walking toward the Nzer, Hagane slid his baton beneath his arm and plunged his arm through the Nzers hide to rip a young man out.

Snapping a light pole in half, Masumi threw the pole through a large Nzer's hide and smiled as Touko ignited the light bulb on the other end. Masumi stood watching the Nzer fry as the rain hit the sparking electricity that was touching something metal. Quickly turning around to avoid a swinging talon, Masumi lifted the Nzer into the air and threw it across the street ripping the large amounts of iron out of its blood before it hit the concrete. Surging the iron into three small spheres; Masumi shot the balls across the street to spear through several charging Nzers. Turning toward another Nzer leaping at his face, Masumi lifted his hand and caught the Nzer before it slammed its talons into Masumi's face. Gazing annoyed at the Nzer, Masumi winked and his spheres speared through the Nzers chest.

Across the street, Hikaru pulled Manabu behind her as she blocked Nzer's swinging talons with Esal's bronze sword. Pushing Manabu backward, Hikaru hopped out of the way to land on her rear to stare up at the Nzer's snarling face. Hopping backward on her butt, Hikaru raised Esal's sword blocking a swing allowing her to quickly stand up missing the next swing. Pulling Manabu backward as he messed with his data pad, Hikaru lifted up her shield to allow her time to gain her breath.

"Manabu Lí, what are you doing trying to get yourself killed?" Hikaru questioned.

"Of course not, Hikaru; I wouldn't be trying to help you if my intentions were to get myself killed! I am simple converting the molecular structure of the Nzers' immune system so that you can pinpoint the precise location of vulnerability!" Manabu stated.

Hopping back to avoid a swinging talon, Hikaru yelled out as the Nzer hammered its arm in between her legs. Kicking the Nzer in the head, Hikaru pulled Manabu away from the swinging talons.

"Meaning what?" Hikaru questioned blocking the Nzer.

"It means the spot of vulnerability is right here . . ." Manabu informed kicking the Nzer between its legs. Watching the Nzer drop to its knees groaning in pain, Hikaru cocked her head to the side and smiled at Manabu. "There you see . . . everything in the world has a weakness!" Manabu stated looking down at his data pad.

"Yeah, but for how long," Hikaru questioned pulling Manabu away as the Nzer stood back up.

"Just do it again!" Manabu stated kicking the Nzer again in between the legs.

"All right, Mister Action Star!" Hikaru chuckled pulling him away. Running up to Kimiko, Hikaru pulled Manabu behind her as she pulled up Esal's sword to slice it through several Nzers.

"Hikaru, can't you put up your shield?" Kimiko questioned looking at her.

"I can't Kimiko, Esal was the one that did all of those things!"

"Hikaru Neijo, you know as well as I do that there is some kind of power inside you and it is not the same kind of power Esal called upon!"

"Kimiko, I can't!"

"Yes, you can Hikaru . . . if you don't do something quick, we're going to be down here fighting these Nzers forever and we won't get a chance to save Yuri or Kimon!" Kimiko declared.

"All right, I'll try . . ." Hikaru stated pulling Esal's bronze sword out of a large Nzer's hide; **"Everyone get over here!"**

Slicing Esal's blade through the ground, Hikaru sucked in a deep breath as she lifted her hands above her head. Closing her eyes, Hikaru began to concentrate as the barrier slowly came down around everyone as they came toward Hikaru, Kimiko, and Manabu. Groaning, Hikaru thought of Esal and Kimon and the city as the Nzers hammered into the shield.

There has to be something else that they are vulnerable to! Hikaru thought quietly as she strained herself trying to keep the shield up and think. There is, they don't like water . . . they wouldn't come in after me when I was in the school pool! But where am I going to get enough water to do anything?

Pinching her eyes tightly closed, Hikaru wrinkled her nose across her concentrated face when a loud rumble started to echo through the Nzer's bellows. Gazing around the street through the barrier, the Hunters listened curiously to the ruckus as it grew louder. Turning around, the Nzers looked down the street attentively when a large wave of water crashed around the corner. Scrambling around the barrier, the Nzers quickly raced down the street trying to outrace the wave when it pushed through them carrying them with as it swept through the city.

Opening her eyes, Hikaru lowered her arms as the barrier disappeared to see her Hunters cheering hysterically. Smiling wirily, Hikaru released a heavy breath as she turned toward the spacecraft floating above the tower. Moving her wet raven hair out of her eyes; Hikaru stared at the dark ship before gazing back at her Hunters.

"This isn't over yet . . . it's only beginning guys!"

Racing around the buildings surrounding the tower, Hikaru and her Hunters walked up to the end of the street to stare up at the large spacecraft hovering above the tower. Whipping rain off her cheeks, Hikaru gazed at the platform where she had first seen Esal and fought back several tears. Sucking in a deep breath, Hikaru started toward the tower with her Hunters close behind. Glancing down at the sword in her hand, Hikaru gazed appalled at the copper blade that had consumed the once beautiful crystalline blade. Tightening her grip around the hilt, Hikaru gazed up at the Latrinian **Warship G-731** with vengeful eyes.

It's Judgment Day! Hikaru thought to herself.

Tuesday, April 29, 2026, 12:00am

54

Latrinian Warship G-731

The same blue marked Nzer that had obtained Kimon rushed up to Kler's seat and dropped to its knee. Dropping its head exposing its small feathers behind its head; the blue marked Nzer quietly hissed. "S-Sire, the vermin Hunters-s-s and their leader are approaching the s-ship!"

"Well we don't want to keep them waiting . . . when they reach the s-ship open the hatchway!" Kler ordered to an orange marked Nzer sitting at the controls.

"Yes-s-s Mighty One . . ."

Earth—Tuesday Morning, April 29, 2026

The rain continued to pour over the city as the Devilry Hunters raced up to the large iron poles holding up the tower. Gazing around the blood-stained grass blades, the Hunters stared at all the dead bodies from men to children lying around the area. Shaking her head in disgust, Hikaru looked to the top of the tower where the spacecraft was hovering. Gazing at En, Hikaru smiled and pointed at the tower's peak.

Looking at the top of the tower, En looked at Hikaru and smiled nervously. Lifting his arms, En shot the wind out around everyone and slowly began to pick them up to lift them to the tower's summit. Lifting everyone up to the top platform at the tower's peak, En gently landed on the concrete and dropped his arms as the wind disappeared.

Looking at the overlook of the city, everyone gazed sadly at all the destruction the Nzers had caused. Large buildings lay in debris heaps, every exit was blocked off or dismantled, and several areas across the city muffled screams trailed up from burning neighborhoods.

Turning away from the city, Hikaru gazed up at the spacecraft as a hatchway opened up. Staring at the entrance as her Hunters walked up to her side, Hikaru cocked her head to the side before she looked at Kimiko and smiled.

Standing around the hatchway waiting for their visitors, over a dozen Nzers flinched with their talons ready when a part of the floor five feet away blew up. Thrown back by the force, the Nzers sat up to stare at the hole as Maya leapt up into the ship and charged toward them screaming.

Pulling herself up into the ship, Hikaru stared around the dark hall when she spied Maya sitting on a large heap of Nzers. Chuckling Hikaru assisted the others up while Maya sat flexing her muscles. Standing up once everyone was inside, Hikaru gaze around the dark hall as Maya stood up and joined them.

"So where do we go?" Touko questioned.

"I don't know I've never been here before!" Hikaru stated.

"Maybe Maya should've left one of those Nzers alive so it could have told us!" Jeremy stated looking at Maya.

"Oh yeah, good idea Jeremy . . . we'll just ask a Nzer which way to go while its talons are coming toward our faces!" Maya stated smacking him in the arm.

"Yeah, it was just a suggestion and don't hit me you hit hard!" Jeremy whined rubbing his arm.

"Guys, hush . . . stop fighting, we'll find a way!"

"Yes, it will not be so hard to find whatever we are trying to find in this dark ship . . . after all if you are trying to find a certain person like Yuri perhaps all you would have to do is use the COM boxes I gave you!" Manabu shouted.

"Oh, good idea . . . if we find Yuri; Kimon shouldn't be too far away!" Hikaru excitedly stated pulling her COM box out. Pressing her thumb on the gray square, Hikaru unlocked the COM box and pressing the red button was surprised to see a map of the ship come up. Smiling, Hikaru pressed her finger against the miniature purple button to see it pop up flashing. "There's Yuri, she's two floors above us and twenty chambers down in the lower regiment it says . . . yeah, can we do this with Kimon?" Hikaru questioned Manabu.

"You should be able to. He's the violet color . . ." Manabu stated as Nzers raced around the corner. "But then again we may not get the chance to try!"

"Guys prepare for battle!" Hikaru screamed.

Watching from the control room, Kler sat upon his seat within the shadows scratching his talons up and down his broken armrest. The impatience in his breathing showed more vividly in his large red eyes as they stared at the view screen unwavering. Digging his long talons into the armrest, Kler bellowed out through the room as he watched the Devilry Hunters dismantle his Nzers.

Stepping back as Kimiko blew the last Nzer into thousands of pieces, Hikaru released a breath when she gazed at all the Hunters. Smiling brightly, Hikaru gazed around the room when her smile slowly faded.

"Where's Manabu?"

Looking up and down the dark hall, the Hunters realized Manabu was missing when Kler's hiss echoed through the halls.

"What do we do Manabu's gone!" Touko panicked.

"First we need to stay calm . . . now we didn't let any Nzers escape, did we?" Hikaru questioned gazing at all her Hunters, "so Manabu probably went to hide somewhere or is exploring the ship or he went to do what he does!"

"What does he do?" Jeremy questioned.

"I'm not sure!" Hikaru giggled. "But we have to find Yuri and Kimon, so we have to get going . . . we'll find him. Remember, we can find him with the COM box or he'll find us!"

Watching the Devilry Hunters through the view screen, Kler smiled maliciously before turning toward its command deck. "Prepare the Hunter collecting!" Kler chuckled.

"Preparing to open throttle doors-s-s . . ." a small Nzer relayed.

"Open them now . . ." Kler ordered bellowing.

Walking down the dark halls following the volts of light that sparked through the ship, the Hunters turned a corner to quickly stop when they saw seventeen-foot stocky Nzers with spiked clubs. Gazing at the Nzers as they bellowed into the darkness, the Hunters cleared the path as a club was thrown down the hall at them. Quickly springing out of the way as the five large Nzers came charging down the hall; the Devilry Hunters spread out into their ring preparing for combat.

Stepping out in front of the others, Hikaru lifted her barrier as the Nzers threw another club toward them. Stepping up beside Hikaru, Touko lifted her hands toward the walls and slowly started to suck the electricity out of the ship to surge it toward the approaching Nzer highlighting the darkness. Once she was able to see the Nzers clearly, Kimiko charged the energy around her hands and walking up to the barrier stuck her hand through it to blast the energy through one of the Nzers.

Racing up to the barrier, one of the Nzers hammered the club against the invisible wall before hammering into it. Bellowing angrily at the Hunters, the Nzer continued to hammer its club against the barrier when En happened to gaze behind him to see more Nzers approaching. Yelling, En raised his arms shooting a strong currant out to slow the Nzers when Maya charged forward.

"We don't have time for this . . ." Hikaru stated once her brother came to her side, "we need to get around them somehow!"

Nodding his head, Masumi straightened his body, "a distraction!"

"What . . ." Hikaru called as Masumi walked to the front of the barrier.

"Kimiko burn a hole in the wall big enough for you to fit through but not the Nzers!" Masumi ordered.

"I'm on it . . ." Kimiko stated racing up to the wall Masumi pointed at.

Walking up to the barrier, Masumi extended his hand started pulling the large amounts of iron from the seventeen-foot Nzers as Kimiko burned a hole through the ship's wall. Stepping away as the melted iron fell to the floor, Kimiko turned to Masumi.

"Done . . ."

"Good, now everyone get in there!" Masumi ordered as he started shooting the metal spheres through the Nzers bodies.

Jumping through the hole, Kimiko gazed around the dark hall before helping the others through. As Hagane crawled through, Hikaru leapt into the other hall and turned around to look at Masumi.

"Come on, you're the last one, Masumi . . ."

Walking up to the hole as his spheres continued to shoot through the Nzers, Masumi looked at Hikaru. "You go ahead. I'll hold them off . . ."

"No, Masumi, you're coming with us!" Hikaru ordered preparing to crawl back through the hole.

Pushing Hikaru back in, Masumi smiled at her, "it's all right Hikaru, otherwise these creatures will find someway to follow us!"

"Masumi, I'm the leader . . ." Hikaru yelled when Masumi pushed her back and stretched one of his spheres out in front of the hole.

Slamming her fists against the metal, Hikaru quickly turned to Kimiko, "burn back through it!"

Placing her hands against the metal, Kimiko looked at Hikaru, "I can't; he's not letting me!"

"Masumi . . ." Hikaru yelled banging against the wall.

Taking Hikaru's arm, Hagane turned her toward him, "Hikaru, you are the leader . . . you need to proceed with the mission! We came here to get Yuri and Kimon so that the Nzers did not destroy the prince . . . Masumi is giving us the chance to get as far as we can without other distractions!"

Gazing at Hagane, Hikaru looked around at everyone else and slowly nodded her head in agreement. Pulling out of Hagane's hands, Hikaru lifted her COM box and looked at the layout of the ship. Hitting the miniature, green button; Hikaru pinpointed their location with Kimiko and started walking in a direction.

Watching from the control room, Kler chuckled conceitedly as he gazed at the Devilry Hunters through the view screen. "One down . . ."

Dispersing light from her body as they walked down the dark hall, Touko couldn't help but start to feel nervous and frightened. Her large navy-blue eyes scanned the hall while Hagane walked close behind her to her relieve. Though Hikaru stood in front of her leading the way, Touko couldn't shake the feeling that they were being watched. As a soft echo reached her ears, Touko suddenly stopped and stared around in the darkness.

"Something's coming . . ."

Inching back against Hagane, Touko yelped as a tiny mouse jumped out of the shadows before her. Hands over her mouth, Touko gazed around at everyone who was watching her. Gazing at En as he started laughing, Touko looked annoyed at him.

"It's not funny En Skilou; I thought something was coming!" Touko stated when a hatchet flew by her face.

Jumping back screaming, Touko pushed Hagane against the floor as a second hatchet flew past where his head was. Gazing down hall into the shadows as Nzers emerged leading several small creatures with frills surrounding their necks. The tiny creatures looked like a frilled lizard to Touko at first until they shot fire at her making her change her mind.

"Where are these creatures coming from anyway?" Touko questioned as they all ducked behind a corner.

"I'm not sure but we can't fight fire . . ." Kimiko stated pulling her head back as a flame shot toward it.

"It's about time we go up a level . . ." Hikaru suggested.

"Thank you, I was hoping we were going to by pass the baby dragons!" Touko replied enthusiastically.

"Kimiko, let's burn through that ceiling . . ." Hikaru replied.

While Hikaru held the barrier around them and Jeremy extinguished the flame throwers; Kimiko stood on Maya and Touko's human pyramid. Standing with their arms entwined, Maya and Touko bore Kimiko's weight as she cut through the ceiling. Knocking the burnt metal away from the others, Kimiko poked her head through the hole making sure there were no Nzers waiting to cut a head off. Pulling herself up to the next level, Kimiko reached back down to take En's hand then Jeremy to protect against anything that may came along. Taking Maya's hand, Jeremy and En lifted her to the next level followed by Hikaru. Quickly standing up, Hikaru looked down as Hagane lifted Touko to the hole when a large Nzer raced around the corner.

"Hagane . . ." Hikaru yelled as the Nzer lifted Hagane away from the hole.

Throwing Touko out of his arms, Hagane watched En and Jeremy catch her, "keep going Hikaru!"

"But Hagane . . ."

"Hikaru go now . . . I mean it!" Hagane yelled as he was pulled out of view.

55

Searching the other floor for Hagane, Hikaru quickly moved away as another Nzer attempted to leap into the hole. Dropping backward, Hikaru screamed at the Nzer as she kicked its arm that was trying to grab her foot. Scrambling away from the hole, Hikaru stepped on the Nzer's hand and raced around a corner with the rest of her Hunters. Gazing around the corner, Hikaru stared at the Nzer as it tried to squeeze its large body through the hole.

"I have an idea . . ." Hikaru stated taking out her COM box.

Pointing the COM box toward the Nzer, Hikaru pressed the red button and quickly pulled it back toward her body.

"What did you do?" Kimiko questioned looking at the COM box.

"Well, I figured that if we are going to be in here for a while it would be nice to know how close we are to the Nzers . . . so I just loaded them into the COM box! See, the closest one is the one around the corner!" Hikaru happily stated.

"That's one Nzer Hikaru . . . what about the rest?" Touko asked.

"They all look the same, do you think the COM box is going to individually mark each one or give every one of them the same mark?" Hikaru smiled.

"So since there are so many of them . . . we'll be able to see every Nzer in the ship! Hikaru you are brilliant!" Kimiko chuckled.

"No, I'm mad; I'm tired of these things taking my friends!" Hikaru stated as she looked at the COM box, "I think we should go that way!"

"Why, is that way clear?" Jeremy questioned looking down the hall.

"It looks to be, but I just don't want to walk past that Nzer!" Hikaru smiled.

Shaking his head with a smile, Jeremy followed Hikaru as she walked down the dark hall. The bellowing and talons scrapping across the metal floor echoed down the hall as the Devilry Hunters walked away from the Nzer leaving it alone in the darkness. Taking a last look at the area where she was separated from Hagane, Hikaru fought back the urge to go back and save him. But the loyal security of all the other Hunters around her silenced her thoughts as she turned away.

"This-s-s is-s-s jus-st too enjoyable; the vermin girl has-s-s now los-st two of her Hunters-s-s, oh how enjoyable . . . let's-s-s s-see; oh, s-she's-s-s heading toward the ships-s-s power cells-s-s! Well s-she'll have company real s-soon . . ." Kler chuckled.

Walking out of the dark hall; Hikaru and her Hunters came strolling into a brighter room containing large electrical mainframes with massive conductive power transformers at each corner. Staring around the wide room, Hikaru stepped down the aluminum steps and started across the vibrating floor when a loud hiss echoed through the hall. Jumping down the steps, Hikaru started running across the room to find it cave in as she stepped on it.

"What kind of floor is this?" Jeremy questioned as he fell forward against it.

Staring at Jeremy as he lifted himself from the floor to see that his frame was still pressed into it, En burst out laughing. "It's a better version of you Jeremy!"

"Shut up En . . ." Jeremy yelled.

Bending down to press her hand into the floor, Kimiko straightened up to stare at her handprint, "it's squishy!"

"No this has to be the power cells that give the ship its power, so in case of a power surge the floors were made of a super pliable rubber!" Touko stated.

"Why is it rubber . . ." Hikaru asked taking a few steps.

"Because rubber is conductive, if anything happened to the power cells over there; none of the ships circuits would get fried!"

"Okay well, I want to get across this funhouse floor and over to those stable stairs quickly!" Hikaru stated jumping on the rubber toward the far wall.

Racing out to the end of the hall, several Nzers stared out across the room to where Hikaru and the Hunters were walking. Thrusting their heads forward, the Nzers bellowed out into the room before lunging over the stairs to bounce on the floor. Scrapping their talons across the rubber floor, the Nzers quickly came toward the Devilry Hunters.

Turning around as the others climbed up the steps, Touko watched the Nzers approaching when her eyes befell the power transformers. Smiling, Touko walked down to the bottom step and extended her hand toward the power cells. Closing her eyes, Touko extended her reach and tore into the electrical mainframes causing them to explode and shoot electrical waves through the air. Sucking the power into her body, Touko shot the electrical volts toward the approaching Nzers and burnt them.

"Touko come on . . ." Maya called as they reached the top of the stairs.

"Go Maya, help them . . . it's my turn to hold off these smelly creatures!" Touko smiled encouragingly.

Staring at Touko hesitantly, Maya nodded her head before racing after En and Jeremy, "good luck Touko!"

Racing down the hall, Hikaru lead her Hunters to a large iron door. Gazing down at her COM box, Hikaru looked back at Maya and nodded. Walking up to the large door, Maya clenched her fists and hammered her hand into the joint that held the two doors together. Pushing her hands through the caved in metal, Maya smashed the joint apart allowing the door to push open freely. Stepping back, Maya smiled triumphantly before kicking her foot against the door pushing it open. Following the others into the chamber, Maya stared up a winding stairwell and whistled.

Gazing back down the hall as a bellow echoed into the chamber, Hikaru looked down at her COM box. Staring at the small visual; Hikaru watched over two dozen white blinking lights quickly approaching the small green dot. Looking up at the others, Hikaru smiled nervously before running toward the stairs.

"Time to go . . ." En chuckled.

Racing up the winding stairwell, Hikaru quickly leapt up the stairs as she heard the Nzers race into the chamber. Following Hikaru up the steps, Kimiko gazed down at the bottom of the chamber to watch with her mouth wide open as all the Nzers raced through the chamber door when En pushed her forward. Jumping up the steps, Maya followed close behind En and Jeremy when her foot crashed through the steps. Falling against the steps, Maya looked down at the hole and slowly pulled her cut leg out. Grabbing the railing, Maya pulled herself up when En jumped down beside her to help lift her out of the hole.

"Is she OK?" Jeremy yelled coming back down the steps.

"Yeah, other than a nasty cut on her calve, she's fine!" En stated pulling Maya's arm over his shoulder.

"Come on, let's go!" Kimiko yelled.

"En, you can't drag me along with you, I'll slow you guys down and the Nzers will catch all of us!" Maya declared.

"I'm not leaving you behind!" En stated.

"En, listen to me . . ." Maya ordered grabbing En's cheeks, "you need to keep going! I'll be fine; I'll make sure that the Nzers don't follow you guys this way!"

"Guys the Nzers are getting closer!" Kimiko yelled.

"Go . . ." Maya ordered pushing En forward toward Jeremy.

Turning around, Maya started slamming her fists into the stairs shattering them as Jeremy pulled En up the steps. Walking backward, Maya continued to destroy the stairs creating a large gap between her and the Nzers as they stopped at the far end of the hole she had created. Slamming her feet into the stairs, Maya started breaking off pieces of the aluminum floor and throwing it at the Nzers. Pausing briefly as she watched the Nzers leap onto the walls, Maya stared annoyed as the Nzers started coming toward her.

"Oh, sure; why wouldn't they be able to crawl on the walls?"

Pulling En through the door at the top of the stairs, Jeremy fell against the wall as Hikaru and Kimiko slammed the door closed. Holding the door closed while Kimiko burnt the seam together; Hikaru looked back at En as he paced the floor with his hands on his head. The bellows of the Nzers echoed up the stairwell as Kimiko finished sealing the seam when Hikaru walked up to En and Jeremy.

"How do they know everywhere we are . . ." En questioned.

"We're in their ship En; they probably have sensors in places we would never imagine!" Jeremy declared.

"What's bothering me is that everyone has been disappearing according to how Hikaru found us!" Kimiko stated.

"What . . ." En replied.

"You guys haven't noticed . . . first Masumi then Hagane, then Touko and now Maya! Somehow the Nzers know us by the way Hikaru found us!" Kimiko explained.

"Oh my god, you're right . . . but that would mean Jeremy will be next!" Hikaru stated looking at the three.

"Thank you Hikaru; I needed to know that!" Jeremy whispered.

Watching from the Control Room, Kler grinned excitedly as it stared at Hikaru, Kimiko, En and Jeremy through the view screen. Its razor-sharp fangs clattered together while its lips twitched slowly as large pockets of drool streamed from its yearning mouth. Widening his large blood-red eyes; Kler lurched forward from his shadows to scratch his long talons across Hikaru's body.

Slowly walking down a hall behind Hikaru while she stared at her COM box; Kimiko, En, and Jeremy carefully scanned the darkness when they strolled out into a room without a floor. Quickly grabbing Hikaru before she stepped onto air, Kimiko turned her toward her and gazed angrily at her.

"Hikaru what are you doing . . . there isn't any floor here!"

"Kimiko, you almost pushed me down there!" Hikaru yelled back.

"Girls, calm down; we just need to turn back and take another path . . ." Jeremy declared turning around to stare at several Nzers standing at the edge of the shadows in the hall. "Oh, man!"

"Hikaru you're supposed to watch for these!" Kimiko yelled.

"Well, I would've if you weren't distracting me!" Hikaru yelled back.

"Everyone jump!" En yelled as the Nzers raced toward them.

"Are you crazy . . . there's no floor En!" Kimiko yelled.

"I said jump!" En yelled pushing Kimiko, Hikaru and Jeremy down the hole before leaping after them.

As they started to fall down the long dark chasm; En pulled a large currant beneath himself and his friends gently stopping them from falling further. Lifting up to the end of the hall; En, Jeremy, Kimiko, and Hikaru smiled as the Nzers leapt for them to fall down the chasm. Chuckling triumphantly, the Devilry Hunters leapt around in the air as En safely brought them to the other end of the chasm. Watching her friends laughing enthusiastically, Hikaru glanced down at her COM box to see more Nzers approaching from the side they were on.

"We've got company on the way!"

Quickly racing around the corner of the hall; a dozen blue marked Nzers dashed up to the end of the hall to look out over the dark chasm. Glancing toward the other end, the Nzers snarled up their lips and bellowed as more Nzers raced up to the chasm. Looking down the chasm, several Nzers started crawling down the walls while others headed up to the upper levels connected to the chasm.

Rapidly spearing its talons through the chasm walls, the commanding Nzer climbed up to the upper hall. Lifting itself into the hall, the Nzer ran its nose against the floor inhaling a deep sniff of the floor to bellow down the chasm before it took off down the hall after the Devilry Hunters. Scrapping its talons across the metal floor, the Nzer noisily pursued the Hunters as several of its minions came along its side.

Lifting Hikaru into a ventilation shaft, Jeremy quickly replaced the grate and ducked as the Nzers raced beneath them. Lifting his finger to his mouth, Jeremy insured that the others would remain quiet until he was sure the Nzers were gone. Fearing to make even the slightest sound, the Hunters held perfectly still while they slowly released air from their lungs. The scrapping of the Nzers talons continued to echo through the hall while; Jeremy, En, Kimiko, and Hikaru lay corpselike within the vents.

Finally as the halls fell quiet, Hikaru lifted her arms before her face and stared at her COM box and nodded. Peeking over Hikaru's shoulder, Jeremy stared at the grid that showed the navigation of the vents before he started moving the direction he was facing. Slowly sliding their legs and hands over the vent floors, the Devilry Hunters quietly made their way through the ventilation shafts while; Kler threw a fit in the Control Room.

Throwing a large chair through the glass navigation grid; Kler lifted the communications commander from its seat and shook him angrily before tossing it against the wall. Following the direction the commander had flown, Kler looked through the large hole it made in the Control Room's east wall. Throwing its large muscular arm through the hole, Kler ripped the commander back in front of its face and snapped its fangs before the commander's mouth.

"Pleas-se run that by me again!" Kler bellowed in the commander's face.

"The vermin have dis-sappeared from our grids-s-s entirely S-sir . . . navigation is-s-s checking to s-see if they found another route . . ."

"You better hope that he does-s-s commander; or you are going to wis-sh that you were down there being killed by the vermin girl hers-self!" Kler threatened.

Throwing the commander back through the wall, Kler turned toward the rest of his commanding officers. Curling its long talons together behind its jutting back, Kler walked across the large bridge stretching over the Control Room.

"Let this-s-s be a warning to all of you . . . if one more of you los-ses-s-s that vermin girl; you will all be s-slaughtered like vermin and hung through the corridors-s-s for our future generations-s-s to s-see the s-shameful ances-stors-s-s that failed to handle a s-single, pathetic, whimpering, vermin girl!"

Quickly turning back to their display screens, all of the commanding officers continued to do their tasks with more anxiety as Kler hovered above them. Rubbing its long talons down the jut of its back, Kler inhaled a long breath as his blue frill expanded around his back. Moving across the bridge, Kler extended his long muscular legs to slowly set them upon the porcelain stones laid over the metal frame of the ship's bridge. Turning his large red eyes toward the view screen; Kler released a low growl from its throat as it stared at the visuals of the ship's bare interior. Turning around, Kler walked back down the bridge to his seat overlaid by shadows and sat down to quietly listen to the hum of the control room's power cells. Moving its eyes toward the left side of the room, Kler stare at the blinking lights flashing across the larger navigation grid and snorted a large breath out of the darkness.

"Commander Tuk, go check on the vermin, prince's-s-s pes-stilential s-sis-ster . . . every time the vermin were in a jam the vermin girl would look at a s-small little box-x! S-see if the young princess-s-s has-s-s one as-s-s well . . ." Kler ordered.

"Upon your command, S-sire . . ." the commander addressed replied respectfully before it disappeared out the archway.

Leaning back against its chair, Kler stared through the shadows veiling it while; it snarled its lips up to flash its razor-sharp fangs. Its large eyes expanded momentarily as it listened to the ruckus of all the commanders within the Control Room carrying out their duties under his watchful unforgiving eyes as the city clock chimed the morning toll.

56

Earth—Wednesday Morning, April 30, 2026

From the occasional volts of light that shot past them in the dark halls, the ventilation shafts were an improvement. Coiling around the top seams of the vents was an illuminative powder that almost seemed to be burnt inside the metal. Other than the dim light from the powder, the occasional passing volts of light beneath the vents pushed through the grates the Devilry Hunters were approaching.

Slowly sliding himself toward a gray light was briefly pushed through, Jeremy released a gasping breath as a musky smell flew up into his face. Nearly vomiting from the smell; Jeremy lifted his white shirt's collar over his nose to breathe as he gazed down through the grate. Turning away as the smell started to becoming more intense, Jeremy gazed at his friends when they suddenly smelled the scent.

"Oh, I think I'm going to be sick!" Kimiko whispered turning away.

"What is that?" En questioned holding his hand over his mouth and nose.

Pushing past the others Hikaru slid up to the grate and lifting it up dropped down into the room below. Landing upon the floor, Hikaru caused a large cloud of mist to shoot up around her frame as she looked around the dark room. Straightening her body, Hikaru rose off the ground and peered around the room when something touched her shoulder. Turning around with a squeal, Hikaru stared at Jeremy as he quickly laid his hand over her mouth silencing her.

"What are you trying to do . . . give me a heart attack?" Hikaru yelled in a whisper whacking Jeremy.

"What are you doing?" Jeremy questioned grabbing Hikaru's arm.

"I want to know what's in here," Hikaru replied.

"No . . . I don't think you do!" En stated pointing to a wall.

Turning toward the wall En indicated, the Devilry Hunters stared at an illuminated large alien body hanging on the wall. Centered in the middle of its long narrow face; the alien's enormous sphere eyes illusively stared at the Hunters making it appear to be alive. Its slender long arms reached far past its extensive torso to the thick thighs connected to jutting hips. Bulky ribs protruded out of the alien's silky skin stretched into a skeletal stomach which then extended to the projecting hips. The huge thighs radiating out of the jagged hips stretched down to shrink into knot knees then into slender sturdy forelegs which would've been held up by two plump flat toes.

Staring at the alien's gangly frame, the Devilry Hunters slowly approached the wall when Jeremy tripped over something. Quickly lifting his body off something malleable, Jeremy jumped to his feet covering his mouth. Jumping backward behind En, Jeremy whipped his hands on his pants and whipped his hands through his hair shooting something wet through the air.

"What is that?" Jeremy questioned.

"Something smelly . . . and now it's all over you!" Kimiko giggled.

"This is far from funny Kimiko!" Jeremy whispered in a fury.

"He's right, this isn't funny . . . Jeremy can you light up this room enough so we can see what's in it, but not bright enough for the Nzers to see us if they're walking by?" Hikaru questioned.

"Yeah, give me a sec . . ." Jeremy stated walking in front of Hikaru.

Releasing a long breath, Jeremy shook his body as his eyes slowly sealed. Inhaling a deep breath, Jeremy opened his eyes and raising his arms into the air slowly started to illuminate the room.

Gazing around the room, Hikaru stared wide eyed as she slowly started to make out over thirty bodies lining the walls. Her brown eyes slowly scanned each alien body as she released a long breath. Gazing down at the floor, Hikaru stared at a fat decaying body which Jeremy had landed on. Pulling a small smile across her face, Hikaru gazed back at Jeremy, who was quietly throwing a fit. Stepping around the body, Hikaru walked up to the wall to inspect each body.

"What are these?" Kimiko questioned touching the smallest alien on the wall.

"These have to be inhabitants of the planets in the Solari . . ." Hikaru declared gazing at the bodies, "But I don't understand why they are in this ship . . . Esal said that the only alien species that was imprisoned in the ship was the last surviving Nzer!"

Walking up to a weird fish looking alien; En wrinkled up his nose, "well we can be sure that these aren't Nzers!"

Gazing at En, Hikaru looked at the alien Kimiko was standing in front of back to the one she was facing, "no, the Nzers did this . . . they were going around killing species, but some of the planets were too protected by the prince's forces! The Nzers's think that once they get rid of Kimon they will be able to finish what they started! It's like they're making a museum of creatures . . . and Earth was next!"

"That's creepy!" Jeremy stated.

"I don't know what's more creepy though; that the Nzers are really doing it or that Hikaru guessed that they were doing it!" En whispered gazing at the alien fish face.

Staring at the alien face, Hikaru turned to her friends, "come on, we've go to stop the next planet collection!"

Turning back to the grate, Hikaru raced across the room and climbed up several boxes toward the ventilation shafts with her Hunters close behind. Jumping onto the top box; Hikaru gazed down at Kimiko, En, and Jeremy when several Nzers burst through the chamber door. Grabbing Kimiko's arm, Hikaru quickly pulled her up and pushed her into the vents to grab En as the Nzers raced toward them. Pulling En onto the box, Hikaru quickly took Jeremy's arm and lifted him up as the Nzers hammered into the line of boxes. Stumbling toward the edge of the box, Hikaru fell to her knees to stare at a large scaly face snarling its lips up at her. Screaming in its face, Hikaru avoided its swinging talons as Jeremy grabbed the back of her gray skirt and pulled her into the vents.

Up in the Control Room

The shadows surrounding Kler were utterly dark until Commander Tuk came rushing under the arch. Trotting up to the seat within the shadows, Commander Tuk glanced around the room when Kler's red eyes opened breaking up the darkness. Leaning forward, Kler pushed its large mussel out of the shadows to snarl at Commander Tuk when it raised a small box in front of Kler's face. Shooting his eyes down toward the little COM box, Kler quickly snapped the box out of Commander Tuk's hand and started trying to open it. Digging its talons through the small seam in the box, Kler tried to rip it open then he started to slam it down against the arm of its chair when the navigation commander turned toward Kler.

"Mighty One . . . the vermin have been found in the S-Sanctity Room!"

"Get them; I grow tired of waiting . . ." Kler bellowed gazing up from the COM box, "I want to kill the vermin princ-ce before it finds-s-s a way to es-scape!"

"Very good, s-sire . . ."

Pulling her legs away from the grate opening, Hikaru watched with wide eyes as the Nzers hammered their talons through the vent's aluminum walls. Scooting back further into the vents, Hikaru pushed against Jeremy as the Nzers ripped the vents open attempting to pull their bulky bodies into the small crawlspace. Turning around to crawl through the vents, Hikaru pushed Jeremy into En and Kimiko urging them to start moving as the Nzers started ripping further into the vents.

Leading the way through the ventilation shafts, Kimiko took a right around the next corner with En, Jeremy, and Hikaru following close behind. Crawling up to a grate, Kimiko paused for a moment to look back at the others when an enormous Nzer arm hammered through the vent where Kimiko would have been. Staring at the Nzer arm in front of her face, Kimiko looked back at the others with a wide gaping mouth. Releasing a tiny whimper, Kimiko gazed back at the monstrous arm and dropping her hand against the talons burnt the hand down to a nub. Quickly sliding past the hole as the Nzer pulled its arm back down, Kimiko crawled through the vents.

Crawling in front of Hikaru, Jeremy glanced up a tall shaft in the vents. Grabbing En's pants, Jeremy whispered for him to stop Kimiko and come back to this shaft. Staring up the long shaft, Jeremy lifted Kimiko up to the upper section of the vents with help from En. Then taking Hikaru's hand, the boys lifted her toward the upper section with Kimiko when Nzers raced through the chamber beneath the vents. Helping En up to the next level, Jeremy took hold of his hand when a blue marked Nzer broke through the vents and grabbed his leg. Pulled out of En's hand, Jeremy hammered into the vent beside the horrendous creature ripping into the shaft. Dropping back down to the lower level, En fell onto the Nzer as it took hold of Jeremy's arm.

"This is one thing that's not going to be part of your collection alien!" En shouted slamming his fist into the Nzer's face.

Quickly grabbing the back of En's shirt, Jeremy saved En from falling out of the vents with the Nzer. Wrapping his arm around En, Jeremy leapt toward the upper section of the ventilation shaft and grabbed Hikaru and Kimiko's extended hands. Pulling Jeremy up to the upper section, Hikaru held her grip on Jeremy while, Kimiko grabbed En's arm lifting him onto the level. Quickly turning, En grabbed Jeremy's shoulders and lifted him to the upper section to get a frustrated look from him.

"What did you think you were doing?" Jeremy questioned as he started to follow the girls through the shaft.

"What, I just saved you . . . last time I checked I still have that right, you are my brother!" En replied crawling after him.

"When this is all over I'm going to kill you, then let Hagane bring you back so I can do it again!" Jeremy threatened.

"Come on guys, this is our floor . . ." Hikaru stated looking down a grate as several small Nzers broke through the vents, "quickly!"

Lifting the grate, Hikaru helped Kimiko down as the boys came toward her with the Nzers in hot pursuit. Grabbing Hikaru's arms, Jeremy lowered her down and dropped her beside Kimiko. Turning to look at the Nzers, En shoved Jeremy down the opening and jumped down after him as the Nzers swiped where they were.

Dropping onto the floor beside Hikaru, Jeremy slowly rolled to his side to see En fall heavily on his arm. Sitting up, Jeremy crawled up to En and gently lifted him off his arm to inspect it as his younger brother groaned in pain. Glancing over at Kimiko and Hikaru, Jeremy lifted En off the floor and pulling his good arm over his shoulder started running.

"Jeremy is En all right?" Kimiko questioned chasing after him.

"I think his arm's broken!" Jeremy stated.

"Please, I'm fine; I just have immense pain shooting through my arm at the moment!" En assured.

"We'll talk once we are in a safe spot, but right now let's get out of here!" Hikaru yelled as the Nzers dropped down on the floor to chase after them.

Watching from the Control Room, Kler stared excitedly at the view screen as the small orange marked Nzers gained on the Devilry Hunters. Scratching his talons across the chair's armrest; Kler whipped his forked tongue out around his fangs while his eyes expanded as he watched the Nzers gaining on the Hunters. Kler carefully watched the view screen when Hikaru suddenly turned around as the other Hunters raced around a corner. Narrowing his eyes, Kler glared at Hikaru and smiled as the Nzers chasing her leapt into the air. Holding its breath, Kler watched stunned as Hikaru severed Esal's copper blade through the Nzer's hides before disappearing around the corner.

Jumping up from its seat, Kler lifted a nearby Nzer and threw it across the room toward the furthest wall. Thrusting its chest into the air, Kler bellowed a frustrated growl out of its throat and slammed it fists repeatedly through the walls.

"I grow tired of this-s-s . . . I want that girls-s-s friends-s-s taken from her now!"

"Pardon my s-saying this-s-s s-sir, but every battalion we s-send the vermin girl des-stroys-s-s one way or another!" A commanding Nzer stated at the wrong time.

Gazing at the Nzer, Kler speared its talons through the Nzer's neck and turned to the rest of the Nzers in the room. "I don't care how it is-s-s done . . . jus-st get her s-separated from the res-st of the vermin, s-so that I can kill the princ-ce!" Kler bellowed.

57

Racing down the dark halls of the spacecraft; Jeremy held En's arm over his shoulder while he securely held his own arm around En's waist. Running in between Hikaru and Kimiko, Jeremy moved around a corner when a loud roar echoed through the ship's whole. Freezing in a dark hall, Jeremy gazed at the two girls when Kimiko quickly bolted to a highlighted door and pushed it open. Following Kimiko inside, Jeremy turned to watch Hikaru run in and push Kimiko down as the sound of talons scraping over the metal floors echoed in the halls outside.

"I'm OK . . . you can let go!" En whispered tugging on his arm.

"Are you sure?" Jeremy questioned carefully releasing En's arm.

"Yeah . . ." En exhaled.

"I think they're gone . . ." Hikaru whispered slowly opening the door.

"Let's go guys . . ." Kimiko ordered with a smile.

Slowly walking out into the hall, Hikaru gazed up and down the area before looking back at Kimiko and nodding. Trotting out of the room, Kimiko ran up alongside Hikaru as En and Jeremy walked out. Watching Jeremy quietly shut the door, Hikaru gazed down the hall when a long string of slobber fell past her face. Releasing a small gasp, Hikaru looked down at the drool stretching across the floor when she quickly looked up to see a large Nzer hanging on the ceiling leap at them.

"Scatter . . ." Hikaru yelled jumping away as the Nzer landed on the floor.

Jumping on the side Hikaru was; Kimiko looked across the hall past the Nzer at Jeremy and En as they quickly moved out of the way. Taking a few steps back, Jeremy moved away from the Nzer as a trap door opened behind him. Falling backward, Jeremy released a tiny yell as he attempted to grab the floor. Turning his head, En glanced over at Jeremy as he fell into the hole.

"Jeremy . . ."

Falling into the hole, Jeremy suddenly stopped when someone grabbed his hand. Looking up at the hall, Jeremy stared at En as he struggled to hold him with only one hand when the Nzer walked up to En. Gasping, Jeremy lifted his free hand and shot a ball of fire across the Nzer's face as En turned to look at it.

"En, I'm too heavy. You need to let go!" Jeremy ordered.

"No, I'm not letting you go when I can save you!"

"En Skilou, I am your older brother and I order you to release me!"

"Just because you're older doesn't mean you're thinking clearly . . . there's no reason you can give me to let you go and become the Nzers prize! I won't do it . . . I shouldn't have left Maya or any of the others, but I wasn't thinking clearly like I am now!" En strained.

"En . . . let me go!"

"How 'bout you stop hanging there telling me to let you go and you grab the bottom of this floor! Pretty soon I'm going to drop you because I have hold of you with one hand!" En yelled.

"Of all the pestilential little brothers I had to have you!" Jeremy chuckled.

"Ooh, you cut me deep . . ." En smiled as Jeremy slid his fingers onto the hall floor, "now help me pull your heavy ass up!"

Lifting himself up beside En's feet, Jeremy watched the Nzer throw Kimiko into Hikaru and charge toward them. "En . . ." Jeremy yelled as the Nzer slammed into his back.

Hammering into the wall, En released a wail and slid down to the floor as the Nzer hovered over him. Bending down, the Nzer grabbed the front of En's shirt and threw him over its shoulder as it dropped to all fours to race past Hikaru and Kimiko.

"En . . . damn it!" Jeremy yelled as he slowly lifted himself toward the floor. Dropping onto the floor, Hikaru grabbed Jeremy's arm and helped him over the edge of the floor when Kimiko came racing up yelling.

"More Nzers just arrived and the one with En went back to hide behind them, I think it's time to skedaddle!"

"No, I'm not leaving, En . . . you guys keep going; find Kimon and kill the SOB that's doing this!" Jeremy yelled as he pushed the girls toward the trap door.

"Jeremy, are you going to be all right?" Hikaru asked as Kimiko started pulling her toward the hole in the floor.

"When I have my little brother back, I'll be fine!" Jeremy smiled as he turned toward the Nzers.

"Come on Hikaru!" Kimiko yelled pulling on her shirt. Trotting up to the trap door, Hikaru looked at Kimiko as she smiled. "Should we try it?" Kimiko questioned.

"We don't have any other choice . . . we've got to get to the other side!" Hikaru stated backing up.

"I bet we can make that!" Kimiko urged stepping back with Hikaru.

"We'll soon find if you're right!" Hikaru yelled as she jumped over the hole with Kimiko along her side. Dropping her foot onto the edge of the trapdoor, Hikaru fell forward and rolled across the floor as Kimiko came right after her and bumped into her side. "Owwww . . ." Hikaru yelled as she stopped rolling.

"He he he, wow that was awesome," Kimiko chuckled standing to her feet.

"Come on, we have to get out of here before more Nzers show up on this side!" Hikaru stated jumping to her feet to race down the hall.

Racing down a long hall, Hikaru and Kimiko quickly raced through the dark halls avoiding traps upsetting Kler while it watched over the view screen. Every attempt was foiled by the girls as they managed to stop each other from falling into traps to springing them. The close bond the girls had could be seen through their physical abilities as well as the mental as they charged through the Latrinian **Warship G-731.**

Trotting out onto a long bridge, Hikaru gazed down at the fifty foot drop between them and the floor as Kimiko ran up alongside her. Releasing a long breath, Hikaru smiled at Kimiko before she started across the bridge. Peering over the porcelain stones laying over the metal frame, Hikaru and Kimiko peered down at all the abandon equipment the Latrinians had to give up when Kler was sealed within the ship. Trailing their eyes off all the equipment, Hikaru and Kimiko gazed over at the cargo bay doors that were marred by long blast bolts.

Staring at the bolts for a few seconds, Kimiko gazed at Hikaru, "what do you think those were for?"

"I'm not sure, but Esal had said that this ship was the last model of a mighty train of warships created in his world. Many wars were probably fought in these chambers that are now plagued by the Nzers!" Hikaru replied looking around the room.

Kimiko gazed at Hikaru for a long minute before uttering the words she had been holding back for a while. "Did you like Esal . . . and I mean in the way that doesn't intend friends!"

Stopping Hikaru looked at Kimiko with sorrow filling her eyes, "I didn't get a real chance to meet him the way I would have liked to Kimiko!"

"I'm sorry, Hikaru. He was a very good guy!" Kimiko stated.

"Good doesn't even cover it . . . Esal was the noblest person I had ever met in my life! He made me feel so dependent and strong and the Nzers robbed me of him!"

"They didn't rob you Hikaru . . . you got the chance to know him enough to where he sacrificed himself for you! If he had fought in so many wars and survived he could have done something else, but he didn't . . . He wanted to sacrifice himself only for you!" Kimiko declared.

"I know . . . I miss him so much Kimiko! Being in his presence was like being with dad again! But to answer your question, no I didn't love him like that . . . Esal had feelings for someone else; just as I do for Kimon!"

Gazing at Hikaru, Kimiko smiled before looking around the large chamber. "So what do you think this was?"

"Probably where they stored the smaller ships they used for battles; this looks like a docking bay!" Hikaru replied looking around the room.

"So where to next . . ."

Gazing down at her COM box, Hikaru followed a path with her finger before looking up. "That way; I think . . ." Hikaru replied pointing toward the northern exit of the bridge, "it should lead us to the lower regiment where Yuri is being held!"

"Hikaru something's been bothering me . . . do you remember when En told Jeremy he wasn't going to let him be the Nzer's prize?"

"Yeah . . ."

"Well, what if En's right . . . I mean you and I are the only ones left!" Kimiko questioned.

"But that would mean . . ." Hikaru stated as she looked down at her COM box.

Sliding her fingers across her COM box, Hikaru pressed the red button signifying Masumi and watched it light up four levels above their currant position. Swallowing an itchy gulp, Hikaru pressed the brown button for Hagane to see it appear alongside Masumi's position. Then one by one; Hikaru pressed the blue button for Touko, fuchsia for Maya, orange for En, lavender for Jeremy, and purple for Yuri. Staring at her COM box disbelievingly, Hikaru watched all the lights flashing in the same area before she looked at Kimiko.

"Every one of my Hunters are in the same area . . ."

"What's going on . . . it's almost like they knew that we were going to come and they had all this planned!"

"And I helped deliver everyone . . ." Hikaru replied breathless, "I left everyone to continue the mission and save Kimon!"

"Hikaru this isn't your fault . . . you didn't know that the Nzers were planning to hold some kind of party!" Kimiko declared.

"Yeah, but we've been racing through this ship for days, probably; and now almost all of the Devilry Hunters are captured!" Hikaru stated as a hiss echoed through the chamber.

"Oh no . . ." Kimiko breathed, "What do we do?"

"I have an idea . . ." Hikaru stated, "Do you trust me?"

"Always . . ." Kimiko snorted.

Racing out onto the bridge towering over the **Warship G-731's** Cargo bay, a battalion of green marked Nzers peered around the chamber. The commanding Nzer of the regiment clicked its fangs together as it extended its long thick legs to stroll up to the center of the bridge and stare down at the floor. Sucking in deep breaths through the small slights on its flat face, the commander slowly turned back to its regiment and nodded toward the northern exit.

Hanging onto the underside of the bridge, Hikaru and Kimiko listened quietly to the clicking sounds echoing through the chamber as the commander's fangs slapped together. Tilting her head, Hikaru softly breathed against her arm as the Nzers talons started scrapping over the bridge to slowly fade away. Peeking around the bottom edge, Hikaru looked at Kimiko and nodded before she released her feet from a metal beam. Taking the side of the bridge, Hikaru slowly peeked around the chamber before pulling herself onto the bridge. Turning around, Hikaru grabbed Kimiko's hand and helped her onto the bridge.

"Let's not do that again . . ." Kimiko stated, "I'm uncomfortable with heights!"

"All right . . ." Hikaru smiled as she pulled out her COM box.

"Out of curiosity, how do you think the Nzers are finding us so quickly?" Kimiko asked Hikaru as she studied the COM box image.

"I'm not sure there may be cameras . . . after all I think ships this big would probably have surveillance of some kind!" Hikaru replied looking at Kimiko.

"Well, do you think it's possible for you to make us invisible from the surveillance?" Kimiko smiled.

Looking up at Kimiko, Hikaru nodded, "OK, I'll try!"

Sitting in the seat veiled by darkness, Kler stared at Hikaru and Kimiko as they pulled themselves out from under the bridge. Scowling with a hissing chuckle, Kler scratched its talons across its chest.

"Clever . . . didn't I s-say that I wanted it s-separated from the others-s-s!"

"There's-ss only one left s-sire, it will be no problem at all!" A small Nzer replied as Hikaru and Kimiko disappeared from the view screen.

Leaning forward in the shadows, Kler grabbed the Nzer's throat and pointed to the view screen, "it might be if it does-s-s that!" Throwing the Nzer across the room, Kler stood up and walked across the Control Room Bridge. "I was-sn't informed that the vermin girl can dis-sappear!"

"S-sir, we weren't aware that it could . . ."

"Well, you better s-start finding out or you all are going to be feeling lots-s-s of pain!" Kler bellowed.

58

S mall volts of electricity flashed through the dark halls as battalions of Nzers raced through the **Warship G-731** searching for the remaining Devilry Hunters. Every chamber was carefully searched for several hours while Kler impatiently walked across the Control Room Bridge. The lights from the navigation grids reflected onto Kler's large scaly hide while it slowly walked above its commanding officers as they continually failed to locate the Hunters running loose in the ship.

"I as-sk you to do one thing and you can't do it . . . maybe I s-should have as-sked s-some of the vermin to as-s-sis-st me, they probably would be doing a better job then my commanding officers-s-s!" Kler bellowed.

"S-sir, we are doing our bes-st, but the vermin have dis-sappeared . . . none of the battalions-s-s have been able to locate the mis-s-sing Hunters-s-s!" The navigation commander respectfully informed.

Widening its red eyes, Kler leapt down from the Bridge beside the navigation commander to grab its neck and lift it into the air.

"I didn't as-sk for an explanation commander . . . s-so don't give me another one, jus-st get the las-st Hunter s-so the vermin girl will come to me!" Kler hissed throwing the navigation commander across the room.

Across the Warship G-731

A long line of orange marked Nzers marched down a wide corridor when Hikaru's long raven hair dropped down with her head from the rafters. Watching the Nzers disappear around a corner, Hikaru dropped down onto the floor to be joined by Kimiko. Slowly stepping backward, Hikaru and Kimiko moved down the hall around the opposite corner and started racing toward the chamber where all the other Hunters were being held. Running down the dark hall, Kimiko followed Hikaru as she stared at the COM box to stop in front of a large door. Grabbing the handle, Hikaru pulled the door open and walked into another winding stairwell chamber. Looking at Kimiko with an annoyed smile, Hikaru started jumping up the stairs as the blinking lights on the COM box started to grow closer.

Halfway up the stairwell, Kimiko slowly dragged herself up the railing when something moving at the bottom of the chamber caught her attention. Glancing down at the chamber floor, Kimiko spied numerous Nzers racing up the stairs after them. Quickly jumping off the railing, Kimiko started rapidly pushing Hikaru up the stairwell to the top of the chamber. Racing through the chamber door with Hikaru, Kimiko quickly slammed it shut and started down the hall Hikaru indicated.

"These things are everywhere!" Kimiko screamed.

"The annoying thing is that I know we've killed a lot of them!" Hikaru replied.

"Then how are there still so many?" Kimiko yelped as a large Nzer snapped at her feet, "shouldn't we be able to move around the ship without running into so many?"

Racing down the hall, Hikaru dropped her foot onto a large silver tile which gave way as her weight pressed against it. Falling through the floor as a chubby Nzer grabbed Kimiko's skirt, Hikaru fell through the trap door pressing her hands and feet against the sides attempting to stop. Groaning as she slowly stopped several feet from the top of the trap door, Hikaru heard the halls grow quiet. Glancing up at the hall, Hikaru watched an orange marked Nzer stick its head down into the trap door. Holding her breath, Hikaru watched the Nzer sniff the sides of the dark chasm to peer down into the darkness that was hiding Hikaru. Slowly releasing her breath as the Nzer disappeared, Hikaru carefully pulled one hand off the wall and lifting her COM box to her face watched Kimiko's position heading for the other Hunters.

Crap the Nzers must have her! Hikaru thought to herself.

Carefully sliding her hands and feet slowly up the walls, Hikaru lost the grip and started falling back down the chasm when a rope dropped beside her. Grabbing the rope, Hikaru slowly stopped sliding down the chasm when a soft squeak called to her. Gazing up the chasm, Hikaru stared at Manabu as he held a rope around his waist and started stepping backward.

"Manabu . . ." Hikaru gasped as she came up to the hall and grabbed the floor, "I thought the Nzers had you!"

"No, I have been wandering around this ship and I have found very interesting things . . ." Manabu declared as he grabbed Hikaru's hand and pulled her up beside him, "I think I know where Kimon and Yuri are!"

"So do I; the COM box shows that direction!" Hikaru stated pointing.

"Oh good, you are using the COM box . . . I am so proud!" Manabu chuckled.

"Yeah, well we have to move now . . . we may be able to catch up with the Nzer that has Kimiko!" Hikaru declared running down the hall.

"Oh, certainly . . ." Manabu urged chasing after Hikaru.

Racing down a long dark hall; Hikaru looked over at Manabu and smiled as she watched his face light up as he observed everything they passed.

"So, what have you discovered Sherlock?"

"Well, considering that there is absolutely no light in this ship, I would say that the Nzers are nocturnal and do not like light at all!"

"I already knew that Manabu!"

"I was not finished Hikaru that was very rude of you to interrupt me like that!"

"I'm sorry, just please explain . . ." Hikaru interrupted again.

"Like I was saying, since the Nzers are nocturnal a bright source of light would come in handy for you to weaken them . . . they're so strong because they have blocked out our sun and every light in this ship is out!"

"Okay, so create a big light source of some kind and it will weaken the Nzers . . . where am I going to get an energy source as bright as the sun?"

"I do not know, I am just telling you something that will weaken them!" Manabu stated as they raced out into an enormous room.

Looking down at her COM box, Hikaru softly replied, "this should be where they all are . . . but I don't see anyone!"

Staring around the wide room, Hikaru slowly walked in to stare up at the dark ceiling towering above her. Slowly dropping her black slipper shoes onto the porcelain tiles laid across the floor; Hikaru looked back at Manabu as he strolled up alongside her. Gazing at the wall ahead of her, Hikaru looked to her left side to stare at the dark shadows covering the western wall when a high hiss echoed into the room. Quickly turning around, Hikaru spied a blue marked Nzer as it hammered into both herself and Manabu. Sliding across the floor, Hikaru rolled over to her side to stare at the Nzer as it sat beside the doorway. Staring at the Nzer puzzled, Hikaru looked toward the ceiling as she heard a whirling click echo above her.

Staring wide-eyed as the ceiling released a long metallic worm; Hikaru quickly pulled herself to her feet when she saw it approach Manabu. Racing across the floor toward the area Manabu landed, Hikaru got hammered into by the Nzer again. Rolling off her back, Hikaru sat up to watch the metallic worm wrap around an unconscious Manabu's chest. Jumping to her feet, Hikaru leapt for the worm as it pulled Manabu off the floor and disappeared into the ceiling's shadows. Staring up at the ceiling when a low hissing chuckle echoed across the chamber, Hikaru looked down into the western wall's shadows to watch a gigantic Nzer walk toward her.

59

The Nzer standing before Hikaru towered twenty-eight feet away from the chamber floor. Upon a pair of massive feet were three talons in front and a smaller talon protruding out of the bottom of the Nzer's calves. The thick thighs upon the Nzer's legs connected to the wide hips stretched out into a bulky chest. The large angrily eye upon the Nzer's face stared coldly at Hikaru as its flat head inched away from its thick neck while the blue frill lining its back expanded.

Raising its lips as a hiss escaped its throat, Kler's eyes enlarged as it stared at Hikaru standing before it. Displaying its razor-sharp fangs, Kler emerged further from the shadows and approached Hikaru. Raising its massive arms, Kler swung its two talons through the air showing off the dark chamber to Hikaru.

"S-so tell me vermin girl . . . what do you think of my vas-st empire?"

Narrowing her eyes, Hikaru gazed at Kler with vengeance in her eyes, "It's you . . . you're the one that's been plaguing my city with your unjust persecution!"

"Correct . . . you s-see I greatly dis-slike vermin s-species-s-s that think they have the right to govern over others-s-s and have an entire planet to themselves-s-s!"

"So you destroy these 'vermin' just because they live alone on a planet . . ." Hikaru questioned, "what makes you think you can toy with peoples' lives . . . No one has that right!"

"You know out of all the vermin I've des-stroyed . . . you have too be the mos-st bois-sterous-s-s and annoying . . . Not even the princ-ce had vex-xed me like you!"

"I'm glad I could play the part . . ." Hikaru angrily spat.

"I've been eagerly waiting for the moment that you and I would finally meet, s-so that I could tear your limps-s-s off one by one; then eat your organs-s-s while you s-slowly die a painful death!"

"There are something's worse than death Nzer."

"It's Mighty One to you . . ."

"My rear I'm going to address you with such dignity; you worthless pile of dung!" Hikaru stated.

"I really don't like you . . ."

"My feelings exactly . . ."

"You dis-sres-spectful vermin . . . I will make you eat your words-s-s!"

Lunging toward Hikaru, Kler raised his large arms extending his talons as its red eyes blazed like fire. Snapping its eager fangs together, Kler stared at Hikaru as she raised her arms lifting her barrier in front of her. Slamming into the barrier, Kler stumbled backward rubbing its face as it gazed back at Hikaru furious. Leaping up to the barrier, Kler hammered its talons across the surface and tried to tear it open with its fangs while Hikaru smiled up at it. Growling angrily at Hikaru as she smiled up at it; Kler jumped back and snorted a large gust of air out of his slender nostrils.

"Hiding behind a s-shield . . ."

"Why not . . . you've been hiding inside this ship the whole time; the real Nzers have been out there doing your work!" Hikaru replied.

Growling angrily, Kler lifted a conceited smirk upon its scaly face, "yes-s-s well, let me introduce-ce you to a real **Leader!**"

Throwing his head back, Kler hissed a long growl out of its throat which echoed throughout the chamber slightly shaking it. Glancing around the chamber, Hikaru watched a dim light cascade down from the shadows at the western wall. Slowly staring past Kler, Hikaru spied Kimon lying unconscious at the foot of a large purple gold-trimmed throne. Distracted by Kimon's presence, Hikaru gasped as she spied Kler lung into her barrier smacking it against her. Falling against the floor, Hikaru quickly separated her legs as Kler hammered its arm through the floor.

Staring at Kler's large arm, Hikaru pulled Esal's sword off her hip and sliced it past the arm. Quickly moving out of the way; Hikaru watched large amounts of Kler's acidy blood fall over the floor burning into it as the arm pulled out of the broken metal floor. Lifting the copper blade that had once been Esal's crystalline sword, Hikaru stared at Kler as it lunged for her. Avoiding the piercing talons, Hikaru swiped the sword at Kler as it lifted its foot to scrap the talons across Hikaru's thigh. Stumbling backward, Hikaru blocked Kler's swiping talons with Esal's sword as the vindictive Nzer hammered its foot into her chest. Sliding across the floor, Hikaru abruptly stopped as Kler grabbed her foot and pulled her toward it.

Lifting Hikaru off the floor, Kler stared at her as she hung upside down in front of its massive body. Snickering through its waiting fangs, Kler lifted its free hand and swiped it at Hikaru as she lifted her sword at the last second. Slicing its hand across the sword, Kler threw Hikaru across the chamber as it pulled its wounded hand close to its body. Glaring angrily at Hikaru as she landed upon the floor, Kler leapt into the air to drop over Hikaru's body. Grabbing the front of her shirt, Kler lifted Hikaru over its head and ripping the sword out of her hand threw her to the floor.

"Oh, this-s-s is-s-s that White Guardian's-s-s s-sword . . . or s-should I s-say; was-s-s the White Guardian's-s-s s-sword!" Kler chuckled.

Sitting up onto her thighs, Hikaru watched horrified as Kler broke the sword's copper blade into tiny pieces. Watching the shattered blade's tiny shards fall to the floor, Hikaru fought back the tears falling to her eyes as she gazed angrily at Kler.

"You know I regret that my Commander Ras-sp died, but I didn't expect for him to actually kill the White Guardian . . . he was-s-s too much like his-s-s mother—arrogantly aligned with the vermin princ-ce! S-so though I los-st the only Nzer in my own image I got s-something better back in return . . . no pes-sky guardian s-stopping me from killing the princ-ce!" Kler smirked.

"Made in your image . . ."

"Oh, that-s-s right this part of the s-story remains-s-s s-secret to you . . . well, once I es-scaped my impris-sonment within this-s-s s-ship; I s-sought revenge agains-st the ones-s-s that des-stroyed my kind and cas-st me away to live ins-side an illuminative jar for over a c-century! S-so I removed a half of my own heart and rib and with the dark magic from the Dark Queen; I made the firs-st reborn Nz-zer, Ras-sp! After that I removed half a heart and a rib from every other Nz-zer and created a grand army worthy of Latira onc-ce we return!"

"That's why there were so many of you creatures . . ."

"Are s-so many of us-s-s vermin girl . . . do you hones-stly think I s-sent my bes-st battalions-s-s down to deal with you? No vermin girl, I s-sent the newes-st Nz-zers-s-s down to des-stroy you . . . all of my older far more ex-xperienc-ced ones-s-s are readying thems-selves-s-s for the invas-sion of Latira!"

"Invasion of Latira . . ."

"You really don't know anything do you . . . I came to your worthless-s-s planet to find the vermin princ-ce there!" Kler explained pointing back at Kimon, "you s-see; the S-Solari thinks-s-s that their princ-ce s-still lives-s-s and is-s-s with them on Latira, imagine the s-shock on the vermins-s-s' fac-ces-s-s when they s-see me s-show up with the young pathetic princ-ce!"

"So why the attack on Earth . . ." Hikaru questioned scooting away from Kler as it approached her.

"Well, I knew that the White Guardian had come to find you, the prince's-s-s protector, hoping you would be able to s-stop me from doing what I currently am doing! Boy, he was-s-s wrong to believe in you . . ." Kler chuckled.

"So if you're winning; what's stopping you from going to Latira?" Hikaru questioned as she watched the long talon emerge out of the bottom of Kler's forearm.

"Killing you; I've been waiting to kill you s-sinc-ce you were found by the White Guardian . . . you aggravated me s-so! But I think you s-shouldn't die without an audienc-ce!" Kler smirked.

Gazing backward as banging metal echoed behind her, Hikaru glanced back to see all her Hunters hanging over fifty feet in the air bond by the arms to the large, metal worm stretched over the ceiling.

"S-see, all your friends-s-s have gathered to watch you die and after I kill you, I will enjoy s-slowly tormenting them making them wis-sh for death!" Kler chuckled when something blasted against his back.

Glancing after Kler to watch it hammer into the far wall, Hikaru turned around to see Kimon lift her off the ground.

"Are you all right?" They both asked.

"Yes . . ." Kimon answered.

"Yeah, but it's coming back!" Hikaru yelled pushing Kimon away as Kler swiped its large talons at them.

"Nic-ce of you to join us-s-s, princ-ce . . . I thought you would like to s-see your vermin girl die before you join her, but if you wis-sh to go firs-st I can grant your wis-sh!" Kler bellowed hammering Kimon backward before leaping at Hikaru.

60

Raising her arms, Hikaru blocked Kler with her shield. Stepping back as the massive Nzer pressed down on the barrier, Hikaru strained herself to keep her shield around her when she heard a familiar voice below her.

"Cleo . . ." Hikaru gasped looking down at her feet to see her stuffed bear sitting there wiggling her tail excitedly.

"YEAH HIKARU; SO WHICH ONE YOU WANT ME TO TAKE?"

"Cleo this isn't a game!" Hikaru shouted as Kler hammered into her barrier throwing her and Cleo across the chamber.

Hammering into the steps in front of the throne, Hikaru rubbed her hand over her head and looked frustrated up at Kler.

"This is a war . . ."

"WAR . . . I CAN DEAL WITH A WAR! POINT ME IN A DIRECTION AND I AM A LEAN, MEAN, FIGHTING MACHINE!" Cleo growled jutting her skinny back up raising the hair slightly.

Standing to her feet, Hikaru prepared to block Kler again when Gobu zipped forward and hammered into Kler's face throwing it across the chamber.

"Gobu . . ." Hikaru gasped as Gobu swirled around in the air dizzily rotating his eyes as he dropped to the floor.

"Gobu to da resku!" Gobu saluted falling backward onto his back.

"I'll yell at you guys later . . ." Hikaru stated picking up Gobu and Cleo, "right now we're running!"

"WHAT . . . I'M A NASTY TYRANT HIKARU; LET ME AT 'EM!"

"Okay Cleo, you want to take on that?" Hikaru asked shoving Cleo's head against Kler's face as it chased after them.

"POINT TAKEN . . ." Cleo stated staring at Kler as it snorted air against her face, "LET'S GET OUT OF HERE!" Cleo yelled whacking her paws across Kler's face before zipping through the air past Hikaru and Gobu.

Growling angrily, Kler swiped his arms under Hikaru grabbing her legs pulling her to the ground.

"Wait, Let's Go Back There!" Cleo bellowed.

"Okay . . ." Gobu gurgled happily.

Quickly turning in mid-air, Cleo shot back toward Hikaru and hammered her enlarging head into Kler. Rocking back and forth as her gigantic head pulled her to the chamber floor, Cleo attempted to lift her shrinking head off the floor when Hikaru lifted her away from Kler's talons.

"Hikaru I Told You That You Need To Stop Making My Head Enlarge Like This, If You Want Me To Be Bigger; Focus On Making My Whole Body Large . . . Not Just My Head!" Cleo bellowed as Hikaru dodged Kler's swinging talons.

"I'll try to remember that next time . . ."

"Thanks . . . Now Will You Make My Head The Right Size Again; This Is Strenuous On The Neck!" Cleo demanded.

Swinging her arms out of the way of Kler's talons, Hikaru dropped Cleo onto the floor as her head started to shrink. Pulling a large, metal pole off the wall; Hikaru quickly blocked Kler's long talon beneath his forearm when Cleo yelled up at her with a small squeaky voice.

"Hikaru Neijo . . . Now My Head Is Too Small! You Are Doing This On Purpose; Give Me Back My Right Sized Head!"

Smiling as she saw Cleo's miniature head upon her larger body, Hikaru slid down into the splits as Kler swiped its talons over her head. Throwing her foot into the air, Hikaru hammered her leg across Kler's head giving her time to stand back up and counterattack the next blow.

"Oh Joy, My Head Is Back!" Cleo chuckled pressing her paws over her face.

"Mesa tinks yousa lookt better with bigga head!" Gobu gurgled happily.

"I'll Show You Who Looks Better With A Big Head!" Cleo growled chasing after Gobu snapping her fangs at his stubby tail.

"No . . . mesa tawl; get yousa own!" Gobu shrieked covering his tiny tail with his sponge arms.

Severing its talons through the metal pole in front of Hikaru, Kler scraped his talons across Hikaru's chest throwing her backward. Licking several drops of her blood off his talons, Kler slowly approached Hikaru and lifted his arms for the final strike. Hammering into Kler's head, Gobu rendered it momentarily stunned when Cleo raced through its feet knocking the Nzer to the ground. Shaking the daze off its spinning eyes, Kler crawled to all fours and leapt for Hikaru.

Sitting up to see Kler coming toward her with its talons extended, Hikaru's brown eyes followed a movement that stepped in front of her. Watching with wide eyes, Hikaru screamed out as Kimon stepped in front of her to suffer Kler's extended talons.

Hanging fifty feet in the air, Kimiko slowly opened her eyes to look down at the far off floor. Releasing a squeal, Kimiko lurched around in her chains as she stared down at the floor. Quickly looking to her sides, Kimiko stared at En and Jeremy's unconscious faces. Sticking her tongue to the side of her mouth, Kimiko lifted her legs to throw them toward Jeremy to kick him.

"Wake up; dang it . . ." Kimiko yelled as Jeremy groaned to slowly open his eyes, "We are hanging very high up in the air!"

"**Jimmy Christmas . . .**" Jeremy yelled seeing the air between the floor and his feet, "what on Earth is going on?"

"Not on Earth . . ." Kimiko corrected, "in the spaceship!"

"Hey; you two, screaming mimmies . . ." Maya's voice called from the other side of Jeremy, "look down there!"

Glancing down at the floor, Jeremy and Kimiko stared at what Maya was indicating to see Kimon get speared through by an enormous Nzer.

"Oh no, Kimon's going to die . . ." Kimiko bellowed as light radiated up from below, "what's going on I can't see?"

"Shut up Kimiko and watch!" Jeremy ordered.

Staring up at Kimon as violet rays radiated away from his body, Hikaru smiled as she watched the rays blow Kler across the chamber. The violet rays fell gently against Hikaru's skin as the white uniform around Kimon's body disappeared. Slightly blushing, Hikaru watched a purple tunic bordered by light lavender wrap around Kimon's frame to be tied off by a golden sash around his waistline. Watching the purple tunic fall over two calve-high raven boots; Hikaru stared at the large rainbow orbs towering over miniature ones trimmed by gold bands. Glancing up at the long sleeves; Hikaru watched rainbow orbs appear over the black gloves that stretched over Kimon's tanned hands. As a long plum neckline fell over Kimon's shoulders; Hikaru peered at two rainbow orbs appear beside the one centering Kimon's chest line to fasten the lengthy red cape to the tunic.

Catching Kimon as he dropped to his knees, Hikaru stared at the violet ray that wrapped around his forehead. A bright light stretched across Hikaru's entranced face as she watched the ray disappear into a golden band. Taking Kimon's shoulders, Hikaru looked under his face to peer into his deep indigo eyes as his raven hair fell over the golden band. Lifting his head, Kimon gazed at Hikaru before looking at his new attire.

Smiling brightly, Hikaru chuckled, "well, I guess you really are the prince!"

Returning Hikaru's smile as Kler's hiss echoed through the chamber, Kimon quickly turned to see the vindictive Nzer lord leaping at them. Rapidly jumping to her feet, Hikaru moved in front of Kimon and lifting her arms away from her sides prepared to finish the task she swore to Esal she would.

Hanging fifty feet in the air; all the Hunters had regained consciousness and were screaming loudly at Hikaru as she moved in front of the gigantic leaping Nzer. Kicking her legs through the air, Kimiko repeatedly attempted to burn her hands free of the metal rope around her hands failing every time. Beside her Jeremy tried uncoiling it to disappearing to also fail miserably while Maya tried to expand her hands and throw her legs up trying to shatter it. Even Masumi couldn't cause the metal wires to obey his commands.

"What does she think she's doing?" Kimiko questioned hysterically.

"Maybe she's going to bring up her shield!" Jeremy suggested hopefully.

"I've been hanging here watching for sometime and that Nzer breaks through Hikaru's barrier!" Maya replied.

"Maybe she's going to do a Chuck Norris move at the last second . . ." En stated to have everyone look at him with confusion, "you know; the 'move-out-of-the-way-and-kick-the-object-in-the-back-of-the-neck' thing!"

"Okay, En you are not watching anymore movies or TV shows again!" Jeremy stated with annoyance.

"Hikaru Neijo!" Masumi screamed down at his little sister.

Standing with her arms extended, Hikaru held her body firmly before Kimon as Kler slowly fell toward them. Tightly sealing her eyes, Hikaru ignored Kimon and all her Hunters screams to try to think of how she could weaken this Nzer. Thinking back to when Manabu rescued her, Hikaru remembered him mentioning creating a large light source.

Where am I going to find I light source as bright as the sun Manabu . . . Hikaru thought to herself as she could feel Kler's hot breath nearly licking over her cheeks.

Create it . . . Hikaru heard a sweet voice echo through her mind.

61

*W*here am I going to find I light source as bright as the sun Manabu . . . Hikaru thought to herself as she could feel Kler's hot breath nearly licking over her cheeks.

Create it . . . Hikaru heard a sweet voice echo through her mind.

Quickly springing her eyes open, Hikaru stared around a cotton valley covered by Lillian flowers. Dropping her arms, Hikaru quickly spun around searching for the ship, her Hunters, Kimon and Kler to see a small river etching past her. Following the river's movement with her eyes, Hikaru spied a tall lean woman sitting on a millstone beside a large waterfall dropping into a small pond that stretched out into the river.

Slowly walking toward the woman, Hikaru gazed around her frame trying to see her face when the woman's voice echoed through the valley in a gentle hum. Like the sound of crystal bells chiming along the wind, the woman's voice reached Hikaru's ears to clearly make out what she was saying.

Tears filled Hikaru's eyes as she listened to the same lullaby her father would sing to her every night to get her to fall asleep. Quickly approaching the woman, Hikaru raced around her frame to stare at an older image of herself. Lifting her hands to her mouth, Hikaru stared at the smiling face of Jocelyn Neijo.

"Hello, Hikaru . . ."

"You're my mother . . ." Hikaru softly breathed through her hands, "I've prayed everyday for such a meeting and as I'm facing the biggest turmoil of my life . . . here you are!"

"Yes, Hikaru, I know of the horror that is going on at this very moment and considering that the fate of all rests on this one moment . . . I thought you should know that you are of higher power Hikaru!"

"I don't understand," Hikaru replied as Jocelyn took her smaller hands in hers.

"Hikaru, the first generation of Devilry Hunters was destroyed because the Dark Queen wanted you out of the way!"

"Me . . . why me?" Hikaru questioned. "The Dark Queen hasn't even met me!"

"No, she hasn't, but she knows where you originate from . . . Hikaru you are a Child of the Solari! You were sent with the reborn princes and princesses so that you could protect them . . . you are a child of light and mercy! And the Dark Queen fears that it is the only thing that can defeat her!"

"But why did she destroy all the Devilry Hunters if you were carrying me?"

"The Dark Queen didn't know who the gift was going to . . . only the White Guardian knew who she blessed with such a gift!"

"So you're saying that I am from the Solari! That I was sent with the prince and his subjects to protect them from the Dark Queen?"

"Yes . . ." Jocelyn replied.

"But why . . . why must I protect the princes and princesses, I don't understand?"

"Hikaru if the Dark Queen should gain the ruling child of every planet in the Solari, she could spread her evil throughout the Universes and destroy them!"

"So what are you trying to tell me mom?"

"Hikaru, there is power in you unmatched . . . if you should unleash this power you can vanquish any foe!"

"But the only thing that can weaken the Nzers is water or extreme light like the sun!" Hikaru ventilated.

Taking Hikaru's cheeks in her hands, Jocelyn smiled brightly, "then create it, my baby! You are the perfect child for this mission Hikaru . . . vanquish your foe and watch over your friends! I love you so much Hikaru and I wish I could've seen you grow into this strong independent woman I see standing before me!"

"I love you too mom . . . I miss you so much!" Hikaru sobbed as Jocelyn kissed her forehead.

"Tell your brother I love him . . ." Jocelyn stated as the valley started to disappear, "good luck my darling child!"

Create it . . .

Staring through the darkness before her sealed eyes, Hikaru thought repeatedly over what she had just heard and seen.

Create it . . . a light source with the intensity of the sun!

Feeling her arms still floating away from her sides, Hikaru heard her friends' cries when Kler's hiss echoed into her ears. Opening her eyes to stare coldly at Kler, the iris in Hikaru's brown eyes was suddenly engulfed by a ring of fire. White waves started to burst away from Hikaru's body to blow around the chamber cutting through the metal worm causing it to release all the Hunters.

"En . . ." the Hunters screamed.

Pinching his eyes shut, En shot a currant of air beneath himself and the rest of the Hunters slowly bringing them to the floor. Staring up at Hikaru as white rays shot out of her body, Kimon looked toward the Hunters and his little sister when Hikaru looked back at him.

"Go Kimon; help them out of their restraints . . ." Hikaru stated as her voice echoed around the chamber. Seeing the look on Kimon's face, Hikaru smiled brightly and nodded her head. "It's OK . . ." Hikaru stated watching Kimon stand to his feet to race toward the Hunters, "I've got this!"

Lifting her hands above her head, Hikaru's brown eyes slowly faded into a bright glow as her body was suddenly engulfed by flames. Pulling her hands down in front of her face, Hikaru clenched her fists with a smile. Looking at Kler as it slowly stopped; Hikaru blasted flames toward it and released a breath as she watched several rays conform from the flames. Pushing her whipping hair out of her face, Hikaru watched the rays spear through Kler's body causing him to wither to the ground.

Small rays speared away from Hikaru's body, leaving small glowing symbols in their stead as a bright symbol of a star appeared on her forehead. Tucking her arms tightly into her chest, Hikaru blasted an enormous ray away from her body to shot through the entire whole of the ship destroying every last Nzer blowing them to ashes.

Pulling the last metal wire off Yuri's hands, Kimon wrapped his arms around her as she leapt against his chest. Gazing over at Hikaru, Kimon stared in wonder as the flames jumping away from her body turned into rays that sprayed across the ship. Lifting himself from the floor, Kimon ran his hand across Yuri's forehead before he raced toward Hikaru. Ducking under several jumping flames, Kimon raced around her front to stare at the bright white light that had engulfed Hikaru's body. Lifting his arm to shield his eyes from the blinding light, Kimon raised his voice screaming out to Hikaru.

Dropping his arm as he watched the rays slowly dissipate, Kimon stared at Hikaru as all the flames and rays disappeared from her body. Staring at her with a smile as she raised her hand to her head, Kimon dove forward to catch her as her body faltered. Smiling brightly at Hikaru as she smirked impishly at him, Kimon looked toward Kler as it slowly stirred. Wrapping his arm around Hikaru, Kimon approached Kler with all the other Hunters close behind.

Coughing large amounts of its acidy blood, Kler's body twitched uncontrollably when it spied Kimon approaching. Dropping its large arms onto its chest Kler gazed vengefully up at Kimon, Hikaru and the Hunters.

"You got lucky, vermin princ-ce . . . you better hope you are as-s-s lucky for the nex-xt time!" Kler coughed spitting blood out of its mouth.

"There won't be a next time Kler . . . you're dying Under Dweller!"

Chuckling through its vomiting blood, Kler looked up at the prince and the Devilry Hunters, "the veil of darknes-s-s es-scapes-s-s through the s-shadows-s-s and returns-s-s when the world res-settles-s-s into a peac-ceful era!"

Then choking on the last spray of blood, Kler dropped his head back against the floor and slowly disappeared before Kimon and the Hunters. Shaking his head, Kimon looked away from the burnt patch on the ship's floor and gazed toward the Devilry Hunters. Smiling as they bowed playfully to him, Kimon took his little sister in his arms as she grabbed his tunic sleeve.

"I owe so much to all of you . . . thank you for coming after us!" Kimon thanked looking down at Yuri with a smile.

"Don't thank us . . . thank Hikaru! After all it's Miss Lightning Bug that saved all our rears!" Masumi laughed.

"Ha ha, very funny . . ." Hikaru stated whacking her brother in the arm.

"That's a cute nickname . . . I think it's what we should call her from now on guys!" Masumi chuckled.

Scratching the top of his head, Manabu softly questioned, "You know I was wondering; how did you create such an enormous light source like that Hikaru . . . Hikaru?" Glancing to his side, Manabu stared wide-eyed as Hikaru was wrapped around Masumi's body with her arms around his neck strangling him.

"I may be able to answer that for ya Manabu . . ." Kimiko replied.

Pointing toward Hikaru and Masumi, Manabu looked at everyone, "should someone?"

"No . . ." came the reply from all the other Hunters and Kimon.

"Like I was saying; when Hikaru gets nervous, powers just pop out of her!" Kimiko stated as Masumi flew past her.

Looking after Masumi, Manabu pointed at him as Jeremy chimed in. "Yeah and there's the fact that she has a major . . ."

Reaching up to grab Jeremy's hair, Hikaru pulled him toward her as she stared at him with an angry expression. "Something you want to share Jeremy?" Hikaru questioned as Jeremy quickly shook his head no, "Good; now let's go home!"

"Home that world has new meaning now!" Hagane smiled as Touko grabbed his arm and smiled.

Earth—Thursday Night, May 1, 2026
11:59 pm and 59 seconds

62

$\int$oyous laughter sparked throughout the kingdoms of the Solari as news of the Nzers's obliteration reached the border of the planets. Large displays of sparking lights filled the skies of every planet as the night lights fell over Latira. Large spraying lights flashed across the dark olive valleys to reflect off the streaming rivers while villagers joyfully spent the night enjoying life. The signing and laughter rang through the halls of Latira's palace as the Holy Priest walked through the Grand Hall.

Walking up to a large stairwell snaking up to the second floor, the Holy Priest found Jeannee hunched over against the side of the rail. Coiling his fingers around his staff, the Holy Priest leaned down to gaze into Jeannee's teary light orange eyes. The front of her shirt was stained with the many falling tears that had streaked down her cheeks to drip off her chin. Her sobs gasped uncontrollably as she cried in the joyous laughter that rang through the halls.

"Whatever is the matter child . . ." the Holy Priest questioned sitting beside her, "the city is sparking of laughter the Under Dwellers have been destroyed, what are your tears for?"

Looking up at the Holy Priest through tears, Jeannee hysterically sobbed, "he fell . . . Esal has fallen!"

"Jeannee, don't shed tears for your friend, for he lives!"

Gazing up at the Holy Priest with wide eyes, Jeannee couldn't find words to reply to his comment. She sat quietly staring at him as the laughter and music continued to ring through the palace's porcelain halls.

Earth—Friday Morning, May 2, 2027

A soft drizzle fell lightly over Tokyo when the sun slowly pushed out from behind the dark clouds dissipating away from the **Warship G-731**. Across the city, citizens all lent a helping hand as they cleaned up the destruction the Nzers had brought to their city. Debris and trash alike were cleaned off the streets as large dump trucks went around collecting the large shards of glass and broken foundations, the task force went around clearing the city of the fallen citizens to take them to the hospitals to await further instructions.

Standing on the bridge lining the park river, Hikaru stared down at several swans and their babies as they slowly passed beneath her. Gazing around the park, Hikaru watched city workers and citizens clean up the area as children once again were found playing in the playgrounds. Looking to her side, Hikaru smiled brightly as Kimon walked up the wooden boards to lean on the railing beside her.

"The city is slowly beginning to piece itself back together!" Kimon softly replied.

Nodding her head in agreement, Hikaru looked up at Kimon and answered, "thankfully for them they don't truly know what was going on!"

Looking down at Hikaru, Kimon's face grew serious, "how are you doing?"

"Me . . ." Hikaru questioned looking up at Kimon, "I'm fine my body doesn't ache as much as I thought it was going to!"

"That's not what I was referring to . . ." Kimon replied.

Quickly looking down at the slow moving river, Hikaru could feel tears starting to come to her eyes.

"I'm . . . I won't lie. I miss him a lot! More so then I could have imagined . . ." Hikaru softly whimpered. "I keep thinking that there was something I could have done if he just let me!" Hikaru stated looking up at Kimon, "I could have saved him!"

Pulling Hikaru into his arms, Kimon tenderly wrapped his arms around her, "Hikaru, I don't doubt that you could have saved him and neither did he . . ."

"Then why did he do it?" Hikaru cried against Kimon's chest.

"I don't know Hikaru, but he knew what he was doing . . . of all of us he knew what he was doing!" Kimon softly breathed.

"I'm sorry . . ." Hikaru softly replied whipping tears out of her eyes, "I got your shirt all wet!"

Looking down at his shirt, Kimon looked back up at Hikaru and smiled, "it will dry . . . personally I think it looks sexy!"

Releasing a small giggle, Hikaru shook her head, "oh yeah, a large wet spot on your chest is real sexy!"

"It would send a message to Claire . . ."

"Oh, what message?" Hikaru chuckled.

"I let another woman cry on me!"

"Oh well, keep it on there and go show her; anything that annoys her makes me happy!" Hikaru chuckled.

"I know . . ."

Leaning her arms against the railing, Hikaru followed the river with her eyes as it slowly faded into the distance. The sun's reflection was a joyous sight as she stared entranced at the bright sphere.

"Now that things are settling down; there's something I want to tell you Hikaru," Kimon stated looking out over the river.

Looking up at Kimon, Hikaru felt her heart leap in her chest when he looked down at her and smiled. Watching him turn around and lean against the rail as he looked down at the bridge, Hikaru could feel her cheeks rapidly heating up. Looking up at the light blue sky, Kimon closed his deep indigo eyes and released a long breath as a smile crossed over his face.

"We've known each other since childhood . . . me, Masumi's friend, Yuri, yours. But once we grew older, I soon found that I would stare continually at you for no apparent reason without noticing until your brother pointed it out to me. As I started to become more involved with certain things, I didn't get to see you very often and it pained me!" Kimon softly stated opening his eyes to look down at Hikaru.

Pushing off the railing, Kimon tucked his hands in his pockets and walked to the center of the bridge as Hikaru followed him with her wide eyes.

"Then I became the Acting Chairman of the Academy you attended and I found that days had become more meaning full from the days that I was away from you! When I am in your presence, my stomach turns to knots, but the countless hours I am away from you I can't think of anything else but when I will see you again, and as I start to think more about you, I can't breathe!" Kimon stated looking out over the bridge at the forest line when Hikaru's hand pushed into his.

Turning around to look at the tender expression on Hikaru's face, Kimon wiped several of the new falling tears from her bright brown eyes. Sliding his fingers along her cheeks, Kimon bent toward Hikaru as she felt her heart bursting.

"I love you Hikaru . . . I have always loved you! You are the woman I have longed to be able to share my life with!"

Rising up on her tiptoes, Hikaru reached up to meet Kimon's lips as he pressed them against her own. Tears fell loosely from Hikaru's eyes as she held tightly to Kimon as he brushed his hands down to her neck.

Walking down the park path, Yuri turned a corner heading toward the bridge when she abruptly stopped. Staring wide-eyed, Yuri smiled brightly as she saw her brother and Hikaru finally kissing. Biting her lower lip, Yuri slowly turned around and taking one last look started walking back down the path through the park.

63

The wind blew gently along Yuri's frame as she walked happily down the sidewalk toward Kimon's and her house. The sweet chirping of the birds and the annoying squeaks from squirrels scampering overhead breezed past Yuri as all she could think of was her brother and Hikaru. Walking down the street, Yuri was nearly at her house when walking by an old abandon house something tugged at Yuri's subconscious. Stopping on the sidewalk, Yuri looked toward the house curiously as a feeling of someone in pain suddenly consumed Yuri's mind.

Walking around the side of the house, Yuri remembered old tales of this house being haunted by ghosts. As a child, Yuri had refused to go inside the house when Hikaru, Kimiko, En, and Jeremy insisted that they try to see the ghosts. Now as the thought of someone in pain filled Yuri's mind, she found herself pulling at the old boards at the back door. Glancing around the backyard, Yuri was relieved to find tall shrubbery covering the fence lines prohibiting anyone from seeing her breaking into this old house. Giving a board one last strong tug, Yuri found she ripped the board away from the house too hard as she fell backward onto the lawn. Releasing a nervous breath, Yuri lifted her self to her feet and slowly closing her hand around the old copper doorknob pushed the door open.

Light poured into the back hall of the house for the first time in probably thirty years as Yuri slowly set her black shoes down on the dusty wood floors. Looking back as the back door slowly creaked closed, Yuri sucked in a deep breath and walked down the hall. Dropping her feet onto the dirty floors, Yuri walked around the corner as dust shot up around her legs to brush along her white thigh-high socks. Pushing spider webs aside, Yuri walked into the house's suggested den to see several mice scurried away to their holes. Shaking her head, Yuri released a long sigh when a soft moan escaped into the house behind her.

Quickly whirling around causing more dust to fly up near her face, Yuri closed her hand around a doorknob and walked into a large dark bedroom still inhabiting all the furniture. Preparing to reseal the door, Yuri walked further into the bedroom as she heard a soft cough and a few deep breathes. Walking across a dusty carpet, Yuri slowly tore through several spider webs to peer around the side of the bed to see a young man leaning against the jut between the wall and the bed. Gasping, Yuri quickly approached the bed and dropped down in front of the young man startling him.

"Wow . . ." taking the boy's arms, Yuri gently laid them back across his lap, "It's all right." Peering at the boy as he stared uncertainly at her, Yuri pushed the bangs out of her face and gently laid her hand on the boy's. "I'm not going to hurt you. I promise."

Glancing down at the young man's white shirt, Yuri saw a large red stain centering his chest. Gasping at the same time as the boy sucked in a deep breath, Yuri reached toward the boy when he caught her hands in his own.

"You're bleeding badly. I need to get you to a hospital!"

Slowly shaking his head, the boy leaned his head back against the bed, "no hospitals . . . I just needed to rest, I'm fine!"

"You're delusional from losing so much blood. I need to get you to a hospital so they can stop the bleeding!" Yuri stated.

"I can't . . . someone will find me there!"

Looking down at the young man, Yuri looked around the house, "you came in here to hide from someone . . . how did you get in here anyway, the building was undisturbed?"

Shaking his head, the young man looked wearily up at Yuri. "You should go."

"You are going to die if I don't get you help!"

"I already told you—" he started to choke on the coughs making him lurch forward.

Shaking her head in frustration, Yuri grabbed the young man's arm, "then I'm taking you home with me!"

"No, I . . ." the young man groaned as Yuri pulled him up. "You don't understand. I don't want you involved!"

"Involved in what?" Yuri practically yelled as the young man fell against her nearly knocking her over.

"I would greatly appreciate it if you would not yell . . ." the young man softly stated in pain, "my head is spinning enough as it is . . . you don't need to add to the torment!"

Yuri looked at the young man's bronzed face as he looked over at her, "all right look, you need to let me help you . . . I won't take you to a hospital or anything like that, but at least let me stop the bleeding!"

Peering at Yuri through his pale eyes, the young man swallowed an agonizing breath and whispered, "OK, but you must swear to me that you won't speak of me to anyone!"

Nodding her head happily, Yuri gently pulled the young man's arm around her shoulders and gently lifted him to his feet. Wrapping her other arm around the young man's waist, Yuri slowly walked beside him bearing half his own weight as he leaned against her. Opening the bedroom door, Yuri walked sideways out into the hall to head toward the back hall.

"By the way my name is Yuri . . . Yuri Youitan!"

Smiling wearily at Yuri, the young man softly breathed, "honored Yuri . . . I'm sorry I can't return the gesture . . . I don't know who I am."

64

Darkness rolled continually through the atmosphere surrounding the Dark Moon of the Solari as large volts of lightning sparked around Seira Moudei, the center core of the Realm. The raven clouds covering the planet released dark veils of rain against the barren valleys surrounding an expansive dark kingdom.

Large stone walls crumbled slowly beneath the illuminating clouds as parched areas with the courtyard quickly began to flood. Dry towering trees collapsed to the ground as lightning frequently struck the large expanding branches reaching toward the dark skies. Shrilling cries from hungry predators filled the night air as the wind howled furiously toward the medieval castle.

Within the cold dry castle, a dark man walked briskly down a raven veiled hall into a wide cavern. Lifting a torch from the wall, the man strolled down a long winding stairwell toward the bottom of the grotto. Dropping his raven boots onto the dusty spider-infested floors, the man stepped into a long canoe and lifting a long oar pushed off the bank into a swampy lake beneath the castle foundation.

The man's long silver hair draped loosely over his narrow hazel eyes that stared contently away from his tanned skin. His armor plated forearms curled firmly as he lifted the long oar out of the water setting it down as he stepped out onto the bank. Lifting his long gray over coat out of the boat prohibiting it from touching the murky water, the man strolled up the bank toward a kindling light flickering around a corner.

Several candles stretched across a sphere cavern bordered by towering mirrors covering the rocky foundation. Within each mirror, a different planet slowly rotated through the Solari atmosphere unknowingly being viewed through these mirrors. Soft clicking of heeled shoes echoed through the cavern as they fell against the porcelain tiles laid as a path through the cavern. Standing in the midst of the circlet of mirrors, a tall dark woman with long red-violet hair stared at the planets before her lavender pink eyes. The Dark Lady's eyes stared narrowly at the mirror containing Earth as a malicious smirk crossed over her blood red lips. Tilting her head to the side as she lifted her soft hands to her chin, the indigo Dragon Tear gem centering the Dark Lady's forehead sparkled brightly through the candle light. Running her finger across her lips, the Dark Lady watched as the mirror faded and brought up an image of Tokyo.

Walking around the corner, the man dropped to a knee behind the Dark Lady before she realized he was there. Raising his head, the man gazed at the nobility of the Dark Lady's malice radiating away from her frame. Gazing up the wide raspberry skirt. The man looked past the raven torso of the Dark Lady's dress as she slowly turned to look at him. Bowing his head, the man smirked up at the Dark Lady as the crystal gems upon her face and neckline sparkled through the darkness surrounding the candle light.

Running her fingers along her raven choker, the Dark Lady looked toward the mirror captivating Earth. Dropping her arms to her waistline, the Dark Lady waved her hands through the long cherry tanned sleeves of her dress. "Thank you for coming . . ." the Dark Lady's voice echoed through the cavern, "General, the final world has come into play! The Nzer Lord failed just as I knew it would, but I never expected the Nzers to wound the White Guardian Esal!"

"Because of that, the Archangel Prince is nearly in your grasp . . ." the man replied with a chuckle.

Turning to look at the man, the Dark Lady smiled conceitedly, "yes, and what better person to send after the young prince than you!" Walking up to the mirror surveying Earth, the Dark Lady swiped her hand in front of the image causing it to ripple. Watching eagerly as Yuri and the young man slowly rippled across the mirror, the Dark Lady smiled as she laid her hand on the younger man. "You dropped the Young Angel Prince into my hands perfectly once before, General Shr. I want you to go reclaim what is rightfully ours!"

Bowing his head, General Shr rose to his feet, "on your Command."

Stroking her fingers along the image of the young man's face, the Dark Lady looked after General Shr. "Remember General, you won't be alone on trying to find the lost prince, so work swiftly and be sure that we are the ones to have possession of the Angel Prince in the end!"

"The others may prove to be useful in this task. After all, the new generation of Devilry Hunters prove to be worthy rivals!"

"Yes, after seeing what they accomplished with our first test, the Nzers' invasion. I'd say that we may need a different approach with how to deal with these . . . children!"

"The Keto siblings would be a perfect choice . . ." General Shr offered.

"Yes, they would be, but I worry about the Neijo children . . . if they are anything like their father, and children normally are, they may prove to be a nuisance!"

"What do you want to do?"

Looking at General Shr, an evil malice twinkled in the Dark Lady's eyes, "Take the Ketos with you and start the mission immediately . . . I'll prepare a counterattack for the Neijo Children!"

CPSIA information can be obtained at www.ICGtesting.com
Printed in the USA
BVOW010226131212

308051BV00002B/282/P